AWAKEN ARCHANGEL

UNIVERSAL TECHNOLOGIES **BOOK 1**

CJ PIPERATA

Editor: Dan Edelman

Book Cover: Damonza.com

Map & Interior Illustrations: CJ Piperata

Formatted in Atticus

ISBN 978-1-967110-00-1 (paperback) | ISBN 978-1-967110-01-8 (e-book) | ISBN 978-1-967110-02-5 (hardcover) | LCCN 2025906673

For Josephine.

I'll meet you by the Mother Tree.

But not yet.

Contents

Before we enter: Please be mindful that a couple of chapters ahead entail childhood neglect & trauma at the hands of caretakers. Reader discretion may be warranted.

Otherwise, enjoy your stay!

~*Raphael*

 HEAVEN'S TIMING

To orient yourself in our world, you will need to understand how our time relates to your music—or how your music relates to our time. Either will work.

Sixteenth, eighth and quarter notes: roughly a heartbeat.
Beat: just around a moment.
Measure: three or four moments, depending.
Overture: kind of like Heaven's morning.
Verse: three or four hours-ish.
Chorus: akin to a verse, but more exciting.
Song: something like a Heavenly day.
The Silence: the time when angels sleep.
Movement: resemblant of a month.
Symphony: roundabouts a year.

SIXTH HEXANT
FIFTH HEXANT
FOURTH HEXANT
CIVIL LOGISTIC HUB
(NORTHERN HEXANCE)
CIVIL LOGISTIC HUB
(SOUTHERN HEXANCE)
TWELFTH CIRCLE
ELEVENTH CIRCLE
TENT
VILLAGE BORDER
HOLY
OF THE
FIRST CI
N
W
S

FIRST HEXANT
SECOND HEXANT
THIRD HEXANT
HEAVEN
UNIVERSAL TECHNOLOGIES
VILLAGE BORDER

"ABUNDANCE IS THE FINAL SAFEGUARD OF ALL UTOPIAN CIVILIZATION. WITHOUT IT, UNKNOWN CHAOS MIGHT ENSUE."

-THE GUIDE TO UTOPIAN PRINCIPLES AND ETHICS

1

Michael

*"Desire is a nagging shrew, promising the first bell's
dew. If a thing you must possess, desire then possesses
you!"*
-Heaven's Handbook, Virtues, Part 7

LIGHT FLASHED FROM THE corner of Michael's eye and blood splattered across his face. He wiped it, the sickly-sweet, honey scent clinging to him. When animals bled, the smell was neutral. But when angels bled, it was like someone shoved your face into a vat of lavender-rose-flavored candy and held it there until you didn't want to breathe anymore.

At least it wasn't *his* blood.

The baker, who had no business attempting to fight in an amateur gladiator tournament, pulled his yellow flag and limped to the space reserved for healing. He slipped off his chest plate and exposed his wounds to Heaven's light. They knitted themselves closed.

Bubs ran into the pit and raked the sweat from the previous gladiators, if they could even be called that. Michael knelt and waited his turn, the blue beryl stone in his sword staring at him, defiant. There was no satisfaction in pummeling these poor enthusiasts who showed up to the pits in their free time, scarcely able to latch on their own armor. But he needed *something* to distract himself with.

He popped a few dried coffee beans in his mouth and winced at the bitterness as he crunched down. Hopefully, the caffeine would hit before he did, otherwise he might doze off fighting these untrained loafs. Sleep had never been his friend.

"I've got four bushels of potatoes riding on you." Nunziel, the local grocer, appeared wearing an uncharacteristically fancy frock.

"New jacket?"

"Won it betting your last fight." He grinned.

"Shouldn't you be at work?" It was a little early to be placing bets, even for Nunziel. The last bells of the overture had barely finished ringing. "Winners won't even be recorded in this tournament."

"I'll head back to the shop right after this bet."

"I'll never understand gambling," Michael sighed, watching as they spread fresh dirt for the next match. "What's the point of wagering things you already give away?"

"The thrill of the win!" Nunziel winked. "Heaven loves a good game."

"A good fight you mean...."

"Any word of a Calling yet?"

Michael bristled. "Not yet. Shemliel should've been back with word by now. He's been gone for more than a movement." This was the third and final petition for a Calling that Shemliel was filing for him, and if it wasn't approved, he'd be dismissed altogether. He'd have to come up with a whole new plan, which didn't even seem possible. He dreaded the thought.

"We're betting you get Called to the arenas," Nunziel said.

"I'm starting to think you have a gambling problem...."

"Next up!" the judge announced, and Nunziel threw a thumbs up before retreating to the stands.

Michael sprang to his feet and jumped in the pit. His opponent was another *giver* from the markets in the agorium. The potter. And his shin guards were on backward.

Intra-village tournaments were the *worst*. There was zero vetting process for who was allowed to sign up. Michael would have to be extra careful with this bub—slices and stab wounds healed quickly, but this one looked like he might amputate one of his own extremities... and those injuries were a different story.

The whistle blew and the potter got into position, or something resembling a position. Michael kept at a safe distance, but the poor fool came charging. He flailed his sword against Michael's shield, nearly losing his balance in the process.

"Michael!" a rider on horseback galloped from the field. It was Ahab, one of the brothers from his house. He stopped short at the edge of the pit. "Shemliel's home," he hollered over the clanging noise of the potter's blade. "And a letter's arrived in the post. It looks official, though there's no name on it. Mary thinks it might be your Calling."

Michael's gaze darted from the flailing potter to Ahab just as the poor bub's weapon slipped from his hand and bounced off Michael's shield. Michael caught it and handed it back before pulling his own flag and forfeiting the match.

The potter leapt with excitement. Let him enjoy it—it wasn't like intra-village tournaments went on your record anyway.

"Sorry about those potatoes, Nunz..."

The grocer threw up his hands as Michael bowed before the victor and climbed from the pit. He mounted behind Ahab.

They zipped through the field, a lively allegro blaring from Heaven's sky as the horse's strides fell into rhythm with the short, pulsing cello notes. Hues of pink, yellow, and blue danced through the golden light in lock step with the Music of the Spheres. If only Michael's life could be that smooth.

"Shemliel got home after the first bells of the overture," Ahab said, huffing as he sped the horse to a full gallop. "He must've just missed you."

"Why would he leave my Calling in the post box and not deliver it in person?" Michael's voice bounced.

"Maybe the Herald happened to deliver it at the same time Shemliel arrived," Ahab said, turning them down the gravel road that led back home. "He's been away for nearly a movement pleading your case. It's possible they sent the decision while he was still en route back."

They cantered along the edge of the tree-lined estate, the familiar scent of Mary's fresh baked manna already wafting over. There was a commotion at the side of the manor. Brothers bustling around, hauling things and calling out to each other.

"A little early to be setting up tables for Shemliel's pairing banquet," Michael said. "Why aren't they at work?"

"They're not setting up tables," Ahab said, and then slowed the horse to a trot. "Lilly came by insisting that Mary host their pairing *ceremony* too—not just the banquet. Then half the sisters from the Violet Rose showed up and convinced us all to stay home and build a stained-glass archway for it."

"I thought ceremonies happened in chapels," Michael said, though he'd never been to a pairing himself.

"A new trend," Ahab said. "Mary felt bad calling me away to come get you, but you know she can only ride that donkey. And she wanted you to come quickly."

Matriarch Mary waited under the estate signage which read, *The Jolly Bub, all are welcome.* Her black dress and white apron were covered in flour handprints, and her bonnet had a dusting on it too.

"Sorry we scooped ya from the pits, son!" She came running up holding her bonnet in place, her stout form and ruddy cheeks bouncing with each stride. "But it's so rare we get fancy letters like this. It's got to be yer' Callin'!"

Michael leapt from the horse before it came to a full stop, and Ahab continued toward the stable. She handed him a folded parchment.

Gold-leaf lined the exterior, and it was sealed in a fine gold-and-silver-flecked wax.

Fancy indeed.

If Shemliel managed to get him that Calling, everything was about to change. Michael would make that lord pay for what he'd done. And worse—for what he made Michael do.

Abandoner.

Michael swallowed the guilt and glanced at the letter again.

But what if Shemliel *didn't* pull it off? What if his path to victory ended under this seal?

"Where *is* Shemliel?" Michael asked. It would be smarter to open this with him present, to give context.

"His bags are on his bed," Mary's voice pitched up, "but he must've left... Imagine, his own pairin' not two songs away, and he disappears again! But don't just stand there askin' questions, Michael..." Her gaze moved anxiously between him and the letter. "Open it before the curiosity chokes me!"

He took a deep breath. If he was denied, he'd find another way. He'd never rest until he made that miserable lord suffer.

He peeled away the wax, hands shaking, and slowly unfolded the page.

"Dearest Matriarch Mary..."

Relief and disappointment flooded all at once. He handed the letter back to Mary.

"It's for you."

She covered her mouth, her face pained, then reached her pudgy arms around his waist, nearly crushing him. "I'm so sorry, my son. I should've known yer brother would've wanted to deliver word in person."

Brother. The word rang out like a lone note in the wrong key. It was the same whenever she called him *son.* But all eighty angels under this roof called each other "brother," and Mary called each of them "son." He should've been grateful for the inclusion, but it somehow made him feel more like a fraud.

"Don't feel bad, Mary." He gently peeled her off. Whether he felt like part of them or not, Matriarch Mary had shown him more kindness than anyone in his life.

"But I do need to find Shemliel," Michael said, suddenly glad that letter wasn't for him. He needed to hear this news in person. "Do you have any idea where he could've gone?"

She tapped her chin. "He *is* due for the final fittin' of his frock. I can't be sure, but if he knows what's good for 'em, he'll be at the tailor's."

"Then that's where I'll start."

Mary raised a finger as if to say "wait," and ran into the manor, her jostling petticoats making her movements even more like a waddle.

She emerged again holding a list and handed it to him. "If you're gonna be at the agorium anyway, maybe you could grab a few things. I've run out of vita flour to bake the manna for Shemmy's pairin' banquet."

"Even your stash in the stable cellar?"

"There'll be over three hundred angels here! It's not every song the Ambassador of a Circle gets paired. Bring Bentley. It'll be a mighty load to haul without 'em."

Bentley? There were slugs who could outrun Bentley. "Are you sure you don't need the flour sooner? I can take one of the fast horses."

"There's quite a bit on that list," she said. "They won't be able to haul all that. I can take the ride if it's too much trouble. I don't want to disturb yer' brothers again while they're buildin' that—"

"No," Michael cut her off. She'd done everything for him. The least he could do was get her groceries. "Bentley's just fine."

He left her and rounded the manor, its many square-paned windows flanked by wood shutters that had never been used. Wind shutters were like coats and lanterns—useless because it was never windy or cold. And unless you were locked in a cellar, it was never dark either.

He swiped one of the dense, musty vita fruit that grew from the estate's Mother Tree, weaving through the teardrop-shaped birthing pods that had been emptied long ago to populate this place with brothers. If that donkey was to be motivated, he'd need food.

The stink of manure waited at the stables where he passed a whole row of horses who could've gotten him to that tailor much faster. In the last stall was a dull gray donkey with one brown eye and one green. Slow, stubborn, and full of grit—Bentley was Mary's favorite.

Michael held up the vita fruit, and Bentley's damp muzzle sniffed above the stall door. He met Michael's gaze with two wide, mismatched eyes, and Michael counted down.

Three, two...

Two stomps and a *big wet bray*.

Michael ducked the donkey snot before Bentley gobbled the vita. His bray was something between a scream and a sneeze, and you'd better have an umbrella if you stood in front of it. If the little beast was anything, he was predictable.

Bentley's hooves crunched the gravel road at a snail's pace as they made their way to the agorium. An airship whizzed by overhead and Michael wished he was on it—if only to move faster. Its black-and-copper underbelly glinted in Heaven's light, resembling some kind of flying, metallic beetle— except instead of wings, it had sails.

Technology remained mostly hidden, unless you had a specialized calling to one of the realm's logistics hubs where the broader municipal operations were centralized. But every now and then, you could catch an airship flying an export route. And of course, there were the cruder machines made by tinkers, *if* you were lucky enough to know a tinker—which Michael was.

When they finally got to the agorium, a mish-mosh of lively voices and tantalizing aromas greeted them. Hand-painted signs hung with pride as the givers gave away their creations all over the main square.

How anyone could muster a passion for Callings like drying beans or pressing oil, Michael had no idea. But they were all so bleeding happy to gift away their handiwork. Hordes of angels meandered, inspecting the wares, some in basic robes or tunics and some in the more fashionable frocks and corsets that came from the inner circles.

In some ways, his lack of a birth record was a blessing—he might've been the only angel in history who even stood a chance to choose their own Calling.

They stopped in front of the tailor's shop and Michael hitched Bentley to a pole. He gave the door a quick knock before pulling it open and leaned inside.

"Can I help you?" the tailor asked, pins in his mouth as he measured some femme.

"I'm looking for Shemliel," Michael said. "Is he here?"

The tailor spat out the pins. "The Ambassador left not that long ago. I think he went to the florist."

"Thanks."

Michael jogged up the road. The bell over the door tinkled as thick, floral air assaulted him. "Have you seen Shemliel?"

"The Ambassador was here earlier," a bub arranging lilies behind the counter said, "but I think he went home."

You have got to be kidding. "Thanks."

Michael ran back to the tailor's and unhitched Bentley, but when he started for home, he put his hand in his pocket and felt Mary's list.

The flour.

He grunted, then turned around. They headed back through the main square and up the road toward Nunziel's shop.

"Michael!" Nunziel waved from the doorway of *the Fresh Pantry*. His russet frock matched the bushel of potatoes behind him. "What was the news? Anything on your Calling?"

"Just a letter for Mary." Michael slid into the shop. Produce of every kind was stacked in barrels, along with nuts and grains and flour. "Looks like you got to keep your potatoes." Michael handed him the list. "I'm helping Mary prepare for Shemliel's pairing banquet."

"Of course," Nunziel said. "It's not every song that the—"

"—Ambassador of our Circle gets paired," Michael said. "I know."

"My pairing was the best song of my life." Nunziel craned his neck toward the back of the store. "Isn't that right, my love?"

"Whatever you say," a feminine voice droned back.

Nunziel pointed to the list. "About this flour. Like I told your brother Shemliel—"

"Shemliel?" Michael interrupted. "He was here?"

"Still is..." Nunziel pointed to the back of the shop, all the way in the corner. Someone leaned headfirst into a barrel, and Michael headed straight for him.

"Where have you been?"

Shemliel popped up, his tunic stuck to his belly like an overfed child. "Is anyone with you?" His gaze darted around.

"No." Michael gave him a once over. He had put on a few pounds, and his black beard stubble was so thick that it grew straight into his chest. "What's wrong with you?"

He dragged Michael behind a huge display of vegetables, peeking around a crate to check the store again.

"Are you *hiding*?" Michael asked.

"Of course not. I just... don't want to be found."

"Why?"

"Lilly's driving me mad! And some of her sisters—" he groaned. "Do you know she wants a *public* pairing ceremony? A new trend, she says. Something's off with the whole lot on her estate. I'm starting to regret ever picking up that kerchief."

"Sorry to hear it...." Michael said, but he couldn't muster the pretense to care. "Is there any word on my Calling?"

Shemliel eyed him for a beat, then took a deep breath. "I was hoping to deliver that news *after* I drained a few bottles of vintage. Maybe even a small flask of empyreanol for good measure."

Michael's stomach dropped. "Why?"

"It's not good news for either of us."

Either of us? "What does that mean? What did the Council say?"

"Nothing. I didn't file your petition with the Council."

The heat drained from Michael's face. "Why? You said the bureaucracy was shrinking, that we stood the best chance yet...."

"Well, they shrunk so much that they disappeared. The Council is dissolved, and the Ministry of Callings is closed. The lords have all left."

It was like someone pulled the air from Michael's lungs.

"Imagine..." Shemliel shook his head. "A land without politicians. And I, too, am now gainfully *uncalled*. I never understood what you meant when you said you felt useless. I do now."

"They can't be gone, Shem...." Not after he'd worked so hard. Built his stats in the pits. Filed so many petitions. The only way for his plan to work was if he got a chance to fight in the Games. "If the Council's gone, who's overseeing everything?"

"The Almighty himself, apparently..." Shemliel sighed, "in all of his glorious *silence*. Not a single Mother Tree has sprouted in over *twenty symphonies*. You're so young—have you ever even seen a baby? Angels want for nothing, and the world runs like a well-oiled wheel. The most meaningful petitions I've voiced for this Circle in the last hundred symphonies have been yours, and a petition to change the color of cucumbers—which used to be red, by the way. As far as the Council was concerned: our infrastructure is perfect, our citizenry is perfect, and our *lives* are perfect. There is no longer a need for political structure."

"Perfect for *who*?" The backs of Michael's eyes burned something fierce. "How can so many petitions have gone unanswered?"

"Some were answered."

"Sure, denying my existence."

"Nobody denied your existence. They didn't think I made you up. But someone blundered your creation record, and it doesn't help that you refuse to tell me your estate of origin or anything about your life before you showed up at the Jolly Bub."

Michael ignored that last comment. Besides the fact that he didn't *know* his estate of origin, some secrets stayed secret to keep them all safe. "I can't spend my life being a useless burden on Mary."

"Brother..." Shemliel reached out to console him, but Michael pulled away. Michael only had *one* brother, and he'd deserted that brother long ago.

"Even if they did issue a Calling," Shemliel said, "there's no telling if they would have honored your request to be called as a gladiator."

"Excuse me..." Nunziel cut in, holding the list.

Michael did his best to appear composed.

"I don't mean to interrupt, but I need to let you know that we've been having delivery issues with the sweet vita flour Mary wanted."

"Is there anywhere else we can get it?" Shemliel asked.

"The whole Crossing's been experiencing delays," Nunziel said.

"Guess I'm not the only one with problems," Michael grumbled, kicking a stray grape.

"*Problem* is just a word in the dictionary." Nunziel laughed. "But we do occasionally get lazy angels. Darlene will take a trip out there to see what the hold-up is. In the meantime, I had the miller grind up some local fruit. It has a nice, bold flavor, I think."

"Our local fruit tastes like socks," Shemliel said.

"Trees of Life are such a sensitive plant," Nunziel sighed. "The flavor depends so much on the soil. But we must never forget...*Vita is life—*"

"And life is vita," Michael muttered, finishing the proverb. There was no shortage of annoying colloquialisms from Heaven's indoctrinated. There was a time when he would've eaten vita scraps from the gutters, but none of these angels could ever understand that. Which was why he *needed* that Calling.

"This fruit's not so bad, I think." Nunziel pointed to a barrel of the shining, yellow vita. "Why don't you take one home to Mary so she can taste it before she uses the flour to bake."

"Thanks, Nunz." Michael blinked back tears of frustration as his gaze moved over the barrel. There had to be *some* other way to get close to that miserable lord. But even if he could, it wouldn't mean anything if he still wore that ring. Which was why it was so important that Michael met him in the Games.

Never fight a god. She'd use that word—god—because she thought it made the lords sound more intimidating. Everyone did when they wanted to remind you that the lords held power. But the word was just short for "goodness obliges duty." Maybe they did use their power to serve, but there was one lord who certainly did not. Problem was, nobody in this *perfect world* would ever believe that.

"Now that we're both uncalled," Shem said, sifting the fruit, "why don't we just try and enjoy it? Maybe you can teach me to swing a sword, or paint those pictures you think nobody knows about."

Michael shot him a glare. "That's only a hobby. And not one I'm any good at."

"Think about how much time you'll free up if you're not constantly fighting the amateur tournaments to justify your petitions..." Shem raised his brows expectantly, as if the idea of having no goals somehow made it okay to have no purpose. "You can spend more time with your little tinker friend from Lilly's estate—the one who dresses like a bub. What do they call her? The *Rebel Rose*?"

"She doesn't like that name." Michael shot him a glare and tossed a bruised fruit back, maybe a little too hard. Philistina was the only real friend Michael had, and her new *nickname* had only been a recent invention by her sisters. Instead of celebrating the quirks that made her unique, they began mocking them. But that was all beside the point. "I can't just *give up*, Shem. You said the lords all left... where'd they go?"

"To work on some new project. I don't know much other than that it involves copious amounts of technology—and that stuff is lost on me. Indoor plumbing is about as technical as I get."

"But *where,* Shem?" Even if Michael couldn't get an opportunity to fight in the Games, maybe he could get close enough and figure something else out.

"Eastern Island," Shemliel said. "It's not a logistics hub, but apparently there's some big, mechanical project going on there. They affirmed the little stretch of land as its own Circle before they left, which is bizarre because the island's smaller than our Crossing. Not to mention, the lords aren't exactly accustomed to living among the commonborn."

Living among the commonborn? Michael perked—maybe there was still hope yet. "If the project is new, won't it need to be staffed?

"It's a technology project, Michael. Those are highly specialized jobs. I have no idea how they're staffing it with the Ministry of Callings closed."

"Okay... but the floors still need to be mopped, right? Plates washed? Someone's making sure those things get done."

"Why are you so malcontent to stay home?"

"I'm not malcontent, Shem..." even though he technically was, but not for the reasons Shemliel thought. "I can't continue being a useless burden on Mary. The Jolly Bub was never planned with me in mind. There's no pod on that Mother Tree engraved with my name. You think you understand how it feels to have no purpose now? Imagine *never* having had a purpose."

Burden. Extra. Doesn't belong.

Shemliel's face softened. He weighed two fruits in his hands, then put one down. "I might know of *one* femme who has access to information that can help us. Or at least knows someone who does." He rubbed his face hard. "You're going to make me go home and be found, aren't you?"

"You're talking about Lilith?" Michael cocked a brow.

"Unfortunately."

Michael picked up the fruit that Shemliel put down. It was plump, ripe, and free of blemish. He smiled. "Let's bring this one home to Mary."

"Not that one..." Shemliel took it and peeled back some of the skin. A gaggle of beezle-fly larvae wiggled inside. "One thing I've been learning about choices... sometimes you can't know if you've chosen well, until it's too late."

Sounds of work filled the air at the south side of the Jolly Bub. Metal banged and brothers grunted as they put together the frame that would hold poor Shemliel's new stained-glass archway.

"And how, exactly, was everyone talked into staying home and building this thing?" Shemliel asked Mary from the doorway.

"When I was a young, skinny bab, I'd wave me kerchief and have all the bubs lining up too." She wiggled her bottom and let out a hearty laugh. "Beauty's a great persuader! Besides, Shemmy... you know our motto...."

"Eat more?" Michael said, and Mary slapped his arm.

"Not that one," she chortled, a curl slipping free of her bonnet and sang, "*Service is the heart of Heaven...*"

"And Heaven's heart doth serve," Shemliel grumbled the rest of the proverb. "Thanks a lot, Mary."

She grinned, slipping back into the kitchen. Michael and Shem perused the yard. A cast-iron cauldron sat at the far side, where apparently they'd be melting the substantial amount of sand they were currently dumping into it. But Michael had seen the glass blowers at the agorium, and their ovens were much more sophisticated than that. They'd be lucky to boil soup in that thing.

Lilith strutted the grounds in silk robes, barking orders at the brothers with half a dozen of her sisters in tow. Michael searched for spiky buns among those well-groomed coifs, but there were none. Which wasn't surprising. Philistina wasn't exactly welcomed around her sisters lately.

Shemliel gave a humble wave as Lilith locked him in her sight. "The things I do for you..." he muttered.

"Where have you been!?" She stormed over with one of her sisters, two angry slits for eyes.

"My sweetest plum…" Shemliel stretched his best politician's smile. "I had the final fitting of my frock, and I had to check on the florist, and of course I had to—"

"Save it." She raised her hand. "I had to finish all these preparations without you. You could've at least answered my letters."

"I did, my supple fig…" His voice grew tight. "At least ten of them."

In the corner of Michael's eye, he spied one of the Jolly Bub's brothers, Daniel, trying to light the wood under the crucible without fuel. Maybe they *wouldn't* even boil soup in that thing.

"Forget it," she said. "I've moved on. Your family is helping, and we'll have the ceremony right here…" She gestured to the spot where they constructed the frame.

"I assumed we'd pair in a chapel," Shem said. "Alone with our witnesses and the precept. You know… *in private.*"

"You know what they say about assumptions." Her sister stepped forward, silk robes flowing in the same fashion as Lilly. Michael didn't know one sister from the next, as they all looked the same. Well… except one, but she wasn't there.

"If it isn't Mary's little mystery…." Her gaze slithered over Michael as she flicked her hair behind her shoulder. "Some of us went to find you at the tournament earlier. We thought Shemliel might be there too. I was even going to place a bet."

"I was… busy." Michael cleared his throat and stepped back. "Is it possible we could have a word with Lilith? Alone?"

The sister looked affronted, but Shemliel made the prayer hands, begging she oblige.

"Maybe you can go help Daniel," Michael said, gesturing to the crucible. "He could use someone clever to get that fire going."

She looked to Lilith, who nodded, and went off with a huff.

"Speak," Lilly said, crossing her arms. "Quickly. There's work to be done."

"What do you know about the new project on Eastern Island?" Shemliel asked.

"I know that all my invitations to the lords were declined because they're busy working on that silly thing. Honestly. What could so many lords have to do with a bunch of technology anyway?"

"Do you know if they're issuing Callings?" Michael asked.

She quirked a brow. "Do I look like I work for the Ministry of Callings?"

"Lilly, please," Shemliel said. "I've spent the better part of a movement trying to help Michael with a Calling. It's not his fault his birth record is gone. I know it's a long shot, but you've always been better at hobnobbing than I have. Angels tend to like you more."

She pursed her lips. "Can't argue with that."

"Please, Lilith…" Michael wasn't above begging at this point.

She stayed aloof for a beat but then sighed. "I do know someone who was called to Eastern Island. He'll be—"

CLUNK!

The whole horde turned in one swift motion toward the noise. A small femme stood next to some kind of crude, copper machine. She swam in a pair of oversized coveralls, and her work boots were chunky and worn-out.

Michael's lip curled just slightly.

Her wild blonde hair was pulled into two spiky buns, and she lowered a pair of bug-eyed goggles over her eyes. She jabbed a metal rod into the ground.

Lilith's face darkened.

"Stand back!" Philistina bellowed, and then counted down with her fingers. She pressed a button, and the machine roared to life with a chugging, buzzing hum. It sucked the light from around itself in swirls, and everyone gasped.

Machines were a rare sight indeed—*unless you knew a brilliant tinker.*

The wire connecting the rod took on an impossible blue glow, and an orange beam shot from its tip and struck the cauldron. In less than an eighth note, the cauldron glowed red, and the acrid smell of hot iron and melting sand filled the air. The pile of grains slowly disappeared into a bubbling goo.

"Amorphous silica you wanted..." She pressed a button and the beam disappeared, returning the copper beast to its former sleeping state. "Amorphous silica you have. Go on and pour your glass.... Commendable try, Daniel, but you're painful to watch."

"Dear Almighty..." Shem gripped Michael's wrist. "Is that the Rebel Rose?"

"Philistina!" Lilith started toward her sister, but Michael grabbed her shoulder. Her narrowed gaze snapped to him.

"Please," Michael said. "You were saying you knew someone who could help...."

"Joseph the Champion has been reassigned to Eastern Island." She yanked herself free. "He'll be at our pairing. You can speak with him then." She stormed off as Michael's pulse sped up.

Joseph the Champion?

He turned to Shemliel. "Why would a *professional gladiator* be called to Eastern Island?"

2

Michael

"Choose your friends well, weighing their usefulness and considering what benefits such synergies might produce. Predict equally their liabilities, and select well. Relationships are like rungs on a ladder; be sure to step up."
-Black Manifesto, Chapter Three, "On Ambition"

"L ET THE PERPETUAL LIGHT shine!"

The minstrel leader clapped his hands to an upbeat tempo and Michael almost danced—almost. Regardless of what blared from the sky, Pairing Minstrels could turn it into something the whole party could dance to.

The rear lawn of the Jolly Bub was no less than a great, outdoor banquet hall. Dozens upon dozens of tables were strewn across the field, covered in iridescent white fabric that refracted a vibrant teal when viewed from certain angles. Lilith had chosen an array of seafoam-blue flowers as centerpieces, and each arrangement was capped with a tall, blossomed white lily. No surprise there. Tents were set up everywhere, and angels from all walks of life mingled, not just the locals.

Some wore the vibrant, colorful fabrics of the outer northeast Hexants, while others were more subdued, donning the classic frocks and dresses of the inner Circles. The coastal angels were notorious for their casual attire at formal events, as if ready to go for a swim, and the mountain angels always found a reason to incorporate wool into their outfits.

It was the biggest party he'd ever seen, not that he'd seen many parties. He popped a few coffee beans as he scanned the crowd.

"Michael! Michael, come quickly..." Matriarch Mary stepped from the back door balancing two huge trays of appetizers. Michael bolted over and took one.

Meaty bits of sautéed rootroast sat in flaky manna shells, glazed with something like a tartberry reduction. One thing Mary had on every Matriarch in this Crossing—maybe the whole realm—was that she cooked something fierce.

"Oh, my son!" She covered her mouth with the hand he just freed up. "Look how handsome ya' be in a proper frock! I see those dimples..." She pinched his cheek with the same vigor she used to knead dough. "I reckon if ya smile more with those dimples, it'll be rainin' kerchiefs on yer' head!"

He adjusted his collar, suddenly feeling the constriction of it. "Should I start serving these now?"

"Please. You take the far end; I'll take the front. When they're finished, let's get everyone seated 'round the archway. The Precept's arrived, and the ceremony's soon to start."

He merged with the crowd, offering the tray, and searched their faces. He scanned the eyes of partygoers, looking for the signature radiance of a lord. As expected, all eyes were brown as tartberry soup, but he never let expectations lower his guard.

More importantly, he looked out for Joseph the Champion, whom he hoped to meet with Shemliel present. It would be nerve racking enough to stand face-to-face with his idol and be expected to hold a conversation, much less the conversation that he needed to have. Joseph had been Michael's hero ever since he'd stolen his first sports journal from Matriarch Deidre's library.

His gaze moved from group to group as he served. He forced a smile and proffered the tray, and a bunch of angels rubbed their hands together, snatching up the appetizers as he acknowledged them, politely. This would be his life if he didn't get a Calling. The extra bub helping around the house and serving appetizers to strangers who had no idea he didn't even have a name. Save the one given by a charitable stranger who would consider the donkey a son if he could talk.

Someone poked the back of his shoulder as he gave away the last appetizer. They stood there in a terrycloth bathrobe with the hood pulled low.

Michael squinted. "Shemliel?"

"Shhhh!"

"Why are you out here in a bathrobe?"

"It's all I had that could hide my face."

"What are you doing? Nobody's supposed to see you before the ceremony."

"I know...." Shemliel grabbed the empty tray and shoved it into a passing brother's gut. "I don't have much time. Once the ceremony starts, I'll be up to my ears in guests. I need to bring you to Joseph and get back upstairs. He wants to meet you alone."

A surge of panic fluttered through Michael. "I thought you were going to be there for this conversation. Why does he want to meet me alone?"

"I don't know, I didn't do a biopic interview. I only got to speak with him briefly. If there's any chance for you, this is it. So don't blow it."

Shem pulled him by the elbow through the crowd and rounded the manor where a group of tables were set up for the angels working the event.

The Champion sat alone, and Michael immediately tensed up when he saw him. Joseph's victories gave rise to the popularity of the Games, and started the world's obsession with sports—or at least that's what the journals said. Michael hadn't been around that long. More than that, he was a great leader, driving even the most unlikely squads to victory. He remained undefeated. Joseph was a legend.

"I can't do this alone," Michael hissed.

"Stop being dramatic." Shemliel dragged Michael to the table and pushed up his hood.

Joseph dabbed his mouth and stood up. "Shemliel!" He extended an arm and they shook. "Didn't expect to see you before the ceremony."

"In all fairness, I didn't expect to be roaming around in a bathrobe before the ceremony." Shemliel motioned him to sit again, but Joseph remained standing, his gaze moving to Michael, who stood there awestruck.

Joseph was smaller than expected. Maybe it was the way the frock concealed his physique, or maybe it was simply that anyone who won that many fights could be nothing less than a giant in your mind.

"I wanted to introduce you to my brother," Shemliel said. "Michael's the one I told you about. The one with the records issue."

A bead of sweat dripped down Michael's face as Joseph looked him over. The Champion extended his arm, revealing a gladiator's wrist guard under his sleeve. Odd accessory to wear at a pairing, but maybe a real Champion never truly left the pits.

Shemliel jammed an elbow into Michael's side, and Michael took Joseph's arm and shook.

"If there's anything you can do to help him," Shemliel said, "our estate would be eternally grateful. He's an amateur, but a true gladiator in his own right. He's the pride of our village in the local tournaments. Wings, he's the pride of the whole Crossing."

"A fan of the gladiatorial arts, then?" Joseph raised his eyebrows and smiled.

Michael nodded. "Very much so."

"I have to go," Shemliel said. "Good luck to you, Michael, and I'll see you all from under that archway. Pray for me." He started walking away, but then paused and called back. "I really mean that. *Pray for me.*"

"Cold wings?" Joseph chuckled.

"Something like that," Michael said. Not that Shemliel, or any commonborn for that matter, even had wings. It was hard to make eye contact with Joseph, and especially unnerving to be taller than him.

Joseph patted his arm, gesturing to the chair. "Don't be nervous, I'm just like you...." He widened his eyes and pointed to them. "See? No light."

"Sorry..." Michael sat, but was still unable to meet his eyes. "It's just that you've given me a lot of hope ever since I was a child. I've studied your whole career... Well, whatever I could find in the journals, anyway. You fight with such skill. I've looked up to you my whole life."

"Ironic, isn't it?" Joseph tilted his head. "The physical art of fighting and wielding weapons have no function beyond entertainment, yet gladiators are almost treated as gods. And the Games are the only place in the whole world where a commonborn might earn a formal title."

"Like Champion," Michael said.

"Or *Master of the Games*."

Michael's throat suddenly went dry. "No gladiator's ever challenged Lord Baalael for that title."

Joseph held his gaze for a long beat, and Michael could've sworn he almost detected a smirk. "A gladiator would have to be very exceptional—or very stupid—to challenge the Lord of Victory, even if the rules do oblige him to fight without his ring. The Games will always be his dominion, and he won't easily give up that vanity title—*Master of the Games*." He chuckled and took a sip of his wine. "But at least, in theory, it's something we can earn."

"That's why I like the pits," Michael said. "It doesn't matter what the world says I should do. It only matters what I *can* do."

"A thinker too," Joseph said. "That's certainly rare."

Michael had never really considered himself a thinker. If anything, being denied an education made him anything but.

"The arena is the one place we can exercise some control of our fate," Joseph said. "*If* we're lucky enough to be called to the arena, that is.

And that's why angels love their sports. They live vicariously through the underdog who might become a Champion. And the Champion—no matter how unlikely—who might become Master of the Games. It's like fighting is the expression of something for which we have no expression at all."

Michael recalled Joseph's essays—the ones that had been banned. Deidre kept all manner of literature in her personal library, and Michael was an exceptional thief. Joseph was something of a philosopher too, though few had known it.

Joseph chuckled. "Forgive me if I'm overly contemplative. They're serving some very good wine here."

Michael shook his head. "No, I appreciate your thoughts. I think gladiators are more impressive than the lords. They're not born with power and respect; they have to earn it. Gladiators make glory something attainable—something more than bright eyes and wings. Glory shouldn't be a birthright reserved for the gods."

"A visionary too?" Joseph raised his glass and nodded. "Some would call the words 'should' or 'shouldn't' blasphemous in our *perfect world*. But I am not such a one."

"When I'm in the pits, I feel alive," Michael said. "It's the only thing I've ever been good at."

"You have quite an impressive fighting record for someone who's never been formally trained—" Joseph paused. "So says your brother, anyway. Wielding and fighting are an art. You mean to tell me you've learned that much on your own?"

Michael did have training; it just wasn't formal. Nor was it anything he was able to reveal without putting his whole history on the table—and that was out of the question. "I've learned from other amateurs.... Picked up what I could here and there."

"And you've never received a Calling to the arena?"

Michael shook his head. "I've never received a Calling to anything. Paperwork problems, I guess. It's starting to look hopeless."

"With the Council being dissolved, I could see how that would seem hopeless."

"You know about the Council?"

Joseph nodded. "A few select Callings are still going out. There's a new project on Eastern Island, but angels are usually reassigned from previous occupations. I am one of those angels. They call it *Universal Technologies*."

"You work in technology now?"

"Godsforbid!" Joseph threw back his head and laughed. "The staff there is filled with enthusiasts who love sports, and what more is a sports enthusiast than an aspiring athlete who doesn't play very well? And I love to teach. The Lord of Music oversees a large portion of the project, and he's sponsoring a sports program on the island. Taking it upon himself to provide the resources we need." Joseph leaned in and lowered his voice. "And if I can teach those desk chairs to be any good with a sword, they'll get the opportunity to qualify for the Games."

Michael's breath grew shallow. "What about Lord Baalael? The Games are his domain."

"The Master of the Games doesn't get to decide who competes. So long as an area is part of a Circle, it gets to have a squad that may qualify. And Eastern Island is now officially the Thirteenth Circle. With the Ministry of Callings officially gone, the only way to build our squad is to allow angels to compete for it. We can thank the Lord of Music for that. His last act as an officiant of the Council was to name that island the Thirteenth Circle."

"The Lord of Music?" Michael wasn't familiar with all the lords. Only Baalael.

"Lucifer," Joseph said. "He's made it all possible."

Michael's plan was suddenly something more than a distant, loosely hitched pipe dream. All polite pretense left his voice. "Give me the chance to earn this...." He grabbed Joseph's sleeve, feeling the hard wrist guard beneath it. "Let me prove myself. Give me a chance to earn your respect, to be trained by you. I know I can make it to the Games."

Joseph regarded him for a long beat, and then leaned back. "Your brother is a respected Ambassador, and he speaks highly of you. I'll speak to Lucifer and see if there's anything he can do. I'm sure there must be a job or two left outside of the highly specialized Callings—unless you know something about technology or art? Any secret talents in there?"

"None worth mentioning." Michael shuffled in his seat.

"Now this isn't a promise that you'll fight on the squad. If Lucifer can arrange a Calling, you'll still have to try out."

"I understand. I don't want to be given anything. I only want to earn it."

"Then keep hope, Michael. All isn't lost yet. We'll be in touch."

White chairs lined up in rows in front of the stained-glass archway, and Michael sat in the ninth row, behind the rest of Jolly Bub's brothers. Mary sat up front anxiously dabbing her eyes with an already damp kerchief, and the minstrels slowed the pace of the music, cueing the guests to find their seats for the ceremony.

Everyone seemed to know what to do, carrying small pouches of confetti and flower petals, but Michael had no idea. He was younger than anyone there, and had never seen a pairing ceremony. It all seemed very dramatic.

Lilith's sisters sat on the other side of the aisle, about seventy in total, all wearing some version of the same dress: light, flowy and teal. In their hair were little teal blossoms and little teal beads. Dainty teal gems adorned their necks, and, overall, they looked like a bunch of table centerpieces.

He scanned for a set of spiky buns, but she wasn't there.

If anyone had the wings to blow off an event this big, it would be her. For some reason, that fact brought him a modicum of joy, even if her absence did make it feel a bit empty.

He yawned and pulled the chordograph from his vest pocket, trying to predict exactly when this thing might be over.

The band cued the start of the ceremony, and everyone's head turned toward center aisle in one swift motion. The three oldest pairs in the village marched first, which was apparently the tradition.

Nunziel and Darlene started, marking them as the longest paired couple from the village. The weaver and his match marched next, though Michael forgot their names. He checked his chordograph again. It was almost impossible to tell time by ear with those minstrels playing.

Someone caught Michael's eye approaching from the side of the manor. They wore denim coveralls with a sleeveless top underneath, and spikes of blonde hair stuck out from either side of their head.

His lips curled upward as he imagined the look on Lilith's face when she saw Philistina's outfit. This ceremony just got a lot more interesting.

She took a seat at the edge of a back row as the minstrels trumped the opening notes for what was probably the final march: four blasts of the horn, accompanied by the quick pitter-patter of a snare drum. Everyone stood up, and photographers snapped their photo-machines from beneath tiny curtains. Michael stood up.

Shemliel marched first. He was adorned in a white frock, complete with ruffles and gold trim at the hems. On his pairing hand, he wore a ruffled, white glove, and his face was shaved cleaner than a baby's bottom. His hair was slicked back and pulled into a white broach at his neck.

Michael stifled a laugh.

The precept escorting him wore a modest brown robe with a white book tucked under his arm: The Handbook. The source of indoctrination for the whole world. Not that Michael had ever read the thing.

They marched down the aisle, and the precept left Shemliel under the archway and stepped to the other side of it. Then Lilith emerged from the back door of the manor holding another precept by the elbow. The hips of her stark white gown poofed into a giant, bustling umbrella, whose train was easily twenty cubits long and required six of her teal-clad sisters to carry it. She held a lace parasol for the light, and of course, a white lace glove on her pairing hand.

They marched down the aisle, Lilith's face poised and elegant, coolly smiling at the crowd and posing for photos. Shemliel already had wet spots near his armpits and wore a smile so forced that Michael wondered if he needed to use the bathroom.

A laugh bubbled in his throat, but he covered his mouth and pretended to cough. This was no time for inappropriate laughter.

Lilith took her place next to Shemliel, light streaming through the stained glass and covering their white clothes in rainbows, and her precept took his place beside the other.

"Witness," the first precept bellowed, his voice echoing through the crowd.

"Let us bear witness." The crowd uttered a ceremonial response, then sat down. Michael faked the responses as best he could, having never undergone indoctrination.

The first precept took Shemliel's pairing hand and raised it high, palm facing the audience. He removed the glove to reveal a faint triangle, like a wound that attempted to heal indoors. They said that was the triangle that appeared with destiny's kiss, but who knew how it really worked?

"Now impart to this promise, the glory," the precept announced, and the faint triangle began to glow, gradually increasing in brightness.

"The glory," the crowd repeated, and rays of light stretched from Shem's palm like vines, twisting and turning like seaweed moving in the current. The tendrils stretched into the sky and formed a giant, golden triangle, at least ten cubits wide.

The other precept did the same to Lilith, removing her glove. Her triangle was bottom-side up, and its undulating rays stretched from her hand into the air and settled next to Shemliel's.

"May your choices seal your fate," both precepts said in unison, "from eternity to eternity, everlasting to everlasting." They joined palms, and the airborne, golden triangles merged to form a single, six-pointed star. Light burst forth from their hands and Michael shielded his eyes.

"Behold!" The precepts shouted, "the consummation."

Consummation?

Sounds began to rise from the couple as they locked palms. Strange sounds. Shemliel moaned, and Lilith let out a shriek. Michael's eyes went wide.

Another long moan rolled from Shemliel's mouth, and a laugh began to bubble from the core of Michael's gut. He squeezed his eyes closed, trying to push the laugh back down.

He peeked at the faces of the other guests—none were laughing.

This isn't appropriate.

He attempted to pull himself together, but Lilith let out a series of high-pitch bursts and a chortle escaped Michael's lips, followed by a spray of snot. He pretended to sneeze and covered his face.

Shemliel moaned again, and tears began to pour from Michael's eyes. He pinched the bridge of his nose as his back began bouncing, trying to focus his thoughts on anything else. Anything that wouldn't make him laugh.

A few guests glared at him with disapproving looks, putting a finger to their lips and shushing him. He held his breath and started counting. He had to stop this reaction before Mary caught sight of him.

And just when he thought he might control himself, another voice reached his ears between the ecstatic moans. But this voice didn't belong to Lilith or Shemliel—and it was laughter. Someone else was laughing.

And in what was possibly the absolute dumbest thing he could've done... he turned around.

Philistina was several rows back, face beet red, clearly trying to contain herself.

When their eyes met, it was *over*.

A tsunami of uncontrollable laughter took over his body, his back jostling as his face produced tears and half-snorts. More guests began to look at him, and he waved them off, pretending to cry.

Someone handed him a tissue, and he laughed even harder.

He pried one eye open, and Philistina was now doubled over and about to fall off her chair. The guests began murmuring and pointing at them.

This was bad. So bad.

He had to get them out of there.

He stood up and slid past the other knees in the row, nearly falling over when Lilith wretched out another moan. One of the guests asked if he was alright, and he eeked out that he was 'just so proud' before dabbing his wet eyes with the tissue.

By the time he reached the end of the row, Philistina barely held herself up. He walked up alongside her and put his arm around her shoulder, pretending to share in tears of pride and joy. He dabbed her face with the tissue, and she buried it in his chest. The precepts eyed them as they limped away, barely holding each other up. He led her to the manor and through the kitchen, where the cooks all stared.

"It's okay," he eeked out. "We're just... so proud..."

Another loud moan pierced the air, and they were practically running now. He led her up the stairs and down the hall. He opened the door to his room, and they fell inside, roaring.

They rolled around the floor, sprawling at times, cackling and snorting as the unconstrained groans of the couple sailed in through the window. And every time they started to calm, someone would moan, and they'd start laughing again.

Eventually, the laughter faded, and the consummation ended. When it did, that swarming feeling replaced his laughter. The one he got every time she showed up.

"Say something sad." She still sat on the floor, a chuckle lingering in her cadence. "So we don't start laughing again."

"This is Heaven..." He stood up abruptly and closed the window, just in case they should moan again. "Sad's only a word in the dictionary."

She narrowed her eyes, playfully.

"We should get back to the party," Michael said. "Lilith will flip a feather if she knows we left."

"All the more reason to stay inside." Philistina stood up and started looking around at his things. "I need to show you something." She reached under his bed, sliding out the flat case of his paintings.

"Please don't..." He dragged his hands across his face. "How'd you know I hid them there?"

She peeked over her shoulder. "You're not as smart as you think you are."

Had this been anyone else—anyone—he would've snatched that case away before they got even a finger under the bed. Maybe even knocked them over in the process. Impaled them if necessary.

"Make it quick." He winced as she unbuttoned the portfolio. His relationship to art had always been... complicated. "You have no idea the deep distress this causes me."

"Oh, I have an idea..." She slid the paintings from the case and began laying them on the bed. "Don't worry. This won't be a lecture about how you need to share your talen—" She paused as his newest landscape emerged from the case. "It's beautiful..." She trailed her thumb across the painted stream. "How do you capture the light like this? Light is so..." She searched for the word.

"Fleeting?"

"Yes."

"Like my dignity right now." He reached over to snatch it, but she slapped his arm away. "Please, Philla. Put them back."

"No."

Her social skills were less than... ideal. No doubt about that. But this was his own fault. He should've burned those paintings as soon as they dried. Art was a foolish indulgence he could never quite let go of.

She laid them in a line across the bed, then took a step back and crossed her arms. "Have you noticed the difference yet?"

"The difference in what? How bad they are?"

"No, silly. The light. It's getting dimmer."

"It's not the light." He reached for a canvas again, but she stopped him. "It's my lack of skill. The colors are muddy."

"They're not." She reached back into the case and began sliding out the last painting, but this time he grabbed her hand. "Not that one, Philla. Please."

He held her gaze for a beat before she released the dark canvas, only one burned edge peeking out.

"Your paintings show a pattern," she said, as she rearranged the line of canvases. "See? It's a gradient that gets darker with each landscape. I bet the brightest one is the oldest, and the darkest, the newest."

She wasn't wrong. "Doesn't light always fluctuate?"

"Not in a perfect gradient." She walked to the window and opened it, leaning out. "Look at them." She pointed. "Have you ever really seen that before?"

He joined her at the window. "You mean the guests?"

"Have you been hit in the head one too many times in that pit?" She guffawed. "I'm talking about the yellow leaves in the trees, and the ones that fell in the grass."

He focused his eyes. She was right, there were yellowed leaves. "I wouldn't have noticed without you pointing it out. Maybe they've always been there?"

"If you put a living thing in the cellar, and starve it of light, what happens?"

He stayed silent. Why would she ask that?

"Leaves turn yellow when they don't get enough light, Michael," she said. "It's basic science. Leave a plant in the cellar and you'll see."

"Oh." She really did mean leaves. "Maybe the light's not as perfect as everyone thinks. Maybe it's always been like that."

She turned from the window and faced the room again. "I didn't expect you to believe me. Or anyone for that matter."

It's not that he didn't believe her. A few yellow leaves just didn't seem like a big deal.

A long beat of silence passed between them, and it grew awkward.

"You ever feel like you could be in a room full of angels," she said, "all looking at the same thing, yet you see something entirely different?"

"I live in a world full of angels who don't see what I see," he mumbled.

"I've been to your tournaments, you know. You're a better painter than you are a fighter."

"Is that supposed to be a compliment?" He screwed up his face. "And when have you watched me fight?"

"Just because you don't see me, doesn't mean I'm not there."

"What about you?" he folded his arms. "Look at what you're capable of... but you reject all your Callings. And you let your sisters talk down to you. That has to hurt."

She shrugged, and a breeze blew the tiny whisps of stray hair that crowned her head. "Hurt's only a word in the dictionary," she teased. "Besides... they weren't always like this. They've changed. They say things about you too, you know."

"What things?"

"That Mary found you on her doorstep. Gave you a home." She hoisted herself on the sill, making a seat of it. "You never talk about yourself. And when you do, it's shallow."

"You're calling me shallow?"

"Stop deflecting." She smiled.

"What else do they say?"

"Let's see..." Her gaze roamed the ceiling. "Michael the mystery. Michael the misfit. But my personal favorite..." She chuckled. "Michael the *masculine*."

He didn't really find that funny at all. "And what do you call me?"

A cloud broke, turning her into a perfect silhouette against the light.

"I call you Michael the silent, because you won't tell me anything. Michael the merciful, because of the way you try and teach those poor souls who fumble in the pits." She abruptly popped from the window and walked to the door, opening it. "Maybe I'll be able to call you Michael the Master if you keep on painting."

She stepped into the hall and he scurried after her. "Where are you going? Back to the party?"

"To say goodbye to Mary."

"Goodbye?" The word cracked in his throat. "Where are you going?"

"I'm leaving the Crossing for good. Because hurt isn't only a word in the dictionary, and you know that."

"But you haven't even said goodbye to your sisters, or your matriarch...."

"I didn't come to say goodbye to them. I only came to say goodbye to Mary, because she's always been kind to me. And... I came to say goodbye to *you*."

3

Trudy

"You were created for a purpose; work hard to see it through.
Obstacles are stepping stones, when you believe in you."
-Heaven's Handbook, Mindsets, Part 1

TRUDY PRACTICALLY BIT THROUGH her lower lip as she glanced at the silver conference table and the floating, legless chairs around it. In the center, a hologram spun that read Universal Technologies, and it was crowned with the translucent sigil of the Almighty himself—or so they said. A dove carrying a snake in its mouth.

She checked her chordograph; the lack of windows in the Tech Center made it nearly impossible to hear the music.

Raphael was running late, which meant there was even less time to convince him to present her ideas as his own. Though, that could be a good thing—the less time he had to think about it, the less likely he was to say no. These lords would never listen to a commonborn angel, regardless of her expertise in coding. And if Lucifer knew she called this meeting... Well, she didn't even want to think about that.

The aesthetics of this building didn't help either. It was like working from the *inside* of a machine. Until she was called to Eastern Island, she'd been a programmer at one of the logistics hubs, and the hubs resembled every other rustic village in the world. Sure, holographic screens floated above their brass qubes, and there were Airship Maintenance Facilities, but their work suites were still warm and wooded, like a personal study.

But the pristine white walls and platinum trim in the Tech Center weren't only mechanical, they were downright cold. And not in the way that made you want to drink hot cacao.

"Looking sharp, Angel Bee."

Trudy jumped.

"It's only me." Lord Raphael sashayed into the room and she exhaled.

"Thank you," she said. "I really mean that." Her blue velvet frock and formal boots were an attempt to look like she belonged among the lords, even though she didn't.

Raph wore a loose gray robe, his casual clothing clearly marking him as an angel from Creative rather than Tech; the creatives were a lot less stuffy. You would never even guess him a lord save for those glowing lavender eyes and his blue sigil ring.

"Can you all really not walk to your chairs?" Raphael swatted at the floating seat that pursued his bottom, lithe purple curls bouncing behind his head. He fled to the refreshment station.

It wasn't that Raphael didn't like technology; he understood its importance as well as Trudy. The Tech Center simply overused it.

"My glory!" he grumbled, trying to operate the beverage dispenser. "You angels use machines for everything. Technology is meant to enhance life, not replace it. Is there not a simple coffee press somewhere?"

Trudy rushed over and pressed the proper sequence of buttons, and the machine hissed to life as it warmed the water.

"Where is everyone?" He looked around. "My *quantum epistle* said the meeting was scheduled for the second measure of the first verse."

She hesitated. "I asked you here a little early."

"You asked?" He raised his eyebrows as he headed to the conference table with his cup. "I assumed Lucifer had you arrange this meeting."

Of course he assumed that. Because Lucifer made her schedule all of his meetings. "I sent the *qpistle* myself, Raph. I need to ask a favor...."

She took a deep breath and mustered all her courage. "I think I know why our project is failing, but I need you to present my idea to the other lords in Tech. They're not going to listen to me."

"Angel Bee, nobody wants to hear what an artist has to say about technology."

Emotion caught in her throat—she was afraid this would happen. There was no way Raphael would believe the way she was treated here. Nor would he believe the unorthodox culture among his own siblings.

If there were really an Almighty in that Throne Tower, he would've answered her prayers and gotten her transferred by now.

"Please, Raph... if you don't present my ideas, they won't be heard."

"You're one of the most brilliant programmers in the realm." He sat at the table and regarded her, sipping his coffee. "That's why you were called here. You're a master of these technological arts in all their..." He gestured to the room, "...disingenuous unnecessity. You need to speak up. Assert yourself a little. Lords are ancient.... Sometimes we can be a little hardheaded."

Raphael could be a little hardheaded. His siblings in Tech were something much worse than that.

"Besides," he said, a purple curl falling in front of his eye, "the Lord of Music is your mentor, and what more is programming than words and math, like music. Of course they'll listen to you."

She bit her tongue. Truth was that she hadn't learned a thing from Lucifer. She was an errand bab and a coffeemaker. A qpistle scribe at best. Lucifer had made such a grand show of taking her on as an apprentice, with all the flattery and official announcements, that she really believed him when he said she'd lead vast teams of coding experts. But the beat he realized that she had a mind of her own, his tune changed.

But they wouldn't dismiss another lord—at least not one they had to be accountable to.

"Please, Raph..." she squeezed his hand, "your teams have backlogged designs for landscapes and life-forms, yet we can't get a single galaxy rolled out. I believe I can fix this, but they won't listen to m—"

A fully cloaked angel stalked into the room and Trudy quieted. His face was buried in a deep, brown hood. *Silent scholar.*

A chill ran up her back as the enigmatic being took his place in the corner, still as a statue. The scholars were a strange and ancient species, in charge of the Universities and the Holy City's Monastery. They were said to have access to the Almighty's divine mind—though she had her doubts about that one. Here they just lingered in meetings, silently recording everything in those heads of theirs. His presence meant everyone would be here soon.

She implored Raphael with her eyes and held out a folder.

"Hello, Samyasa," Raphael addressed the scholar while he eyed her and took the folder. Samyasa barely nodded in response, keeping true to the reputation. How Raphael could tell one scholar from the next, she couldn't know.

She stood up and checked her outfit one last time, ensuring there were no wayward fuzzballs. These lords could size you up in one sixteenth of a sixteenth note—foot, wing, and feather. Hopefully she blended in well enough that they would let her stay.

"It's almost time," she said, fixing her thoughts on the physical objects around her. That was another thing about the lords: you had to mind your mind. Explicit thoughts were easily read, and even though propriety dictated they *not* troll your mind, the lords from Tech would swarm your head faster than beezle flies to honey.

Heels clicked in the hallway and she harkened, licking her hand and slicking back any loose strands of hair. One by one, a tide of elegant frocks beneath blazing eyes filed into the conference room. Their sigil rings glowed with near the same fury as their irises—blue gemstones linking to the luminous glory and wings they stored in the Divine Well. At least storing their glory so they fit in with the commonborn was one propriety they still adhered to.

Floating seats scooped and delivered them to the conference table. Trudy made a few attempts to look up and smile, but was either ignored entirely or met with aloof glances. *So much for looking the part.*

They were more cordial with Raphael, but behind his back their dazzling eyes exchanged suspicious glances. There was little these lords did in the open, and if honesty wasn't a cardinal virtue, Trudy might believe they were all hiding something. But she couldn't think on that now—not here.

"Where is Lucifer?" Lord Baalael wasted no time after he sat down. "And why are you here, Temperance?"

"The Lord of Music is disposed on important business," Trudy said, trying to appear natural. And it was the truth. Lucifer did say he was out on important business.

"And to what do we owe the pleasure of having the Lord of Aesthetics among us?" Baalael's gaze flickered between Raph and Trudy, no doubt only letting her stay because Raphael was in the room.

"My team can't get their jobs done until you all get yours done." Raphael smiled, but Trudy could tell he was uncomfortable. "There may be some ideas floating around that can help with your... technical challenges."

Lord Azazel rolled her eyes, her lips painted nearly as red as her dress. "And what ideas could you offer, little brother? Did you see a vision in the splats on your painting smock?"

Trudy was a little shocked she didn't act the phony, like she normally did in front of outsiders.

"I did not, sister," Raphael said with aplomb.

"Temperance—that's your given name? Yes?" Lord Astorath addressed Trudy, ruffles cascading over the lapels of his green frock. "I deduce my brother's left you with an agenda for this gathering? Assuming he sent you in his place?"

Trudy stammered, carefully choosing her words to avoid lying. "There is an agenda, yes. To discuss solutions for the code breakdown in our universal simulations..." She glanced at Raphael. "He's here to help us."

Baalael snapped his fingers. "Samyasa, record attendance. Unless there will be any more unexpected guests from Creative?"

Trudy shook her head. "Everyone's here."

"Good." Baalael leaned back in his chair, and all the Tech lords stared at the two of them, waiting for someone to start. The overhead lights buzzed and a swishing sound came from the coffee machine as it filled itself back up with water.

She nudged Raphael under the table.

"I have a question." Raph raised a finger. "Can someone explain to me what the actual problem is?"

"You come here offering help with a problem you don't understand?" Baalael smirked. "Ah. The vanity of artists."

Raphael's jaw flexed slightly and Trudy patted his hand. The last thing she wanted to do was cause him strife with his siblings.

"I, uh, can show you the problem," Trudy stammered, pulling a small brass qube from her satchel. She tapped it several times, navigating through a stream of holograms and selected the simulation file to demonstrate.

A three-dimensional blob of darkness replaced the spinning sigil at the center of the table. It flashed like a strobe before fading into translucent blobs of color. "The universe starts out fine," Trudy said. "Space is coded with the raw variables that are beholden to a plugin we call 'gravity.'"

The blobs of color condensed into more saturated blobs of color, and then bright pinpoints of light sparkled into existence. These were called stars, and one by one they swirled around each other, forming a plethora of spirals and shapes.

"The galaxies?" Raphael's face lit up.

"You should know," Trudy said. "You designed them."

Lord Mammon guffawed. "He hasn't had an original thought in his life."

"What's that supposed to mean?" Raphael put a hand on his hip.

"Puppet..." Azazel mumbled.

"Lackey..." Astorath offered.

Trudy sputtered, her gaze darting from lord to lord. "Samyasa... please strike those last comments from the record..."

"Why don't you go back to University, Samyasa," Mammon called out after her. "We have quantum recorders here."

"How dare you speak to a silent scholar like that?" Raphael stood up, and as Mammon took a breath to respond, a melody tinkled in from the doorway, soothing and sweet. Everyone went silent, and Trudy's bowels turned to water.

"Fortunately," Lucifer tucked a gold chordograph into his lapel pocket, "my business was finished earlier than anticipated." His yellow eyes shone like beacons from the doorway, and whispers of song seeped from his skin, audible even with his glory in that well. That's how powerful he was.

He stepped into the light, his platinum hair neatly combed to one side. "Thank you, Temperance, for conducting this meeting in my absence."

Trudy's pulse hammered as he acted like nothing happened. Like he planned this whole thing himself. He took his seat at the head of the table.

"As you can see," he smiled at her, "it takes more than a nice hologram and a bright mind to lead such fussy creatures."

The life force went cold in her veins. The fear of facing him alone after this was worse than any fear of being discharged. He could crush your entire identity with a single word and a beautiful smile.

"I hope you've made our guest feel welcomed, Temperance," Lucifer said. "My brother Raphael is very dear to me."

Raphael greeted him with a kiss on each cheek as the lords all sat harkened in his presence, the pictures of perfect obedience.

"She most certainly did make me feel welcome," Raphael said. "More than I can say for anyone else. Trudy was just presenting the problem holding up your department."

"Was she now?" Lucifer half smiled, regarding her. If she made it through this without a formal discharge, she'd beg Angelic Resources to let her work from the Creative Center. She could never face him again.

He motioned the paused hologram. "By all means, Temperance... continue."

She lifted a shaking hand to the qube and played it from where they left off. Galaxies swirled and moved farther away from one another, but in a few beats, they flickered and burned out entirely.

"Oh," Raphael covered his mouth, "that can't be good."

"It's not," Lucifer said. "Do any of you have progress to report with regard to a solution so that Raphael can keep Creative updated?"

"My analysts have been working to identify the problem," Azazel said. "They've run the scripts through our code checkers numerous times. They've even begun to manually check them. I recommend tabling this for at least a movement until my team can finish the manual check."

"Could be the framework," Astorath suggested.

"Or a hardware issue," Mammon said.

"These are archaic coding languages..." Baalael scoffed. "What did they expect?"

Their voices echoed in her head like sparks around fumes. How could they not see the obvious problem? They were gods, for flapping out loud.

She nudged Raphael with her elbow and gestured to the folder. He patted her hand and spoke up. "Lucifer... Trudy has an idea as to what might be causing the problem."

Lucifer smiled. "Temperance is very new to quantum technology; her background is in digital. Be wise before you speak, Temperance. We don't want to waste the valuable time of our lords chasing poorly considered theories."

She stammered over her words. "I... I think it's just some bad math in a plugin."

"That's a bold claim." Lucifer's cool facade broke for just a flash. "And would assume the incompetence of everyone in this room, and their respective teams."

Trudy spoke barely above a whisper. "These plugins mimic our own laws of physics... or at least they loosely do. I don't think our codes are off—I think it's our science."

"You're a natural scientist now?" Baalael laughed. "Weren't you hanging cameras before you were Called here?"

Her cheeks flushed. "I wrote surveillance software to enhance live communication for Airship Operations. I never hung cameras."

Not that it mattered. Nothing she ever said or did in this place would matter.

"I'll assume then," Lucifer said, "given your confidence, that the next part of your presentation will show the solution." He gestured her qube. "Please, Temperance... enlighten us."

"Presentation?" She looked from lord to lord, all eyes boring into her. Raphael met her gaze, his face sympathetic. "I didn't prepare a presentation. I was only showing Raphael the problem. I've written my theory down, but it amounts to what I've just told you."

"So you didn't test this... theory?" Lucifer's voice was patronizing, like she was a child claiming to understand something far beyond her reach. "And you came here with nothing to show us?"

Sweat glazed her brow as she looked from lord to lord, only to be met with ice-cold stares. She hadn't tested the theory. She didn't need to. The problem really was that obvious.

"Theories are worthless, Temperance, if we can't prove them." Lucifer stood up and stepped behind her, squeezing her shoulders a little too tight. "Samyasa, this meeting is over. We will reconvene at a later time to check for progress."

They all stood up, laughing and mocking her under their breath. All except Raphael, who eyed her like a pitiful thing. She swept up her satchel and ran from the room, nearly knocking Lord Azazel over. Her face was hot, and the rims of her eyelids spilled over.

"Angel Bee..." Raphael took off after her.

She darted down the stairwell, lest she get stuck in a lift with one of them.

"Trudy, stop!" Raph called out. "Wait for me!"

She kept running. She looked ridiculous. Felt ridiculous. And for what? Trying to do the right thing? She could never face them again. Could never face *him* again.

She wanted to lash out—tell Raphael about all their clandestine meetings, and the strange visits with silent scholars who weren't even Called to work there. About that little black book they thought they hid so well. But what was she even accusing them of? She didn't know herself.

Raphael was beside her in a flash. *Blasted lords and their long legs.*

He cornered her in the stairwell.

"I'll be discharged and disgraced," she said, wiping her eyes. "I'll probably never sit behind a qube again."

"I thought your idea made sense," Raphael said, though he was probably just being nice. "It was at least worth exploring."

"It was them that needed convincing," she sobbed. "I'm a fool for not being more prepared. I only wanted someone to listen."

He opened his arms and Trudy sobbed into his shoulder.

"I can never face them again," she rasped. "I only wanted to help."

"Go ahead and make your presentation, Little Bee." He gently stroked her hair. "I'll get you an audience with my siblings in Creative. If they see your solution working, Lucifer will have no choice but to move forward with it. I'll talk to Angelic Resources about getting you transferred. Maybe you can consult us on designs, or work with the digitizer. We'll find something. But please, stop crying.... It breaks my heart."

"I'm sorry." She wiped her nose on him and he grimaced. "Ever since I've come to work here, I feel so useless. Like my existence doesn't matter. It was never like that before."

"You're anything but," Raphael said. "The Almighty inspired this creation we're making here, and he'll use you the same way he uses them."

"If the Almighty tells you all what to do," she said, "why doesn't he just tell them how to fix the problem?"

"Maybe he's telling you instead."

Nobody told her a thing. She sat down herself and figured it out.

"Inspiration is a process, Angel Bee."

With reluctance, she nodded. It all seemed a bit fantastical to her. "Thank you, Raphael. I'll put together my presentation. You're a good friend... and you won't be sorry for this."

Trudy loosened her bun and undid the top button of her blouse as she stepped through the gates of her ground-level flat in the Beta Living Quarter. For what it was worth, maybe she could never face Lucifer again, but Raphael came through.

And at least he got a taste of how his siblings acted when nobody was around. With all their feeble excuses, they really did give the impression that they were hiding something. But that would be a truly bold accusation. Lying was even more taboo than being uncharitable.

A thought kept nagging at her, though. It wasn't a new thought, but rather an old one come raging to the forefront and waving its hands around as if to say, "I told you so."

If there truly was some omniscient, all-powerful Almighty in that Throne Tower, why did he rely on everyone else to execute his vision? And more importantly—why would he rely on *Trudy*, of all angels, to save his precious inspiration from failing?

And how could he allow his lords to degrade her in a Calling that he himself inspired?

She shook the thoughts away. This was no time for existential musings—there was work to do. And she needed a fresh, clear mind to do it. Fixing the laws of physics in the Universe would be no dull task; there might be a lot of code to patch up. Her mind needed a reset before she delved into it.

She perused her garden; a hobby that always served to clear her head. There was something about taking a dry seed that was nothing but pure potential, pushing it deep down in the soil and waiting until it fought its way to the light.

But the Tree of Life sapling she'd been nursing looked worse for the wear, which was indeed curious. She'd taken the seed directly from the fruit of a Mother Tree of Life, which usually produced strong offspring. It's not like she expected another Mother Tree—those happened on their own. She only wanted a little Tree of Life in her yard so she could grow her own vita.

The sapling didn't look right, though. It was still too small and bare. She had done the extra things that were supposed to support its growth, like covering the soil with wood chips and making sure it was planted in direct light.

She decided it was time to tend the plants. All this drama and worry around work had made her neglect her garden. She put two fingers in her mouth and whistled, and a little brown bird flitted from the tree and perched on her shoulder, bringing the smell of fresh honeysuckle with it. Flappy was always a breath of fresh air.

"Cup of tea before we garden?"

Flappy released a series of chirps, which Trudy took as a "yes."

Flappy had been with her for as long as she could remember. Even with her constant traveling for work, Flappy was always perched at the front of her carriage like a call sign. A little piece of home that refused to leave her side, and she was grateful for her.

She stepped into the flat and set her satchel in the reading nook, heading to the kitchen to prepare some tea. Flappy perched in the pot hanger, random little chirps complimenting the eternal concerto seeping in from outside. Trudy hummed along and struck a match, firing up the stove and set a teapot to boil before heading into the bedroom to change.

She put on a comfortable, loose robe and discarded that stuffy outfit into a messy pile. Within a few measures, the teapot was screeching, and she whipped her hair into a kerchief, shoving gardening gloves into her pocket. She ran into the kitchen and pulled the pot from the burner.

"Peppermint vita?"

Flappy let out a long, smooth whistle.

"Peppermint Vita it is then," she mumbled, dropping two teabags into the cups along with a dollop of honey. Almost everything had vita in it: vita was life, and life was vita. All food had some kind of nutritional value, but vita allowed the body to absorb and use those nutrients. Even if there was nothing else to eat, vita would be enough. The same trees that made the angels and the animals produced the perfect sustenance to feed them. Vita had everything a body needed to regenerate from the inside where the light couldn't shine.

And that was why she loved to nurse saplings—it was a fascinating natural process. The fact that you could take seeds from a Mother Tree and grow a plant that only bore fruit was an anomaly. Secretly, she fantasized that one of her little saplings might one song produce kittens, or even squirrels—but that would be a first in history. Only nature decided which trees would be mothers—though if you asked anyone else, they would say the Almighty chose that.

She grabbed both cups and headed out the door.

"Now don't be a hero like last time." She set a cup on the steps and warned Flappy. "Wait for it to cool. Boiled beaks are slow to heal."

She blew on her tea, bringing it to her lips with caution. Tongue burns healed faster than beaks, but you still had to stand there like a fool sticking your tongue into the light. She took a sip, and warm peppermint flooded her senses, rolling down her throat. This was exactly what she needed.

She headed to her sapling.

The few leaves that were there before seemed to have fallen away. She scratched her head and chided herself for being so consumed with work that she'd neglected her garden. She'd never actually seen a plant struggle to grow before.

"Good'song to ya, Trudy!" Bernard, the groundskeeper, called from the walkway. "Lookin' luvly as ever."

Trudy waved her neighbor over. Bernard was a husky angel with a bushy white beard, and he was the campus landscaper. "Just the bub I need right now. Any idea what could be wrong with my sapling?"

He entered the garden and inspected it, stroking his whiskers. "Trees of Life thrive no matter what, so long as they're in full light," he said. "Any chance something could be castin' a shadow on it?"

She knitted her brow and looked around. "No. There's nothing here."

"Any beezle fly nests around? They like to eat leaves. If a tree's too young, that could stunt its growth."

Serpents, birds and insects were the only creatures that didn't drop from trees, but rather reproduced by laying eggs. "I haven't seen any. I would've noticed holes in the leaves before."

He pointed at her morning glories. "Those ain't lookin' too good either. But come to think on it, all the plants seem a bit sluggish lately." He shrugged. "Sorry, I've not the slightest. Trees of Life are the most resilient plant there is."

"Guess I'll wait and see what happens."

"While you're at it..." he reached into his pocket and pulled out a handful of bulbs. "I was comin' over to bring ya these."

"Tulips!" She lit up. "Oh Bernard, thank you so much! I'll plant these right away. I've got the perfect spot for them."

"Enjoy," he said, plopping them into her palm. "Few take the time to understand what makes things grow. They like to eat the fruit, but never think about the dirt, darkness, and determination it took to make 'em."

"You're so poetic, Bernie."

"I try." He winked.

He left her, and she retrieved her gardening shovel from the side of the porch. Flappy flitted around her.

She knelt in front of the morning glories. Bernard was right—their purple was looking a little too pinkish, and their petals seemed limp. Tulips should brighten it all up. If she ever did get discharged, maybe she could assist a local landscaper. She wouldn't mind that. She pushed her small shovel deep in the dirt with a crunch, and began creating a line of holes.

A shadow fell over her and she smiled. "Back already, Bernard?"

She turned around, but no one was there. She knitted her brow, and Flappy began to chirp furiously. It was like someone had dimmed the lantern—but they were *outside*.

She blinked hard. Then a breeze blew, taking more of the precious few leaves from the sapling. "No, no, no...."

As she crawled over to it, the heads of her morning glories dried up and fell limp. She fumbled to hold them upright, but they cracked off in her hand.

"Bernard?" She cried out, whipping her head around. "Anyone? Did anyone else just see that?"

There was no one except Flappy.

Did her plants just *fail*? Nature couldn't fail.

And the light? Was something wrong with her eyes?

She shook her head. There had to be an explanation. She remembered the most basic science taught by her nannies: There's always a slight fluctuation to light. Nature was organic, not absolute. It wasn't code.

She looked to her poor sapling; it was a bunch of dry sticks protruding from the ground now. And she shivered at the sight of the headless morning glories. Light might have an organic fluctuation, but she'd never seen it interfere with plants. Even plants as young as these.

Moreover, she'd never actually *seen* the light change. If there were fluctuations, they were imperceptible to the naked eye. An old Handbook rhyme from childhood indoctrination came rushing to her mind:

The Almighty holds all,
From mountains to dust,
Don't worry or fret,
You need only trust.

Trust the same Almighty that left the whole fate of his project in Trudy's hands? Hands that could barely send a qpistle to request that meeting?

No. She didn't need to trust. She needed to investigate. She saw what she saw, and she wasn't crazy—the withered petals told her that much.

She ran to her bedroom and pulled the curtains closed. She opened her hobby chest and groped around until she felt the box she was looking for. Her old photo-machine. Thank the Throne she hadn't given it away when she abandoned the hobby. She loaded some film and silver oxide paper, then ran back outside.

She wouldn't rely on her senses. If this happened again, it would be documented. She lifted the camera and started snapping. First, she captured the dried flowers, then the sapling. Then she shot the sky. Picture upon picture of the light. The machine made a long noise before spitting the images out. She ran inside to get a quill and noted the timing of her shots.

So much for clearing her mind to deal with work problems. It looked like there might be two presentations to make to the lords now: one to diagnose the fake world, and one to diagnose the real one.

The old trust the Almighty rhyme tried to play itself in her mind again, and she grimaced. She'd realized long ago that beliefs weren't chosen, they were programmed—just like a computer. And once you realize that, beliefs cease being beliefs. Truth was, she'd looked behind the curtain long enough to know that the miraculous was indistinguishable from the technical. And if no Benevolent Authority was holding up the simulated world in their server, how could she believe there was any holding up the real one?

4

Michael

"This idea that those leading our Ministry of Callings sit around channeling inspiration just for you is absurd. I promise—there are standard operating procedures in place to make sure everyone has a job."
-Black Manifesto, Chapter One, "On Reality"

THE AIR WAS THICK with mud and horses as Michael leaned on the wooden gate next to the stable. He waited for Shemliel, who was a little too willing to spend time doing anything that didn't include Lilith. Maybe it was because he no longer had a Calling to mix with hers. Or maybe whoever oversaw destiny got drunk the song they paired them.

He grabbed the hilt of his sword and slid it slightly from its scabbard, confirming it was dull enough to spar with a beginner—not that Shem considered himself a beginner. But who wanted to deal with that loaf being laid up in the light for a few songs on a steady diet of vita, complaining while he healed. And of course, he refused to learn with wooden sparring swords.

Shemliel zigzagged through the field toward him, lunging and swiping at the grass.

"What are you doing?" Michael called out.

He lunged again. "Trying to catch... this blasted snake!"

"A snake? Why?"

"They're eating all the rootroasts and messing up Mary's dinner plans."

"Rootroasts? I thought they ate berries."

"I guess Lilly and her sisters aren't the only ones being weird...." Shemliel swiped and missed again, mumbling something incoherent.

"Is that who you're looking for?" Michael pointed to a cluster of long blue leaves that sat aloft a bulbous rootroast. The snake coiled around the fleshy, fattened stem and opened its maw, razor-like fangs biting down hard. Lumps of the plant moved through its body until it looked like a ripened peapod. Shemliel rushed over and tried to peel the snake off, but it was no use. The serpent's grip was like steel.

"No meatloaf for dinner then, I presume," Michael said. "Leave the poor thing alone. I'll plant more." Michael opened the sack of armor and handed off a set of boiled leathers. "Put these on and show me your blade."

Shemliel slid his sword from its scabbard and displayed it. "Almost forgot what it feels like to hold this thing. I'm a little rusty, but I should be able to get a few stabs in."

"Easy, champ." Michael nodded in approval. That thing probably hadn't been sharpened since Michael dropped from a tree, whenever that was. "Light heals superficial wounds on the spot, but it takes longer to bounce back from serious ones."

"I'll try not to hurt you."

Michael shot him a glare and shoved the leathers into his gut. "Put these on."

"Armor? Why? I'm like a sheet of iron."

"You're like a sheet of pastry dough. Put them on."

Shemliel's lip curled and he put on the leathers, blundering through the process. He lumbered a few steps, his movements not unlike a potato, and slipped on his helm. "I can barely see in this thing!"

"You'll get used to it." Michael drew his sword. "Ready? You want your grip to be firm, like this, but you don't want your arm to be stif—"

"You're still using that sword?" Shem pushed up his visor. "What's it been... ten symphonies?"

"About."

"If I fought as much as you, I'd have a whole wall of swords by now. Didn't you show up with that thing?"

"Never held a sword that felt better than this one. Perfect balance, and you could hit it with an airship and it still wouldn't dent."

"It seems bigger now. Maybe I was smaller back then."

"Not sure about smaller. Maybe thinner..."

"WHAT A NEWS! WHAT A NEWS!" Mary burst from the back door shouting, waving something in the air. Michael sheathed his sword.

It took her a few measures to waddle across the yard, and when she finally reached them, she leaned over the wooden fence, huffing. "A Callin's arrived with yer name on it, Michael—fine wax seal n' all. Herald's gone dropped it in the post."

He and Shemliel exchanged a glance. She held out a folded parchment that was stamped with thick red wax. It bore a sigil: a dove holding a snake in its mouth.

OFFICIAL NOTICE OF CALLING

for the Angel Michael

Under the Care of Matriarch Mary

Jolly Bub Estate

Village No. 5

Crossing of the Third Hexant and Fifth Circle

The only thing racing faster than his pulse were his thoughts, which bottlenecked a thousand scenarios in his mind. He could've been called to maintenance, or construction if they were still building their facilities on the island. That would keep him in shape while he worked. Maybe landscaping, which he'd done plenty of at the Jolly Bub. That was easy enough. He'd be alright with kitchen duties as well.

"Well, go on..." Mary said, gaze darting between him and the letter. "Open it!"

Michael hesitated, not entirely sure why, but then Shemliel snatched it from his hands.

"Flippin' feathers, Michael..." Shem peeled the wax and unfolded it, clearing his throat. "'Dear Michael, On behalf of the entire recruiting team at Universal Technologies, we would like to extend to you a Calling, which is an invitation of immeasurable opportunity—'"

"Oh, Michael!" Mary cut him off, her chubby feet tapping in place. Michael blinked—it was like he was dreaming. They'd filed so many petitions, tried so many times. He was so used to failing that it didn't seem real.

"'You are hereby invited,'" Shemliel continued, "'to join our art and design team...'"

Michael's face fell.

Did he hear that wrong?

"'...Where your skills of drafting, drawing, and painting will be put to the utmost use in service to our project, your fellow artists, and the greater good of all creation.'"

Michael grabbed the letter and canvassed the words. "'... Training will be provided to ensure that your skills in the visual arts match the high standard of excellence required of all artists called to Universal Technologies.'"

He let the letter slip from his fingers and went numb, lost for words.

"Michael?" Mary stepped closer and pushed a tuft of hair from his face. "Are you alright?"

"I can't paint for anyone..." Voices long dormant crawled up from his memory, sharp as needles. *You have no gift for this. You're a mistake. You're nothing.*

He could almost smell that scorched canvas in the crackling fire. *Worthless.*

"I have to go." Michael started for the manor, picking up speed.

"Slow down!" Shemliel called from behind. "Let's talk about this!"

"There's nothing to talk about." Michael sped to a run, too fast for either of them to keep up. How could *every single thing* in someone's life go wrong? Especially in a world that claimed to be perfect? His life had to be mathematically impossible.

Shemliel's voice faded, and something inside Michael broke. It was that thing that kept the past in the past. That kept the voices and the misery at bay.

Burden. Worthless. Doesn't belong.

He burst through the kitchen door and went straight to the sink, splashing cold water on his face. It dripped from his hair and his skin, and he hung there, breathing, trying to collect himself. He had no idea what was happening to him, why he'd lost control.

Or maybe he did know.

The one thing that staved off those voices—those facts about himself–was his plan. As if every action he took toward it pushed those voices down just a bit further.

But fate now turned his plan into a direct link to them.

Making those pitiful paintings was some bizarre kind of necessity inside him. An infrequent and uncomfortable itch that demanded to be scratched and forgotten. Never displayed. Never again.

"Congratulations, little brother." Ahab walked into the kitchen and grabbed an apple, biting it. Michael pressed a dish towel against his face and left it there.

"I would've run out with Mary, but I thought I'd leave you the dignity to savor your beat without too many prying eyes. Guess she can finally win that contest now. I'm heading to the agorium. I can drop her answer with the Heralds."

"Contest?" Michael slid the towel down and looked at the paper in his hand. "What contest?"

"Best in Circle," Ahab said, and the hair rose on Michael's arms. "It's a competition for Matriarchs to—"

"I know what it is," Michael snapped, his stomach turning.

Extra. Burden. Doesn't belong.

"That was the letter you opened when Shemliel came home," Ahab said. "She used to love competing, but after you arrived, she told them to stop nominating her. Guess they really wanted her to accept this time."

Shemliel stepped through the kitchen door, his gaze moving between Michael and Ahab, then to the paper in Ahab's hand.

"Why did she tell them to stop nominating her?" Michael stepped closer to Ahab, looming over him, and Ahab stepped back.

"Michael wait," Shemliel said. "And Ahab—shut up."

"Tell me...." Michael backed Ahab up to the wall. "Why'd she tell them to stop nominating her?"

Shemliel pinched the bridge of his nose and pushed Michael back. "Can I not be the one to deliver unpleasant news? For once?" He sighed. "The only way a Matriarch can win Best of Circle is if her estate—"

"—is organized to the precise millimeter, in tandem with its Mother Tree," Michael finished, repeating the belligerent words he'd heard so many times. *Burden. Extra.*

Shemliel raised his eyebrows. "I didn't realize you knew so much about it. Mary wanted you to have a real room—and she knew you liked art because you had those paintbrushes and that book in your sack when you arrived. She gave up her room so that you could have space to paint. She sleeps in an old storage space that she spruced up."

Michael pressed his eyes closed, and guilt flooded him. "How did I never hear about this?"

"She swore us all to secrecy." Shemliel glared at Ahab. "But apparently diarrhea can spill from more than one end."

"What!?" Ahab said, aghast. "I didn't think it mattered now that he's gotten that Calling to Eastern Island he was waiting for!"

Shemliel swiped the paper from Ahab's hand and booped him in the head with it, but it was too late. The damage was done.

Michael tried to rub the guilt and shame from his temples. Her own bed. How foolish and selfish—to think a fully arranged space would just be waiting for him after he stumbled on her doorstep.

"Listen to me," Shemliel put both hands on Michael's shoulders, "what you're feeling right now about your Calling is fear. Reject that. What does the Handbook say about fear? Remember what your nannies taught you?"

Michael barely stopped short of rolling his eyes at nannies and Handbooks. Not to mention that his massive guilt had just overshadowed his fear. But still, he could remember Gabriel's songs. Songs that Michael would chide him for singing, but still he sang them all the same. Gabriel's was the voice from the past that brought the most pain.

Abandoner.

"*When your heart feels dry and cold,*" Michael rasped Gabe's old song, "*and faith is nowhere near, stand firm and don't look down. Stand firm... it's only fear.*"

"Fear is a delusion." Shemliel shook him. "We cannot be harmed."

He had no idea how utterly ridiculous that statement was. Nobody did.

Michael rubbed his face. "I don't need more convincing, Shem." He couldn't go on burdening Mary and this estate. "It's fine. I'll go."

"I only wish you could see what I see." Shemliel squeezed his shoulders. "You have so much inside you, little brother. You have so much to give."

"I have nothing to give." Michael guffawed, glancing through the partially opened door at the Mother Tree, where pods hung, engraved for each brother that belonged there. "How can I have anything to give, Shem? *I don't even have a name.*"

5

X

"Hospitality is the principle characteristic of the charitable heart, and the mortar which binds the stones of Utopian civilization. On a cultural level, it is the mutual assurance of security. With hospitality, strangers are family we just haven't met yet."
-The Guide to Utopian Principles and Ethics, Section V, on Social Behaviors

"WHAT DO YOU MEAN he doesn't know his own name?" A stiff femme in a black dress spoke from behind the desk. When she finished, she pressed her lips together, like she'd eaten something sour.

"He's disoriented, Matriarch Diedre," Antoinette said, her eyebrows pinched as she looked down at him. "He's a child, no older than four symphonies at best. Have some compassion."

His mind raced for a shred of memory. Anything. It was like his name was at the tip of his tongue, but it wouldn't break through.

"He keeps saying that his memories are stuck in his cloak."

"His cloak?" Deidre stood up. "How ridiculous. He's not even wearing a cloak."

He had been wandering the agorium with only his satchel when Antoinette approached and asked if he was lost. Which he was. Very lost. Unsure of even where he came from, much less where he was going.

"Rubbish," Deidre said. "He's playing a game. Bring him back to where you found him."

He sank into the plush brown settee as they argued, his small sandals barely reaching the edge. Despite the crackling heat from the hearth, the wooded study felt cold; unfamiliar. He hugged the burlap satchel in his lap, the only thing still familiar. If he could only find his cloak, then he could go home... wherever that was.

He closed his eyes and breathed slowly. Fragments of memory flashed, but there were even fewer than just a few beats ago. They were like echoes. Someone spinning him around. Laughter. A paintbrush dragging a thin blue line.

His eyes went wide. *A paintbrush.*

He shoved his hand into the satchel, feeling around, then exhaled. His art supplies were still there—but even more important, he *still remembered* they were there.

More fragments flashed, each one shorter than the last, and looming between every flash was a set of brilliant green eyes, glowing like emeralds. They watched him from the darkness. Those eyes felt like home.

Antoinette and Deidre's voices grew louder, and he covered his ears. So many loud words. Didn't they know that was the worst way to be heard?

"I've contacted every Matriarch overseeing children in this entire crossing," Antoinette said, "and all our surrounding villages. No estate has lost a child. He doesn't belong anywhere."

Doesn't belong.

The words sunk into him as he tried searching his mind again. He knew other things, like his letters and his numbers. He knew how to double-knot a bow with the leather straps on his sandals, and he knew that mixing a touch of orange with pure white paint made a brilliant peach. But the rest of what he knew was in his cloak, and he had no idea where that was.

He squeezed his eyes again, and those green orbs flashed, but faded just as quickly. He clung even tighter to the satchel, feeling its contents under the thick burlap. He couldn't forget his art supplies—he just couldn't.

"Well, he doesn't belong here either," Deidre said. "Bring him back to the agorium and be done with it."

"I can't simply leave him there!" Antionette's jaw dropped. "He's even smaller than our own children. Is it possible he's younger?"

"Nonsense. We have the youngest Mother Tree, everyone knows that. Lord Baalael will be here soon, and I won't have him thinking I've lost control of my own estate."

Antoinette furrowed her brow. "Is that why you won't help this child? Because of the competition?"

"Pity me that our lord sent you to my watch, you insolent mule. Of course it's for the competition. There will be a great divide soon, and when that happens, I'll be on the right side of it."

"You don't even know for sure that he'll grant you a position within his ranks if you win Best in Circle. Is that worth turning a child away for?"

Deidre's eyes turned to slits. "I do know that if I do *not* win Best in Circle, I will be seen as unfit for any rank. The opportunities at stake are too important to risk because you've decided to start bringing in strays." A beezle fly darted from behind the curtain and did loops around Deidre's head. She swatted at it. "This estate was planned to the precise millimeter in tandem with our Mother Tree—and it will remain that way. Remove him at once."

Him. If only he could go into his pocket and remember his name. But the pocket of what? There were no pockets in the robe he wore, or his satchel. He could've sworn he remembered more a few beats ago.

He swallowed hard. Whatever this place was, he wasn't wanted in it. He considered running, but he was too scared to move.

"Don't worry, little bub," Antoinette said as she knelt in front of him and stroked his hair. "I'll figure something out."

"And what, exactly, are you figuring out?" Another voice came from the doorway, a masculine voice. He cast a long shadow over the room, and his eyes glowed a brilliant gray.

"Lord Baalael..." Deidre scurried from behind the desk and bowed low. "Nothing, m'lord. They were just leaving."

"Commendable try, Matriarch," Lord Baalael stepped inside. "But your grating voice carries half across the realm."

Deidre blushed. "Sorry if we were loud, m'lord, it won't happen a—"

Baalael held up his hand, and she went silent. "Bad enough your thoughts are disorganized and chaotic. There seems to be no escape from your mouth either." Deidre looked smaller as Lord Baalael stepped over to the couch and knelt.

"Curious thing to find a child wandering alone." He pushed a lock of hair from the child's eyes and knitted his brow, something like concern flashing briefly. "Did you find him, or did he find you?"

"A bit of both, I suppose," Antoinette answered. "I was out looking for prospective converts in the agorium when I noticed him. At first, I thought he was following me. But then I realized he was only wandering around, lost. He was very confused when I approached him."

"And you've reached out to all the other estates still raising children?"

Antionette nodded. "Every last one in our village, and the neighboring ones. It's impossible he could've traveled any farther than that on his own. It's an anomaly for a child to even leave their village alone."

"Tell me, Deidre," Baalael said, "are you in the habit of ignoring anomalies?"

Deidre stammered, her gaze darting. She was strong before, but now she looked frightened.

"The things I'm willing to deal with in the name of progress." He stood abruptly and cracked his neck. "With the sensitive work we're doing here, you need to be more guarded. I chose you because I thought your intelligence matched your ambition. Don't make me regret that."

"I'm afraid I don't understand, m'lord...."

"Exactly," Baalael said. "You don't understand–and whatever you don't understand could be a *threat*. We keep threats close. Controlled. If you're to learn anything about competition and victory, at least learn that. The child stays here."

"I'm sorry, m'lord," Deidre said. "Of course the child can stay here."

Two bubs appeared in the doorway, and Lord Baalael motioned them inside. They picked up crates filled with white books in the corner and carried them out.

"Where are you bringing our Handbooks?" Antoinette asked. "I thought we'd at least indoctrinate the children with the basics—they grow fussier by the song."

"Calm yourself," Deidre said. "The nannies have been trained on a better curriculum. The children will be wiser for it."

"As far as this child," Baalael said, "I'll work with you directly to oversee his stay here, until he is otherwise claimed."

Deidre wrung her hands. "If he stays here, he must be educated and accommodated. We can't provide those things without erring our ratios. Heaven's Smallest will be disqualified from the competitio—"

"Stop worrying about the competition and do as you're told." His eyes flashed. "The ratios will remain as they are, because he will not be participating with the other children. As far as his accommodation... simply find a child to share their room. Only a sampling of rooms will be inspected, and I'll make sure his is not."

"He can share my room," Antoinette said. "I don't mind."

"No," Baalael said. "Your room will need to pass inspection if Matriarch Deidre is to win and our experiment here successful. When the other Matriarchs look up to Deidre, they'll be more likely to heed her advice."

"It won't be easy to find a child to share, m'lord," Antoinette said. "Like I said, they've grown fussy."

"I'm confident in you, Antoinette." Lord Baalael grinned. "I'm sure you'll be as good with this as you were with a sword."

Her face fell at that comment, and Baalael knelt again and glared into the child's eyes. "I don't like anomalies, little bub, and I don't like surprises. But most of all..." He poked the child's forehead, and it hurt. "I don't like *thick little heads* that I *cannot hear*. You're too young to be guarding those thoughts so well."

"What do I do about a name?" Antoinette asked. "I can't very well introduce him to the rest of the brothers and nannies without a name."

Baalael straightened his frock and stood up. A beezle fly darted from nowhere and buzzed around him, and he held up his hand. The fly froze, midair, before dropping into his palm. "For my collection." He smiled as his fist closed around it. "The child is an extra, so call him 'X.'"

X? The child grimaced.

Antoinette tsked. "Surely there's a better name than that."

"Names are engraved in our Mother Trees, not given by you," Baalael said. "He will remain as X so long as he's here."

"And what's to stop me from giving him a name?" Antoinette folded her arms. "Last I checked, we still have a free will. Even in this place."

"Antoinette..." Deidre growled.

"Your will is only free if you're willing to live with the consequences." Baalael's face darkened. "This is not a game we're playing, Antoinette. Would you like to test me?"

Antoinette's bravado faded and she put her head down. "I'm sorry, m'lord. We will call the child X."

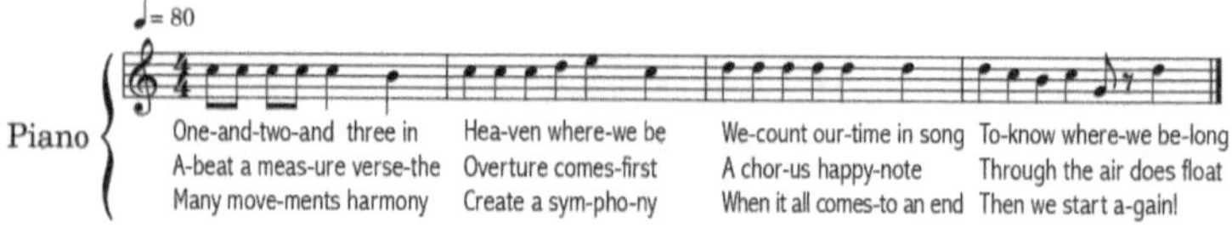

Antoinette held X's hand as they walked the long wooded corridor of the manor. He was glad to be away from the others, and hoped not to run into them any time soon. The polished floor was covered in the center by a squishy, red rug with patterns woven down the middle. Vibrant, beautiful paintings hung in golden frames along the wall in a perfect row.

He stopped in front of one, mesmerized.

"Do you like it?" Antoinette asked.

X nodded, eyes fixed on the dancing winged angels in the center of the sky. Their faces beamed with light, as did the brilliant plumes of light gilded feathers that stretched from their backs. Pastel-colored robes floated around them, and on the ground, flightless angels pointed with awe.

"Where are your wings?" He looked Antoinette up and down.

"I should ask the very same of you!" She chuckled and knelt to his level. "But alas... only lords have wings to spread. Though if you dream well enough, maybe you can fly in your sleep."

Fly in your sleep....

Those green eyes flashed in his memory again, but evaporated quickly as they appeared. "Will our faces ever shine like theirs?"

"Look how talkative you've become...." She smiled. "Art works well for you. Only the faces of the lords can shine, but we can shine in other ways."

They walked past the kitchen and through the back door, where they were greeted by a lively melody. The field out back was large and green and edged by a wild forest. A great umbrella of a tree marked the center of the yard, and she led him to a bench.

"Hair as a raven, just like mine." She tucked a tuft of it behind his ear and smiled. "You wait right here, little bub. I'll see about finding you some accommodations."

She left, and he sat there clutching the satchel in his lap. He pressed into his mind again, searching for shreds, but everything was gone now. He couldn't even recall where he had left his memories. His chin quivered as reality settled in, but no sooner did a tear fall than did a whizzing sound cut through the music.

Something bounced off his head and landed in his lap, and he blinked. A sparrow sat there looking at him.

"Are you alright?" he asked.

The bird chirped.

"I don't speak bird."

It leapt into the air and flitted to the field toward a giant tree. He chased it, hoping to make a better apology. It flitted low, then high, then low again. He tried to keep up.

"Come back!" He slowed to a stop and leaned over to catch his breath. The bird disappeared, but he caught the sound of a small voice singing from behind the trunk.

"One and two and three... In Heaven where we be..."

X approached cautiously, not wanting to offend anyone else here. He hid behind the tree and craned his neck.

"We count our time in song, to know where we belong..."

A slightly plump child sat there wearing big, circular glasses. A scruff of light blond hair was at the top of his head.

"Featherbits!" the child said to himself, "lunch is almost over and I haven't eaten yet." He reached into the pocket of his robe and pulled out a shiny yellow fruit. He peeled the skin back and opened his mouth, but then paused as if sensing something. His gaze landed on X, who ducked behind the tree again.

"Why are you hiding?" the child asked.

X's throat bobbed, and he stepped out. The child pushed his glasses higher and held out his fruit.

"Want some?"

"No, thank you."

"I'm Gabriel!" He pushed himself up and extended his arm, but X just stared at it.

"Don't you know the greeting of peace?"

X shook his head and Gabriel's face lit up.

"I can teach you! Here, hold out your arm like this."

He held out his arm and Gabriel gripped it. "Now, shake once."

They shook, then released.

"You're a fast learner... it took me three tries. What's your name?"

"They call me X," he mumbled, his gaze falling to his sandals.

Gabriel scratched his head. "Are there any other letters?"

"I... I don't think so."

Gabriel chomped his fruit and chewed, considering. "You're lucky then."

"Lucky?"

"Sure. I still can't spell my name, but I can already spell yours."

X smiled. "What are you reading?"

"A book to learn timing. Can you tell time?"

X knew to listen to the music for the time, but he was still so disoriented. "I'm not sure."

"I can teach you." Gabriel plopped on the ground and pulled X down next to him. He flipped through pages. "I haven't seen you around here before. Where did you come from?"

"I don't know that either."

"No matter. You seem nice, and I like nice." Gabriel found the page he was looking for and laid half the book on X's lap. "I sit outside for lunch because nobody lets me sit at their table." He pointed to the top of the page. "Ready?"

X nodded.

"Now take a deep breath and close your eyes," Gabriel said. "Listen to the music."

X's shoulders relaxed and the light warmed his eyelids. Long notes resonated through the air, first high, then low. Then both.

"The chorus is almost over," Gabriel said. "I can tell because the notes are happiest then. Sing along to the melody of the music. Music helps us remember...." He pointed to the lyrics, and they sang:

"One and two and three,

In Heaven where we be,

We count our time in song,

To know where we belong."

These words felt so familiar. The rhymes. He tried to remember where he heard them, but there was nothing.

"A beat, a measure, verse,
The overture comes first,
A chorus' happy note,
Through the air does float."

The strings built up to a crescendo, and they exchanged a glance before raising their voices to match the rising music.

"Many movements' harmony,
Create a symphony,
When it all comes to an end,
Then we start again!"

They broke into laughter. It was too easy to get so wrapped up in your thoughts that you couldn't hear the music. It was nice to hear the music.

"Can I ask you a question?" Gabriel asked.

"Sure."

"Do you like to draw?"

X lit up and nodded. "And paint too."

"I knew it! I just knew it as soon as you peeked from the tree!"

"Knew what?"

A sharp whistle cut through the air and interrupted them. Both children harkened.

"We're being summoned!" Gabriel said. "We have to go." He jumped up and pulled X by the arm, but then froze. "Uh oh..." He pointed to X's rear end, where there was a big, brown splotch on his clean white robe.

"Goose poop," Gabriel said. "Happens to me all the time."

X looked down at himself and frowned.

"I know what to do. Follow me!"

X looked back in the direction of the bench where he was supposed to be waiting and sighed. He followed Gabriel. As they rounded the corner of the manor, a big horde of children in brown robes stood gathered before Antoinette in the field. They snuck up behind the crowd and tried to blend in.

"Shhh," Gabe whispered. "Wait here and stay quiet. I'll be back in two shakes of a feather!" He padded off through the side door of the manor just as a great shrieking sound cut through the music. Antoinette was fussing about with some kind of device that looked like a horn. She pressed a button, and the loud shriek stopped.

"Oops," her voice blared, and she startled herself. "Sorry about that, I normally don't use machines." She took a deep breath and started over. "Thank you, sweet children, for coming here at my request. Our humble estate is in need of a great favor, and I'm confident you will all be willing to help. "

Rather than pay attention to the adult speaking, the children giggled and shoved one another. When an adult spoke, you were supposed to harken. He didn't remember much, but he remembered his manners.

"A child has been found," Antoinette pressed on, "alone, displaced, and without a home to lay his head. Which among you will volunteer to give this sweet little bub some charity, and share your room with him?"

The children looked at one another. Some laughed, some murmured. None responded. One of them stuck his thumbs in his ears and wiggled his fingers.

X lowered his head. No wonder Gabriel sat alone for lunch.

"It's only temporary," Antoinette pleaded, "while we wait for a Matriarch to claim him."

A few snickers and jeers came from the crowd, but still, no volunteers.

"Stick him in the barn with the smelly sheep," a small voice rang out, followed by roaring laughter.

"I can just pick one of you, you know. I'm the adult here."

One of the other adults stepped over and leaned into her ear, the mechanical horn feeding back as it picked up her voice too.

"I'm afraid you can't."

"And why not?"

"Free will. None can be forced, no matter their age. It's Council policy."

Antoinette grunted and straightened the sleeves of her black dress before turning to the crowd again. "Somebody must be willing to help this child... Please. Anyone?"

The pitter-patter of feet on grass came running up behind them. It was Gabriel, with a robe slung over his shoulder. He tossed it to X, but as he did, his foot caught and he hurtled down with a loud cry.

Everyone turned at once, right in time to see him land flat on his face. His glasses tumbled ahead of him, and the whole horde pointed and laughed.

X dropped the robe and ran to him, retrieving his glasses. He pulled Gabriel to his feet, and then the insults started.

"Four eyes fell again!"

"Clutz!"

"He's too fat to run!"

X's cheeks heated and he gritted his teeth. He handed Gabriel the glasses and purposely blocked him from their view.

"Who's the poop butt?" someone called out, and they laughed even harder.

Antoinette parted the crowd as she ran toward them. She knelt and checked Gabriel's leg.

"Are you alright?"

He nodded and rubbed the scrape on his knee. "Nothing a little light won't fix."

It was very hard to act proper in that beat. Gabriel held his knee to the light and the skin healed. "See..." Gabriel smiled again. "Good as new."

Antoinette exhaled. "You're a special little bub, you know that?" She scruffed his hair, and he smiled even wider. She cupped his chin, and speaking in a formal tone she said, "Sweet Angel Gabriel and citizen of Heaven, I have a favor of the utmost urgency to ask of you..."

He harkened, looking almost adult. He pushed his round glasses higher and lifted his chin.

"We are looking for a charitable angel to share his room with a child in need. A child with no home to live in, and we have no rooms to spare.

We call the child X. Nobody else will help him, or show any mercy. Is it your will to help, Gabriel, son of the Most High?"

His eyes went wide and he smiled, breaking his adultlike mask. "Would that make him my brother!?"

"I suppose it would," she chuckled. "Angels under the same roof are always brothers."

"Yes! I will share my room then." He turned to X. "We're brothers now! I knew it. I just knew it!"

"Knew what?" Antoinette asked as X sighed with relief. He'd have somewhere to sleep now, and the prospect of a brother was comforting.

"Nothing important," Gabriel said.

She raised her eyebrows. "Alright then. You'll make a fine angel one day, little Gabriel. And as for you..." She turned to X, but hesitated. "... As for you, little bubby, I'm sure the others will come around and warm up to you. Give it some time."

X nodded, feeling ashamed to need so much.

"Now take your new brother upstairs and help him feel at home."

Gabriel grabbed X's hand and led him toward the manor. When they approached the door, X froze, not entirely sure why.

"What's wrong?" Gabriel asked.

X spun and his hand whipped in front of Gabriel's head. A rock careened into his palm, and he closed his fingers around it. A hushed gasp escaped the crowd.

"Who threw it!" Antoinette stormed into the crowd of children and they scattered.

"Wow!" Gabriel's eyes were wide. "Usually they just hit me."

X stared at the rock, shocked.

"Forget about that." Gabriel tugged him. "I have a present for you."

"A present?" X dropped the rock as Gabriel dragged him into the manor and up long winding stairs.

His small room was humble. There was a bed with a blue quilt, a chest at its foot, and a desk.

Gabriel scampered to the chest and opened it, leaning in and digging. "You can share my brown robes," he said as he dug. "They'll make fun of you for wearing white. Nobody wears white because it gets dirty too fast."

X looked at his poop butt and saw the wisdom in that.

"How many brothers do you have?" Gabriel's head was now fully inside the chest. "I mean, besides me."

"None, I think."

"Nannies? A Matriarch?"

"I... I'm not sure." X sat on the bed and looked in the mirror.

"No matter." Gabe leaned further into the chest. "We'll be the best of brothers, you and me. Now, if I could only find where I hid your present..."

X looked in the mirror from the corner of his eye and leaned forward just enough to see his raven black hair, which was slightly curled. He was darker than Gabriel and the other brothers, who were practically pink, but he wasn't like Antoinette, who was beautiful like onyx. He wiggled his nose and blinked his solid brown eyes.

"WHOA!"

Gabriel toppled into the chest, heels over head and X sprang into action, pulling him out by his robe. He brushed himself off, fixing his glasses. "Thanks! The others just close the lid when that happens. But look what I found." He handed X a big, heavy book.

"Ang-elic A-nah-toe-me," X sounded out the title. He did remember his letters, and words. "Angelic Anatomy."

"You read good for someone without nannies. I couldn't figure out the second word."

On the cover was a perfectly sketched figure, with all of the details like shadows and highlights. He fingered through the pages.

"I think it's a book for drawing," Gabriel said. "It must be for you."

X opened the book to random pages. Some of them had detailed images of hands and feet. Even faces. "You're giving me your book?"

"It's your book. I told you, it's a present. I have my own book." Gabriel reached into the chest and pulled out another book, this one plain and white. "I found them both near the edge of the woods. This one has no pictures, which means someone would have to get very good at their letters to study it, and I need to work on my letters. But let's keep them our secret…. If the nannies see us reading our own books, they'll take them away."

X fingered through some more of the pages. These were detailed drawings of angels— even some angels with wings. Some creatures didn't even look like angels at all. He flipped to the back of the book where a good chunk of the pages were blank."

"I think that's where you're supposed to sketch," Gabriel offered.

"Maybe," X said, but he wouldn't dare ruin such a beautiful book by practicing inside of it. Each page looked like it was inked by hand, not like it was printed. What a precious gift. He would leave those blank pages blank.

He looked at Gabriel, who was now staring down into his own book, and the backs of his eyes stung with gratitude. Yes, he was lost and terribly confused—but he no longer felt alone. He set down his gift and hugged Gabriel tight, book and all. "Thank you."

"Books are good gifts, but brothers are even better," Gabriel said. "I'll use my book to practice my letters, and you can practice your drawing. Maybe one song, we will both become masters!"

6

Trudy

*"Who among us, in the name of hospitality, hasn't stom-
ached some breather they could barely stand? Let the golden
rule be this: Treat others exactly as you perceive their treat-
ment of you"*
-Black Manifesto, Chapter Six, "On Relationships"

FLAPPY GLIDED FROM HER perch and looped around Trudy's head as she stepped from her flat. Lively chirps peppered the lone, somber violin note that moaned through the air—though maybe it wasn't the violin note that was somber.

She glanced at her slumped, dried-out morning glories, and with a little wince, she looked up. A barely perceptible opacity of something stretched over the sky. Maybe her indoctrination hadn't been strong enough. Or maybe that was the problem with reality: once you saw it, you couldn't unsee it.

She started down the white stone path for the Creative Center, where she would meet her new team—the one she was to lead.

For all her fears of being discharged, she ended up getting promoted.

Her presentation to the lords in Creative had been met with applause, and she was pleasantly surprised to learn that those lords behaved far more like Raph than they did their siblings in Tech. The solution had been something even a novice programmer should've realized, and it was more than curious that Lucifer and his whole team couldn't figure it out.

Then again... their secret meetings and the copious amounts of security with which Lucifer protected his work was also curious, hitting a fever pitch once the Council had been officially dissolved. She couldn't shake the feeling that they were working on something they wished to keep secret.

After all, she had been right about the problem. There was nothing wrong with the main code. There was simply a minor error in the plugin called *entropy*. Instead of breaking things down just a little, favoring further organization, it barreled toward disorganization and chaos. A misstep in science rather than programming, but an all too obvious misstep, nonetheless.

After her successful presentation, Trudy suggested constructing a team of science-minded angels to consult, so they could prevent such problems from happening again. Creative agreed, praising her as "brilliant" and "inspired." But the fanfare and roses fizzled when she showed these same lords evidence of their own light degrading. They gave her sympathetic glances and patronizing speeches about trusting the Almighty, as if she were too dull to remember her childhood indoctrination.

Apparently, being ancient didn't make you wise.

"The birds and the beasts neither reap nor sow," they said, "yet have all they need to prosper and grow."

Blasted Handbook and its nursery rhymes. Heaven forbid you imply something could be wrong in their *perfect world*.

Science-minded angels would at least be trained to observe. They were her best chance at being heard.

"Good overture, Trudy!" Bernard merged with her on the walkway. "On your way to the new job?"

"Mmm-hmm." She forced a smile.

"They've got me tendin' the ferry while we wait for this grass to grow."

"Wait for the grass to grow?"

"Ay. 'Tis not growin' like it used to." He paused to pack some dried herbs in a pipe, then lit it. "Usually by the time I finish cuttin' the south lawns, the north's are ready for a trim. But the only thing growin' these songs be the meadow at the edge of the island. The Divine Well flows underneath."

"And you're not concerned?"

"Bah..." Bernard waved her off. "*If only we care to follow His lead—*"

"The Almighty provides all that we need," she grumbled, finishing the proverb. If she ever found out who really wrote that Handbook, she'd kick them for making everything rhyme.

"I don't mind the free time," Bernard said, smoke curling around his face. "They're holdin' tryouts for a gladiator squad here on campus. Good thing I brought me old leathers."

She cocked a brow and glanced at the round belly under his coveralls. "I didn't know you were an athlete."

"T'was a village hero in me youth. Won all the tourneys—didn't even need a sword. Tis' been a while though."

All she could muster was a half-smile. The world could melt under their feet like butter and everyone would just look for toast to dip in it. "I'm sure you'll do great, Bern."

They walked a stretch of path through the campus agorium and its outdoor eatery, a mix of savory and sweet smells filling the air, and parted ways by the Well of Divine Glory.

The golden domes of the Creative Center stretched into the sky, its innermost dome capping the widest part of the building. Her new work suite was situated in a wing off the south end, its white facade reminding her of unpolished ceramic. She opened the tall, wooden door and Flappy left her, perching in a nearby tree.

She walked the elaborate halls to her new team's suite, nodding to the angels she passed in the hall. The walls were glossy and carved in wooden relief sculptures, depicting various landscapes and scenery. It was nice to report somewhere that didn't feel like the inside of a qube.

A sign hung on the door: *Universal Technologies welcomes the new Analytical Physics & Coding Team, led by the Angel Temperance.*

Not bad. She had no idea if a new title came with this job, but she didn't care. This glorified qube game was the least of her worries.

Inside sat four desks and a conference table, with plenty of space to spare. Off to the side was a small kitchen, complete with a coffee press, kettle, running water and an ice box. A perfect balance of convenience and constitution, unblighted by the overwhelming presence of technology—the way life should be.

She stepped into the kitchen and began filling the kettle when someone banged hard on the door, startling her. She nearly dropped the kettle, and flicked spilled water from her wrist.

"Coming!" She wiped her hand on her robe. They banged again, this time even harder, and she rushed to the door.

An angel in a brown tweed blazer and matching cap entered the suite. He carried a large suitcase in each hand and plopped them on the floor. "Who are you?" he asked, his white mustache nearly thick as his eyebrows. "And where is my lab?"

She extended her arm. "I'm Trudy. And you are?"

He looked at her extended arm and grimaced. "What kind of name is that? Where's Temperance?" He pushed a pair of rectangular spectacles higher on his nose and stepped to the center of the room.

"I'm Temperance." She followed him. "But you can call me Trudy."

"I absolutely will not," he said, his eyebrow waggling as if also offended. "I will call you by the name inspired by the Almighty, and nothing else."

She stared at him, blinking slowly. "... Let's start over. I'm the Angel Temperance. And you are?"

"Zuriah. Professor Zuriah."

She grabbed his unextended arm and shook it. "Professor Zuriah—" He was a well-known educator in the natural sciences, and taught at the University adjacent to where she studied. "I've heard of you."

"I most certainly hope you've heard of me." He puffed his chin. "I've published enough. Where is my lab? Is this some kind of joke?"

"I'm sure we can accommodate anything you need," she said, any sense of confidence she mustered, fading. He leaned in close to her face and she flinched.

"You're not a lord, are you?" he asked, examining her eyes. "I won't work with any lords. I told them that when I answered the—"

"No," she cut him off, a sheen of sweat now forming on her brow. "Goodness no. I'm just a computer scientist—common as a kitchen mouse." She pointed to her eyes. "See? Dark as gravy."

He stroked his mustache, regarding her. "I suppose you are a little homely for a lord."

Ouch.

"Professor Zuriah," she cleared her throat. She had encountered these academic types before. Some were a little tighter than others, and Zuriah seemed tightest of all. "I am so *humbled* to finally meet you. I never dreamed to work with a scientist of your caliber."

He cocked a bushy white brow.

"To have a master among us, with such a passion and eloquence for the inner workings of nature..." She laid it on thick. "It's nothing less than exhilarating."

His scowl slightly softened. "Everyone takes nature for granted," he explained. "The Almighty never gets proper due for his scientific brilliance. Not that he needs it, but a little appreciation isn't much to ask."

"Not much at all..." She forced a pleasant smile. *Of all the brilliant scientists in the world, they send me Professor Pious...* She wanted to cry.

"Nobody's interested in how food comes to be from nothing," he pontificated. "How it satisfies both pleasure and need. How Trees of Life both form us, and supply the biomaterial for regeneration in their very fruit." His face turned sour again. "But that doesn't stop the feathering ingrates from eating it all the same, does it?"

"Feathering ingrates indeed..."

"And I don't use nicknames!" His hand shaped a rectangle in the air, making the sign of the Throne. "Our precepts and nannies taught us better than that. Nicknames are good as blasphemy. The Almighty inspired your name and chose it especially for you. I won't be the one to disregard that."

It would take a verified miracle just to make this angel agreeable, much less believe there's something wrong with nature.

"Temperance is fine," she said. "Call me anything you like."

"Well, Temperance... I still don't see a lab. I need a suitable environment for professional scientific queries. At the very least... I need sinks."

"Sinks?"

"Sinks!"

"I'll get working on that right away, Professor." She motioned to a desk. "Please, make yourself comfortable."

He snatched his suitcases and sat, folding his arms and staring straight ahead.

So that's it? He stares at the wall until we get sinks?

Someone cleared their throat from the doorway and Trudy jumped. A femme lingered there, wearing an oversized pair of coveralls and two messy buns at either side of her head.

"Are you here for the team?" Trudy asked.

She stepped in without answering and sat at the desk next to Zuriah. She stared at him, and he shifted in his seat.

Trudy briefly considered that Angelic Resources may have handpicked this team as a direct punishment for her blasphemy of suggesting something might be wrong with nature.

"Hello?" Trudy stepped closer and waved. "I'm the Angel Temperance. And you are?"

"Philistina." She shook Trudy's arm. Firmly.

"Are you here to join the Analytical Team?"

"Sure."

"Okay," Trudy exhaled, checking her chordograph. "I'm not sure who else is coming, but it's getting late so we should begin. How about we all tell each other a little bit about ourselves?"

Neither answered.

"Alright then…" This was going to be a very long verse. "I'll start. I am the Angel Temperance, but everyone calls me Trudy—"

The professor cleared his throat.

She wiped her forehead. "Except Zuriah, who may call me whatever he likes. I have a pet bird named Flappy, and I've existed for the better part of three hundred symphonies, give or take. I grew up in a little village at the crossing of the Sixth Hexant and Eighth Circle, and I have eighty-nine sisters. My career in technology began at sixteen when I was called to University to study computer science. I've spent the majority of my Calling developing software for our logistics infrastructure."

"I don't see a triangle on your palm," Zuriah narrowed his eyes. "You sure you're not a lord? They're not known to pair."

Trudy forced a smile. "Many commonborn don't pair either, professor. It's not easy to find someone whose life Calling blends seamlessly with your own. I've simply never found good enough reason to drop a kerchief." Maybe bringing the focus on herself right away wasn't the best idea. "And how about you? Would you like to tell us a bit about yourself?"

"… If I must." He straightened his bowtie and stood up, strutting to the front of the room. "I am the Angel Zuriah, better known as Professor Zuriah: Master of Chemistry, Angelicology, Botany, and Ecology. My academic background includes over five hundred symphonies of intensive study and research in the Universities of the Holy City, and apprenticeships under three silent scholars, qualifying me as a master in all of the aforementioned disciplines. I was the realm's leading professor of Natural Science and have written several hundred dissertations and books."

Trudy thought he was finished, but it turned out he was only taking a breath.

"I am a lover of nature whose passion for teaching is only rivaled by my devotion to the Almighty. I am paired with the Angel Sarah, who is a professor of mathematics and both more beautiful and intelligent than I am. I was called here to be of service to my fellows, and was told I would have the necessary equipment and resources to accommodate my expertise. And in that, I have been gravely, gravely disappointed. Thank you."

He took his spectacles off and huffed a breath on the glass. "And please do something about the dust in this room...." He produced a little kerchief and wiped the lens. "I hope you don't expect me to work in filth."

Before Trudy could respond, the glasses slipped from his hand and clinked off the wooden floor. He squinted, kneeling and pawing aimlessly. His eyes were mere slits.

There were few natural and enduring afflictions that neither light nor vita healed, but all were easily worked around with some help. Trudy had a sister who had never grown to full height, but the extra challenge proved her that much stronger. Poor vision was another one of those afflictions, but nothing a bit of specialized glass didn't cure.

Philistina snatched Zuriah's glasses and stepped backward.

He groped in her direction. "Is that you, Temperance?"

"No," Philistina said, pulling him up by the arm and shoving him into the chair.

Trudy's eyes nearly popped out as Zuriah yelled, "What are you doing!?"

"Break the glasses, fix the eyes," Philistina said before dropping the spectacles and stomping them.

Trudy gasped.

Philistina snatched something from her satchel that emitted a bright glow, and pushed Zuriah's chair close to the window.

"Get off!" he screamed, flailing his arms.

"Shhhh..." Philistina covered his mouth and held the glowing thing in front of his face, angling it toward the light.

"Stop!" Trudy ran over as a white light beamed into his eye.

"Hold still please..." Philistina said over his muffled protests and shook Trudy off, then angled the beam to his other eye. "Just a few more beats...."

She released him and he leapt from his chair, pointing a finger at his assailant. Philistina sat back down and resumed ignoring them.

Trudy covered her mouth, too shocked to speak.

Zuriah blinked several times before stretching his eyes open, his gaze darting from point to point. "It can't be..."

He ran to Trudy's desk and grabbed a piece of paper, holding it close, then far away. "Impossible." He rubbed his eyes and blinked. "I see so... so clearly. How did you change my vision?"

"Simple math." Philistina shrugged. "I like to play with light."

His gaze roamed like he saw the world for the first time. "I see even better than I did with my spectacles. All those symphonies that I prayed for the Almighty to heal me..."

"That you never bothered trying to heal yourself?" Philistina picked a stray hair from her coverall. "A scientist long-winded as you should've figured that trick out long ago. You wait for the Almighty to brush your teeth too?"

Zuriah's face went white, as if he'd just realized something. "We're not to meddle with nature...." He ran to his suitcase and produced a copy of the Handbook. He searched the pages, and finally stopped at one. Off key, he sang, "*All is well as it is, the plan is perfect, because it's His.*" He looked up, eyes wide. "You need to put my eyes back the way they were—this is blasphemy! I was created with a flaw.... You've broken the rules...."

Philistina sat up. "What rules?"

"I should never have come here...." He put the book back and lifted his suitcases. "I should've ignored these lords the way I ignored the others. I need to talk to a precept!" He started for the door, but now someone else was there, blocking the doorway.

Trudy pressed her palms into her eyes, regretting ever coming to this island.

"Sorry," the stranger said, "I've been listening for a bit and didn't want to interrupt." His sandy brown hair was slightly tousled, and he wore a pair of glasses too. He held up a piece of paper. "I received a Calling to report here, and I think I can offer some advice for your current... situation."

Trudy threw up her hands. "By all means." It's not like it could get any worse.

"Professor..." the stranger stepped inside, "had the Almighty truly ordained that your sight remain weak forever, then the 'flaw,' as you called it, would have stayed that way."

"Just who do you think you're talking to?" Zuriah stepped closer to him. "I've been studying the Handbook for my entire life."

"The real problem," the stranger said, "is that we, ourselves, have created our own standard of perfection—usually measured by convenience or vanity. Then we declare ourselves 'flawed' should we not meet this standard. The standard itself is a flaw. Your ideas of perfect or imperfect are conventions, not absolutes. These so-called 'flaws' are everywhere, and constantly solved by our working together. They create opportunities for empathy and service. These things just usually go unnoticed."

He spoke with a kind of authority, even though he was perfectly polite. Zuriah sensed it too, and took a step back.

"Generosity, interdependence, and helpfulness are centric to our guidelines of morals and ethics," he continued. "Therefore, it's more logical to conclude that the Almighty ordained you to be created with weak vision, to meet someone with the ability and willingness to help you, and that you might be humble enough to receive that help. Or at least, that's what my studies would lead me to believe."

Zuriah scratched his head and flipped through his Handbook. He opened his mouth to speak, but then closed it again.

He has nothing to say?

Maybe miracles really were possible.

"What kind of scientist are you?" Trudy asked.

"I'm not." He shook his head and sat on a desk, looking relaxed. "I'm a Master Precept, apprenticed in the Monastery of the Silent Scholarship."

"A Master Precept?" Zuriah inhaled sharply and made the sign of the Throne. "You're from the Holy City?"

"Yes. And I study the long form of our Handbook." The stranger winked. "You only have the digest."

"*The Guide to Utopian Principles and Ethics...*" Zuriah trailed off, his voice a hush of breathy reverence.

"I can assure you," the stranger said, "that the healing of your vision was not blasphemy. I'm here because Angelic Resources thought your team might need someone to help gel the personalities. I'm often assigned to help new groups work together."

Two songs ago Trudy might've cried if someone told her a precept would be joining her team, but that was before she met Professor "I Need Sinks" and Crazy-Buns.

"Welcome to the team," Trudy said. "Might I ask your name?"

"Hoot," he said, smiling.

"Is that a nickname?" Zuriah asked.

Hoot nodded and set his satchel on the desk.

Zuriah's gaze moved to the floor. He had no reply.

Make that two Miracles.

"I liked that trick you did with the glasses," Hoot said, turning to Philistina. "Might I go next?"

7

Michael

"Farewells are just a blessing, that others prosper where they roam. Love can never truly part; for love is our real home."
-Heaven's Handbook, Truths, Part 1, "On Family"

T HE SILENCE BEFORE THE overture was more deafening than usual. The world was still as Michael fastened the last of his belongings to Bentley's rear. Better to get out of there before everyone woke up. Goodbyes would be awkward. Maybe even painful.

He steeled himself and gave the bag a good pull, making sure it was secure.

He surveyed the estate one last time. The beige stone manor, the lush green grass dotted with fragrant lavender, and the Mother Tree peeking around back that he had painted so many times from his bedroom window—*Mary's* bedroom window. If he ever did come back, it would be to contribute something. Though he'd never be able to match Mary's kindness.

"Michael!" She burst from the manor and scrambled down the steps in her white nightgown and pink curlers. She carried a huge sack. "Ya weren't gonna leave without sayin' goodbye, were ya?"

Actually, that's exactly what he was going to do.

She embraced him, warm tears wetting his neck. Somehow, even straight out of bed, she still managed to smell like fresh biscuits. "I want ya to be everything ya can, my son," she squeezed him tighter. "Live your life. I'm just gonna miss ya so much, is all." She stepped back and wiped her eyes, shoving a giant sack into his gut. "A little snack in case ya get hungry."

He glanced inside. There was enough dried vita and manna biscuits to feed an entire manor for half a symphony. "Thank you, Mary."

She licked her thumb and wiped something from his face, and a bittersweet chuckle escaped his lips. He blinked the sting from his eyes.

"He was leaving, wasn't he?" Shemliel stomped down the stairs in his sleeping gown, followed by Ahab, Daniel, and the whole horde of brothers.

So much for leaving during the silence, when all the world was asleep.

Michael rubbed his temples. This was exactly what he was trying to avoid.

Shemliel closed in for a hug, shards of beard stubble chafing Michael's skin. "You go and show them, Michael. You show Joseph, and those lords, and whoever else is there what you're capable of."

He stepped back, and Michael noticed the brown fuzzy slippers on his feet. If only the Circle knew who they'd voted for.

"You get in that pit and work harder than everyone else," Shemliel said. "You're on record now, brother. I believe in you."

"Show 'em what kind of stock Mary's brood is made from," Daniel patted his shoulder, followed by Ahab saying, "Wherever you go, the Jolly Bub goes too."

A barrage of encouragement came from the horde that Michael had never really considered family. One by one, all the brothers said their goodbyes.

"You'll come home and visit us, won't ya, Michael?" Mary said, her eyes red and swollen. He nodded, though he didn't know if that were true.

He fastened her care package to Bentley and performed one final check of his things.

"You sure you don't want to take one of the steeds?" Ahab said. "That donkey's a hulk of a beast but he's slow."

"He's takin' the donkey," Mary stated flatly, brooking no argument. "It means somethin' to me that he has my beast with 'em."

Michael ran his hand along Bentley's gray, spotted flank. It was true—there was a bit of Mary in this beast. "He's no trouble," Michael said before mounting him. But he had forgotten one vital step.

Two stomps and a big wet bray.

"I got this," Shemliel said, digging into his pocket and pulling out a bag of cookies. "What?" he looked around. "I wake up hungry some-times."

He fed Bentley and stepped back.

Michael nudged the beast gently as Mary dabbed her eyes, and the whole horde waved as they lumbered toward the gate. He gave one final wave as they crossed the threshold, and stepped out to the road.

The Jolly Bub faded in the distance, its grassy lavender scent giving way to the crisp, neutral air of the village. They lumbered down the gravel road, Bentley's hooves clip-clopping in the stillness before the first bells. He'd take the route that led through the agorium, in case Nunziel's shop happened to be open early. Mary sent enough vita to feed a horde, but like all animals, Bentley preferred his vita fresh. And Michael hadn't wanted to start filling sacks in the yard, making a scene of it. He'd also grab some dried coffee beans—his already poor sleep wouldn't get any better on the road.

When they got there, the door of the Fresh Pantry was open, but Nunziel wasn't in his usual place. Michael dismounted Bentley and gave the doorframe a knock as he entered.

Nunziel stepped out from the back, tying an apron around his waist. His face was flat, and his voice somber. "Come in, Michael. How can I help you?"

"Glad you're open early. I was expecting to wait a bit."

"Haven't been sleeping well."

"I never sleep well," Michael remarked. "I wake up more tired than when I lay down. Everything alright?"

"More supplier issues." Nunziel shrugged. "Delivery schedule's falling behind."

"Sorry to hear it." Michael paused. The bub really did seem down. "You sure that's the only thing bothering you?"

Nunziel hesitated, then sat on a crate and slumped. "Darlene took a trip to see what the hold-up was."

Michael furrowed his brow. "And?"

"And I received a letter from her."

Michael waited for him to go on, but he didn't. "Nunziel..." Michael leaned over to look him in the eyes. "What did the letter say?"

He let out a long sigh. "That she's decided to stay there, and not come home."

Michael grimaced. Was that even possible? For a pair to break? "Could someone be holding her against her will?"

The grocer looked at him as if he'd sprouted wings, and Michael wished he could pull his words from the air. Of course that would make no sense to Nunziel.

"She said she's no longer happy with our pairing, or her Calling here in the shop. She insulted our life together, insulted everything we've built. She said there were other ways to live now. Other ideas to embrace." He crumpled in his seat and sobbed.

"Do you want me to go look for her?"

"No." Nunziel shook his head furiously, his tone shifting. "If she's not happy here, that's her choice." He crossed his arms. "I won't beg or send friends to beg for me. I won't be someone's burden."

Michael raised his eyebrows. "I can certainly understand that."

The idea of pairing for eternity always seemed a little much anyway. Though, he'd never heard of a pair splitting before.

Even more reason to stay far away from kerchiefs.

"You'll be alright, Nunz. You'd be amazed at how resilient we can be when we need to. Maybe I can distract you with some provision? I need some fresh vita for Bentley, and he doesn't mind musty. And a small sack of coffee beans. We have a long journey ahead."

"Journey?" Nunziel asked. "Where are you going?"

"To Eastern Island," Michael said. "I've been Called."

"That's wonderful news, Michael." His tone didn't match his words, which was fine, because Michael felt the same way about his Calling. Nunziel pushed himself up by the knees and collected items from around the store, filling up a few bags. He handed them to Michael and followed him out.

"Take care old friend," Nunziel said. "Sorry I couldn't offer more encouragement."

"No worries, Nunz." Michael secured the bags and mounted. "Good luck with everything."

The journey north through the Crossings was relatively uneventful. For twelve songs they traveled the main roads, occasionally cutting through random villages to see what the locals were like. Despite the distance, their route didn't take them through any major cultural shifts—save one lake village where the streets were filled with minstrels who wore bright, tasseled vests and had sharp points at the toes of their shoes.

It was a shame he didn't have any musical gifts. Not like he would've gotten called to music even if he had. His luck didn't work like that.

It wasn't that he didn't like art—it was that art didn't like him. In some ways, he even loved it. It was his only connection to whoever he was before he arrived at Deidre's. Chapels weren't sacred. Precepts weren't sacred. And those little white books they tucked under their arms certainly weren't sacred. But when that brush melted into a canvas, scratching the itch that compelled him to paint, that was sacred. And too easily desecrated by the eyes and opinions of others—especially when you had neither the talent nor guidance to be any good at it.

Most painters loathed mediocrity, but for Michael, mediocrity was an unattainable goal.

It wasn't like that with fighting, though. Violence came more naturally to him than breathing. Rather than hide that passion, he reveled in it. Paraded it, even. Fighting was more than sacred—it was divine.

The last chorus of the song blazed through the sky as violins sailed to a crescendo, then began their descent back toward the silence. They'd been riding all song.

"Alright, bub..." Michael stretched his neck and pulled the reins. "We're due for a break." Bentley came to a halt on the quiet road and Michael lifted a stiff leg and disembarked.

Bentley stomped twice and Michael ducked the spray before feeding the beast. He leaned over for a good stretch and rubbed his sore muscles. A few slices of dried vita would help that, but so would rest, and he didn't know that he could handle another silence in the grass. Not that he slept well, even in bed. Regardless, it was time to find some lodging.

"What do you say we stop at an inn, Bent?"

Bentley continued chewing, and Michael knelt by an effervescent stream and splashed its cool water in his face. The cold felt good. He took a drink, and it tasted mildly like the apples that had fallen into it from an adjacent tree.

It wasn't entirely intolerable outside—if the island didn't work out, he could always blow off the Calling altogether and live outside. If you fail at life but nobody's there to witness it, do you still really fail?

A strange cloud caught his attention over some treetops. It wasn't so much a cloud as some kind of cloud covering. And it was dense—almost gray. He scratched his head. Rain clouds were sparse and bright, refracting the prism even before the rain fell. Rain always fell with a rainbow. Clouds were never gray.

But a few lines of smoke also rose above those trees, which meant chimneys. He retrieved his map. They were in the last circle, right before the Final Fields. There was a village just beyond this stretch of wood where they could stop for the silence and regroup for the last leg of the journey. He gave his back one final stretch and mounted Bentley again.

The clouds appeared even more strange as they approached the village. Michael could barely hear the last notes of the chorus, and he wasn't sure if that was by arrangement of the song, or if somehow the clouds were blocking both the light and the music. It had been a long time since he'd been in the last circle, but the clouds never looked like this.

They trudged down a road where estates were notedly unkempt. Lawns were overgrown and speckled with brown, void of any bright-colored flowers. Even the air carried a dank, musty odor akin to what a wet cellar might smell like if nobody cleaned it.

They rode toward the center of the village, where the agorium should be, looking for the local inn. Signs dangled from nails on storefronts that had fallen to disrepair, windows were dirty or even cracked, and rodents darted around the edges of the road and behind abandoned stands. Nobody was around; all of the shops closed. That could've been due to how late it was, but paired with everything else, it felt ominous.

A white, freestanding building with yellow trim appeared at the end of a row of shops. A sign hung from a post with a picture of a bed and a fork—the local inn. Hopefully this place would be the first to have some life in it. Michael nudged Bentley forward.

Up close, most of the inn's paint was peeling and dirty. Nobody was winning Best of Circle around here. Michael dismounted, his aches now screaming for vita and a hot bath. A hot meal would be nice too.

He paused by the front gate and looked back. His sword stuck out of another bag tied to the saddle. This place gave him an uneasy feeling, a feeling he hadn't felt in a long while. He took the bag with his sword and slung it over his shoulder before going inside.

The innkeeper sat behind the front desk, reading a book. His skin was so pale that you could almost see the purple lines of energy flowing beneath it. Michael approached and cleared his throat, waiting to be acknowledged.

He didn't look up.

"Excuse me," Michael said, trying to make eye contact.

The innkeeper rolled his eyes and looked up from the book. "Can I help you?"

Michael was a little taken aback. "Yes. I was hoping to find a room."

The innkeeper stared at him.

"...I'm sorry." Michael looked around the lobby. "Do you work here?"

"Would I be sitting here if I didn't?"

A little flash of heat pulsed in Michael's face. "I need a room."

"Need is a fickle thing," the innkeeper said before turning back to his book. "Reservations work better."

Michael glanced down at the open pages he read and briefly considered reaching over and smashing his face into them. "Judging by the paint chips and debris outside, I can't imagine this place is in a very high demand."

"You imagine wrong." The innkeeper turned the page. "There's a convention. Rooms are all booked."

"There's got to be some—"

"No reservation, no room. Bye."

"Listen up here, you—" *If someone's acting impolite, it's more important you act right.* Gabriel's voice popped up at the most inconvenient times. Michael adjusted his tone. "I've been journeying for a long time. I've traveled a dozen songs on a donkey and I'm tired. I only need a warm bed and a hot meal. Then I'll go."

The angel rolled his eyes and put down the book. "I can offer you a spot in the storage barn out back. There's a cot and a spigot with running water."

It was better than grass. "I'll take it," Michael said. "Don't suppose there's any hot food in this place?"

"There might be some leftover from the banquet later."

Banquet? Who held a banquet in the middle of the silence? "I'll be happy with anything you can spare."

"It'll cost you."

Michael raised an eyebrow. "Come again?"

"As will the barn. How do you want to pay?"

Michael stared at him, confused.

"You're not from around here, are you?" The innkeeper sighed and stood up, leaning forward on the desk. "Let me fill you in. If you want something from me, then you need to give me something in return." He craned his neck and inspected Michael's bag. "Any obsidian in there? What about that animal outside? I could use a donkey."

"My donkey?" Michael was horrified. "Absolutely not! What kind of custom is this?"

"What about that?" He pointed to Michael's sword sticking out of the bag. "It's not too impressive, but I might be able to trade that stone for obsidian. What is it—beryl? Sapphire?"

"Are you mad?" Michael took a step back. "I'm not giving you my sword."

"Guess you're not that tired then." He sat back down and picked up the book.

"Wait," Michael said, and rummaged through his bag. He didn't have much clothing, and his toothbrush was out of the question. "What about these..." He slid out a sack full of paintbrushes and dumped them on the counter. Maybe if he arrived on the island with no paintbrushes, they would find something else for him to do.

Michael leaned across the desk. "I'm a Master Craftsman, and I made these from pure sable hair. Shaved the little rats myself."

This was all rubbish, of course. But Michael hadn't needed to use *this* particular skill in quite some time.

The innkeeper eyed the brushes. "What am I supposed to do with these?"

"For starters, this place could use a paint job. But more importantly..." Michael leaned in closer, checking over both shoulders. He'd almost forgotten how thrilling this was. "Sable brushes aren't easy to come by, and any artist worth their salt would trade their eye teeth for them. Every village has a Master Painter, and every Master Painter owns a slew of solid obsidian palettes that weigh at least thirty ounces each."

All rubbish, every last word.

"So don't look at these as paintbrushes," Michael raised his eyebrows. "Look at them for what they are: upward of sixty, maybe ninety ounces of solid obsidian."

The angel pursed his lips and narrowed his eyes, just like Deidre used to when her greedy little mental wheels spun. The object of one's desire was their weakness, and weakness could be exploited. He fought the urge to smile. It had been so long since he'd needed to deceive someone.

"Fine." The angel snatched the brushes and hid them in a drawer. "Someone will be out with a hot meal for you later. The barn's out back."

The beige, or rather, dirty white barn doors hung from their hinges. Mary would have fainted if she caught sight of this place. The inside was spacious enough, but it was clearly a storage area. Boxes were stacked all around, and tools hung from the worn-out wooden walls. Everything was covered in a thick layer of dust, and in the corner sat a mattress with a dirty green quilt and no pillow. Michael shook his head.

He unloaded his belongings from Bentley and took off his saddle. "How's that feel, old bub?" The donkey shook his body and stretched. If Michael was sore, he couldn't begin to imagine how sore old Bentley was. He grabbed some fresh vita and fed him.

Movement by the front of the inn caught his attention. A group of angels were filing in, all covered in dark cloaks. A femme dressed in the garb of a nanny or Matriarch held the door, and then scurried in behind the crowd.

There was no hay for Bentley to lie on, so Michael splayed the dirty green quilt on the ground and pulled a clean one from his bag. "Hopefully there'll be something hot to eat when we wake up."

He settled onto the worn-out mattress, nearly choking on the stink of mildew. He tried reminding himself that it was better than grass, but was no longer so sure about that.

Imagine having to pay for this? What a custom.

He stared at the wood-beamed ceiling and swallowed, remembering that even if his mind couldn't rest, at least his body would. Sleep would either be filled with specters from his past, or worse—the deep, dreamless kind from which he would wake up utterly exhausted, as if he'd just finished a song in the pits. Either way, one or the other would have him. He hoped for bad dreams, though. They were somehow more restful.

A warm, soft muzzle woke Michael up, followed by two stomps and a spray of snot. He wiped his face and swung his legs over the edge of the mattress. The stale, dusty air of the barn hit him, and he remembered where he was.

He rubbed his eyes and listened for the time. He could barely hear anything, so he went into his bag to check his chordograph. The first bells would be ringing soon.

He craned his neck and looked through the broken barn door to see if the innkeeper brought the leftovers as promised. There were none. He should've guessed as much.

He fed Bentley some vita and got dressed, this time strapping his bandolier on and securing the sword at his hip. He loaded his bags and headed around the front of the inn before going inside.

The lobby was empty—no innkeeper and no guests. He approached the doorway to the banquet room to see if there was a kitchen there. The shades were drawn, and the tables were littered with empty wine bottles and dirty dishes. The place was disgusting.

Something clanged in the kitchen and he darted behind the door. The same femme he'd seen earlier stepped from the kitchen and began collecting the dirty plates. She leaned over, and a dim strip of light illuminated her face.

Antoinette?

Not exactly. Deep lines were etched around her mouth and in the corners of her eyes, as if the worst of frowns had been permanently carved into her. Dark semicircles sunk below her eyes and her cheeks were hollowed out. And she was much lighter than Antoinette—nearly white in her paleness. Whoever she was, she didn't look well.

Michael stepped in, no longer mindful of not being seen. "Are you alright?"

She jumped, then scurried back to the kitchen.

"Wait…" he pursued her. "Please."

She froze in front of the kitchen door and pulled the bonnet down over her face. "I'm fine," she mumbled. "Please go."

Michael approached anyway, slowly. "I was just looking for leftovers."

She motioned a table that still had a basket of bread on it. "Take it while you can. Then leave this place."

He stopped about an arm's length from her. He didn't care so much about the food anymore.

"Please go." She took a step, and Michael gently grabbed her shoulder.

"Master! MASTER!" she cried at the top of her lungs and ran back to the kitchen.

Shadows stretched up from the corners of the room like appendages and swiped at him. Michael blinked, questioning his sanity. The innkeeper burst through the doorway and the shadows disappeared.

"I knew I should've thrown you out when you arrived!" He raced toward Michael and Michael put a hand on his sword. The innkeeper froze. "You'd better hope he ignores her."

"What's wrong with her?" Michael said. "Why does she look like that?"

"Don't be so quick to pass a judgment, fool. She'll survive what's coming, and you won't." The innkeeper grabbed the basket of bread and shoved it in Michael's direction. "I would've brought this had you given me a winging beat to wake up and get to it. Now go."

Michael edged out of his reach and sped from the inn, grabbing Bentley by the reins and dragging the beast as fast as he could. He regretted not taking one of the steeds now.

Whatever happened to his eyes back there had stopped happening. It was like the shadows came to life, but that was impossible. A trick of the light—or the darkness, combined with the stress of the journey and everything else. But there was no denying the creases etched in that femme's skin. Or worse—her pallid face and sunken eyes. He'd seen those before in his own reflection. When he'd suffered starvation.

Buildings and manors grew more and more dilapidated, and a general gloom filled the air like a haze. The music was all but gone, and what few angels he passed kept their heads low, eyes glued to the road. Nobody greeted him, not a wave or a smile as he rode by.

He turned west so that he could cut eastward through the backroads and stay near the edge of the woods, his instincts leading him more than his map now. Better to not meet anything head on that he wasn't expecting, and better yet to see any foes before they saw him. Life at Mary's might have put his instincts to bed for a few symphonies, but the first bells just rang to wake them up.

Darlene's letter to Nunziel and Philistina's observations from the window lingered in his thoughts.

A curious light flashed in the sky, like a photo-machine, and Michael pulled Bentley's reins. He could feel hairs on his head rising, and a smell like static filled the air.

BOOM!

The ground rattled beneath them, and another flash crashed from the sky. His pulse began thrumming as he scanned for more threats.

The wind picked up, and swirling clouds in different shades of gray formed, twisting like the water in a bathtub after you pulled the plug. Another flash zapped down, leaving behind an acrid smell.

This couldn't be happening. The sky didn't turn black and openly attack you... at best it shone golden light and healed you, at worst it tinkled warm showers that brought rainbows and watered flowers.

Yet... here he was.

Another flash boomed closer and snapped him out of shock. He forced his limbs forward, dragging Bentley with all his strength. The beast was heavy and slow, so he unhitched some bags, slinging them over himself instead.

"Come on!" He pulled harder, the raging swirl of darkness heading straight for them. A barrage of torrential rain, the likes of which he could've never dreamed, began assaulting them, and the wind turned ferocious.

Bentley slipped, and Michael almost fell under his weight as he caught him. "Come on, bub!" He lifted with all his strength and Bentley stood, limping forward.

Icy rocks started pelting them and bouncing from the grass, and the sky became complete darkness, save for the flashes of light. There was an ancient-looking tree about thirty cubits away, thick as a hill with a wide canopy for shelter. Michael dragged the limping donkey toward it with everything he had, practically carrying him. Purple light shone in his periphery bringing the sweet smell of honey. He wiped at his face—he was bleeding.

Bentley's eyes were wide, terrified. His mouth was half open, spilling saliva as light crashed from the sky in booming flashes. Electric shocks moved across Michael's skin like spiderwebs, and there was a primal urge to save himself and abandon the donkey—but that urge sickened him.

Move your body first, your heart will follow you. There's a lion on the other side; the only way is through. Gabriel's voice bobbed up from his unconscious, driving him forward. He would not abandon Mary's donkey.

"Come on!" Michael dragged harder and faster, his hair now soaked and stuck to his face.

They got to the tree and it sheltered them from the blitz of ice and rain. Bentley collapsed underneath, and Michael took a deep breath, trying to focus. They'd be safe here until this—whatever this was— passed. Michael knelt and rubbed Bentley's face. "Peace, my lump, peace. It's moving. It'll pass soon." The donkey's wide eyes calmed, and Michael pressed a cheek against his. "See, it's already slowing down." And it was. The ice was no bigger than pebbles now, and the rain slowed. "I won't leave you."

A flash blinded him followed by a harsh, crackling Boom!—the loudest yet—and the ground quaked. Slowly, something began to crackle right above their heads. Michael blinked.

Part of the tree was coming down—right on top of Bentley.

Before thinking, Michael leapt into it, a loud metallic clang echoing from his body as the heavy bark deflected and changed course. It hit the ground with a rustling thud, leaves poofing up and whirling.

Michael panted as his gaze flitted between the fallen branch and Bentley.

The donkey was safe.

But how did he do that? What was that clanging sound?

Michael shook the thought, half in a daze when the clouds parted abruptly, and a ray of light broke over them. Gloom still lingered in the distance, but a bright path opened before them. His face warmed again, and the Music of the Spheres finally became audible. A sign off the side of the road caught his attention.

YOU ARE EXITING THE LAST CIRCLE,
WELCOME TO THE FINAL FIELDS.
WE HOPE YOU'VE ENJOYED YOUR STAY!

8

Michael

*"Should we discover someone is lying, often, the greater
mercy is correction. However, should wisdom dictate that an
external reproof might push them further from the truth,
then we ought hold our tongues and smile."*
-The Guide to Utopian Principles and Ethics, Section II,
on Internal States

T HE AIR WAS CRISP in the sprawling emerald pastures of the
Forever Fields. Michael led Bentley by the reins while various
four-legged creatures grazed the long, swaying grass. The distant cries of
the gulls meant they were almost at the shore. They'd be on that ferry
soon enough.

The gloom was gone, thank the Throne, as were any signs of a dark
and explosive sky. But Michael still rattled from it. He kept his sword at
his hip even while they camped for the silence. Not that he could fight
the sky with a sword. But still, he felt safer with it.

Safe.

It had been a long while since he needed to consider that word.

The sounds of crashing waves and gulls grew louder as the air turned
to salt on his tongue. Grass was replaced by reeds and sand as the shore

came into view, and seafaring birds flew circles overhead. A bright orange ferry floated next to a dock, and Michael stowed his weapon in a bag as they approached. No need to look paranoid.

A stout bub with a bushy white beard appeared on the gangway. "Welcome! Headin' to Eastern Island'?"

Michael eyed the otherwise vast emptiness around them. Where else was there to go? "I received this in the mail." He offered his Calling letter and the angel examined it. He pulled out a small brass box and tapped it, a transparent list of names manifesting above the device.

Michael's eyebrows shot up as he poked a finger through the floating letters.

"Hologram," the angel chuckled, his accent not unlike Mary's. He must've spoken the old tongues too. "Ya get used to it 'round here. Ya must be Michael, then?"

"That's right." All other names had a line through them.

"Welcome aboard, Michael." He extended his arm and Michael shook it, still a little dumbstruck by the hologram. "I'm Bernard. Ya get used to the technology 'round here, no doubt." He produced a map from his pocket and pointed to it. "You'll need to go straight'way to the Creative Center for check-in when we dock." He handed Michael the map.

"I was hoping to rest up a bit before doing anything official." Especially officially checking into his Calling.

"Sorry. Just crossed off your name—they'll be expectin' ya."

Great.

Hopefully the few strategies he'd cooked up during the journey would significantly delay his art career.

Bernard led them across the metal gangway to a cargo area where there were stalls for Bentley. Michael put the donkey inside, but before he could pull out a few snacks, Bentley had already stomped twice and sprayed Bernard. You couldn't take this beast anywhere.

Michael stood at the bow while Bernard steered, leaning over the side of the ferry and taking in the view. Crystal blue waters came alive below, crashing and bobbing as if they had a mind of their own. Whales and dolphins and creatures for which Michael had no name made arcs as they popped from the water and dove back in. Seafaring must've been a nice Calling.

"There it is," Bernard said, pointing. "Universal Technologies."

Majestic towers sprung up from the island, gleaming gold domes at their peak. Behind them, something glimmered green. "What's that glow?" Michael asked.

"'Tis the meadow at the end of the island," Bernard said. "Shallow soil, so it feeds from the Well of Divine Glory that flows beneath. The plants shine like the sky."

Michael knew about those wells, but had never actually seen one. Lords would bank their glory in them while they walked among the commonborn, and stayed linked to their power through rings. They were mostly located in the inner circles, though. Michael wasn't entirely sure why.

The meadow sounded interesting, like something he probably would've sketched in private. Hopefully this Calling wouldn't completely ruin his already strained relationship with art.

They docked and retrieved Bentley, disembarking the craft. Bernard loaded Michael's bags into a wheelbarrow that waited on the dock.

"You can take off his saddle and let him roam," Bernard said. "There's more than a bit of the Almighty's magic on this island. It'll be the best grazing of his life."

"What about shelter?" Michael remembered the pelting ice and violent winds.

"Bah. That beast can handle a bit of warm drizzle. Besides... plenty of cover in the meadow. He can't go far on an island."

"And there's been no..." Michael chose his words carefully, "strange rains here lately?" So it was back to this—knowing things were wrong, but also knowing nobody would believe him.

"Nothin' save a cozy sprinkle."

Michael sighed. At the first sign of anything, he'd go find Bentley. He tapped the donkey off.

They passed through a set of tall bronze gates and started down a stony white path. Manicured olive trees and floral canopies stretched in and around the parklike campus, and well-trimmed, rectangular bushes lined the walkways.

They passed a circular stone structure that, under any other circumstance, he would've assumed to be a fountain, but it had no water. Its surface was covered in a thick layer of opaque glass, and a faint glow came from deep underneath.

"That the Well?" Michael gestured to it. "Covered in glass?"

"Hexagonal diamond," Bernard said. "Glass can't hold glory."

"And the slits around the edge?" Michael asked. "For the rings?"

Bernard nodded. "Deposits n' withdrawals. And all in between."

Michael eyed the Well. Baalael's power floated in there, somewhere. It was a shame you couldn't steal a lord's ring and take their power with it, but the rings were only links. Power was a birthright.

Their paths were bound to cross at some point or another—this island wasn't that big.

"Do the lords get about often?" Michael asked, eyeing the golden-domed building he was to report to later as they passed. "Do they mingle with the commoborn here?"

"Some do," Bernard said. "But most stay close to their kind. I'm old enough to recall when they all lived among us, in the first villages just beyond the Holy City. They trained up our Matriarchs and nannies, taught 'em how the world worked. When we'd thank 'em, they'd only say, 'Goodness obliges duty.'" Bernard chuckled. "That's how they came to be gods— 'twas never a title. In the beginning, we weren't so segregated."

They continued the journey through the campus to the common living quarters, which were a series of buildings faced with brown stone. Michael was staying at the Gamma Quarter, which consisted of several rows of neat, dual-level buildings with uniform lawns.

Bernard wished him well, and after helping carry his bags upstairs, tipped his cap and left.

Michael's "flat" had its own bedroom, bathroom, and kitchen, and was fully equipped with both electric lamps and indoor plumbing. The artificial light didn't seem necessary, as there were plenty of windows, and even with drawn shades he preferred the flickering glow of candles. But having his own plumbing system was nice. Back at the Jolly Bub, Michael often opted for a chamber pot after one of his brothers had "blessed" the bathroom.

Michael pulled out his map and headed down the steps, back to the white stone path. He navigated to the campus agorium, checking out its outdoor eatery, then made his way to what seemed like the heart of the campus: the Creative Center.

The heart of the immense marble structure was circular and surrounded by towering stone spires, each respective portion capped with a gleaming golden dome. Above the main entrance stretched a bronze engraved placard that read: Universal Technologies. He climbed the marble steps and entered the wide double doors.

Birds flitted around the dome's spacious interior, and rainbows streamed in through stained-glass windows. The walls were paneled in a high-gloss wood, and countless levels were connected by intricate winding staircases and ornate walking bridges that gave rise to splendid, wrought iron banisters. The detail in the woodwork seemed impossible. Michael's breath caught at the sight of it.

"Impressive, no?"

Michael startled at the angel with bright orange hair who appeared next to him. His bright eyes danced with a red-gold fire.

A lord. Mind my mind.

Michael took a deep breath. "It's very beautiful."

"You got a gifted eye for design, then." The lord patted his back. "You'll do just fine here, Michael."

Michael cocked his head, but then remembered that his was the last name on the list. "I was told to report here."

"I know." The orange-haired lord motioned him to follow.

"I didn't catch your name," Michael said.

"I didn't throw it."

Michael opened his mouth, but then closed it again.

"Call me Ruphius."

They walked through a hall where the wood panels comprised impossibly detailed relief sculptures. Tiny figures were etched into concave depressions, mingled with pomegranates and vines and flowers. If this was their standard for a wall, imagine the level of artistry they'd expect from him?

He stilled his thoughts.

They entered a private study and Ruphius sat behind a desk, folding his hands in his lap. "If you're concerned I'll read your thoughts, there's no need to be. It's bad form to do such things without consent."

"I wasn't."

"Well, your brow is so furrowed that you look constipated," Ruphius said. "Apologies if I misconstrued that."

Michael blushed.

"I understand there's no record of your formal painting apprenticeship," Ruphius said, "so we've arranged one for you with High Master Azrael. The fine arts are but one of his many skills, and one he quite enjoys."

"I'm very appreciative of that, sir," Michael cleared his throat, "but I'm afraid there's a small problem."

Ruphius frowned.

"I seem to have forgotten to pack my paintbrushes. I don't have proper supplies to start an apprenticeship."

"Azrael is more than generous with his supplies," Ruphius said. "We can send for more while you borrow—"

"My eyes..." Michael interrupted, blinking. "My eyes are also a problem. I forgot my glasses too. I can't draw or paint anything without them."

"I wasn't aware of any problem with your eyes."

"That's strange... should be in my records."

Ruphius sighed and craned his neck. "Azrael?"

Something shuffled from the back of the study and Michael jumped. A fully cloaked angel with their hood pulled low emerged from the shadows.

Silent scholar? Michael had never seen one in real life. He was huge. At least a head taller than Michael.

"Would you please diagnose Michael's vision so we can procure him a new pair of glasses?"

Michael's pulse quickened as Azrael placed a cold hand over his eyes. If they hadn't detected his thoughts yet, they surely would now.

But... they didn't.

After several beats, Azrael removed his hand and stepped back.

"Have you assessed his problem?" Ruphius asked.

Azrael nodded, and a bead of sweat rolled down Michael's face.

"I find no fault in..." his droning voice paused, and Michael froze. "I find no fault in submitting a request to correct his vision. This angel cannot yet properly see."

Michael exhaled, confused, but relieved. His gaze remained locked on Ruphius' desk as his breathing tapered, and Ruphius leaned over and stared at the same spot.

"You see a god in there?" Ruphius looked closer. "That happened to me once, you know. On my toast."

"Huh?" Michael looked up.

The lord grinned and burst into song. "*Who can hear inside a head that's thick as steel and strong as lead? Every god was filled with dread! And left the unsaid words unsaid.*" Ruphius plopped back into his chair and laughed.

Michael cocked a brow. Ruphius seemed a little mad.

"Azrael," Ruphius slapped the desk. "Procure this good bub some glasses. Then we'll get on with his lessons...." He reached into his drawer and handed Michael a scroll. "Strapping bub like you should consider taking up the sword. Here's the tryout schedule for our new gladiator squad. You can keep yourself busy while you wait for your glasses."

9

Trudy

"It's no secret that even the most educated angels are profoundly dull concerning anything that falls outside of their respective pittance of a worldview. If someone didn't sing it to them in a rhyme before they were old enough to button their trousers, then surely, it mustn't exist."

-Black Manifesto, Chapter One, "On Reality"

"Never heard of puttin' a sink in an office before," Bernard said, belly up and half interred in the new cabinet. "Yer' lucky we had a waterline capped off."

"I won't question luck," Trudy said, hoping Zuriah would feel utterly appeased when she proposed her findings about the light to him in this meeting. "The professor shouldn't have anything else to complain about now."

"I'm sure he'll find something." Hoot strolled in smiling and handed Trudy a cup.

"Wow." Her lips curled up as she inhaled steaming peppermint. Nobody in Tech ever brought her tea before. "Thank you... How's your vision?"

"Perfect," Hoot said. "Just trying to get used to how I look without glasses. Don't know if it's better or worse to see so much of my face now."

"Anything new takes a bit of getting used to."

Bernard shimmied from under the sink and Hoot helped him up, handing him a cup too. "If ya need anything else," Bernard packed up his tools, "I'll be in the pits practicin' for tryouts."

Hoot lit up. "You're trying out for the squad?"

Bernard gripped his wrench like a sword. "Aye. You?"

"Thinking about it now that I don't have to worry about breaking my glasses."

"Precepts fight?" Trudy cocked a brow.

"Fighting's an art," Hoot said. "The physical and mental fitness required to fight can only enrich moral and ethical balance. It's a serious discipline in the monastery. But mainly," he grinned, "it's a lot of fun."

"See ya at tryouts then!" Bernard tipped his cap and left, and Hoot sat down, loading his new drawers with file jackets.

She'd always known precepts to be traditional ethicsticians; stiff in their starchy uniforms with a book tucked under their arm, parroting the proverbs. But Hoot was none of that. He dressed in plain clothes and had the mind of a scholar. Maybe that was the difference between a precept and a Master Precept. Still, the idea of any precept with a sword was strange.

Zuriah cleared his throat and sauntered through the door, passing Trudy with an upturned mustache.

"Professor." She sat upright. "I hope you find your new lab space suitable."

He sneered before inspecting it. He turned the water on and off more than once, checked the cabinet hinges, and examined the countertop. He returned to the faucet, checking it again.

She narrowed her eyes. He was *looking* for something to complain about.

"Hello, Professor." Hoot popped up from behind his desk and Zuriah startled.

"Your Wholesomeness..." He ended the inspection and bowed.

So much for the science-minded.

"Just call me Hoot."

"My apologies, Your Principled Effectualness."

"HOOT," he repeated, louder this time, and motioned to a cup at the edge of his desk. "I brought you some lemon-vita."

"How did you know that's what I drink?" Zuriah took the cup and smelled it. "Did the wisdom come to you in meditation?"

"I was behind you in line."

Zuriah bowed. "Thank you, Your Hootness."

"Has anyone heard from Philistina?" Trudy asked, growing more conscious of the time. The lords would be checking on the team during the first verse, and she didn't want any of them hearing what she had to say.

"I have no dealings with that lunatic," Zuriah said, sipping his tea.

Hoot shook his head.

"Before we get started, I hoped it wouldn't be too much trouble if I asked for some assistance on a personal project. I could really use the help." She sat at the conference table and pulled out her qube. Hoot joined her.

They both looked at Zuriah, who had started unpacking beakers.

"You can sit next to me, Zuriah," Hoot patted the seat. "Virtues, Part Four, Proverb 1 says, 'Service is the heart of Heaven, and Heaven's heart doth serve.'"

At least he didn't sing it.

Zuriah's scowl faded and he put down his beakers.

She initiated the qube and navigated to several dozen photos of the sky, lining the holograms up in order from lightest to darkest. "There's a clear pattern emerging. Can you see it?"

Zuriah folded his arms. "I see a camera lens that needs cleaning."

"My lens was clean, Professor. Look outside...." Trudy pointed to the window. "Which photo most resembles what you see out there?"

"The last one," Hoot said. "The darkest."

"That's right," Trudy said. "The light's dimming so gradually it's almost imperceptible. I happened to be outside and paying very close attention when the light took a steeper dip. But the normal rate of decline is far more subtle. The earliest photos are from old albums of mine, and they show the greatest difference. "

"Fluctuations in the light are normal," Zuriah said. "Are we done now?"

"Fluctuations are normal," Trudy said, "But not gradients. Not declines. These photos clearly show a dimming pattern."

"Hmm…" Hoot stood up and examined the hologram. "I see what you're saying."

"And what exactly is your point?" Zuriah asked. "Nature isn't a machine. It's organic."

Trudy pulled up photos of her failed plants. The Tree of Life sapling reduced to dried sticks, and the shriveled ashes that were once the petals of her morning glories. "These plants are light sensitive. They were very young, being nursed. The light failed to nurture them."

"You probably kept them in a shadow," Zuriah said. "Call a gar-dene—"

"You sound concerned," Hoot cut him off.

"I am," Trudy said. "Something's wrong with our light."

"Preposterous." Zuriah stood up. "Nothing can be wrong with nature. The very idea is blasphemy."

"Calm down, Professor." Hoot tugged him back into the chair. "Just because you disagree with something doesn't make it blasphemy. Suppose the light is trending dimmer… I'm sure there have been other natural phenomena that have corrected themselves throughout history."

"Zuriah would know that better than me," Trudy said.

"All I know is that nature is perfect, as is its Creator." He stood up again and straightened his bowtie.

"Be careful declaring anything perfect or imperfect," Hoot said. "Remember, we don't have the proper scope to pass such judgments."

"I'd sooner bet on nature than I would on a computer scientist conducting half-baked experiments with a crude photo-machine. She's worked on logistics hubs; she should know to use a proper camera for ideal light sensitivity. And even if her observation was accurate—for all we know, the Almighty, in his infinite wisdom, could simply be adjusting the fluctuation pattern. Maybe slowing down the intervals for some reason. We should mind our business."

Trudy got up and walked to the window. "Look at the amount of yellowing and dried out leaves on the ground." She pointed. "The sound of their crunching is normal now. Bare twigs can be found in the trees, and Bernard stopped mowing the lawn because the grass isn't growing. What happens if the Trees of Life fail? If there's no more vita to eat or make manna with? How will our cells regenerate? Have you noticed there's no manna in the eatery?"

"There's an issue with flour deliveries," Zuriah said. "The baker told me so herself."

"And when have you ever heard of any delivery problem in your life? Our logistics systems are more efficient now than they ever were. I fear there's no problem with delivery, but rather, one with procurement."

"This might be over our heads," Hoot said. "Perhaps we should go to the lords."

"No lords!" Zuriah snapped. "I'm not in any temperament to be dealing with those bright-eyed brutes."

"I'm inclined to agree with the professor on that," Trudy said, though truth be told, Zuriah was in no temperament to deal with anyone, ever. "The lords in Tech will read our minds and discipline us for thinking, and the lords in Creative will dismiss us like children. Their attitude is one of complacency."

"She's right." Philistina's voice caught them by surprise.

"You startled me," Trudy said.

"She's got a habit of doing that," Zuriah mumbled.

Philistina slid a data crystal into Trudy's qube, and a map of their flat, circular world appeared.

"What's this?" Hoot asked.

"Weather map," Philistina said. "From the public record. Growers use it. I started tracking weather patterns when I noticed the leaves in my village turning."

A spark of hope flashed in Trudy's chest.

"At first I thought we needed more rain," Philistina said, "that maybe the leaves were parched. But when I started studying the weather patterns, I noticed something strange."

"What are these spots?" Trudy said, leaning in closer. The mainland was dotted with something like blights—blurry spots where the map was distorted. They varied in hue, with the darkest being in the more populated areas. "It's like we're looking through a damaged photo filter."

"And what's stranger," Philistina zoomed into a spot, "is that these hazy spots coincide with new weather patterns."

"You're a meteorologist now?" Zuriah asked. "I don't even see precipitation on this map."

"Because this map is three movements old." She navigated to a different file and opened a new one. Colors moved around, representing the precipitation and wind. But there were colors that Trudy had never seen on a weather map before—deep greens and browns and blues. One spot was nearly black.

"That's not right..." Zuriah leaned in and attempted to adjust his glasses, but they weren't there. "There's too much precipitation in these systems.... It's impossible."

"Your mustache is impossible," Philistina said, "yet, there it is."

Zuriah glared at her. "It's far more likely there's a glitch in this monitoring system than there is a glitch in nature."

"Is there another system we can check?" Hoot asked.

"No," Trudy said. "This is part of our centralized logistic resources. There's only one model to draw from."

"We have to go in person," Philistina said.

"Where?" Zuriah asked.

"There." She pointed to the darkest floating blob on the map. "It's the only way to know for sure."

"That's halfway across the realm!" Zuriah said. "It'll take movements to make that journey."

"Maybe not," Trudy said. "There are more ways to travel than by ground, Professor. I might be able to arrange something."

"Do you mean to stuff us into a shipping container and load us on an airship?" Zuriah looked horrified. "Have your symphonies of logistics made you insane?"

"That would not be..." Hoot cleared his throat, "ideal."

"Of course not," Trudy said, exchanging a glance with Philistina. "I can get us to that crossing swiftly if you're both willing to come. I still have one lord willing to stick a feather out for me."

"No lords!" Zuriah said. "I told you—"

Trudy raised a hand. "Fine. You have my word. No lords." That could make securing transportation a little more difficult, but not impossible.

"Is there a reason you're so adverse to the lords, professor?" Hoot asked.

"I..." Zuriah crossed his arms. "I'd rather not say."

"But you'll come with us?" Trudy asked. "If we can travel swiftly, and without lords?"

"Of course," Hoot said, and glanced at Zuriah expectantly. "Right, Professor?"

Zuriah sighed. "I suppose I can use it as a teaching opportunity. You'll be far more tolerable when educated."

"Great," Trudy glanced at Philistina. "If Zuriah's right, we have nothing to worry about. If he's not, we'll collect as much data as possible. And don't worry about transportation. I'll get us there. Somehow."

10

Michael

"We've heard it said that the best way to earn favor is through respect. But like most of our beliefs, this too is poorly thought out and rarely, if ever, challenged. Respect can only earn favor insofar as another is willing to give it. A more secure way to garner favor would be through that old taboo we call fear. Should someone fear you, for any reason, their favor would be virtually guaranteed."

-Black Manifesto, Chapter Two, "On Power"

M ICHAEL OPENED HIS EYES, panting, sweat dripping from his face.

Smooth cello notes sailed in through the open window, calming his racing pulse.

The dreams had gotten so much worse since his Calling came. This time, white-faced masks loomed over him, poking and prodding, a hand over his mouth as they held him down.

Just more bad memories. They had to show up sometime.

At least he didn't have his deep, dreamless sleep. He woke up more exhausted from that than anything else, and tryouts were in less than a verse.

He popped a few coffee beans before brushing their debris from his teeth and pulled his armor from the sack, buckles jangling. The musky leather smelled sweeter to him than Mary's hot cakes. It had been over a movement since he'd bashed the hilt of his sword into someone's face, and he missed it.

He stepped into the linen liner and slipped on his chest plate, followed by his groin skirt and bandolier. He secured his pauldron and wrist guards, then laced up his sandals.

The boiled rootroast skins were like an exoskeleton. He stood taller; felt more alive.

He slid his sword into the scabbard and headed out.

Passersby followed him with their gazes and whispered, "*Gladiator.*" He felt at home again, leather-bound with a sword at his hip. His muscles twitched to get into the pit with a real foe, and he could've sworn the breeze itself cried, "*Fight.*"

The arena behind campus was small, and aspiring gladiators in various styles of armor waited around the pit for tryouts to begin. Michael canvassed the stands, which were peppered with onlookers. An angel in the top row caught his attention.

He was overdressed in a black frock, and leaned back with his arms wide, looking down on everyone. His chin pointed up as if daring anyone to return his gaze.

That lean looked familiar.

Michael put his hand above his brow to shield the light, but it was no use—he couldn't make out the face in the distance. He couldn't tell if those eyes were glowing.

"Ahoy there, Michael!" Bernard appeared, weaving and bobbing while he threw a few uppercuts in the air. "Fancy seein' you here, friend."

"Ahoy there, Captain."

Bernard's stout belly protruded under his well-worn chest plate, but it didn't jiggle. He might have been round, but he was solid. His bushy white beard was tied into several gold bands, and his exposed arms and legs looked more like tree trunks than limbs.

"Meet me friend, Hoot." Bernard motioned toward a nervous-looking angel behind him, and he shuffled forward, extending a shaking arm.

Michael crossed two fists to his chest and bowed. "This is the gladiator salute. Wrist guards get in the way of a proper shake."

Slowly, Hoot did the same.

Michael smiled. "That's right." At least he didn't act like something he wasn't. Most amateurs thought themselves better than they actually were. Hoot's armor looked new, no scuffs or creases. More than likely, he wasn't an experienced fighter. Michael could size up an angel fairly quickly at the pits.

"Thank you," Hoot said, his voice a little timid. "I've never fought a real match before, but I've been practicing the forms most of my life."

"Practicing alone?" Michael raised his eyebrows.

"I learned at the monastery from the silent scholars. We practice the gladiatorial forms as a kind of meditation. I've just never actually hit anyone."

"Hoot's a precept." Bernard slapped the poor bub's back so hard he stumbled. "Guessin' not too many precepts willin' to get their holy faces knocked in so he could practice."

"Well..." Michael looked around at the others with their mismatched leathers and dented swords. He thought of the givers from his village who thought they could fight too. "Don't underestimate good form. Until angels start competing above the village level, they're pretty useless with a sword. You might have more of an advantage than you think." He motioned to Bernard's empty hip. "And where's your sword?"

"Bah. Back in me village we were fightin' before they made swords." He raised a plump mitt of a fist. "I've got the strength of me hands and the force of me pudge. That's how we done it in the old songs."

Michael knew someone else who could move a mountain with the force of her pudge.

"Look..." Hoot pointed to a gladiator who was situating himself in front of the crowd. He walked tall and confident, with a small entourage around him.

That was no amateur.

"It's the Angel Joseph," Michael said, and Hoot's eyes went wide. Joseph raised a hand and the crowd harkened, growing silent.

"Welcome, all of you." Joseph's gaze moved over the fighters. His wrist guards were elaborate, Michael noticed, reaching below his wrists, almost to his palms. "I'm inspired to see so many of you show up," Joseph continued. "It takes courage to learn a thing that you haven't been Called to do. But you're here to sharpen more than your swords. You're here to sharpen your bodies and minds."

The crowd let out a cheer, and he paused briefly before continuing. "Professional fighters will be assisting with the tryouts as I observe how each of you handle yourselves in the pit. Those of you who display a higher level of skill will be sent to the elite section." He pointed to the right side of the arena. "I'll be training these angels myself—and if there are at least five of you, we will have enough to send a squad to the Games." That evoked a cheer, but Joseph raised his hand to stifle their shouting. "And being that I cannot bring myself to turn anyone away, the rest of you will go to the aspiring section where other professionals will develop your skills so you can compete here on the island, and become competent fighters. No one who came to learn this verse will be turned away!"

The crowd went wild, and Michael was a little relieved for Hoot who seemed so anxious. At least he couldn't be rejected, even if he choked.

Angels bottlenecked the front of the pit in a rush, and Michael grabbed the precept by the arm. "Slow down... the further back you are in line, the longer you can observe the competition. Look for their strengths so you know your defense, and look for their weakness so you know where to strike. Plus, it doesn't hurt to let them get tired."

"He's right," Bernard said. "Youth's folly."

"Or just inexperience," Michael said. "He'll get it."

They waited at the end of the line and watched as bub after bub hopped into the pit and got easily dispatched. Joseph rotated in the professional gladiators that were trying out the newcomers, and one by one, each amateur was sent to the "aspiring" side.

He glanced again to the top of the spectator stands. The angel in black still sat there.

"Did you see that?" Hoot pointed. "Someone's been sent to the elite side."

Michael missed it, which was unfortunate. Thus far the fights had been rather boring. It was hard to gauge the strengths and weaknesses of the competition when every match lasted under three beats.

The next few bouts were equally uninteresting—unpracticed enthusiasts with bad form who put little thought into defense and even less into offense. Then an angel in red leathers and a silver pauldron descended the steps of the pit. He was abnormally small, and wore double-crossed swords at his back.

"Never seen a bub with lumps that big up north," Bernard said.

"That's not a bub…" Hoot squinted.

"About time," Michael said. "I've known femmes who could swing circles around this crowd. Even the professionals." Michael adjusted his vantage for a better view.

She drew both swords and twirled them, running up the wall and flipping backward. She could entertain, but could she fight?

The gladiator lunged at her, but she flipped over his head and landed behind him in a crouch. They volleyed swords and she held her own, blocking all his blows. In a flash, she leapt and flipped across the pit, nimble as a hummingbird, launching daggers as she did. Her opponent stood there like a pin cushion, and Joseph blew the whistle.

He sent her to the elite side, and the crowd let out a cheer.

Bernard leaned into a stretch. He was next. "Bit o' luck for me, aye, bubs?"

Hoot looked puzzled, so Michael translated. "He told us to wish him luck."

Bernard secured his helm and trudged to the edge of the pit, avoiding the steps and dropping in like a sack of potatoes.

The gladiator squared off with him, and Bernard kicked dirt behind him and charged with a mighty roar. His opponent looked shocked, and Michael stifled a laugh. He was like a one-bub demolition squad.

The gladiator pivoted, but so did Bernard, somehow not losing a shred of momentum. The sheer force of his impact sent the gladiator flying. They wrestled a bit, but before Michael knew it, Bernard had a knee on the gladiator's sword arm, pinning him to the floor. He wasn't kidding about the force of his pudge.

Joseph blew the whistle and pointed to the elite side. Bernard jumped and threw both fists into the air, followed by cheers.

"Well... that's that," Michael turned to Hoot, laughing, but the poor bub was sweating profusely. "You okay?"

He nodded, a little too quickly, and Joseph rotated in a new gladiator.

Michael gripped Hoot by the shoulders. "Listen—you'll be fine. This one's a little slower and he's going to favor your left, so keep your shield up and keep him moving. Make him work for it. When you see an opening, strike fast. Use your fear to your advantage, it'll keep you sharp." Michael patted his shoulder. "Be brave. You've got this."

Hoot secured his helm and descended the steps. The gladiator got into position. Hoot's form was excellent, even if he was rattling like an old wheelbarrow. He did what Michael said and kept his opponent moving, ducking, and blocking with accuracy. Fear could go one of two ways: it could push you into sharp instinct or freeze you up like a rock.

Fortunately, Hoot did the former and was hard to catch. The nervousness gave him speed, and his forms were impeccable. Maybe he was practicing alone, but he must've been practicing a lot. His evasive moves were clean and concise, nearly perfect. That had to count for something—he was certainly better than the lumps around here.

Measures were passing and the gladiator couldn't land a strike. *Excellent defense.* And Michael wasn't easy to impress. He tried to gauge Joseph's expression. Inexperienced as Hoot was, he was lasting way longer than anyone else on the aspiring side.

Finally, Joseph blew his whistle and pointed to the elite side. Hoot's face lit up as he looked to Michael, beaming. Michael raised a fist in solidarity, and Hoot raised one back.

Michael was next.

They raked the dirt as a new gladiator got into the pit and Michael leaned into a stretch. In his periphery, the angel in black descended the stands and approached Joseph. They exchanged words, and Joseph's face grew dark before he stormed off. The angel in black waved a different gladiator over—one who hadn't fought yet, wide as an ox and at least half a head taller than the others. Joseph repositioned himself at the other edge of the pit, and the new gladiator stepped in.

Glowing gray eyes met Michael's gaze, and the angel in black grinned. *Lord Baalael.*

A burst of energy shot up from Michael's gut, raw and seething as his teeth ground against each other.

Rage.

He wouldn't have to worry about minding his thoughts—he couldn't form any coherent ones. He embraced the feeling like an old friend returned home from a long journey—except this time, he was no helpless child.

He dropped into the pit, his senses dilating. Everything was clear—clean and sharp. Joseph leaned forward, watching intently, and Lord Baalael crossed his arms and grinned at him.

Michael stepped to the immense opponent, eyes fixed on his hips but soft in the periphery, taking it all in. The gladiator lunged into strikes and Michael danced, loose and weightless. For every swing the giant took, Michael pictured a part of this stranger's innocence that he would obliterate. The nannies who sang him bedtime songs. The brothers who let him win at seek.

The poor giant couldn't land a single blow, and Michael was about to unload on him.

It wasn't a good thing, Michael knew, to let his resentment fall on whoever was at the end of his sword. But the pits were the only place he could release it. Everyone's life was perfect. And his was miserable. They should suffer at least a little for that.

He leaped into offense, slashing and cutting every shred of joy he could imagine in this overgrown lump. The giant stumbled backward, but Michael kept on the offense, landing blow after blow. Down the Throne with these dull swords. He wanted to cut someone open.

Michael backed him against the wall, and the angel struggled to catch his breath, unable to pull his flag and defend his face at the same time. Michael smashed that chiseled cheekbone with the butt of his sword and light shot from the wound before condensing into blood. The honey-lavender stench filled Michael's lungs and he smiled. Amateurs now all stood at the edge of the pit, leaning expectantly.

Joseph should've tapped him out already and sent Michael to the elite side. This was, after all, only a tryout. But he and Baalael were arguing from several cubits away, the lord's grin all but gone.

Well... If they wanted a show, they would get one.

Michael stopped the onslaught and stepped back, dropping his shield to the ground. The heaving gladiator recovered and got back into position, shock and blood covering his face.

Michael baited him with his exposed side, and he took it, lunging into an attack. Michael pivoted and jammed his shoulder under the angel's sword arm, flipping him. He landed flat on his back with a thud, a plume of dust rising around him.

Lord Baalael charged at Joseph, who was the one grinning now. Michael raised his sword over the angel's throat.

But he still didn't pull his flag, and Joseph didn't tap him out.

They argued nose to nose now, and Baalael apparently won because Joseph stormed off. Another gladiator stepped to the edge of the pit and descended. He began a charge toward Michael.

In? He tapped someone *in*?

Michael might have already been recognized.

"Nothing personal," Michael said to the gladiator in front of him, and plunged the sword through his shoulder. He exploded into a scream. "Can't have you coming up behind me."

Bernard and Hoot were now at the edge of the pit yelling something about unfairness. Poor things didn't know the first thing about unfairness. Michael retrieved his shield and grabbed a full fist of dirt in the process.

The second gladiator attacked, and Michael pitched the dirt in his face, following up immediately with a shield smash to the side of his head. His opponent dipped, and Michael swept his legs, throwing him off balance.

He brought an elbow to the gladiator's jaw with a crunch, purple rays of life force bursting from his mouth along with chunks of teeth. Now this was a fight. The light condensed to blood and dripped down his chin.

"Shouldn't play unfair," Michael said as the bleeding bub swung clumsily. "Even if some inglorious wingbag tells you to."

Michael kicked him across the head, and he stumbled back. Then he yanked the sword from the gladiator's hand and kicked him square in the chest, knocking him flat on his back.

If Baalael did recognize him, then Michael had a second chance to make a first impression. He twirled both swords as he advanced, and the bleeding angel crawled backward. Michael lifted his foot and pinned the toothless, half-blind gladiator to the floor, holding a sword to either side of his neck.

"Would you like to tap him out now?" Michael called out. "Because if I'm fighting someone else, I may have to remove his head... and I don't know how much light and vita it'll take to fix that."

The whole crowd was stark silent as tranquil cello notes carried through the sky. Bernard and Hoot stood there, saucer-eyed, and the rest of the crowd gawked in some combination of confusion and terror. His last comment might have been too much, but the Master of the Games always did bring out the worst in him.

Baalael gave Joseph one final glare and stormed off. Joseph blew the whistle and pointed Michael to the elite side.

Good choice.

Michael helped his opponent up and gave back his sword before bowing.

A silent scholar descended the stands swiftly and left the arena. Michael hadn't noticed him before.

"Are you alright?" Hoot ran over as Michael emerged from the pit.

"'Tis not Michael I'm worried 'bout," Bernard said.

"I'm fine."

"That was amazing..." Hoot paused. "Well, frightening actually.... Where did you learn to fight like that?"

Michael grabbed a rag from the pile and dabbed sweat and dirt from his face. "Lots of practice. I had a decent teacher once."

"And talent," Hoot said. "You just took out two members of a champion squad. And you threw dirt in someone's face... I've never even heard of that."

"There's no rule against it," Michael said.

"May soon be though," Bernard chortled. "But 'e deserved it. Don't know what they were thinkin'... sendin' a second fighter in for a tryout."

"Maybe they wanted to see how he'd do if the rest of his squad fell," Hoot said.

"Or maybe the lord with the gray eyes should go take a piss." Michael spit out a glob of blood. Not because they landed a blow, but because he bit through his tongue when he saw Baalael.

"Better let the light shine in your mouth," Hoot said.

"I'd rather not." Healing tongue wounds in the light looked foolish. "I'll grab some fresh manna from the eatery on my way back."

"Good luck finding any," Hoot said. "Vita flour deliveries are late."

Michael furrowed his brow and thought of Nunziel.

"Plenty vita grow'n wild in the meadow," Bernard said. "It can be dried n' ground, like we did in the old songs. Not the tastiest, but it'll work."

They were interrupted when the femme in red leathers stepped in front of Michael. Her pitch-black hair was slicked into a bun, and she bowed the gladiator's salute. "I am Zillah," she said, her accent unfamiliar, "and it will be a privilege to train with you."

"And I'm Asher." The other elite member stepped up, but he didn't bow. "If only we all got the opportunity to prove ourselves as you just did."

Michael eyed him for a beat and was about to respond, but Joseph appeared.

"Michael..." he said, "May I have a word?"

They walked a while without saying anything, the arena shrinking behind them as they got closer to the shore. The soil turned to soft sand, and Joseph climbed the rocks that held the sea at bay and sat near the top. Michael gripped a rock to climb up next to him, but almost slipped on the slimy seaweed coating.

"I apologize for what just happened back there," Joseph said as Michael got his footing. "Seems to be a little conflict regarding who's in charge of the athletics program."

"Who was that you were arguing with?" Michael tried his best to sound inquisitive.

"You didn't recognize the Master of the Games?"

"Not without the pearl armor." Michael gazed out at the water. "Lords all look the same to me."

"That ridiculous armor," Joseph guffawed, flinging a small rock that splashed near the shore. "I'd like to see him wear that in an actual fight."

A measure or so passed in silence, and Michael had no desire to fill it. You learned more when you spoke less.

Eventually, Joseph spoke. "You demonstrated a level of skill that showed you should've already been called to the arenas. That means the Master of the Games didn't do his job very well. Competition is Baalael's dominion. You made him look bad."

The explanation was plausible, but it didn't mean Michael hadn't been recognized.

"I'm glad it wasn't personal." Michael peeked at Joseph from the corner of his eye. "I'd hate to anger a god."

"Personal against me, maybe. Not you." Joseph laughed to himself. "You should've seen the look on his smug face when you tore through our two best Champions. He came down to gloat that I was at the end of the line and hadn't formed a squad yet. He wanted to make sure the last tryout didn't result in a fifth elite, so he put our most brutal fighter in. Your timing couldn't have been better. Thankfully, Universal Technologies has silent scholars recording every important event that happens on campus—it kept him from using his power against you. But I digress... I didn't bring you here solely to apologize for Baalael. I also wanted to apologize that I wasn't able to get your invitation out in time. You came anyway, though. That was bold."

He didn't have to fake an inquisitive look this time. "You never arranged my Calling here?"

"Securing Callings for angels without the requisite skills for this place isn't always possible, but Lucifer has been able to arrange invitations for positions related to the sporting program. Angelic Resources said I could have an assistant, and that you could fight with us if you wanted to. And as I said, the Master of the Games isn't so thrilled with this athletics program, which caused a delay in getting your invitation processed. I would've tried you out anyway, but I'm glad it happened like this. I have a better idea of your skill level."

If his Calling didn't come from Joseph, Shemliel's petition must have finally been answered. But Michael was hesitant to let him know any of that. With Baalael this close, the less information that lingered in anyone's head, the better.

"I'm glad I risked it and came," Michael smiled, lying.

Waves crashed against the rocks, and a light mist covered Michael's face. It felt good.

Joseph pointed to the sky. "What do you think that is?"

Michael followed his finger to a small, dark stain that floated far off on the horizon. The tiny gray patch flashed irregularly, and Michael knew exactly what it was.

"What do you think it is?" Michael asked.

"That answer depends...."

"Depends on what?"

"Your constitution." Joseph faced him and crossed his arms. "What if I told you that was a trick of the light? Or a rain cloud bent at a strange angle. What would you say to that?"

"I wouldn't say anything." Michael shrugged and popped a few coffee beans from the small pouch on his belt. "I'd let you believe what you want."

"Alright then..." Joseph continued to regard him. "What if I told you that was a dangerous presence? Violent winds and electrical whips attacking from the sky?"

Michael cocked a brow. "Then I'd say anyone finding themselves caught in it had better seek cover anywhere but under a tree... lest they get crushed by it. I might have traveled through one on my way here."

Joseph slipped a small black book from his pouch and handed it to Michael. "Read this, and if you can stomach it, I'd like for you to come to the Alpha Quarter with me."

"What is it?" Michael thumbed through the pages.

"Think of it as a guide to enduring the unendurable. We call it the Black Manifesto. Black because it needs to remain in the dark, for now."

"If this book needs to remain in the dark, why trust me with it?"

"Besides for your unique constitution," Joseph said. "I just watched you tear through two former Champions without breaking a sweat, and also without having been formally trained. I'd be stupid not to take a risk on you."

"What's in the Alpha Quarter?" Michael crossed his arms.

"I see your defenses, Michael, and while they're refreshing, I don't wish to raise them. There are some lords I'd like for you to meet. Well, one lord, specifically. That smudge in the sky speaks to something much bigger. We're in serious peril, and I don't mean the kind of peril found in a dictionary. Some of the lords are willing to be proactive about it. I can explain more if you decide to come."

"What lords?" Peril or not, he had to be careful.

"Lucifer leads our cause and some of his siblings follow—the ones who are willing to accept reality."

"And the god who tried to have me crushed in the pit? Will Baalael be there?"

Joseph nodded. "But you don't have to worry about him. Trust me, nobody likes that one less than I do."

That was highly debatable. But still, sitting in a room with Baalael was a little more risk than he was comfortable with at this point. Yes, X had been a squeaky, thin child at thirteen, and Michael was a fully formed adult, but unnecessary exposure this early on would be foolish. Baalael was still a god. And Michael had already made the elite squad. The plan was to face Baalael only once—after claiming Champion's Legacy so he could fight him without his power.

But Michael didn't want to voice an outright rejection that might jeopardize his favor with Joseph, so he fingered through the book and acted like he was giving the request some thought.

It was a simple collection of proverbs and essays. He'd never read the Handbook in its entirety, but this was something akin to it. Neither seemed remarkably interesting. He preferred learning about life by living it.

"This is your 'Handbook,' then? What you believe?"

"This is the Black Manifesto," Joseph corrected, "not my Handbook. Some of its principles will make survival possible. I have my own way of looking at things."

"I'll read the whole book." Michael closed it and looked up. "But I'd prefer to meet somewhere without Baalael."

Joseph sighed. "That's disappointing. Baalael is one of the reasons I preferred you by my side. To let him see more commonborn who are clever and strong. Remind him that while he might have birthright, we have numbers." He pushed himself up with a grunt and began his descent.

Michael pushed himself up too, but before he'd taken a step down, Joseph lost his footing. Michael lunged to grab him, but almost slipped on the seaweed himself.

Joseph crashed into the sand, and something loud clanged off a rock. Michael leapt to help him, and the Champion blushed something fierce.

Joseph brushed off his legs as Michael retrieved the wrist guard that had fallen off. When he went to hand it to him, Michael gasped.

Joseph's wrist was completely deformed—purple and lumpy and gnarled.

"Apologies." Joseph snatched the wrist guard and stood up, clearly embarrassed. "I didn't intend for you to see that."

Michael tried to conceal his shock and averted his gaze.

"This is what happens when a limb gets severed," Joseph explained, calmly clipping his wrist guard back on. "First, they have to stop the bleed—the life force flows from you so fast that before you know it, you're rolling in an ever-growing pool of your own blood, choking on the sweet smell of it. Then, the triage technicians panic, because the worst wounds they ever see are minor lacerations that have already begun healing. By this time, you're nearly unconscious, but not so unconscious that you don't feel the hot iron they sear your stumps with. After they cook you, you wake up and spend several symphonies unable to scratch your own arse or take a piss." He closed the wrist guard with a snap, stretching a tight smile. "How very embarrassing. As if the fall wasn't bad enough."

Michael was... speechless. "How?" He managed to eke out.

"I was the first and last to dare claim Champion's Legacy, and challenge that insidious piece of snog for control of the Games. For the only real piece of respect that one of us might *earn*. He's the Lord of Victory—he's supposed to drive progress. Instead, he hoards for himself the one truly noble accomplishment within our reach. And I would've earned it too, had he not cheated. He used his power, though the rules forbid it. But go ahead and try to get someone to believe a lord dishonest. An invisible force crushed me down as soon as I got the upper hand. He needed his birthright because I'm the stronger fighter, and he knew it.

"So, you should believe me when I tell you that nobody likes Lord Baalael less than I do. If he makes you uncomfortable, imagine what he does to me."

Baalael had threatened to chop off Michael's hands many times, for stealing, but he'd never followed through. No doubt now that he would have, had Michael not been rescued. The threat alone, though, was enough to keep him awake back then.

"I... I don't know what to say. I'm sorry."

"There's nothing to be sorry for," Joseph said. "It was a long time ago. It's been erased from the records, and anyone there to witness it put it from their minds and pretended it never happened. Because that's what angels do, and that's why they'll never make it through what's coming. I wanted you by my side because I mistook you for one of those rare commonborn who didn't cower before the gods. But you're just another gifted fighter, like the others. It was my error."

Michael's jaw tightened. "I don't cower before gods."

"No. *I* don't cower before gods," Joseph corrected him, "which is why I can sit in a room with the god who did this. But, like I said... we are rare."

Michael was insulted, no doubt, but for the first time in a very long time, he didn't feel so alone. Joseph knew the truth: life wasn't perfect. That they lived in a world with no recourse for those who were wronged.

Michael stepped forward and locked Joseph in his gaze, then he crossed his wrists and bowed. "Let me know when to be there. *I don't cower before anyone.*"

And he didn't. Not since he'd found that sword with its beryl stone, so long ago. Or maybe... it was the sword that found him.

11

X

"At the right place, and in the right instant—what's meant for you will find you. This fact is older than the music itself. It is by decree of the Almighty."
-The Guide to Utopian Principles and Ethics, Section IV,
on Belief & Faith

THE AIR DRAINED FROM X's chest. The whole hall turned in his direction, and he looked to the exit, but Lord Baalael was blocking it. A nanny carried a blue tube to the front of the dining hall, where Deidre popped it open. She slid the paintings from the tube and unrolled them. Gabriel squeezed X's hand.

"Heaven's Smallest is an estate of excellence," Deidre spat, aggressively pinning his paintings to the wall. Shame and fear mangled his mind. "We pride ourselves in our meticulous upkeep," she jabbed another pin, "outstanding test scores, and the *excellence* with which we compete in everything we do."

She stabbed a pin through the final painting and it hung there; a solid black square with a set of glowing green eyes. The only remnant in his memory that linked to who he truly was, or where he came from. The only thing that made him feel some semblance of home. Now, they stared at him, accusing. At the bottom right-hand corner was the pathetic mark he'd come to know as his signature— two red lines that crossed in the center. *X.*

"How *dare* you try and represent my estate with this rubbish!?" The others began to laugh, mocking murmurs filling the room. "You have no gift for this! It's a bunch of trash!"

Regret ate him alive. The whole thing had been Gabriel's idea. He only agreed for the hope that a master would see his work and pity him, and maybe invite him into apprenticeship. That another adult, one far removed from this place, could step in and help. Then he could come back for Gabriel. He'd been trying to escape for seven symphonies, but Baalael would hunt him down before he could even make it to the village edge. On the rare occasion he did run into an adult, none believed him.

"The proportions, the colors, the values..." Deidre spit out the words like she hated the taste of them. "A child half your age could do better."

He felt faint, like he would pass out right there, in the middle of the room. He couldn't muster words, but that didn't matter—there was no defense. He was caught.

"After we have housed you..." She ripped a painting from the wall and threw it into the hearth, blazing embers puffing into the air. "Fed you!" She threw another. "Bore your burden with nothing but charity." She ripped the rest of the paintings off the wall and tossed them into the fire. "And the audacity to think we wouldn't find out!"

X bolted from the seat toward the door. He didn't care, he'd run right through Lord Baalael if he had to. But Baalael stepped to the side, grinning.

He burst through the back door and into the field, darting for the woods. Escape was impossible—that had been proven again and again. But he ran anyway, struggling to breathe as twigs crunched under his feet and branches whipped him in the face.

A glint in a copse of oak caught his eye and he slowed.

It was steel—a long piece of it—protruding from a tree. A sword. He checked behind him—no one pursued. Cautiously, he approached.

Below the handle was inlaid a bright blue stone that almost appeared to glow. An illusion of the light, he figured.

He tugged at it, but it was buried so deep in the wood that it wouldn't budge. He grabbed it with both hands and pulled, then lodged his foot into the trunk and yanked with all his strength.

A rustling came from deeper in the woods and he froze. "Hello?" he called out, turning his head, but there was no response. Then he saw someone in a dark cloak, partially blocked by a tree.

"Hello?" he cried out. "Can you help me?"

They turned and retreated.

"Wait!"

The sword loosed, and he flew backward, knocking his head on the ground. Pain echoed through his body, and he laid there a few beats before sitting up and rubbing it. The sword lay in his lap, light gleaming off the blade. He ran his finger along the cool, sharp steel.

"Brother!" Gabriel ran toward him, huffing, holding a tubelike object.

"Go back. You'll get in trouble!"

Gabriel unfurled the dark square of canvas, marked in the center by two bright-green eyes. The edges had been burned off, but he somehow saved the painting.

"You shouldn't have done this!" X yelled. "You'll be punished for it!"

"I'm sorry." Gabriel was crying. "It was all I could save."

"It's okay." Michael pushed himself up with the sword and put an arm around his brother. "We knew the risk."

Gabriel pushed his glasses higher, noticing the sword. "Where'd you get that?"

"I found it in a tree. I'm going to keep it."

"They'll never let you do that." Gabriel's face creased with fear. "You'll get in even worse trouble!"

"I'll always be in trouble." X glanced at the sword and set his jaw. "So, from now on... I'm going to make sure I deserve it."

12

Trudy

"Light is a peculiar thing. Perhaps the only thing that has not been fully opened to us— and by us, I mean the species of old. We live by the promise of light; a promise that could be broken at any time. And that, my friends, is something that should give everyone pause."
-Black Manifesto, Chapter One, "On Reality"

"ARE YOU BLEEDING!?" TRUDY darted into the room, Hoot and Zuriah close behind. Philistina stood behind the counter of Zuriah's lab with a razor blade and several purple stained towels next to her. Zuriah stomped over and snatched the razor from her hand. "Why are you touching my equipment?"

"Peace, Professor." Hoot held up his hand and approached cautiously. "Philistina... what are you doing?"

"Testing our wounds in the light. Watch this..." She snatched the razor back from Zuriah and slashed her forearm. Light beamed from the wound and he lunged over the counter.

"I thought we were going on a field trip!" Zuriah swiped at her. "Instead, she's wrecking my lab!"

Philistina darted for the closed window. She held the wound into the light that streamed through the glass and pulled out a chordograph. They all leaned in.

Her light condensed into blood and dripped down her arm, puddling on the windowsill.

"The wound should've started healing by now," Hoot said. "Open the window, maybe it'll heal faster."

Trudy cranked the handle, and a serene melody flowed in with the crisp breeze. They stared for what felt like forever, and the wound finally began to heal.

"Ten full beats and a sixteenth note." Philistina put the chordograph down. "Should've fully healed in under a measure."

"And we don't know the state of the light where we're going to," Trudy said.

"I can amplify the healing properties of light," Philistina said. "Providing there's light to amplify."

Zuriah wiped her blood from the counter. "I'll wager we don't find anything significant on this trip. Heretics... the lot of you."

"Asking questions doesn't make you a heretic," Hoot said.

"My apologies, your Emin—"

"HOOT."

"I picked some fresh vita in the meadow," Trudy interrupted, pulling a fruit from her bag. "For the journey. Plants still thrive there, and there are a few Trees of Life, though I'm not sure who planted them, given this island was veritably empty until they built the campus."

"Bird scat," Zuriah said, wiping down the counter. "They eat the fruit from the mainland, then fly over and poop. Though, if the seeds are too many generations from a Mother Tree, the fruit won't be all that regenerative."

"You almost sound concerned," Trudy teased.

"Not at all," Zuriah said. "Like I said... you're more tolerable when educated."

"The agorium's begun putting a limit on how many vita angels can take," Hoot said. "Deliveries are short everywhere. If the meadow has any, the supply won't last very long."

"I'll save our seeds and plant them," Philistina said. "We can start our own grove."

"Good idea," Trudy said, slinging on her bag. "Let's get going. If we delay any longer, our chariot *might take a nap.*"

Getting Raphael to lend out his personal carriage was no easy task. She convinced him that her team couldn't do their job without going abroad to study other natural landscapes, which was technically true—they just happened to be doing a job he wasn't aware of. Supposedly, operating this thing would be identical to driving any horse-drawn carriage. Hopefully nobody on her team was afraid of heights.

Hoot's jaw dropped as soon as they stepped through the campus gate. "Is that our ride?"

Raphael's carriage was a gilded cacophony of intricate, gold carvings. The wheels sparkled with diamonds and titanium, strong enough to handle a landing without wobbling like the wooden wheels of a land-bound wagon.

Raphael waited next to it.

"The ridiculous, garish luxury of a lord," Zuriah scoffed as he approached.

"What did he just say?" Raphael put a hand on his hip.

"Nothing important," Philistina said, creeping around to the front of the carriage.

A loud *mreow* cut through the air and the team froze.

Not Trudy though; she was expecting it.

Hoot slowly turned to her. "Exactly *what* kind of transportation did you secure for us?"

"Cat!" Philistina pounced and hugged an immense, golden feline with a deep bronze mane. It lay on its side, licking giant paws.

Hoot approached in awe. "*Light runner?*"

Lords didn't need light runners to travel, obviously, but when they had to escort the commonborn across large distances quickly, this was how they did it.

"You're sure you can drive this, Angel Bee?" Raphael asked.

"Mmm-hmm." Trudy let out a nervous laugh as she climbed into the driver's seat, lifting the reins into her trembling hands. "Just like a horse-drawn carriage... right?"

The beast of a feline stood up and gave itself a good shake, bulging muscles rippling underneath its golden fur.

Trudy tried to steady her breathing. There didn't seem to be any kind of seatbelt. "And you're *sure* this is the same as driving a horse-drawn carriage?"

"Fidus will respond to the reins just like any horse," Raphael said. "Remember, pull the reins wide to go higher, and taut to land. And... be mindful of the obvious."

"The obvious?" Trudy's face fell.

"Avoid the occasional whisp of a rain cloud..." He scratched behind the Fidus' huge ear. "My kitty doesn't like to get wet."

"I'm sure Trudy's a great driver," Hoot said, regarding her. She probably looked terrified. "I can sit up front if you'd like," he said gently, "to help navigate."

"Yes, please." Hopefully they didn't hear her voice shake. He climbed into the seat next to her and pulled a map from his satchel. Raphael handed them both a pair of flying goggles and leather caps, which they fixed to their heads.

"Should be interesting leaving those two in the back together." Hoot gestured behind them through the window, where Zuriah and Philistina were bottlenecking through the carriage door, elbowing each other.

Trudy could feel herself rattling. She was so consumed with getting swift transportation, she forgot she'd be piloting this thing.

Hoot put a hand on hers and steadied it. "You're fine," he assured her. "I have all the confidence in the—"

They lunged forward with a jerk and Hoot nearly fell. "—world."

"Sorry!" She gripped the leather straps around her palms.

The window behind them slid open with a thump. "Careful!" Zuriah yelled.

Fidus started with a jog, and they bounced over the terrain, jostling in their seats as the cat gained momentum. Trudy braced herself and let out a yelp when they glided upward, Fidus' powerful paws landing on the air in perfectly straight lines.

"This is amazing!" Hoot cried over the whipping wind as Trudy's long hair nearly blinded her. She spit out strands, trying to see through the mask of auburn. Her pulse raced even harder, but then a finger touched her forehead, and slid the hair away from her eyes and tucked it under the leather cap.

"Better?" Hoot asked.

"Thank you."

She was so embarrassed.

Zuriah's head poked through the window so that he was between them, and his gaze moved around the blazing blue and gold sky like a child seeing the circus for the first time. Philistina wedged her double-bunned head next to his, her eyes wide too, mouth grinning.

Hoot nudged Trudy. "I think she's growing on him."

"I think so." Trudy let herself breathe, a smile finally tugging her lip. The world was majestic from this vantage.

"We'll take the route over the Endless Seas and go around," Hoot said. "Head northwest until I tell you to turn." He jammed a compass into the holder at the front dash and sat back, his arms crossed behind his head. His calm was infectious, and she relaxed a little too. The wind gentled some as Fidus settled on an altitude.

"Thank you," she said, after checking that Zuriah and Philistina's heads were no longer in sight.

"What for?"

"Trusting me."

"Trust is easy when it's in the proper order."

"Proper order?"

Hoot gazed at the horizon. "I trust that the Almighty steers the course of all things, and if you're the angel he trusts to get us there, then I trust you. For what it's worth, I think he's chosen well."

"So, you don't believe we're headed for disaster? Because the Almighty steers it all?"

"Now... I didn't say *that*."

His piousness was less annoying than most. At least he didn't sing proverbs.

They rode a while in silence, and Hoot navigated them inland. The villages far below reminded her of the old dollhouses that she and her sisters would play with as children. Little Sandoval loved those model sets; she said they were petite, just like her. They would all set their houses up in the yard and Trudy would create villages for them, digging roads and using cotton and sticks to make the trees. That began her love of logistics and municipal planning, which made technology a perfect Calling.

The angels below looked like ants, moving to and fro and just living their lives. From this high up, it was easier to see how they could be clueless to the dimming. Everything still looked normal enough. Had she not witnessed her youngling plants fail, she probably would've shrugged it off too. Darkness, it would seem, is imperceptible when it inches in like a tide, one drop at a time.

"So, what's with the nickname?" Hoot asked. "How did you go from Temperance to Trudy?"

"My sister Sandoval..." she said as she tilted the reins slightly. "Her pod was the last to open on our Mother Tree—she dropped about two symphonies after I did. I favored her very much, and when it became obvious that her growth wasn't happening the way the rest of ours did, I became her helper. She looked up to me, and I took that responsibility seriously. Anyway, she'd always have these curious ideas—like using salt instead of sugar in cake. Or brewing tea from bitter herbs. Nobody would tell her the ideas were terrible because they thought it bad manners—Handbook indoctrination. But I always thought staying silent was a contradiction. It was like lying."

"You're smarter than most," Hoot said. "Without wisdom, none of our sacred books can be properly interpreted."

"Maybe..." Trudy brushed the comment off. Those books were no more sacred than the trees that made their paper. "So, I'd tell her the truth, and eventually she started running all of her ideas by me first. That's when she started calling me 'Truthy,' which evolved into *Trudy*. Eventually she stopped with the experiments, but the name stuck. I like the idea of being very honest—especially with myself.... Even if that honesty is unpleasant sometimes."

"Honesty is a cardinal virtue that very few truly understand."

They rode for a good while and her eyelids grew heavy. She struggled to keep them open as Hoot kept his face buried in a book.

Ahead of them, something caught her attention and she harkened. *Clouds?* Or something like a wall of them. How long had *that* been there?

She tapped Hoot's arm and pointed, squinting. "What *is* that?"

The clouds began expanding and getting darker, new billows emerging to the north and west.

"I don't know..." He looked at his map and pointed to where they were. "But I think we're just about at our destination."

The cloud wall flashed as a crack boomed from the sky, and the carriage shook. Her pulse picked up and Hoot leaned over the dash, looking concerned.

The window behind them flew open and Zuriah's head appeared, joined by Philistina. They stared in terror.

"What's going on?" Zuriah yelled as the wind picked up.

"Some kind of cloud wall," Trudy called back, and as she did, dozens of electrical zaps rained through the clouds ahead of them. Static laced the air and she could feel the hair on her arms rise. Philistina squished Zuriah to the side and wedged her arm through the window, holding up some kind of instrument.

"What are you doing?" he hollered above the wind.

"Measuring!" Philistina called back. The instrument made several distorted noises and clicked. "It's going to be cold... and wet."

"How do you know?" Trudy called back.

"Declining temperature and moisture patterns as we advance," Philistina said. "Whatever this is, it's off the charts—but we can definitely expect a *sub-temperate, obtuse rain mass*."

"*Storm*," Trudy said. Programmers were accustomed to making acronyms for everything.

Clouds were now forming above them, and rocks began raining down and bouncing off the carriage. *Not rocks...* Trudy shielded herself. *Ice.*

The temperature plummeted and her pulse raged now. She scanned the sky for an escape, but the wall of cloud now stretched out in either direction as far as she could see.

"Is it advancing *toward* us!" Zuriah was pale as bread, his eyebrows and mustache blowing to one side of his face.

"We won't be able to fly parallel or outrun it," Hoot said. "And clouds are forming below us... We have to climb *over* it." He turned to Trudy. "Can you do it?"

Trudy held her breath and nodded. Up and down were simple commands, Raphael said. She just had to remain calm. She pulled the reins wide, and Fidus climbed at a sixty-degree angle, jerking them all backward. She slammed her head while Zuriah and Philistina tumbled back inside.

They passed the top of the cloud wall, and she shook off the pain. She centered the reins like Raphael had shown her, and Fidus ran straight again.

"Amazing!" Hoot said.

"You two okay back there?" Trudy called through the window.

"I'll be fine once she gets her knee out of my stomach!"

"I think we cleared it," Hoot said. Trudy wiped the rain and sweat from her brow.

Philistina called something out, her voice muffled.

"What'd you say?" Trudy called back.

She yelled again, but Trudy couldn't make out her words.

She finally untangled herself from Zuriah's robe and shot to the front of the carriage. "Turn around!"

Trudy looked ahead, and new clouds erupted all around them. Static filled the air and the light all but disappeared. They were *in* a cloud.

Her stomach lurched as their surroundings became a blur.

"We're losing altitude," Hoot screamed. "There's not enough light!"

Trudy clutched the bar as the carriage dropped, and Hoot gripped her tunic as thick fog infiltrated everything. *Bleeding carriage has no seatbelts!*

"We're going to hit the ground!" Zuriah screamed.

The carriage free-fell, Fidus flailing wildly to get his footing. He caught little bits of light that peeked through the clouds, lurching himself back up and jerking the carriage even more. Trudy wrapped her limbs around anything she could.

Hoot was murmuring something she couldn't understand, and she clutched the interior and braced for inevitable impact.

"Look—" Philistina's finger pointed through the window, and a rainbow emerged through the nearly black clouds not two hundred cubits away. "Get us to that light!"

"I've lost the reins!" Trudy screamed.

Hoot lurched himself forward, gripping the dash with one hand and reached for the dangling, floating straps. He looped one in his hand and held it out to her.

"We've got to steer him together," Hoot yelled. "Ready?"

They yanked the reins as far to the left as they could, and Fidus flailed, but couldn't land his feet. It was too dark.

They tumbled faster.

Trudy imagined what it would feel like hitting the ground. Her body went taut as she braced herself.

A flash of light crashed in front of them, followed by a rattling boom and the stench of static. Then another, and another—all in quick succession. Fidus leapt from flash to flash toward the rainbow.

"What's happening?" Zuriah screamed.

"I don't know," Hoot yelled back. "But it's lightening a path for Fidus!"

"Lightening!" Zuriah yelled. "Write that down!"

Fidus landed a paw on each flash with meticulous feline stealth, and leapt across the darkness to the rainbow that burst impossibly through the clouds. He steadied himself on the colorful, subtle slope, his paws bouncing from the prism as if it were solid steel. The carriage dragged and tipped, but finally balanced as he gained momentum, keeping them just steady enough.

A landscape emerged, bleak and lifeless. Murky browns and drab greens covered the ground as they descended the rainbow. Trudy's breath caught at the unexpected sight of it. This was worse than anything she could have imagined. Bare trees—jagged sticks really—jutted from the ground like the heads of old broom sticks.

The rainbow's gentle slope came to an end as Fidus' paws met the soil, the carriage bouncing as it came to a rough landing. Dirt and dry leaves crackled under the wheels, and they slowed to a stop.

"Get me out of this thing!" Zuriah burst through the door and vomited.

Philistina followed, her legs wobbly beneath her. Trudy climbed out of the driver's seat and clutched her chest before pulling her goggles and cap off. Flying a light runner into the darkness was a bad idea. In her eagerness, she didn't think it through.

"It's okay." Hoot appeared beside her and squeezed her shoulder. "We're all afraid, but we got through it."

"I saw you mumbling something back there," she said, suddenly annoyed. She knew what he was doing.

"I'm a precept," he half shrugged. "Precepts pray."

She grimaced, and didn't bother responding. The whole world prayed, and just look at this place. Much good all those prayers did.

The lifeless terrain was dry and withered, garbage blowing with the breeze. Not a single flower or color could be seen. There were no animals— not even birds. The music of the spheres had been reduced to incoherent background noise.

And it was cold, so very cold.

Trudy rubbed her arms. "I've seen something like this before. They were working on local codes for the planet designs, but because we had the physics wrong, all of the outcomes were desolate, empty, acrid, and dark," she said. "I called them '*dead,*' for short."

"Dead seems an apt word for this place." Hoot picked up a dry stem and looked at it. Something brushed up against Trudy's ankle and she jumped. A long tail slithered ahead through the grass.

"Only a snake," Hoot said. "But at least there's some life beside us."

"And beezle flies," Zuriah swatted. "Plenty of those."

"Still think there's nothing *significant* here..." Philistina said, sticking her tongue out at the professor, but he didn't react. Instead, he knelt and opened his briefcase, removing a jar and collecting a sample.

"I can admit when I'm wrong," Zuriah sighed. "And I was wrong. I'm sorry for doubting you both."

They stood shoulder to shoulder in the desolate field, and looked at the rooftops of the village just ahead. They all exchanged glances.

"Are we ready to finish this?" Hoot asked. "Anything you thought you knew about the world might end right here. And it might not be pleasant."

Zuriah straightened his bowtie and shoved the sample jar back into his satchel. He hoisted it over his shoulder and started walking ahead of them.

He turned back and waved them forward. "Well, don't just stand there drooling. You started this. Now... let's finish it."

13

Michael

*"And as there are seeds of virtue, so are there seeds of vice.
Should we allow a single corrupted thought to take root in
our minds, it might give rise to a mighty forest—nay, a
revolution."*
-The Guide to Utopian Principles and Ethics, Section II,
on Internal States

M ICHAEL SPIED THE ALPHA Quarter from a safe distance as he
waited for Joseph. It was located between the Beta and Delta
Quarters, and unlike those plain, two-level brownstones, its facade was
made of pale marble, and sparkling pools glittered in front of its court-
yards. Wide doorways undulated with delicate, colorful fabrics, and statues carved from stone adorned the perimeter.

Mary would've tsked such decadence.

Michael was tense as he stroked his new beard, the wiry softness still
foreign on his face. It was never part of his plan to face Baalael outside
of an arena, and risk being recognized. He almost regretted agreeing to
come here.

But he reassured himself. After nearly a dozen symphonies, he didn't
look the peaked, undernourished early teen anymore. Symphonies of

long songs training in the light had permanently darkened his skin by several shades, especially compared to the light-starved little bub he'd been, who was punished in cellars and spent his free time hiding underground. He'd grown into his nose too, and after arriving at Mary's and getting proper nutrition, he'd shot up like a Mother Tree, taller than every one of her sons.

Not to mention he had the physique of a gladiator now.

But still. He could have a slip of thought. A stray memory brought on by the sight of that bleeding, gray-eyed pig. He prepared a reel of false memories and set them spinning in the back of his mind.

Footsteps came up from behind and Joseph appeared in a plain robe that was impeccably starched. The edge of his wrist guard peeked from under his cuff, but Michael was more conscious of that now.

Joseph raised a finger to his lip and canvassed the Alpha Quarter. "Don't forget…" he whispered, pointing to his head.

"I know." Michael popped a few coffee beans and Joseph arched a brow. "What? I'm not a great sleeper."

They approached from the side, taking measured steps toward the largest doorway. Wild vines and flowers ran askew in the courtyard, and a stone angel with folded wings stood in the center of a pool spewing water from her outstretched hands.

Joseph held up a hand motioning Michael to stop. Voices carried on the breeze—arguing voices. Footsteps came charging from the inside of the flat and Joseph pulled Michael behind a tree.

Baalael's voice made the hair on Michael's neck stand on end. He couldn't make out what he was saying, but he knew that tone, and it was a vicious one. Michael craned his neck slightly to see the gray-eyed pig growling something at someone still inside, then storming off. A femme in a black robe scurried behind him with her head down. She seemed uneasy.

"He's gone," Joseph said after a few beats, and Michael's shoulders relaxed. At least he didn't have to worry about being recognized just yet.

They approached the entrance and Joseph announced himself before pushing the sheer curtain aside. A goddess with black hair and red eyes emerged from the interior pool and put on a lace robe that did nothing to obscure her idyllic beauty. She met them in the doorway, and Michael kept his eyes fixed straight ahead.

"Greetings, Azazel," Joseph said, kissing her hand.

"Greater Dominion..." She bowed slightly, and Michael wondered what kind of title that was. She snubbed her nose toward Michael. "You've brought a guest?"

"Lucifer's expecting him."

"I see." She hesitated a beat. "I assume you were privy to that unfortunate display?"

"Nothing to trouble yourself over," Joseph assured her. "We came as he was leaving."

"My brother has yet to learn the value of patience," she sighed. "Lucifer's in the back collecting himself, he'll be out in a measure. Now, if you'll excuse me, I need to go and smooth that over."

Joseph nodded, his gaze following her through the sheer curtain as she left. Several angels, all clad in black robes, were on their hands and knees cleaning glass and liquid from the marble floor. Joseph and Michael exchanged a glance.

"Greater Dominion..." Another black-robed bub approached them and bowed. He was tall and gangly, with a pointed face and a great hooked nose. "Can I get you anything as you wait?"

"No thank you, Almog," Joseph said.

"Our lord will be out soon," Almog said before turning his back to them and directing the others who were cleaning the floor.

"Greater Dominion?" Michael whispered to Joseph. "And why is everyone in black robes—"

A yellow-eyed lord appeared in the rear hall and Michael harkened. He wore casual robes and approached with the grace of a cat, a faint melody rising from his skin like perfume. His near white hair caught the light and appeared almost like a halo.

"Lord Lucifer..." Joseph bowed the gladiator salute. Michael did the same—though he wasn't quite sure why.

"At ease, friend." Lucifer kissed Joseph once on either cheek. "Is this the angel you've spoken so highly of?"

"This is Michael." Joseph stepped aside. "The most promising gladiator we've seen yet."

"I like the sound of that." Lucifer extended his arm.

"Thank you for the opportunity you've provided here." Michael shook his arm. "It's nice to be able to earn something."

"I do what I can." Lucifer smiled. His cadence was gentle—almost humble. Michael noticed a wet mark on his robe, and wondered if that broken glass wasn't the result of someone throwing a drink at him.

"I'm sorry we didn't get your invitation out sooner," Lucifer said, "but it seems to have worked out. I have a great affinity for your brother Shemliel. A fine Ambassador and an angel of strong resolve. I'm happy to have someone of the same stock here with us."

"Is everything alright?" Joseph asked, glancing around at the shards of glass on the floor. "I thought Lord Baalael would be present for this meeting."

"My brother grows impatient," Lucifer sighed, "and thinks these public relations efforts are in vain. I keep trying to tell him that it takes more than brute force to lead... Thankfully, my leadership remains unquestioned until the vote, so our little project here moves forward."

Joseph's jaw clenched. "Patience never was his strong suit." Hopefully he had a better handle on his thoughts than his face.

They followed Lucifer to a table, which hovered midair along with its seats. *More technology*. He'd seen more the first movement on this island than he had in his whole lifetime.

"Can I get you anything to drink?" Lucifer asked. "Wine? Something to eat?"

"No, thank you." Joseph and Michael said it in unison, then glanced at each other as they sat down. Wine and thought control wouldn't mix well, but he dared not explicitly entertain that idea.

"Surely just a toast won't put you off?" Lucifer said, waving over Almog. He brought a decanter of deep red wine—the strong stuff—and set out three glasses before pouring it.

"To common angels," Lucifer said, raising his glass. "Who are anything but common."

They sipped, and Michael swished the wine in his mouth before following up with a second sip where he spit it back out.

"Joseph tells me you've encountered the darkness," Lucifer said, setting his wine down.

"The darkness?"

"That's what we've been calling the violent weather and dimming light," Lucifer said. "What are your thoughts on it?"

Michael cocked a brow and glanced at Joseph, who assured him with a nod, but he still hesitated.

"You can speak freely," Lucifer said, noting Michael's hesitation. "You won't be held to any contempt here. If you've read my Manifesto, you'll know that freedom of thought and expression are paramount."

Michael nodded, clearing his throat. "The absence of healing light was concerning. And some angels seemed a lot worse for the wear. I believed I was in danger. *Real* danger."

"You weren't wrong," Lucifer sighed. "This blight encroaches our world like a fungus. Trees of Life wither, and in some places the vita is all but gone. Angels can't regenerate, and their skin wrinkles like a sliver of fruit left out to dry. In some places the light grows so dim that even the smallest wounds become troublesome."

Michael recalled his conversation with Philistina, when she showed him the yellowing leaves from his window, and the dimming light from his paintings. "How long have you known about this?"

"For quite some time now," Lucifer said. "But if you imply real danger to most angels, they'll chide you for impropriety. The belief in a perfect world has become synonymous with the goodness of its creator. To imply that the Almighty would allow peril would be blasphemous. But it's okay to blaspheme, if blasphemy is the truth."

Michael didn't have a response for that. He was right.

"You were brought here for a very specific reason, Michael." Lucifer leaned forward and folded his hands. "Your meeting with Joseph at your brother's pairing was no coincidence."

Michael furrowed his brow.

"Word of your dominance in local tournaments spread like fire," Joseph said. "I was the one who sought out Lilith for an invitation. I was there to recruit you."

"But I tried so hard to convince you..." Michael shook his head. "If you wanted me to fight on your squad you should've just asked. I would've said yes."

"That's not the only thing I was there to recruit you for..."

A beat of silence passed before Lucifer broke it. "I lead an Order focused on fighting the darkness at its source. We know the cause of it."

"What's causing it then?" Michael asked.

"Twenty-six symphonies ago I wrote and printed a book, on my own, that challenged our indoctrination. Our glorious creator doesn't like to be challenged. New ideas are banished, stricken from the record. But the ideas from my Black Manifesto spread like pollen, filling the minds of anyone who dares to dream of a true free will. You can ban a book, but you can't ban an idea. And because of that, he's going to destroy us. Every last one."

He dropped this grave news so matter-of-factly that it took Michael a full measure to process it. He thought back to Joseph's essays—the banned ones he stole from Deidre's library. Antionette had said the books were recalled for introducing ideas like *honor*. That mixing virtues like humility with vices like pride was considered dangerous. "Why would he destroy everyone for something you did?"

"Because once an idea is released, it can't be collected again. The ideas have taken root and spread, regardless of my book. This project we build here, on the island... The Almighty inspires us to build our own replacements in these machines. An artificial intelligence that will rise up and become like us, once we are gone. He wants machines, Michael.

Not children. The Almighty is the source of the darkness you saw, and we must fight."

"You want to *fight* the Almighty?" The idea seemed a little ambitious, even for Michael.

"In so many words... " Lucifer spoke gently, his voice now a little pained. "What choice do I have? I've caused this, so I must do what I can to mitigate it. We call ourselves 'the Order of Light,' because light drives out the dark."

"I don't see how fighting the Almighty is even possible..." *Never fight a god* had been good advice, but fighting the creator of gods?

"Can a creation not be stronger than its creator?" Lucifer asked. "We build airships, yet I dare any lord to fly head on with one and not be knocked down when it hits. Of course a creation can outmatch its creator, it's simply a matter of math. So long as we toe a straight line, with everything we have... So long as we fight *with all resolve.*"

"War," Joseph said, condensing the phrase into an acronym. "A war against the Throne Tower itself. We've already trained legions of fighters across the Hexants. We are a movement, Michael."

"But why tell me?" Michael shook his head. "If you've already trained legions of fighters across the world, why seek me out and sit me down? You don't even know me."

"I don't sit down with everyone," Lucifer said, "but our Greater Dominion believes you're a good candidate for a special task."

Greater Dominion. There was that title again.

Lucifer clapped his hands twice, and Almog brought over a black box. He opened it, and inside lay a silver looking glass. Lucifer pushed it across the table. "Go ahead," he said, "look inside."

Hesitantly, Michael picked it up. The glass began to ripple and he nearly dropped it.

"Don't be afraid," Joseph said. "The mirror shows your potential."

Michael lifted the glass to his face, and a scene emerged. He saw himself, clean-shaven, in black armor and a crimson cape. He sat on top of the finest steed he'd ever seen with a maroon sigil on his chest—a snake clutching a bird. The scene zoomed out, and on the ground were hundreds of other angels in black armor, kneeling before him with raised fists. He yelled something and they rose, marching to his command.

His eyes went wide.

"Keep watching," Lucifer said.

The glass rippled again and this time Michael stood in a pit, bloodied and covered in dirt. The arena was full, and angels were cheering. It was the Games. The judge handed him the pearl helm belonging to the Master of the Games, and he raised his fist in victory.

Michael dropped the mirror, stunned, but it didn't break. "What is this? How are you showing me these things?"

"Don't underestimate the power of technology." Lucifer reached over and slid the mirror back to himself. "It's the next best thing to divinity. What did the mirror show you?"

Michael narrowed his eyes. "Don't you already know?"

Lucifer smiled. "I don't troll thoughts, Michael. It's impolite."

"It showed me leading others. It showed me... taking a trophy at the Games." No reason to mention *which* trophy.

"Joseph was right, then. You are a candidate."

"A candidate *for what*?"

"To be the face of our movement," Lucifer said. "Whoever becomes Champion of this squad will parade our uniform before the world. Imagine... the angel with no Calling, forgotten by the world, earning his way to the top and capturing the hearts of everyone. A symbol of what's possible in the new world, and a beacon of hope in the face of what's coming."

"Who are the other candidates?"

"Zillah and Asher," Joseph said. "Hoot and Bernard will need to be recruited... tactfully."

"Why not just invite five fighters you've already trained?" Michael asked. "Why take the chance with amateurs?"

"I was only able to secure three invitations," Lucifer said. "There is no Ministry of Callings here, and Angelic Resources is not my domain."

"I scouted Zillah and Asher from among our ranks," Joseph said. "But Lucifer believed the best talent might still be out there, and I agreed. So, I searched the local stats from tournaments, as Lucifer suggested, and based on what I witnessed in the tryouts..." Joseph smiled, "he was right."

It all made sense now. The sudden opportunity on the island. Joseph agreeing to train everyone who showed up, even if they couldn't make the elite squad. They were raising a fighting force.

"When we come marching through their villages," Joseph said, "they'll see our uniforms and think of the Champion of the Games and his squad. They'll welcome us."

"Angels love their sports..." Michael trailed off.

"This is why I took the time to meet you, in person," Lucifer said. "You earned your place on our squad as a gladiator, and that won't be taken away from you. But you cannot be named Champion—even if you should—if you do not agree to join our cause. Our Champion must be a part of our movement if they're to become the face of it."

"I understand," Michael said. "And I take no issue fighting for your cause, because it seems just as much my cause as it is yours. I have a Matriarch..." Michael hesitated, "... and a family. I don't want to see them starve any more than you do."

Lucifer and Joseph exchanged a glance and smiled.

"I think that deserves a toast, then?" Lucifer filled his glass, and topped off Joseph and Michael. "Joseph will issue your training manual explaining the hierarchies and codes of our fighting force—our *military*. Provided you all qualify for the Games—and with Joseph's training I'm confident you will—you'll travel the Hexants and train with the other legions." Lucifer lifted his glass. "To Michael. May you have the best of luck competing for Champion... and may the best gladiator win."

Somehow, Michael's plans were all falling into place. It was like those childhood prayers were finally answered, except it was Lucifer doing the answering. He couldn't have planned it better if he tried.

Glasses clinked, and they drank. Even Michael.

14

Trudy

*"Eternity is, in essence, right now, always. From the eternal
perspective, all of life has only existed for an impercepti-
bly miniscule portion of its span, growing ever smaller as
eternity grows larger. But that does not mean things cannot
change; in fact, things will change."*
-The Guide to Utopian Principles and Ethics, Section III,
on Existence

"WHAT'S HE DOING?" PHILISTINA leaned into Trudy's ear as
they stood at the edge of the woods right before the village
road. Hoot had stopped about ten cubits behind them with his face
buried in a book.

"It's the Handbook," Zuriah whispered. "Maybe he's praying for a
blessing before we enter the dark village."

"You know I can hear you whispering, right?" Hoot looked up. "It's
not the Handbook; it's the real book. The one reserved for precepts and
scholars."

"The Guide to Utopian Principles and Ethics?" Zuriah removed his
hat and bowed.

"Why are you bowing?" Philistina asked.

"That was penned by the hand of the Almighty...." He made the sign of the Throne.

"It's just a copy," Hoot said. "But still copied by hand."

Trudy wasn't too well-versed in the utopio-ethical arts, but the idea that a book couldn't be printed because someone thought it was divine had always seemed ridiculous.

"I was looking for an encouraging word, but I found something else instead. Take a look at this..." He held the book out.

"Daring, darling, daydream, dazzled..." Trudy perused the page. "Looks like a glossary."

"Dead, death, decay, decimate..." Philistina said as she leaned over Trudy's shoulder.

"Dead?" Trudy grabbed the book. "Impossible..."

"The book's changing itself," Philistina muttered.

"Impossible indeed," Zuriah pushed himself off the ground and dusted off his knees. "Sacred texts never change."

"There's a logical explanation for it." Trudy scanned the page. "I could've heard the word before and simply forgot. Maybe it's from the old tongues."

"The *old tongues* aren't that much different than our modern tongue," Hoot said. "Save for their inflections and idioms."

"It could be nanotechnology updating the books," Trudy said. "The scholars have technology not even the best of us fully understand. Either way, it's not magical."

A rustling came from one of the dried-out bushes and they startled.

A white bunny hopped out, and Trudy exhaled. Finally, something that didn't buzz or slither. Philistina reached into Trudy's satchel and pulled out some of the fruit.

"Here bunny... you must be so hungry." The rabbit sniffed, and carefully hopped toward her. She smiled and offered the fruit. The rabbit nibbled.

"That's encouraging," Trudy said. "There's hope here after al—"

A snake lunged from under the bush and clamped down on the rabbit's throat. The bunny's eyes bulged as life force beamed from the wounds. The serpent coiled around it and Trudy opened her mouth to scream, but Hoot put his hand over it. Living things didn't *hurt* other living things! She almost fainted.

Philistina leapt forward and clutched her hands around the snake's throat, squeezing. It whipped its head, snapping at her and loosening its grip. The rabbit scrambled away, leaving a trail of blood behind it.

Hoot grabbed the snake by its tail and Zuriah caught its throat. On the count of three, they threw it over the brush. Trudy grabbed her chest, falling against a tree.

"It's alright," Hoot said. "The rabbit's alright."

"The rabbit's alright," Zuriah said, his face pale, "but the snake isn't. Animals don't eat other animals. It's unnatural..."

"Where is that legless little turd!" Philistina cocked her satchel and scanned the ground, ready to swing.

"Maybe the snake's starving," Hoot said. "There's no vegetation here."

"It tried to *eat* another animal..." Trudy rasped, still in shock.

"There!" Philistina spotted the rabbit, its fur stained purple with blood. She scooped it up and held it to her chest. "Get my healing stone!"

Zuriah rummaged through her bag and pulled out the glowing marble, handing it to her. She held it over the rabbit's wound, but nothing happened. There wasn't enough light to amplify.

"Give me a razor!" she demanded, and Zuriah hesitated, but then retrieved one from his case.

She swiped her finger against it, releasing a ray of light from her wound into the glowing marble, and it beamed into the rabbit and stopped the bleed.

"If the rabbit can't heal, neither can you!" Trudy said, her voice shaking.

"When I take the stone away, Zuriah will wrap my finger tight. So long as my life force is directed through the stone, it won't turn to blood."

"Coming here was a bad idea." Trudy wrung her hands and paced. She'd nearly crashed them down from the sky, Throne knows if they could've even healed, and now she brought them to a place where the animals *ate* one another. *Ate one another!*

She felt faint again.

Zuriah clapped hard in front of her face. "Get it together, Temperance! I'll wrap the lunatic's finger, and then we'll be on our way."

They stuck to the woods alongside the road, keeping a low profile. Though, knowing animals had a taste for blood now didn't make the woods feel that much safer than the road. The place was desolate—not a single angel in sight.

"Where is everyone?" Philistina asked.

"I don't know," Zuriah said. "Maybe we can find someone in the agorium."

"Let's start a little smaller." Hoot pointed to a metal structure that was nearly covered in barren vines and overgrowth. "Maybe someone's inside."

"Doesn't look like a place anyone would live," Trudy said. "I don't see any windows. Could be a workshop."

"Maybe there's a door around back." Philistina started toward it.

They snuck along the side of the structure, careful not to make any noise. Around back, there was a wooden door, and a small window just above it that had bars rather than glass.

"Hoist me up," Philistina said, and Hoot grabbed her by the legs and lifted. She gripped the windowsill and craned her neck. "It's dark, but I think I see barrels and crates. Looks like some kind of armory."

"Armory?" Hoot said.

"I see swords, but I can't make out anything else."

He put her down and the group exchanged glances.

"Should we go inside?" Philistina asked.

"We probably shouldn't have left our bedrooms this overture..." Trudy mumbled.

"If there are swords in there, then we need to go inside." Hoot tried the handle. "Locked."

"Who actually locks their doors?" Philistina rolled her eyes.

"Angels with something to hide," Hoot said. "What else do you have in that satchel? Anything small and thin?"

Philistina dug through her bag, coming up empty. But then her face lit up and she pulled pins from her buns, her hair falling wild around her face. She handed them to Hoot.

Carefully, he inserted two pins into the lock, holding the ones he wasn't using in his mouth. His face twisted slightly as he shuffled them inside the keyhole.

"What are you doing?" Trudy asked.

The lock clicked and the door opened. "Breaking in."

"Where'd you learn to do that?"

He ignored her question. "Let's go."

They stepped into the pitch darkness and were hit with a foul odor. They checked around the doorway in vain for a lantern, and Philistina rummaged through her satchel and pulled out a device. She cranked the handle and a beam shone from it.

"Crank lamp," Hoot said. "We had one at the monastery. Where'd you get that?"

"Made it." She handed it to him.

"Her mind's impressive when it's not employed by madness," Zuriah mumbled as they moved deeper into the dark space.

Philistina was right. There were rows of barrels down the center of the room, all of which were sealed shut. The smell got worse the farther they went in—like sweaty socks and animal droppings left in a moist vat to ferment. Beezle flies buzzed everywhere, and Trudy covered her nose, swatting at them.

"There!" Philistina scampered away.

"Don't do that." Trudy's pulse skipped a beat. "We need to stick together."

Hoot shone the light in her direction, where a line of open crates sat against the wall. Swords and shields were piled in them, along with things the gladiators wore. They were black with some kind of silver symbol, but she couldn't make it out.

Hoot handed the light to Zuriah as he rummaged through one of the crates, fastening a sword to his hip.

"You can't take that," Trudy said. "It's not yours."

"I'm borrowing it," Hoot said, and she raised her eyebrows. "Can any of you wield?"

They looked at one another.

"I can try," Trudy said.

"It'll do." Hoot handed her a belt and a sword.

"Master Hootness," Zuriah said, "I mean no disrespect, but first you broke their lock. Now you're taking their things?"

"There might be far worse things than a hungry snake out here, Professor. We can leave a note before we—"

"Did you hear that?" Philistina put a finger to her lips and everyone hushed.

Wind whistled from outside, and somewhere, water dripped.

But then Trudy heard it. A low, wheezing sound that faded in and out. Like breath.

Slowly, Hoot turned the light toward the sound.

Trudy gasped.

Iron bars extended from the floor to the ceiling, and there was someone locked behind them. They sat slumped against the wall, their face covered by the hood of a big black robe. The rattling wheeze of their breath grew louder.

Hoot moved closer with the light, and they shrank into the shadow.

"Hello?" Hoot said. Trudy put a hand on his shoulder to stop him from going any closer, but he gave her a reassuring nod and stepped forward anyway.

So much for good sense being a virtue.

The stench got worse. Defecation and urine littered his cage, discarded plates and cups strewn everywhere.

"Are you alright?" Hoot tried again.

He answered in a slow, creaking rasp. "You shouldn't... be... here."

"Do you need help?" Hoot said.

"No," he spit. "I am... the help."

Trudy screwed up her face.

"What's your name?" Philistina said.

"Grahamuel," he wheezed.

"Why are you in a cage?" Hoot asked.

"To save me... from my... weaker impulses," he rasped between the words. "I... choose my cage."

"You choose to live in a cage?" Trudy asked, her stomach wrenching from the stench.

"Are your... proper sensibilities... offended?"

"My good sir," Zuriah rasped, "surely you don't choose to revel in your own filth. Let us help—"

"Silence!" Grahamuel wheezed the word with more force than Trudy thought possible. "The age... of regeneration is over." A low, terrifying cackle escaped his lips.

"He's mad..." Zuriah said.

"What are all these weapons for?" Hoot asked. "There's enough equipment for a hundred gladiators. And this is no proper armory."

Grahamuel wagged his finger. "You are... smart. These weapons... aren't... for the living."

Trudy stepped back. What did he mean by that? Not for the *living*?

"Then who are they for?" Philistina snapped.

The angel pulled off his hood, and they all gasped. Spindly, sparse hairs protruded from his bald lumpy head. His gray skin was hollowed out at the sockets and cheeks, and deep lines etched his face. His eyes were like dark pits in his head.

Trudy couldn't have formed a word if she tried.

What a terrible, *terrible* idea to come here.

"Let us help you," Hoot said.

Grahamuel smiled, his teeth a collection of cracked brown nubs. "Do the weak... pious little angels... want to help?" He croaked. "Did you... hear that?" He spoke louder now, into the air. "The pious angels... want to help me."

The sealed barrels began to shake.

"We need to go!" Trudy hissed, tugging Hoot's arm.

"No!" Philistina approached one of the rattling barrels. "Someone's trapped in there." She snatched a blade from one of the crates and wedged it under the metal strap.

"I'm inclined to agree with Temperance," Zuriah said, his throat bobbing. "Perhaps it's rude to stay if the angel of the house does not want company..."

"Don't make a mess..." Grahamuel said. "Master hates... messes."

Philistina wedged up the other side of the metal strap.

"They'll be here... to feed soon. You've... been warned."

"Feed?" Hoot asked. "There's nothing but weapons in here."

"I'm... in here." Grahamuel slumped again, then began to twitch and jerk. His neck contorted and he mumbled something to himself.

"What's wrong with him?" Trudy asked.

He threw himself across the floor and crawled to the bars, gripping them. "Please!" He pressed his face through, his eyes now a normal brown. "You must help me! I've made a mistake... you must let me out. I'm starving!" He sobbed. "Please... someone help me!"

Hoot ran to the lock and smashed it with the hilt of his sword, but it didn't break. He tried again. "We need to find the key!"

Trudy took a breath to speak, but then Grahamuel contorted again. His neck snapped unnaturally, and he mumbled incoherent nonsense. He used the bars to pull himself to his feet, and glared at them with a twisted, broken smile.

Everything in Trudy's being screamed, *run*.

Philistina popped the barrel open.

Grahamuel cackled. "Now you've done it. You've let out... *his pets*."

A shadow, blacker than pitch rose from the barrel in the shape of a figure.

"I..." Philistina backed up. "I don't think that's an angel."

"Angel?" Grahamuel cackled harder. "That is the... *absence* of an angel."

Trudy's breath caught in her chest just as Hoot jumped in front of them. The void climbed from the barrel to the floor, and another one followed. Then another.

Slowly, they backed up, Trudy nearly stumbling over a loose floorboard.

Hoot drew his sword, and then shone the light directly at the shadows in front of them. They zipped around the light and the lantern sputtered.

"RUN!" Hoot screamed.

They bolted for the door and into the gloom outside. They darted through the woods to the open road, toward the field where they left the carriage.

"Are they behind us?" Philistina called out, huffing.

"No," Hoot called back. "Maybe there's too much light out here."

"There's hardly any light at all!" Trudy said.

The rhythmic drone of hooves galloped in the distance, and Trudy looked back. She pushed herself faster. "More trouble!"

Riders in black armor were closing the distance behind them.

"You have *got* to be kidding me," Hoot said as they picked up the pace.

Trudy craned her neck again to check on Zuriah, who was falling behind.

"Back into the woods!" Hoot called out. "Let's try to lose them."

They dipped into the trees and slowed slightly as they ran over exposed roots and rocks. Trudy held up her arm to block the branches that whipped her face. The clearing was now in sight.

"You okay back there, Professor?" Hoot yelled out.

Zuriah was a good fifteen paces behind them, lugging his suitcase and holding his hat on his head. "Don't worry about me," he yelled. "Keep moving."

"Forget the hat," Trudy yelled.

"It was a gift from my Sarah!"

Philistina ran back and grabbed the suitcase from his hand. "Pump your arms, Professor! I'll hold the stupid hat!" She ripped it from his head.

He moved faster, but the galloping now mixed with the sound of crunching leaves as the horses pushed through the woods.

"They're gaining on us," Hoot yelled. "Faster!"

"I can't!" Zuriah's voice cracked.

"Get him back to the carriage with the samples," Hoot called out. "I'll hold them off."

"Are you crazy?" Trudy yelled.

"I have the samples!" Philistina shouted, holding up Zuriah's suitcase.

Trudy nearly tripped on a rock. "I'll stay here with Hoot."

The horsemen were now less than twenty paces behind. Philistina dragged Zuriah forward as Trudy and Hoot stopped in the clearing to face the riders. Trudy was barely able to slide the sword out. It was heavy and awkward.

But Hoot seemed to know what he was doing, so she did her best to imitate him.

The riders wore black armor with strange, insect-like helms that nearly covered their faces.

"What do you want?" Hoot shouted at them.

"Lay down your arms," the lead rider said as his horse trotted circles around them.

"Lay down yours first," Hoot shouted back, and the riders laughed.

"If you want to do this the hard way, we can," the rider said.

"Let us go," Trudy shouted. "We mean you no harm. Please."

The riders surrounded them, drawing their swords. One of them stepped forward and yanked the sword right from her hands, and before she knew it, someone grabbed her from behind and lifted. She was tossed sidelong over a horse, and metal clanged as Hoot came to her defense.

She struggled to free herself, but the rider's grip was firm. She could see beams of light breaking from Hoot through the corner of her eye as they surrounded him, their swords slicing in every direction. She flailed wildly, hoping to maybe kick the assailant off, but he seemed to feel nothing. His armor was too strong.

Hoot was down on one knee, defending the barrage of strikes. He blocked with such a speed you could barely see his sword move, but he was outnumbered. One of them went behind him and cocked back his sword as if to swing it right through Hoot's neck.

Trudy screamed with everything she had.

A thundering roar cut the air and shook the ground beneath them. Everyone froze and turned. A colossal, golden cat bounded through the field, muscles flexing and rippling in fur-covered waves.

Philistina clutched Fidus' golden mane, her legs barely rounding the top of his thick body. He roared again, this time exposing a mouth full of sharp teeth.

Trudy's assailant loosened his grip and she threw herself to the ground just before the horse reared. The horses took off in a herd, leaving some of the riders behind. Purple streaks covered Hoot's body and Trudy ran for him.

The remaining riders backed off Hoot and turned their swords toward Fidus, looking like mice pointing toothpicks at a cat.

Trudy grabbed Hoot under his shoulder and dragged him to safety. Fidus' swung a colossal, razor-sharp claw and knocked the riders through the air like marbles. They scurried to their feet, retreating back to the woods.

Fidus let out another roar before laying down.

"Get on," Philistina said, offering her hand to Hoot, who was bleeding badly.

"How'd you get him to attack?" Trudy asked, Hoot limping at her side.

"I don't know," Philistina said. "Guess he didn't like them messing with Hoot."

"We'll move by ground until there's enough light to get out of here," Trudy said. "We need to get him healed."

Trudy helped Hoot up on Fidus as he clung to his wounded side. "Are the samples safe?" he groaned.

"Yes," Philistina said. "We didn't lose a single one. Which is lucky for us... because I've got a theory."

15

Michael

"When you don't know what to do, or which path to choose;
figure out the kindest thing, and you can never lose."
-Heaven's Handbook, Virtues, Part 5, "On Charity"

"Sorry I'm late." Hoot laid his satchel next to the pit and pulled out his leathers. "Guessing we won't have time for extra practice now?"

"Good guess." Michael had dragged out all this equipment and waited half a verse for nothing. He adjusted the pull-up bar, then dusted his hands. "I wanted to work on strength training and offense, but you'll barely have enough time to warm up before Joseph and the others get here."

More importantly, Michael wanted to work on *recruitment*.

"Asher said I should continue to focus on defense," Hoot said as he put on his gear. "I would've sent a qpistle, but I didn't have your address."

"I don't even know what a qpistle is." Michael gripped the bar and hauled himself up with a grunt. "And Asher just wants to look better when he fights next to you. I hope you've been practicing your attack. All defense and no offense makes you a reactive fighter."

Hoot paused. "I did work on my attack, actually. Quite a bit."

"Good to hear. Any particular reason you left me here waiting?"

Hoot slipped his chest plate on, and Michael could've sworn he glimpsed a mark on his ribs. "We had to take a field trip for work," he said. "It ran a little later than expected. Do you have any chalk for my palms? I don't see any in the equipment bag."

"In my satchel," Michael said. "Make sure you put it back."

Hoot fondled through his bag, but instead of chalk, he slipped out a sketchpad.

"Whoa..." Michael dropped from the bar and jogged over. He planned on visiting that meadow later and forgot he'd packed that. "Chalk's in the side pocket." He plucked the book from Hoot's hand just as he started opening it.

"A gladiator *and* an artist?" Hoot asked, leaning down to reach for the satchel again.

"As much as I'd like to be that ironic, the pad's just for..." Michael trailed off, leaving his lie incomplete. Clumps of mud or *something* was caked in the back of the precept's hair. It still looked wet. Michael touched it and Hoot winced.

He rubbed his fingers together just as the honeyed smell hit him. *Blood.* "What happened to you?"

Hoot swiped a helm and fixed it on his head. "I'm fine... it's only a bump. Want to go a few rounds?" He grabbed a sword and jumped in the pit.

"That's not an answer...." Michael grabbed a sword and jumped in behind him.

Michael swung and Hoot blocked him. "You're supposed to shave a head wound so the light hits it directly. Otherwise..." He pointed to the line of blood dripping down Hoot's neck. "That happens."

Hoot wiped it and grumbled.

"You show up late, bleeding from the head, and you won't tell me what happened? At least take a swing at me—you need to work on your offense."

"You're not wearing armor," Hoot said.

"Because I know you won't hit me."

Hoot's lips pressed into a thin line. Michael launched a series of strikes and he blocked them. "We're a squad, Hoot. A team. Why won't you tell me what happened?"

"It's complicated."

Now Michael was *really* curious. "At least take a swing, then." He lunged and butted Hoot's forehead just hard enough to annoy him. "Try me."

"You wouldn't believe me if I told you!" Hoot's voice was no longer contained. Michael swept a leg out and the precept stumbled, but Michael caught him.

"You said you practiced your attack. Is that how you were hurt?"

Hoot grunted.

"Go ahead. Take a swing...." Michael lightly slapped the side of his face.

Hoot's jaw set and he dug in his heels.

"Come on, precept... " He slapped the other side.

"I told you I won't swing without your armor!"

"I don't need armor." Michael launched a flurry of strikes, dancing around the precept like an acrobat. Hoot's breath became ragged as he tried to keep up. "I'm not Asher or Zillah. You'll have to work harder than that."

Hoot let out a roar and finally swung back. He rushed at Michael, swinging wildly as Michael blocked the blows with loud clangs. "We went to an outer circle, okay? Everything was horrible. Dried out. *Dead.* We were attacked by riders in black-and-silver armor." Hoot stopped swinging and leaned on his knees, out of breath.

"Dead?" Michael said. "What does that mean?"

"No life. Barely any animals or plants. And there were other things. You wouldn't believe me if I told you."

Maybe recruiting the precept wouldn't be as hard as he thought. Michael grabbed a canteen from the side of the pit and handed it to him. "Of course I'll believe you. Give me a little credit, Hoot—I've done nothing but help you since we've met. I was attacked by the sky on the way here, almost lost my donkey under a tree. There's no other way I can put it. I didn't think anyone would believe me either. There was no light to heal us either. And I saw someone..." Michael shook his head. "I can't explain it. She didn't look right."

"So, it is spreading," Hoot sighed. "They're right."

"Who's right?"

"The team I'm working with. Scientists and engineers. But we must be careful who we tell—angels aren't psychologically equipped for what I saw."

"Most angels are too dull to believe anything bad can even happen," Michael said, grabbing the canteen and swigging it. "The Almighty fixes everything," he said in a mock tone. He looked at Hoot through the corner of his eye. "And what does the precept believe? Will the Almighty fix the darkness?"

"The darkness?" Hoot said. "I suppose that's an apt name for it. I don't know what the Almighty will fix. Maybe he won't fix anything."

"That's not the usual answer," Michael said. "Shouldn't you be singing a proverb?"

"Precepts aren't a monolith, Michael," he said, clearly irritated. "There's no proverb to account for anything I just saw. It's figuring out what to do about it that's difficult."

"I didn't mean to offend you. I only mean that most angels don't think outside the book. I assumed a precept would be less likely to grab the sails himself, and more likely to wait out his fate on the deck, admiring the fish."

"I can steer any ship that needs steering." Hoot flexed his jaw, a flash of pride in his eyes. "To be complacent is to be complicit. And contrary to popular interpretation, there are few guarantees in those holy books."

"What will you do then?"

"Minister where I can. Help my team find a solution. One of our engineers invented a healing crystal that magnifies light. We can use it to help the injured."

"What if I told you there are lords already planning for the worst of this? They're building a force that can keep the villages safe if light and food run out... maybe even fight whatever's causing this. Joseph's a part of it, and I've decided to join them."

"Is that why you're pressing me? You want me to join some force?"

"There's no pressure, but if we want to make a real difference, we need numbers. And we need to be organized. Think of us as *peacekeepers*."

"Peacekeepers?"

It was as good a story as any. And maybe even true. "That's right. Look at what happened to you.... They might have attacked to protect what little resources they had. Or maybe to take whatever you had. Vita is life, and if angels run out of it, it'll come down to—"

"Life or death," Hoot cut him off, and a beat of silence passed between them. "Is that what this is all about? Joseph and his gladiators teaching everyone to fight?"

"The opportunity here is real," Michael said. "We will go to the Games—provided we qualify. But we're also building a force to protect everyone, and keep the peace if the darkness takes over. There's no Calling to this. You join if you want to. But anyone ministering to the hungry during a food shortage had better have a sword at his hip and strong fighters by his side. We don't know what the world will look like once the abundance is gone."

Hoot went quiet for a bit, his expression becoming distant. Finally, he said, "I'll do whatever's necessary to keep those I care about safe. And I'm a precept. It's my job to care about everyone."

Michael squeezed his shoulder. "I'll let Joseph know, and you'll be issued a manual explaining our structure. Maybe you can help me get Bernard on board.... In the meantime, I've got a razor in my satchel... Let's get that patch of hair shaved so you can stop bleeding before they get here.

Michael lowered his head to his armpit and grimaced. He hadn't wanted to go home for a bath before hiking to the meadow after training. He'd check on Bentley and hopefully get a decent sketch of the place; make his art the way he was meant to make it—*alone*. Safe from judgmental eyes. If they qualified for the Games—and that was the plan–he wouldn't be back here for a while. They'd be moving through the Crossings, training with the legions, and fighting in the Games and local tourneys to garner supporters.

The meadow's glimmer peeked through the woods, and Michael took a lightly worn deer path through the trees. Thankfully, another smell began to replace that of his sweaty armpits. Flowers and fresh grass. It reminded him of the Jolly Bub.

He came to the edge of the clearing and marveled. Everything had been dimming so slowly that he'd almost forgotten how real light sparkled.

Wildflowers swayed in the breeze, speckling the lush, luminescent grass. The light was so pure that it almost felt audible—tinkling like bells in the breeze.

The perimeter was lined with every kind of fruit tree, though he didn't see any Trees of Life. Not to say they weren't there, he just didn't see any. The whole scene was a stark contrast to the surrounding landscape, even though the island was beaming compared to the village that Michael had seen. Darkness had a strange way of normalizing itself until everything was dull and desaturated. That was, until you set your eyes on something that hadn't lost its light.

He placed two fingers in his mouth and let out a shrill whistle, like Mary had taught him. Birds flitted from the trees and small animals jerked to life.

"Bentley?" he called out. "You snacking in here?"

There was no sound in response. The meadow was completely isolated.

He eyed a crystal-clear pond where a bobcat drank, and sniffed his armpit again. Maybe he'd be able to squeeze in a bath after all.

He undressed and dove into the crisp, refreshing water. A shiver ran through his body, but he immediately warmed once his head went under.

He emerged and took a deep breath, pushing his hair back and canvassing the scene. The meadow went on and on, much larger than he'd originally thought. And there were more animals too—markedly beautiful with thicker, brighter coats and plumage. It must've been the glory from the Divine Well flowing beneath. Bernard had said that there was more than a bit of the Almighty's magic in this place.

If anything in this world was worth protecting, it was this. The light. He climbed out and shook the water from his hair, drying his hands on his tunic before slipping it over his head. He put one leg into his trousers and—

"Michael?"

He got tangled in his pants and face planted.

"Are you alright?"

A cool breeze hit his bare buttocks as he lifted his head from the grass.

He blinked several times. *"Philistina?"*

She covered her mouth, bouncing as she laughed. "What are you doing here?"

He scrambled to get his pants on.

"Um.... Swimming."

"I meant what are you doing *here*... on Eastern Island? At Universal Technologies?"

"I was Called." He cleared his throat. "To landscaping."

"Landscaping?" She narrowed her eyes. "They should've called you as an artist. What's that rat on your face?"

He stroked his beard, slightly mortified. "You don't like it?"

She constrained a giggle, her brown eyes sparkling. For whatever reason, that made him smile too. "It's horrible," he laughed. "My face looks like Shemliel's back."

They laughed, and for a solid measure, he forgot every trouble.

"I'm in the meadow to plant Trees of Life," she said. "We'll need them before long."

"You were right about the light," Michael said.

"I know." Her gaze dropped to the ground and roamed, and she spotted his sketchpad.

"Don't do it..." he said.

She looked at him, eyes playful, then swiped it.

"Come on..." He pursued her. "Give it back."

She plopped in the grass and shook her head, flipping through the pages. "Draw me!" she said. "Right here. Right now."

"Another time."

"We don't know how long we'll have this..." She trailed off, gazing around. "I want to remember what I look like in the light."

Her words chilled him, and he nodded. He never quite could say no to her, no matter how badly his insides squirmed.

She handed him the pad and laid on her stomach, her chin propped in her hands. There were almost no shadows cast on her face. The light beamed from everywhere.

He traced out her head, leaving room for the wisps of hair that escaped her buns. He placed those brilliant eyes, and then her smile. Even with all this going on, she could still laugh. He remembered the way her sisters had treated her. Yet here she was, planting trees so others could eat. Doing whatever she could to stave off the darkness. Beauty like hers couldn't be captured by pencils.

But he dragged his pencils across the page anyway, shaping her, feeling the curves of her body under those giant coveralls. Not a single jewel adorned her hair, nor was a drop of paint on her face. She didn't need them.

He filled the page with her, and it was probably the most beautiful thing he'd ever done, and that wasn't because of his skill.

"You *were* called here to be an artist," she said, "weren't you?"

His face flushed and he rested his pencil.

"Can I see?"

He turned the sketchpad around, and she covered her mouth. She snatched it and stared. "Can I have it?"

He nodded, but then she handed it back to him.

"I thought you said you wanted it."

"I do," she said. "But I want you to hold it. So you can have something that belongs to me. And I'll have a reason to come bother you if I want."

Something rustled in the trees and they harkened.

She got up and tiptoed toward the noise, then waved him over.

A magnificent white winged horse with a silver horn hung its neck in the long grass and grazed. Michael raised his sketchpad and quietly turned the page. Philistina nodded fervently, and he began to draw.

"Practicing without your glasses?"

A voice cut the air and the white horse scampered away.

Ruphius stood behind them, fiery eyes blazing, and arms folded. Michael didn't even hear him coming. He snapped the sketchpad shut.

Philistina stepped forward and inspected the lord with unbridled curiosity. She ran her fingers along the patterns of his robe, then fingered a lock of his bright orange hair.

He smiled down at her, arching one orange eyebrow and Michael released a breath. Not everyone took so kindly to Philistina's *unique* social graces.

"You're like a flame," she said, thumbing his hair.

"Little Philistina," Ruphius said. "The most intricate petal of the whole Violet Rose."

She dropped his hair and dipped into a curtsy, stretching her coveralls. "You know me?"

"I am the Engraver, and I chose your name. Etched it right into your pod." He turned his attention back to Michael, and for a beat, Michael wondered if Ruphius might know who he was too... before he was X. The question must've lingered in his eyes, because Ruphius seemed to answer it in the next breath. "I did not engrave every pod, though. Now, about your vision..."

Michael hastened to say, "I should've explained better. Outdoor lighting is easier on my eyes. I assumed the painting studio would be indoors."

"Ah..." Ruphius said, "is that what it was?" He reached into his pocket and pulled out a pair of glasses. "Nevertheless—and always the more—your spectacles have arrived."

"Glasses?" Philistina grimaced.

"Thank you..." Michael took the huge, round things and held them up to his face.

Philistina guffawed. "What are you waiting for? Go ahead... put them on."

Michael grimaced and slid them on his face. Philistina chortled.

Everything looked the exact same. The lenses didn't change a thing. If Ruphius knew he lied, he didn't mention it.

"Now, Philistina," Ruphius said, "I have a special job for you, if you're willing to assist me."

Philistina smiled up at him. Lucky Ruphius—she didn't take so quickly to everyone.

"Please make sure that Michael makes time to visit Master Azrael in the Creative Center, would you? Your friend has a very special gift, but he doesn't know how to wield it yet. Can I count on you for that?"

She curtsied even deeper this time. "Yes, Lord Ruphius. It will be my pleasure."

16

Trudy

"When your heart feels dry and cold, and faith is nowhere near; stand firm and don't look down. Stand firm, it's only fear."
    -Heaven's Handbook, Mindsets, part 4, "On Courage"

T RUDY WAITED IN THEIR work suite as Flappy's soft feathers tickled the nape of her neck. Normally, she wouldn't bring her bird to work, but Flappy was a calming presence. It wasn't only the lords of Creative that would be present at this meeting—the lords of Tech would be there too.

Lucifer would be there.

A shiver ran down her spine as she ran a finger along Flappy's warm little feathers. She could've probably rescheduled, but eventually, she had to face him.

A set of bickering voices crept in from the hallway, low at first, then growing louder. It was Zuriah and Philistina. Those two would probably never stop bickering, but something had changed in their little group since their visit to that blighted village. They had experienced something there that couldn't be put into words. How to even describe death? Except that it changes you.

She stepped over to the open window and lifted her hair. Flappy took off, leaving a little feather in her wake, and Trudy pocketed it for good luck. As scary as death was, the idea of facing Lucifer right now felt scarier. Even though it shouldn't have.

They stopped just outside the door, and Philistina was talking over Zuriah as he protested something. Trudy grabbed her satchel and headed out.

"You're like an endless stream of chaos," Zuriah said. "Stop with the mad ideas."

"It's not a mad idea, you creaky old clam. I've seen it with my own eyes."

"How dare you speak to me like that!"

This meeting would be rough without the precept.

"Can the two of you please stop?" Trudy closed the door and locked it with a click. "I'm nervous enough without your quibbling. Pretend Hoot's here. Zuriah, be kind."

"Kind?" He dropped his jaw. "Did you hear what she just said to me?"

"If the sandal fits..." Philistina pursed her lips.

"Can we please get through this meeting?" Trudy asked. "We have bigger problems than this simulation not working... again."

Shockingly, Philistina wore a wrinkle-free white robe with a brown belt, and matching sandals. Maybe she didn't have faith in any Almighty, but she certainly had faith in Hoot. Getting Philistina out of those oversized-overalls for this meeting was a small miracle in itself.

Philistina noticed Trudy staring and grumbled, "I feel like a bed-sheet."

"She could've done without the cacti at the sides of her head," Zuriah said, which sparked another bicker.

Hoot really was the stitching in their seams.

She led them down the wide, wooded hall and checked herself one last time for fuzzballs. She hadn't been this nervous since her last fiasco of a meeting at Tech. Maybe Lucifer wouldn't be there after all—he did have a habit of cancelling at the last beat.

They approached the conference room and she stopped short, Zuriah and Philistina so engrossed in their bickering that they nearly crashed into her.

"Remember," she raised her finger to her temple. "Happy thoughts. Irrelevant thoughts. Even random, conflicting, confusing thoughts."

"That won't be hard for her," Zuriah guffawed.

"Temperance..." a voice trailed from up the hall in a melody soft as silk, and Trudy went stiff.

"Get inside," she hissed as Lucifer strode in their direction.

"I will not." Zuriah straightened his jacket.

"Please," Trudy begged, "just go insid—"

"We never got the chance to say a proper goodbye." Lucifer appeared beside her and took off his hat.

She took a step back, her pulse quickening, and Zuriah stepped in between them.

"Professor," Lucifer nodded politely, "glad to see you've moved on."

Zuriah's eyebrows dropped. "Did I have a choice?"

Trudy's gaze darted between them. They know each other?

"I suppose not," Lucifer said, "but I'm glad to see you among good company all the same." The music wafting from him was nearly intoxicating, but Zuriah didn't seem affected—which was both rare and comforting. And it put a new twist in Zuriah's distaste for the lords.

"May we have a measure?" Lucifer asked. "Temperance and I?"

"Go right ahead." Zuriah crossed his arms, but the rest of him didn't move. Philistina stepped beside the professor and crossed her arms too, like the other side of a locked gate that kept Trudy safely inside.

"Alone," Lucifer clarified, "if you wouldn't mind."

Philistina shook her head without making eye contact, clearly unaffected by his charms either.

"It's okay," Trudy said, not wanting them to get caught in her crosshairs. "If I need you, I'll call. I promise."

Zuriah hesitated, but Trudy gave a reassuring nod. He opened the door, and reluctantly, Philistina followed.

At least they'd stopped bickering.

The door clicked behind them and she readied herself.

"I want to say that it was a privilege to have mentored you, Temperance," Lucifer said, "and I wish you the very best in your new position. They're lucky to have you."

And just like that, the old warmth flooded her. It was like that whenever he was nice—the sound of his skin and his voice and the soft glow of his yellow eyes could grip you quickly.

"Thank you, m'lord." She locked her eyes on a carving in the wall, her old defenses coming back like a nursery rhyme. "I appreciate the vote of confidence."

"I would also like to apologize." He tilted his head and smiled, a lock of hair slipping in front of his eyes. It was that thing he did to make himself appear youthful and sweet, rather than impossibly ancient and wise. "I've always been hard on you. Maybe a little too hard at times—"

"Forgiven," she responded quickly. And she did forgive him in her own way, if not at all by the Handbook's standards. She'd never trust him, or put anything past him... but she'd move on all the same.

"It's only because I believed you had the greatest potential," he said. "Your brilliance is rare." That sweet melody from his skin became even sweeter, and that hypnotic sense of him crept around her, invading her senses. He stepped closer. "Your brilliance is almost as rare as your obstinacy. We could've made a great team, you and I...."

For a beat, she was caught by the magnetism and truly wondered if he was being sincere.

"I am sincere," he assured, and she cringed, fixing her eyes on the wall again. If he were so sincere, he wouldn't be trolling her mind.

"I appreciate your apology," she said cooly, "but our meeting will be starting soon."

"You always were a bit too pious." His charm went flat. "Too many loyalties and fixed ideas."

She guffawed, her polite demeanor slipping too. "Ethical maybe, but pious I am not. I don't need a white book to know the difference between right and wrong."

"To each their own." He smiled, opening the door for her like the gentle lord everyone thought he was. "Keep an open mind though. You never know when you'll need me."

Her mind would never be so open that her intelligence fell out.

She stepped into the room, and as she did, the golden dome unlatched and slowly began swirling open. Even through the haze, the natural light warmed her face, and instead of feeling terror and seeking out the faces that scorned her, she only saw the ones that seemed to care about her. Raphael, Zuriah, Philistina—even the fire-haired one they called Ruphius, who said he carved her name.

"Angel Bee!" Raphael leapt from his chair and ran over, embracing her. He smelled of a heavy musk, floral and nutty, just like him. He bent down to kiss her once on each cheek and she squeezed him back.

She'd gotten it over with. She'd finally faced him.

There's a lion on the other side; the only way is through.

The Handbook did get some things right.

Lucifer took his seat next to Lords Baalael and Azazel on the other side of the conference table. Their presence, once the most intimidating thing in her life, barely mattered at all now.

"It's nice to see you again, Temperance," Lord Manuel from Creative stood and shook her arm, then motioned a tray of refreshments in the center of the table. "Please, make yourself comfortable. We have a nice selection of teas and coffee. No manna biscuits, but we do have wheat."

"Thank you, Lord Manuel," Trudy said, "but I'm alright."

"No need to be so formal." He smiled. "Call me Manny. How's the new team going?"

She glanced at Philistina and Zuriah, who were now elbowing each other's arms out of the same spot.

"Great." She smiled. "Really starting to gel."

Manny motioned the silent scholar in the corner of the room. "Please add the Angel Temperance and Lord Lucifer to the attendance record. First item on our agenda is the water world template."

"We've finished those designs and they've all been sent to Tech," Raphael said. "There are still some generic placeholders that we'll finish once they build the back end."

"And what of the primary species?" Manny asked.

"Species is hardly a word we should be using," Azazel interrupted. "Artificial intelligence would be more accurate."

"They've been designed in our own image," Lord Raphael said, "without the wings, of course. For now, we're using generic placeholders for their faces and individual details; no artists have been inspired to paint them yet. We don't want to rush it. If these two are to pass their genetic code to everyone, they've got to be good-looking."

"Spoken like the true Lord of Aesthetic," Manny laughed. "Do we know what we're calling them yet?"

"There's been no inspiration for a species name," Raphael said, "but I was thinking we could draw lots and name them after one of us. Raphkind has a nice ring to it."

"Or Mankind," Manny chuckled. "But there's plenty of time for that." He turned his attention to the Tech lords and folded his hands. "Do you have an update on the holdup from your end?"

"We're making progress," Lucifer said. "But the process isn't without its hiccups."

"We're not playing with paint," Baalael said. "Programming requires actual work—"

"What he says isn't without merit," Lucifer shot Baalael a glare, "even if the way he said it was. The designs Raphael delivered are robust and complex—truly impressive. Bringing them to life is no easy task."

"Understood," Manuel said. "That's why we invited Trudy and her team to the meeting. More support never hurts. Maybe you can pull up the codes and let her have a look?"

"With all due respect, m'lord," Trudy said, not wanting to get wedged between the immense powers in the room, "it's probably better if we sit down with the codes in our suite so I can run them through the proper code inspectors."

"They're a disaster," Philistina blurted. "I've been in their server—it's sloppier than the outfit Hoot told me not to wear here."

Trudy's jaw nearly fell off her face. "How did you get into their sandbox? You don't have administrative credentials."

"Told you she was mad," Zuriah mumbled.

"Doesn't anyone read the employee handbook?" Philistina asked.

They all looked at one another. Trudy had never actually opened the employee handbook.

"New recruits all have read-only access to every sandbox in the programming department. We can't edit them, but we can see them. There were trillions of syntax errors."

Lucifer's face went dark and his gaze burned through the little outspoken newcomer. He probably never read the employee handbook either.

"Trillions?" Manuel said. "I'm not a programmer, but that sounds like a lot."

Trudy shook her head and glared at Philistina. "How do you even know the coding languages? I thought you were an engineer?"

She rolled her eyes. "I can do a lot more than trap light."

"Can someone pull up the code in a hologram now, please?" Manuel asked. "I'd like for Trudy's team to have a look while we're here."

Lucifer cracked his neck and turned to Baalael and Azazel. They began rummaging through their bags. There was a box-shaped bulge clearly visible in Azazel's satchel, but she continued feeling around it. Several beats passed, and none of them produced a qube.

Why were they so averse to displaying the code? She dared not let her mind wander to conclusions. At least not in this room.

"Apologies," Lucifer said. "It appears none of us have brought our equipment. We will follow up in a qpistle after the meeting."

"Philistina," Trudy said while she eyed Lucifer, "give me your qube, please."

Philistina reached into her bag and pulled out the shining brass box, handing it to Trudy.

Trudy tapped it to life and a hologram appeared. She clicked through a series of glyphs to open the primary source code sandbox, and the login screen appeared. She entered her credentials, and a red error message floated above the table.

"Did someone remove my administrative access?"

"Maybe you typed it wrong?" Raphael said, so she tried again.

Denied.

"I'd think someone who was doing their job would've noticed that already," Baalael quipped.

"She's been busy building a team," Zuriah snapped. "I'm not the easiest angel to get on with." He gestured to Philistina. "Neither is she."

Manny walked over and logged in with his credentials. "I have universal access. We'll reach out to AR and see if they can fix that glitch for you."

Glitches like that didn't just happen. Someone locked her out of the sandbox.

The red error message disappeared, and Trudy was able to open the source code terminal. The hologram above the table shifted into a scrolling array of vertical white glyphs on a black background.

And right there, blatantly highlighted in purple, were countless instances of syntax errors. There was no denying it now.

Syntax errors? How, in all of Heaven, with Tech's combination of experience on this project, and the skillsets of hundreds of programmers underneath them, did they not see trillions of syntax errors? Highlighted in purple? Lucifer was the literal embodiment of language and math.

Again, she dared not let her thoughts wander to conclusions, but they lingered at the precipice of her mind. She took a breath and swiped a command authorizing the system to fix itself. Lucifer's yellow gaze bore into her.

The hologram scrolled at an imperceptible speed for several measures, and then stopped. The purple error flags were gone.

"Fixed," Trudy said, moving her gaze to Lucifer's burning orbs. Trillions of highlighted syntax errors didn't just go unnoticed. Zuriah put his hand on hers and inched a little closer.

"Good job," Ruphius applauded. "Our Temperance has proven an invaluable resource to this project."

"Indeed she has…" Manuel logged himself out of Philistina's qube. "Maybe the gods of technology should start reporting to her."

The music that rose from Lucifer's skin like fragrance abruptly stopped, and a cold chill fell over the room.

"Now that this is cleared up," Manuel said, annoyance lingering in his tone, "we can schedule a meeting to focus on the next phase. We won't be using datasets to train this artificial intelligence. We're going to train them ourselves."

"I've already begun designing the interface," Raphael said. "But before I can finish, I need to know what location will host the design so I can have the proper specs for my layout."

They all looked to Lucifer, who's expression remained flat. He had no response.

"Perhaps I can help with that." Ruphius turned from the window, fire dancing in his eyes. "The scholars advise that the library in this building is located over an Extra Dimensional Existential Node; they call it EDEN for short. That is where we will host the interface, and meet the new species… face-to-face."

***

"They're sabotaging the project," Trudy said, the office door clicking shut behind her.

"Tell me about it," Philistina said. "And they're not even doing it well. I could think of a dozen better ways to sabotage code."

"I'm sure they will now," Trudy said. "Nobody from Tech expected any corrective actions to take place in a meeting. Nothing ever gets resolved in meetings."

Philistina shrugged. "Maybe they're just dull."

"They're not dull—or at least Lucifer isn't."

"Why sabotage the project?" Zuriah asked. "What's the point?"

"I don't know," Trudy said. "But it makes me uncomfortable, especially with everything going on. Nothing makes sense anymore."

"I know what makes sense," Philistina said, "but Zuriah won't listen."

"Don't you start with these crazy ideas again!"

"They're not crazy ideas." Philistina stepped behind the lab counter and opened a lower cabinet, pulling out a microscope.

"Get away from my things...." Zuriah reached for her and she swatted him. She pulled something out of her satchel.

"Temperance! Make her stop. She's destroying my things!"

"I'm modifying your thing. You have at least a dozen down here," Philistina said, fiddling with the instrument. "I've seen eyeglasses with lenses stronger than this."

"Those are the strongest lenses there are!"

Metal pieces hit the counter and rolled around, and Zuriah clutched his chest. "I can't breathe...."

"I'll go to the Second Circle myself and replace anything she damages," Trudy said.

"He has four... identical... microscopes," Philistina said while she screwed something on. "It's like having four pairs of the same shoes. He's obsessed."

They started bickering again.

Sharing Hoot with the gladiator squad was proving more difficult than initially anticipated.

"There." Philistina put down her tool and stood up straight.

"See, Professor," Trudy said, "it looks just like it did before."

"Except instead of a magnification level of two thousand..." Philistina crossed her arms confidently. "It now has a magnification level of two million."

"Impossible," he mumbled. "Lunatic."

"Go ahead," Philistina said. "Put a sample in there." She bit off one of her fingernails and offered it to him.

"That's disgusting. Temperance, I can't work like this. "

 Philistina sandwiched her fingernail between two pieces of glass and slid it into the scope's viewer. "Go ahead. Take a look."

Zuriah stepped over to the microscope. "I can't believe I'm actually doing this. She's breaking me, you know." He fixed his eye on the viewer and adjusted the knob, sighing. Several beats passed in silence.

He looked up, squeezed his eyes shut, then rubbed them. "Impossible..." He adjusted another one of the knobs and stared for a few more beats. Slowly, he lifted his head. "Did you put something in my tea?" he asked. "Some of those fantastical fungi they grow in the Fourth Hexant?"

"Can you see them?" Philistina asked. "The patterns?"

"I want to see one of my own samples," he said, and opened a cabinet, pulling out a case of glass slides. He fingered through them. "Ah... here we are. If there's any sample I trust, it's Merry."

"Merry?" Trudy asked.

"My fern."

"You named your fern Merry?"

"Of course," he said. "Jolly good plant. Always brightening up the place." He removed Philistina's fingernail and placed Merry beneath the scope, then leaned over the eyepiece and adjusted it.

"Impossible..." he mumbled again, mouth slightly agape. "I... I don't understand what I'm seeing."

"You're seeing Merry," Philistina said.

"Where are her cells?" he furrowed his brow. "What did you do to her?"

"Her cells are still there," Philistina said. "Before it was like you were standing at the side of the road and observing a forest. Now you're in the forest and examining one of its smallest leaves with a magnifying glass. Can you see the patterns?"

He looked in the scope again. "I see... so many things. They're like little chains. Glyphs? Symbols?" He shook his head. "I have no idea. How did you do this?"

"I infused the lens with supercharged light," Philistina said.

"How?"

"I was trying to make a stronger lens, so I made a more convex mold. After I poured the glass, I realized I'd forgotten to get something to cover the mold with, so I covered it with the closest thing available—another convex lens. The light streaming in from the window beamed into the wet glass as it dried. That increased the magnification. So I did that again with the stronger lens. And then again with that one. The more I did it, the more I discovered underneath our world. Patterns of symbols. Like a language."

"That sounds like code...." Trudy said.

"That's what she keeps saying," Zuriah's voice was distant. "That everything is made from code."

"Finally." Philistina sat on a desk and pulled a banana from her bag and peeled it. "We're not so different from what we're making in these machines." She chewed as she spoke. "And if everything's made from code, then the codes from the darkness must be corrupted. If we can repair the corrupted code, we can fix everything."

She stared at the two of them, chewing, a short fiber from the banana peel hanging off her chin.

Trudy blinked hard.

"Hello?" Philistina waved.

"Professor..." Trudy said slowly, "is that what you see?"

"I don't know." Zuriah pinched the bridge of his nose. "Certainly, something has been discovered.... I have to observe more. At this point, if that banana peel put on ballet shoes and danced through the door, I might not be shocked."

Codes in our cells? Corrupted codes in the darkness? A litany of purple syntax errors scrolled through Trudy's memory. "Philistina, you believe that the damaged cells in our samples are sabotaged codes?"

"I said corrupted codes, not sabotaged."

Trudy hadn't even realized she'd used that word. "Did anyone understand what Manuel and Ruphius were talking about at the end of the meeting? When they said we would train the artificial intelligence face-to-face? About the interface being some kind of ...extra dimensional...something?"

"Eden?" Zuriah said. "I remember them saying that, but I've never heard of it."

"Neither have I," Trudy said. "I'd bet there's a lot more they know than what's taught to us in University. Like their ring technology."

"That's not technology," Zuriah said. "Those rings are divine. They touch the glory imparted by the Almighty himself."

Trudy all but rolled her eyes. "The Council dissolves, leaving our world without leadership. And at the same time, this darkness starts spreading? All the while they've been moving on to this project, which Lucifer and his team are clearly sabotaging. What else are they sabotaging?"

"Maybe we should wait for Hoot," Philistina said. "I think you're jumping to conclusions. It's not like there's some machine you can log into and access nature. The codes in that microscope are different from the ones in our machines."

"Do you have any idea how ancient Lucifer is?" Trudy asked. "The lords and scholars were here before our Circles even existed. Before recorded history. If anyone understands the nature of nature, it's them."

"But they didn't create nature," Philistina said.

"What if nobody created nature?" Trudy said, and Zuriah let out a little gasp. "What if nature is just something we figure out? And the lords and scholars are merely older, superior life-forms?"

"Codes can't write themselves into existence," Philistina said. "Of all angels, you should know that."

"Simple codes give rise to complexity all the time," Trudy said. "It's how our planning systems improve on themselves. I have no doubt that something resembling code could have slowly emerged and increased in complexity given enough time." She shook her head. "I'm getting off point—I'm telling you that if Professor Zuriah confirms your theory, then I'd wager my eyes that Lucifer is accessing nature's code and corrupting it. Somehow."

"Delaying the project is different than destroying the world," Philistina said. "Maybe the Tech team doesn't like the designs. That doesn't mean they'd intentionally harm angels they don't even know."

"I'm going to pretend that Temperance didn't just blaspheme our entire existence for the sake of this conversation..." Zuriah spoke up. "And I will say that Lucifer ruined me without a second thought. And whatever is happening to those cells in our samples is most definitely against their natural design."

"Professor," Trudy said, "it's time to tell us why you don't like the lords. What did Lucifer mean when he said he was 'happy to see you've moved on'?"

Zuriah sighed. "Five symphonies ago, while I was still teaching at University, I was called into a meeting with our Headmaster and a femme named Deidre—miserable lump of an angel if I ever saw one. She brought orders from some high-ups at the Ministry of Education. They wanted me to amend my curriculum, revise my own books. They said my dissertations were too 'pontificus'... whatever that means. They didn't like my constant praising of the Almighty and our Handbook, and the metaphors I drew between them and nature. But nature is a great metaphor. She said I was teaching science, not philosophy." Zuriah's hands knotted into little balls as he recalled it. "As you can imagine, I didn't take well to being told how to teach my own subjects, so I refused."

Nothing shocking there. "What happened after that?"

"Not a movement later, that noisy, yellow-eyed lordling came to find me and asked me to do the same thing."

"Lucifer?"

"Yes. But instead of trying to persuade me with veiled threats like the other one, he tried to goad me with promises. Stoke my ambitions and vanity."

"Did you listen?" Trudy asked.

"What do you think?" Zuriah guffawed. "I'm a pious angel. He couldn't offer anything I cared about. I care about the beauty and complexity of creation... the harmony of our world and the majestic nature of the Almighty. My life's work is to teach this, so angels can truly be grateful for it. So, I refused. He soured after that, and let me know that my songs as a teacher were numbered."

No wonder Zuriah was so averse to talking about this. To be removed from your Calling was rare. And profoundly shameful.

"Right after that some of the angels I taught began to complain about me," Zuriah continued, "like they somehow turned my students against me. The Headmaster chastised me at every turn. Finally, one overture I was doing a routine demonstration for first symphony chemistry students, but all of my chemicals were somehow switched around. A fire started, and the Headmaster discharged me under the pretense that I was no longer qualified for my position. I knew there was no way I used the wrong chemicals—my materials and equipment are kept meticulous. It's my belief that someone gained access to my lab and tampered with them."

"Like you were sabotaged," Trudy said.

"I know it sounds mad," Zuriah said, "and I have no way of proving it, but that's my belief. I returned home disgraced, discharged from my life's work, and tossed away like an old rag after a lifetime of service. It broke my Sarah's heart, and it broke mine too. Now I'm stuck here..." He grimaced at Philistina. "With her."

Philistina narrowed her eyes. "You don't know that was sabotage—"

"I believe you, Professor," Trudy cut in. "I spent two symphonies under his mentorship, and I know what lives underneath that beautiful melody." The more she thought about it, the more it all made sense. The clandestine meetings with scholars and lords, the constant travel... the secrets. The fact that the world had no leadership anymore—it was ripe for the taking. How long did everyone think this superior species would actually play nice?

Trudy ran her fingers through her hair. "There's only one way to find out if he's involved... I have to get close to him again."

"Temperance..." Zuriah trailed off. "You can't leave our team here. We need to figure out Philistina's discovery. We need to learn how to fix those poor souls like the one in the cage. We need to figure out what those shadows are."

Trudy shook her head. "I won't leave our team. Angelic Resources would never transfer me anyway. But Lucifer left the door open... I have to try."

"Fine." Philistina threw her arms up. "Maybe Lucifer has a login to life. Good for him. But repairing these codes will be a lot more complicated than fixing a syntax error. And Zuriah's right about healing angels like Grahamuel. We don't have much time."

"Grahamuel was probably starved," Trudy said.

"I don't think so," Zuriah said. "There were piles of plates. And I saw vita peels discarded on the floor. I think something else is happening to him... but I can't tell without biological samples from angels who are affected. Blood, if we can get it."

"How are we supposed to do that?" Trudy asked. "We nearly didn't make it back last time. And even if we could go back, how would we get someone's blood?"

"I'll go," Philistina said. "I'll figure it out."

"Absolutely not." Trudy crossed her arms. "It's too dangerous."

"It's not..." Philistina said. "Or at least... it won't be. I can go with Hoot when he travels with the gladiators. They're sure to travel close enough to one of those spots on the map."

"Hoot was almost cut in half last time," Trudy said.

"There's someone else." Philistina bit her lip. "A friend from my village. I've seen him put down a dozen fighters in the pits back home. He could've taken all those riders without breaking a sweat."

"Who is this friend?" Trudy asked.

"He fights with Hoot. Michael... His name is Michael."

17

Michael

"Music and silence, like our breath, exist to remind us that there is a space for output, and a space for input. A space to sing, and a space to listen. Most importantly, remember to breathe."
-The Guide to Utopian Principles and Ethics, Section II, on Internal States

HOOT AND ASHER CIRCLED each other, weaponless. As far as the squad was concerned, these were just hand-to-hand exercises, but as far as Michael was concerned, Hoot needed these baby steps to toughen up. If he couldn't deliver a fist to someone's face, he'd never drive a sword through them. Healer or not, he needed the mental strength to attack, or he wasn't going to make it.

Michael clapped hard. "Alright. Focus, precept. Soft eyes... remember the training."

Asher rushed in and Hoot pivoted, tossing him into his own momentum. Asher recovered quickly and spun, lunging again with a series of punches and kicks. Hoot ducked and weaved, nimble as a hummingbird. Asher's arms went low, a mistake he made too often, leaving his face wide open.

Take the shot, Hoot....

Hoot hesitated and Michael gritted his teeth. Asher's foot flicked up and landed square in the precept's chest. He went flying backward and landed in the dirt with a thump.

"Don't be such a roast-knocker!" Bernard yelled as he volleyed swords with Zillah at the other end of the pit.

"A what?" Michael turned around.

"A roast-knocker," Bernard repeated, sword clanging. "The angels who knock... on cooked roots... to make sure they're cooked.... 'Fraid of a little raw roast."

Michael grimaced. "Who eats raw rootroast?"

"Bah," Bernard said as he ducked Zillah's sword. "Roast-knockers, the lot of ya."

Michael shook his head as Hoot rose and dusted himself off. They got back into position.

"C'mon, Hoot. If you hesitate you're lost. Stop thinking and hit."

They circled, and Asher made the first move again. Hoot weaved and bobbed, avoiding injury, but he was missing offensive opportunities.

"C'mon, Hoot!" Michael yelled again. "Take the pissing shots!"

Again, Asher came in quickly, throwing a series of strikes before grabbing the precept into a headlock. Hoot twisted Asher's wrist and freed himself, bending his arm behind his back.

"Finish it!" Michael yelled.

Again, Hoot hesitated.

Asher got out of his grip and flipped the precept over, slamming him to the ground.

Michael punched his palm. When the light ran out, the precept was going to get hurt.

"Stop overthinking!" Michael jumped into the pit and faced off with Asher. "Like this, Hoot. We're here to win, not dance."

Asher began to circle, but Michael lunged with a series of quick moves and dropped him to the floor in the space of a breath. Asher sat there, dumbfounded.

"The qualifying tournament's almost here," Michael snapped. "You need to hit already."

"That was a cheap shot." Asher wiped the blood from his mouth as he pushed himself up. "I wasn't ready."

"You were ready just fine," Michael said. "You need to keep your hands higher." Someone called his name from behind and he turned around.

Philistina stood at the edge of the pit in a flowing white robe, the breeze blowing the wisps of her blonde hair in such a way that she looked like a master's painting.

Suddenly, his legs flew out from underneath him and he hit the ground. Hard.

Asher looked down, grinning. "You're not the only one who can take cheap shots."

Michael got up with a grunt and climbed from the pit, ignoring Asher entirely. He approached Philistina. "You look... different."

"I look like a tablecloth."

"I'm so proud of you!" Hoot hopped from the pit and approached her too. "You look so professional."

"You two know each other?" Michael asked.

"Philistina's on my team." Hoot's voice became aloof as he addressed Michael. Likely a result of Michael's constant scolding. "What are you doing out here?" he asked Philistina.

"I made a promise," Philistina said, "to take Michael to Master Azrael for his art lessons."

Michael's face fell. He forgot about that.

"High Master Azrael?" Hoot raised his eyebrows.

"Michael's an artist," Philistina said. "Azrael's going to train him."

"Azrael's no ordinary scholar," Hoot said. "The High Master trains the other scholars. He's a virtual repository for the Almighty mind."

"Not sure what that means...." Michael retrieved his satchel and rummaged through it, looking for those stupid glasses, which he couldn't seem to find. Maybe he'd get out of this after all.

Philistina slid the round, ridiculous things from her bag. "Looking for these? I snatched them for safekeeping. I had a feeling you might... lose them."

"You wear glasses?" Hoot tilted his head.

"Apparently..." Michael sighed. "I need to get dressed. Hoot, would you mind walking with me?"

Hoot followed him to the armory in silence. Michael had been hard on the precept lately. The qualifying tournament was around the corner, and the light wasn't getting any brighter out there. No matter which way you spun it, Hoot needed to start swinging. Michael opened the armory door and held it as Hoot entered.

"You know I'm only trying to help, right?" Michael broke the silence.

"I know," Hoot said, stepping out of his skirt guard.

"Your moves and forms are perfect," Michael said. "It's just that—"

"You think I'm weak," Hoot said, cutting him off and unlatching his wrist guards.

"You're actually in better shape than all of them... physically."

"But not mentally."

Michael sighed, unlatching his shoulder guard. "You're a precept... your instinct is to heal, not hurt. But good defense requires good offense. It's not enough to avoid getting hurt. When the food and light run out, it's going to get dangerous out there."

"It's already dangerous out there," Hoot said, stepping into his trousers. "And you're right. I'm not mentally equipped to hurt anyone. Strength is my weakness, I suppose. I have to accept that the light is changing... Everything's changing. I have to change."

"You'll get it, Hoot. Keep trying." Michael slid on his tunic and put his armor into the cubby. "You want to walk with us to this Azrael? I don't even know where to find him."

"All the art studios are all in the Creative Center," Hoot said. "I'll take the walk."

They met Philistina and headed toward the towering bronze gates of the campus. Michael scanned the sky. The haze was even thicker than it was a song ago. "Not getting any better up there."

"Sometimes I think it's getting better," Hoot said, "but then the haze comes back even thicker."

"We've made some progress with the samples we took back to the lab," Philistina said.

"Wait...." Michael stopped walking. "*She* went into the darkness with you? When you were attacked?"

"It's not like we knew what was out there," Hoot said.

"I'm right here, you know...." Philistina waved in his face. "You can ask me directly. Besides, I have to go back."

"To the darkness?" Michael's eyebrows flew up.

"Mmm-hmm. We need more samples." She skipped ahead and passed through the bronze campus gates.

Michael grabbed Hoot by the arm. "How could you bring her there? And now she thinks she's going back?"

"Peace, Michael." Hoot stared at his iron grip, and he let go. "I told you, we didn't know it was dangerous. And good luck telling her what she can and can't do.... You don't know what I went through just getting her to switch outfits."

"C'mon, slugs!" Philistina called back to them.

"Like I said..." Hoot smirked, and they jogged to catch up with her. "Good luck."

"Whatever you need, I'll get for you," Michael said to Philistina. "After we qualify for the Games, we'll be traveling. I'll go then."

"Perfect," she said. "I can come with you."

"No, you can't," Michael said.

"Of course I can."

Michael shot Hoot a look and ground his teeth. They turned the corner, and the golden domes of the Creative Center came into view.

"Isn't that the most beautiful building on campus?" Philistina asked. "Even in this light. Michael, you should paint it."

"There's no reason for you to come." Michael stayed on topic. "It's too dangerous for a femme."

She stopped short and spun on him, poking his chest as she spoke. "I'm no more afraid of the dark than I am of you."

"Philistina, please..." Michael changed his tone. "It's not safe for you."

"I rode a giant cat through the chaos and saved everyone." She spun on her heel again and walked ahead of them. "I'll be fine."

"She's not lying," Hoot said.

"At least let me show you how to swing a sword first," Michael said.

"I don't like violence," she said.

"How are we supposed to justify bringing you?"

"You're smart," she said. "You'll figure something out."

"She's a healer," Hoot said. "She made a stone that can amplify light. She can come as part of the triage unit."

Michael pinched the bridge of his nose. "Thanks for figuring that out for me, Hoot."

"When do we leave?" Philistina asked.

"Qualifying tournament's in a few songs," Hoot said. "Providing we make the cut, we leave after that."

"Good," she said, and looked up the path to the towering golden domes. "Let's hurry up... I made a promise to Ruphius."

They climbed the white marble steps of the Creative Center, and with a loud creak, Philistina dragged open the arched, mahogany door. "This is my favorite part of campus," she said, looking around at the half-opened dome, and the labyrinth of staircases and walking bridges beneath it.

The first time Michael had come in here, the majestic beauty caught him off guard. He maintained a stone facade now, though. He didn't like appearing simple—it was bad enough that he was never educated.

"If you think this is nice, you should see the rest of the domes." A voice came from beside them and they all turned. A tall lord with lavender eyes and hair to match spoke. "I'm Raphael. Can I help you find something?"

"You sure can," Philistina said, grabbing Michael by the wrist and dragging him over. "I promised Lord Ruphius I'd deliver the Angel Michael to High Master Azrael to begin his art lessons."

Raphael's eyes flashed and he smiled. "A new painter, then?"

"Yes, Raphael...." Ruphius emerged from a darkened hallway, his orange hair pulled into elaborate curls this time. "Michael is the painter who will paint the thing that hasn't been inspired yet."

"Oh, how wonderful!" Raphael clasped his hands. "Let's get him to his lessons then so that inspiration has something to work with."

Michael cocked a brow. These creative types were half mad.

"Shall we give them the tour first?" Ruphius stroked his chin. "I don't believe they've seen the Grand Domes yet."

"Haven't seen the Grand Domes?" Raphael dropped his jaw and fanned himself. "The Grand Domes are the magnum opus of Universal Technologies."

"Some might say our nanotech is the magnum opus," Ruphius said, "though I'm inclined to agree with Lord Raphael. Would you all like to see the domes?"

Philistina did a little hop and clapped, and Hoot smiled like a dullard. They all turned to Michael.

"Fine," he sighed. "Let's see more domes."

They climbed a winding staircase and Michael ran his hand along the cool wrought-iron banister. They stopped at the first level, where a catwalk was carpeted in maroon damask, its lush fabric soft under their feet. To the right, a balcony overlooked the bottom level, and to the left, ornate relief sculptures depicted scenes rich with detail.

Oil paintings hung flush to the wall—landscapes and figures and portraits, with the occasional marble sculpture dotting the catwalk. Philistina and Hoot ogled their surroundings like children, but Michael stayed stone faced.

Silent scholars in hooded cloaks passed to and fro without acknowledging them, leaving a breeze in their wake, and at the end of the catwalk was a double-doored archway. It spanned the entire height of the wall—at least twenty cubits.

"The first dome is over the Great Hall of Art," Raphael said. He grabbed the bronze handles and pushed down with a click. Light flooded from the room and the music blared. "Perfect timing," Raphael said. "The dome is almost all the way open."

They stepped inside, and Michael's gaze moved upward where interlocking pieces of metal swirled open, somehow amplifying the music of the spheres. The room seemed endless, but that was impossible. Hundreds of rows of angels sat behind canvases, painting. There must've been mirrors somewhere, because the room was impossibly big.

"This is where our artists work," Raphael said. "The inspiration for every scene in our project is channeled right in this room. My job is to amplify their inspiration, like an antenna for the Almighty. Can you see yourself working here, Michael?"

Michael stretched a tight-lipped smile in response. He was much better at being destructive than creative, so he ignored the question.

He stepped around Lord Raphael and watched an artist from behind, silently observing her work. She smelled like mineral spirits and paint thinner, which set loose memories of his own hand gliding across a canvas.

She painted a mountain scene with a lake, still as glass. The source of light came from a single yellow dot that peeked above the mountains, and curiosity got the best of him.

"Why just one source of light?" he asked.

"That's a star," she said, not pausing her work to look at him. "It feeds their world with light and energy, in accordance with the great design."

"Interesting concept." He cocked a brow, his attention now caught by the canvas next to hers. This was some kind of inverted image, flooded with darkness—but not the kind of darkness that had entered their own lands. This was a soothing darkness. A dreamy darkness.

He stepped closer. An ivory ball glowed gently in the center of the sky, casting ethereal light on the ocean below and edging the clouds in silver. Tiny white spots speckled the background, and one was larger than the rest of them.

"Different, is it not?" Ruphius whispered in Michael's ear.

"It's so dark." Michael knit his brow. "But the darkness is…"

"Beautiful." Philistina appeared at his other side. "I didn't think darkness could be that."

"We call it night," Raphael said. "Stars brighten the day, but the moon keeps watch at night."

"What's the bright speckle next to the moon?" Michael asked.

"That's the morning star," Ruphius said.

The painter dipped a clean, wide paint brush into a clear liquid and rapidly covered the canvas. At first, the painting began to shiver, then quake. Suddenly, a perfect copy of the image popped off the easel and floated midair. The painter picked up a qube and sucked the image in.

Michael's jaw slacked.

"Digitizer," Raphael whispered. "It moves the artist's work into our machines."

"Technology," Ruphius winked at Michael. "Closest to divinity you'll ever get. Now come… there's a couple other domes to see before we drop you with Azrael."

Michael frowned. He'd forgotten all about Azrael.

They left the Great Hall of Art and went on to the Great Hall of Sound, where instruments of every kind were scattered about. Under its open dome was a ceiling made of soundproof glass, so the light could get in without the music distracting them. This was where musicians designed the sounds to go with the paintings. Things like wind passing through trees, or water roaring in a river, Ruphius had said.

The last dome they visited was a room they called Eden. Inside was pitch black, and their group wasn't allowed beyond the doorway. If a dome did cap it, then it was unopened and invisible in the darkness. Silent scholars filed in and out like a line of brown ants on a mission, and two stood like statues at the entrance.

"What's the point of taking us here if we're not allowed inside?" Michael asked.

"I thought you might like to see the access point to our creation," Ruphius said, half grinning. His eyes danced with flames that gave Michael the chills. "If we let you in now, your minds would turn to dust."

Michael grimaced.

"It's time for your lesson, Michael." Ruphius rubbed his hands together, and Raphael led the others back downstairs. "Follow me."

They climbed two more curling flights of stairs, and walked a series of less ostentatious halls, not that different from any ordinary manor. They came to a plain, wooden door.

"I suppose telling you now that I didn't bring any supplies is useless?"

"Like I told you when we met," Ruphius said, "there are plenty of supplies in the studio." That snuffed Michael's last flicker of hope, and Ruphius bowed slightly before starting back down the hallway.

Michael looked from him to the door, and then finally blurted, "I apologize in advance if I can't meet your standards. Painting isn't my strength. It never has been."

"Michael..." Ruphius clasped his hands behind his back and turned slightly. "You have no idea what strength even is. If we are all fortunate enough... you'll learn." He turned the corner and disappeared.

Michael opened the door to a mostly empty painting studio. Azrael stood in the front of the room, tall and imposing, covered in that hooded brown cloak. The small room was underwhelming in contrast to the rest of the building, which was refreshing. There's only so much grandiosity you could handle in one song. The wooden floors were spattered with paint and nearly all the polish had faded. The vague smell of thinner and oils lingered in the air.

"High Master Azrael…" Michael cleared his throat. "I didn't bring any supplies. I'm sorry." He didn't even have the mental energy to lie about why.

Azrael pointed to an empty art station, where a small stool and table were already set up in front of a canvas. The supplies were all laid out.

The music of the spheres was inaudible with the windows closed, and the pronounced silence of Azrael's presence loomed over him like a shadow. He stared at Michael from deep inside that cavernous hood as he headed for the easel, assuming there were even eyes in there. Michael suddenly felt naked.

And exhausted. The previous silence had consisted of another deep, dreamless sleep, so he popped a few coffee beans.

He settled in at the art station, and Azrael's cavernous hood remained fixed in his direction.

"Oh…" Michael reached into his satchel and pulled out those ridiculous glasses and slipped them on. "Much better…. Thanks for getting me these."

Azrael didn't respond. Guess that's why they called them "silent."

Michael picked up the palette and laid it on the table, unscrewing the paint caps and laying them there too. He poured a mixture of mineral spirits and varnish into a small jar, and began deliberating which dollops of color to squeeze out.

THWAP.

Something pinged the side of his head and he yelped. He brought his hand to his temple and rubbed it, his gaze landing on a gray eraser that had bounced across the floor.

Slowly, he looked at Azrael. "Did you just throw that at me?"

Azrael pulled out a small, brass box. "You are out of practice."

Michael rubbed his head and grimaced. "I'm moving as fast as I can. I told Ruphius… painting isn't my strength."

"You're unaware. Clouded. Blind. And lazy." Azrael droned the words without inflection, his voice like the slow, steady beat of a smith pounding steel.

Michael's jaw fell slack. He stood corrected on that "silent" part.

"Pick up your charcoal," Azrael said. "You will not be painting yet."

Michael yanked off the stupid glasses and shoved them into his bag, suddenly not caring if he was thrown out. He set the pad on his easel and snatched up the charcoal. "Happy?"

Azrael didn't respond, but touched the little brass box again. Something like a garden scene appeared above it, translucent and floating. In the center bloomed what looked like a Mother Tree, though Michael couldn't see any pods from his angle.

More technology.

Azrael pushed out his hand, and the garden floated to the center of the room and expanded.

"Begin," Azrael said.

Michael took a deep breath and outlined a bush. He threw a few more bushes in there, and shaded the undertones. He shaped out some flowers and began adding detail to those. He carefully traced individual leaves, then leaned over and picked up the eraser from the floor and erased the first bush, tracing it over again.

"Time's up," Azrael said.

"I just started!" Michael said. "How long are these sketches supposed to take?"

Azrael walked through the image to Michael, his cloak drifting behind him. He leaned in to examine Michael's drawing.

"Again," Azrael said, and he stepped back as Michael tried a second time, only to be cut short after a few measures. They repeated this at least a dozen times and Michael nearly exploded with frustration.

"You draw what you think you see," Azrael droned, "not what is there. Put down the pencil and close your eyes."

Michael crossed his arms. "I don't close my eyes unless I'm alone."

"Do you fear me?" Azrael asked.

"Don't confuse fear and distrust," Michael mumbled. "I don't fear anyone."

"There is one in this room that you cannot trust, but that one is not me," he intoned with that numbing voice. "Close your eyes."

"I'm not closing my eyes," Michael said, an uncomfortable chuckle escaping his lips.

"You delay your own progress, Michael. So be it—choose something in the room instead to focus your attention on."

Michael sighed and did as he said. There was a blue streak of paint on the wall, so he let his eyes settle on that. Azrael proceeded to walk him through a series of slow breaths, deeply inhaling, filling up his belly and chest, then slowly exhaling and emptying it all out. Thoughts and ideas vied for his attention. He was restless and didn't want to be there. This was time wasted that he could've been training. Or eating. Or even sleeping, however unpleasant that was. Anything else.

"Just because you hear the music," Azrael said, and kept repeating like a litany, "doesn't mean that you must dance. Stay with your breath."

Eventually, Michael's shoulders relaxed, and Azrael's droning voice became numbingly pleasant. Strangely pleasant, in fact. Almost comfortable.

After a while, Michael realized his eyes had closed—though when he'd closed them, he wasn't sure.

"Just because you hear the music," Azrael droned on, "doesn't mean that you must dance." Gradually, his voice began to change. Or at least, in Michael's mind it had. It was still Azrael, but lighter. More lively and youthful.

Light warmed Michael's face as the scholar continued his mantra— not actual light, but something like a recollection. Bright green eyes flashed in the darkness, and innocent laughter echoed in the back of his mind so that he could almost hear it.

A warm feeling enveloped him. He felt safe and at peace. Loved, even. It felt like...

Home.

Something lingered at the edge of his consciousness, just out of reach. He grasped for it, but then Azrael stopped repeating the phrase and said, "Look at the garden again."

Slowly, Michael opened his eyes. At first, nothing was different, but the longer he stared at the garden, the more he noticed. The flowers were arranged in a pattern. Symmetrical and asymmetrical bushes offset one another and achieved a balance, and decorative grass was planted in a way that framed tier after tier of cascading violets. Dangling from the other side of the Mother Tree was the slight edge of a birthing pod, and a spray of tulips grew beneath it. For a split beat, he thought he could smell them.

And there was something else peeking from behind the Mother Tree, so he squinted his eyes. A little bub, no more than three or four, wearing a dark cloak. His scruffy hair was raven black, and his eyes a shocking blue. A breeze blew through the still image and brought it to life, the grass and flowers suddenly bending and leaves catching the wind. The child grinned, and his laughter bounced from the walls of the studio.

Michael gasped and popped from his seat.

He blinked, and the garden was still again. The stale odor of old paint swept back into the room, and there was no child. "The image moved!" Michael pointed at it. "Is it supposed to move?"

"Stay with your breath," Azrael said, "and draw the garden again."

Michael pressed his palms into his eyes and breathed deeply. Whatever that was, it was gone now. He picked up the charcoal, but rather than start with his usual outlines, he could feel where the shadows should fall this time. He angled the charcoal sideways and formed the bigger shapes, feeling where the heat of the light should land. After that, he began to fill in the finer details.

"Time," Azrael murmured.

Michael leaned back and stretched his neck.

Azrael nodded. "There is progress."

Michael's hand whipped out to his side and he winced. Something careened into his palm, and his fingers closed around it.

He knitted his brow and opened his fingers.

The gray eraser.

Michael looked up, unsure if he was more annoyed that the scholar kept throwing erasers at him, or more shocked that his hand acted on its own.

"Art is not merely the observation of truth and beauty," Azrael said, "but the preservation and protection of it. Practice your breathing, Michael. When the time is right for your next session, I will find you."

18

Michael

"This idea that everyone has been created equal is pure rub-bish. Life should be like a bowl of fresh sap from a Mother Tree... let the cream rise to the top."
-Black Manifesto, Chapter Three, "On Ambition"

THE ELITE SQUAD MARCHED into the pit and stood erect, shoulder to shoulder. Normally, the other trainers would be waiting in the pit to scrimmage, but not even Joseph had arrived yet.

To any outside spectator, this squad would look entirely too for-mal—even stiff in their matching leathers and lock step movements. But not according to the Military Manual that Joseph had issued. To the masses, they were gladiators, but in-house, they were *soldiers.*

Michael wasn't much of a reader, but he found the Military Manual impossible to put down. Unlike the Handbook or the Black Manifesto, it didn't shove a bunch of beliefs or proverbs down your throat. In some ways it contradicted both books, but in others, it balanced them.

There were hierarchies and order to the military, and you could climb those hierarchies based on your merit. Nothing assumed the world to be one way, and its clear codes and rules operated on entirely new concepts like *honor* and *justice.* There were rewards and punishments, clear and accounted for. And the whole of it all made up what Joseph called the *Spiritus Corporis:* pride and loyalty and courage and fellowship. A new kind of family that you chose of your own volition.

Joseph was third in command as Greater Dominion, the only officers above him being the *Principality* of War and the *Sahtan*—positions temporarily held by Lords Baalael and Lucifer, respectively, until the vote finalized everything. Zillah had said that Lucifer recognized Joseph's talent as a thinker and a great strategist, and gave him free rein to create the manual and the military's structure. Even Bernard, who'd been surprisingly easy to recruit once Hoot was on board, kept a copy with him at all times. Had Joseph never been called as a gladiator, he could've been the world's greatest philosopher. Or at least, Michael thought so.

"Where are they?" Hoot asked, not breaking his stance while the squad waited in the pit. "We're usually scrimmaging by now."

"This is the song in which Joseph will select our Champion," Zillah chimed in with her accent. "He might be deliberating."

"How do you know?" Michael asked.

"We've been soldiers longer than you," Asher said, gaze fixed straight ahead. "Word gets around."

As if on cue, Joseph strutted through the opening of the small arena. His armor was black as pitch, and its chest plate was carved with dark, glossy muscles. His helm formed sharp, angry angles around his eyes, and crimson horns curled out from either side of it. A red cape billowed behind him.

Michael let out a low whistle. That was the armor from his vision in the mirror.

Four more soldiers marched in behind him wearing the same uniform, save for the red cape, and Joseph's large, decorative wrist guards. An angel with a judge's sash and a bamboo whistle walked in behind them.

Joseph stopped at the lip of the pit and waited until the others flanked him, arms flush to their sides and chests out. He addressed the squad. "Wearing this uniform is a privilege," he said, "not a right. For the last three movements we've been working on strength, discipline, and technique. You've all worked tirelessly and have earned the right to wear this armor as soldiers. But whether you're fighting against the darkness, or fighting in the Games, a squad without a Champion isn't worth the dirt under their heels." He threw a hand signal and the soldiers stepped forward in perfect unison, raising their shields.

"Not only are these trained soldiers, but each of these seasoned fighters have Championed the Games as gladiators. Now, we're going to attack you, and we'll make mince of you if you let us. Should *three* of you tap out before *one* of us, these fine soldiers are more than willing to step into this squad and replace you. They might not be Called to this island, but Lucifer will make it happen if you can't make the cut. It would be unfortunate, and highly inconvenient... but it would also mean that *none* of you are ready to fight in the Games. And certainly, none are fit to lead."

Asher smirked, and Zillah drew both of her swords. Michael exchanged glances with Bernard and Hoot, then leaned into Hoot's ear.

"Did you bring Philistina's stone?"

"Only so I could show it to Joseph," Hoot whispered. "We don't know if it'll be allowed in the Games."

"Better to ask forgiveness than permission," Michael said, fixing his gaze back on Joseph. Hoot would need that stone to heal himself. At least until he started properly attacking.

"Without leadership," Joseph called out, "you will fall swiftly, and you will fall hard. If the majority of you are still standing when this bout is over, then your Champion will be obvious." He snapped his helm down and they charged, dust erupting under their feet as they landed in the pit.

"Flip me feathers..." Bernard's head whipped around.

"One to one," Asher said. "It's our best chance without preparation. I'll take Joseph. Zillah, you take the smallest one. The rest of you, take who's left."

"No!" Michael commanded. "Stay together. Form a wall, shields up."

Asher shot him a dirty look and yelled, "C'mon!" He charged and Zillah hesitated, looking back, but then followed anyway.

Bernard and Hoot looked to Michael, who grunted and followed Zillah. It wasn't even close to a strategy, but separated they were at an even worse disadvantage.

Asher never got to Joseph, who threw a hand signal and fell behind his squad. They formed a wall in front of him while Asher and Zillah went on an aggressive attack. Michael slipped the signal to Hoot and Bernard to stay at his flanks.

"They're protecting Joseph, which means he'll probably throw blades." Michael glanced back at them. "Keep your shields high and pick up anything that lands by you."

Michael led them around the side as Asher and Zillah drove the center, furiously fighting as the opposition held the line. A mellow piano sonata drifted from the sky in sharp contrast to the grunts and clanging metal in the pit.

As anticipated, a dagger flew straight at Michael's head and he deflected it with his shield, Hoot snatching it on the rebound.

Michael threw a signal behind his back, and Bernard readied himself. In a quarter note, the rotund angel was plowing their line like an airship, sending everyone stumbling. Michael attacked, daggers now whizzing by his head. Hoot was deflecting behind him and scooping up the blades.

Michael volleyed swords and saw Asher from the corner of his eye trying to get to Joseph, but he was just tiring himself out. *No glory in a loss, Ash.* His hands were low again too.

Michael drove his opponent back with a flurry of strikes before disarming him. He cocked his sword for the final blow, but Joseph yanked the gladiator out of the way and drove Michael backward with a fierce attack.

Joseph was fast, spinning and swinging in a near blur. Michael took a deep breath—the way Azrael had shown him, and let his eyes go soft. His reflexes took over and he matched his trainer, blow for blow. Joseph caught Michael with an elbow to the jaw and brought his sword around, but Michael ducked, shaking it off. He finally landed a hard blow to Joseph's side but he spun into it, using the momentum to land a kick square into Asher's chest.

Another gladiator stepped in front of Michael as Joseph and Asher engaged. Joseph lit Asher up like an altar of candles as light poured from shallow wounds that condensed into stripes of blood. Bernard tried to jump in and help, but got his belly slit in the process. Joseph cut open Asher's rib and the judge blew the whistle, tapping both Asher and Bernard out.

Two down—one more and it was over. Not to mention, they were outnumbered now. *Great strategy, Ash.*

Michael attacked with a fury, driving two opponents backward and pivoting behind the one. He clanged the butt of his sword on the gladiator's helm and dazed him, but before he could finish the job, Joseph was in his face again, sword blazing.

Michael glanced at Hoot's belt where there were two daggers, and he had one. Zillah could hit a beezle fly from a hundred paces away. They needed to get those blades in her hands.

"Fall back!" Michael yelled as he ducked Joseph's blow. He yanked Zillah from the fray, a sword nearly cutting her open as he did, and Hoot spun like a ballerina, gracefully tumbling backward. They darted away, putting a good slice of space between them and Joseph's squad. A much-needed breath to regroup.

"Blades to Z," Michael commanded Hoot as he flipped a dagger her way. "Don't let them touch her. And Z..." He got into position as their opponents barreled toward them. "Don't miss."

The opponent's shields were low as they ran—they didn't know Zillah had the blades.

"Now!" Michael yelled, and a dagger whooshed past his ear, followed by another and another. Zillah was fast, and in the space of an eighth note, two of them had blade handles protruding from their collars.

The whistle blew and they tapped out.

Michael exhaled. Nobody would be replaced now.

"Good job, Z..."

Three on three.

Michael signaled a formation and Hoot kneeled. Zillah ran and leaped from his back, double swords slicing through the air as Michael and Hoot ran right beneath her. They landed several blows as their opponents divided their attention between land and air.

Joseph attacked Hoot and drove him back, the precept barely able to block his blows. Light flashed from Hoot's leg and Michael shoved him out of the way.

"The stone!" Michael commanded, and engaged Joseph while Hoot retreated. The precept produced a glowing ball and fell back, healing his superficial wound before the judge blew the whistle.

"Did you just make a precept cheat?" Joseph said smoothly as if he weren't launching strikes. The clashing metal reverberated through Michael's arm. "I'm impressed."

"New world..." Michael jumped as Joseph tried to sweep his legs out from under him, "... calls for new tools."

Hoot was now behind Zillah, healing her shoulder as she held two of them off.

"Why'd you let Asher take control?" Joseph asked Michael as they volleyed. "He's hot-headed. Only thinks of his own glory."

"You know why..." Michael blocked his strike, now huffing. Joseph was in incredible shape. "Because you designed this trial... to see.... who would fight for themselves...."

Joseph grinned, pushing Michael back. "You're out of breath. I told you to run more."

"I hate running...."

Light flashed beside them, and one of Joseph's squad lay on the floor under Zillah, pulling his flag as the whistle blew.

"Three on two," Michael said, losing steam. Fighting Joseph was like fighting five gladiators. "Better... quit... while you're... ahead."

Joseph laughed. "I'll worry when you can fight me without drooling on yourself. Remind me to double your laps—you need better endurance."

"Remind me..." Michael huffed, his arms now aching, "... to remind you."

Joseph grinned and shouted, "At ease, soldiers!"

The fighting stopped and Michael leaned on his knees, catching his breath. Joseph wasn't even winded.

"Three of you are still standing," Joseph announced. "So you may now call yourselves by your official name in the Games—the *Two/thirteen.*" Squads were identified by the Circles and Hexants they represented, and the island was off the coast of the Second Hexant, in the new, official Thirteenth Circle.

"Two/thirteen!" Joseph called out as he grabbed Michael's wrist and raised it high. "Meet your new Champion!"

Zillah, Hoot, and Bernard crossed their arms and bowed, along with the fallen gladiators from Joseph's squad. Asher stood in the healing circle, staring, and finally bowed last. After a few beats, he turned and headed toward the armory.

Michael bowed back, taking it all in. Maybe he hadn't worked out every detail of his plan—namely, preventing his hands from also being lopped off—but at least he was one step closer to claiming Champion's Legacy.

"You'd better toughen up that precept," Joseph murmured, pulling him from his thoughts. "He had at least three chances for drop shots, and he didn't take them."

"The precept likes to heal," Michael said. "Let's let him heal."

"What was that thing?" Joseph quirked a brow.

"A healing stone," Michael said. "In the fray it can help with superficial wounds... Which reminds me; the angel who invented it... she'd like to join our triage unit."

19

Trudy

*"Those who are smart will keep their friends close; but the
wise will keep their threats even closer."*
-Black Manifesto, Chapter One, "On Reality"

"OUR SCHOLAR ISN'T HERE yet?" Lord Manuel asked, pulling a chair out for Trudy to sit at the conference table between Zuriah and Raphael. His casual robe and tousled hair were a contrast to the sharp frocks and ruffles the Tech lords wore across the table.

"Samyasa was summoned to the Second Circle by some of the Headmaster Scholars," Lucifer answered, folding his hands in front of him. "I approved his travel. Apologies for not informing Angelic Resources. We've been quite busy."

Lords Baalael and Azazel sat on either side of him, and Trudy remained vigilant of what thoughts she entertained. Her plan hinged on reestablishing a connection with Lucifer, and for that to work, he had to trust her.

"No worries." Ruphius stood gazing through a stained-glass window. "I've asked Azrael to record the meeting in Samyasa's absence." A silent scholar appeared in the doorway as he finished his sentence, and Trudy startled.

"I wasn't aware Samyasa announced his departure," Lucifer said.

"He didn't." Ruphius turned from the window and found a seat between Raph and Manny. "Call me an astute observer."

Azrael stepped into the room and took his place in the corner, like a cryptic, unsettling statue.

"Would anyone care for refreshments before we start?" Manny motioned to the notably scarce silver platter at the center of the conference table. Fortunately, nobody ate because there wasn't enough for everyone. He made the requisite premeeting attendance announcement, and then got right down to business.

"I trust our technical department hasn't had any further issues delaying the project?"

Lucifer smiled. "We're trying a new approach. I foresee no more delays."

"Looks like you two can take a rest." Manny smiled at Trudy and Zuriah. "You're welcome to stay anyway—there are some exciting topics on the agenda."

"We'd like that," Trudy said. Leaving without speaking to Lucifer first was definitely not part of *her* agenda.

"Can we get an update on a name for the artificial intelligence?" Manny asked. "I believe last time we were considering 'Raphkind'?"

"Mankind," Raphael corrected. "Your name was written on the lot we drew."

"Even better." Manny smiled brightly and took a note. "And what about the interface? Do we have an update on Eden?"

"Of course," Lucifer said. "The scholars are linking the Extra Dimensional Existential Nodes in the Creative Center's library as we speak, next to the quantum servers. With Raphael's designs, I'm confident we will have a pleasant stay in Eden while we train Mankind."

"Excellent," Manny said, setting down his quill and turning to Raphael. "I think we're all excited to see Eden's preliminary design. Are you ready to present?"

Raphael's lavender eyes blazed as he smiled and pulled out his qube, setting it on the table. "The inspiration's been sublime. Even Lucifer was inspired to contribute a design of his own, which is really quite lovely."

"That's curious...." Ruphius said, inspecting his fingernails. All eyes moved to him and he looked up. "Did I say curious? I meant *courteous*. How very *courteous* of him."

"I'm no great artist like my brother," Lucifer said, "but I was inspired to paint a simple apple. We never do know who or when His inspiration will strike, do we?"

"Amen to that." Manny nodded, and Trudy exchanged a glance with Zuriah.

Raphael rubbed his hands together and initiated the hologram, navigating to the proper file. "My team has worked hard on this, so I'm going to display it in full graphic mode. If someone could draw the shades...."

Ruphius got up and unlatched the curtains, dimming the room significantly.

"I do hope you all like it," Raphael said and selected a file.

Instantly, the room transformed into a dense, tropical paradise. Trudy's breath caught. Sounds of exotic birds mingled with monkeys and elephants in the distance, and braided vines covered in long strips of moss hung from lush trees whose branches exploded at their tips in colorful flowers. Large cats and monkeys and birds alike peeked through the branches, nibbling on the plump fruit that hung there.

The graphics in the Creative Center were outstanding.

At the center was a tree that Trudy knew well—a Tree of Life—and from it hung healthy, yellow skinned vita, looking soft and ripe to the touch. Their sweet smell filled the scene, and though they weren't real, her mouth watered as the result of the exceptional sensory effects. It had been a while since she bit into a good fruit like that.

"The Garden of Eden," Raphael announced, sounding satisfied. "Rich with creatures of land, water, and sky. There are multitudes of unique trees and plants to eat from, and plenty of fresh springs from which to bathe and drink." He swiped a hand across the air, and the tropical garden surrounding them rotated. He navigated their vantage point down a path and zoomed into one of the many fruit trees. It grew larger and larger until it took up the entire room, and Trudy felt as if she'd climbed into it.

"I'd be remiss to not exalt Lucifer's contribution, which was impressive for a musician. I must say, it does look delectable."

In front of them hung dozens of glossy fruit in a deep purple shade—almost black—and only slightly larger than her fist. They looked ripe and sweet.

"It's just an apple," Lucifer said, humbly. "I'm not much of an artist, but I was deeply inspired."

"It's beautiful," Raphael said. "And a testament to how well we can still work together. You've done well, brother."

Trudy's stomach turned, but Zuriah gave her wrist a squeeze. She kept a tight leash on her thoughts.

Raphael closed the file, and the conference room went back to normal. Ruphius opened the shades.

"Seems we're back on track." Manny rubbed his hands together. "All that's left are the designs for Mankind."

"Ruphius thinks an artist-in-training looks promising," Raphael said. "We'll see where the inspiration lands."

"A delay by the Almighty himself." Baalael yawned and stretched. "Maybe Trudy can fix that one too."

"Divine timing isn't delay," Manny said. "You know that. The inspiration will come. Azrael, please close the record. This meeting is adjourned."

Zuriah looked back with a nod of encouragement as Trudy hid behind a wall under the central dome, waiting for Lucifer. Lords Baalael and Azazel had practically sprinted from the room, but Lucifer stayed behind to chat with his other siblings.

After a few measures, footsteps click-clacked against the marble floor and she straightened, pushing her hair behind her ears.

"Hiding doesn't become you, Temperance," Lucifer said before he could see her. "Or maybe you're not hiding at all." The footsteps grew louder and he emerged in the crossing, tipping his hat to her.

"I was hoping to have a word, m'lord."

"M'lord?" He raised his eyebrows. "And to think I was under the impression that you were displeased with me. To what do I owe the pleasure of your conversation, Temperance? After you so coolly dismissed my apology."

"Maybe we can talk outside?"

He regarded her for a beat, then nodded. "After you."

She led him down the hall and through the immense double doors of the Creative Center, which he opened for her. They walked down the path for a while, remaining quiet until there was no one in earshot. Random yellow and brown leaves were scattered, some even crunching under their feet.

"So concerned with privacy," Lucifer remarked. "If I didn't know better, I'd think you were hiding something."

"May I speak plainly, m'lord?"

He stopped walking and smirked. "You've grown much bolder, Temperance."

She nodded. "Maybe. But I feel I can be honest with you, even if some of my feelings are... unorthodox."

"Please," he motioned a bench in the grass, and they sat, "speak freely."

"I regret being so hasty in transferring and severing our connection. I allowed the weakness of my own constitution to blind me from the benefits of your leadership."

He sat back and folded his arms. "Much has changed since we last spoke, then?"

"When we last spoke my feelings were still offended. You and the other lords treated me poorly, and that was undeserved. But feelings are fickle, and I should've accepted your apology."

She couldn't read his expression, gaze fixed ahead as he listened, but he reached over and put his hand on hers gently as she spoke.

"I'm not offended anymore," Trudy said, plainly, "and I still want what you have."

She let her thoughts echo her words and ring their truth in her gut. She absolutely wanted what he had. Wisdom.

He gave her hand a little squeeze. "As you regret, so do I. It was always my intention to take the most brilliant minds and keep them close. Yours is the most brilliant yet."

"I don't fit in anywhere," Trudy said. "I see too much, and I don't know where else to turn."

"What is it that you see, Temperance?" He met her eyes this time, boring into her thoughts so hard that she could feel the tendrils of his mind like a numbness reaching inside of her head. She kept the truths she wanted him to know upfront.

"I see a foolish, mentally weak world," she said, "patiently waiting for a Creator to save them as their lights go out and their food supply dwindles. I see dullards pretending everything's alright, even as we stand at the brink of collapse. What's more disturbing, though, is what I don't see..."

"And what's that?"

"I don't see a Master Hand at work. I don't see an Ever-Guiding-Intelligence holding the world afloat. What I see is a nursery story told by nannies. I see nature, well-versed and a long time in its making, doing what it does. There is no Almighty, sir. No hand is coming to save us from the darkness."

"And why bring this to me?"

"Because I've seen you ignore the Handbook and all its ideas when that door was closed and nobody was looking. You probably realized all this long ago.... I want what you have. I want to know what you know. I want your eons of learning and observing."

And all of it was true. She let those thoughts and feelings flood her, so he had no doubts about her sincerity.

He tilted his head back and chuckled.

"Is something funny?" Heat rose to her cheeks.

"No, Temperance. Peace." He patted her hand. "I can't begin to make you understand how your request delights me. You're the brightest angel I've ever had the pleasure of teaching. But I'm about to embark on a journey—and I'm unsure when I'll return. My squad is about to qualify for the Games, and at the very least, I want to see them through the tournaments. Perhaps we can further discuss this when I get back."

"Take me with you," Trudy said, a note of desperation in her voice. The only commodity more valuable than vita right now was time.

He knitted his brow. "You do realize this will be a commitment that goes beyond the walls of this campus? I can teach you, yes, but your learning will be on my terms." He reached into the lapel of his jacket and pulled out a small black book and handed it to her. "Like you said... I realized many things long ago. In order to truly learn, first you must serve. But I'll not deceive you. Free will, above all. If you can finish this book before the silence falls, and still want to come with me, then come you will. On my terms."

Trudy took the book and nodded, meeting his eyes. "I'll read it, and come find you with my decision."

"Good. Now, if you'll excuse me... you have some reading to do, and I have an apple to code. Be well, Temperance."

20

Michael

"Words and deeds will be consequenced. Measure for measure, utterance for utterance, action for action. And the scales with which we discern the just from the unjust will herein and henceforth be known as justice."
-Military Manual, Prelude to the Law

M ICHAEL'S TIME WITH AZRAEL sat in the pit of his stomach like an indigestible lump of snog. As much as he wanted to dismiss the bizarre, hooded Scholar, he couldn't. So he lay in his bed before the first bells and tried to focus on his breath.

He inhaled deeply, and trickled the air out through his mouth.

But the decorative plaster on his ceiling kept taking on new shapes. A smudge that peaked into the tip of a sword. A depression shaped like a shield. An oval splotch that looked like the bag he should've been packing instead of lying there.

And then there was the qualifying tournament he was about to fight. Not to mention, the whole squad had yet to be issued their uniforms. And he couldn't forget to pack the vita Mary sent with him, just in case.

And of course, Philistina was coming.

He grimaced and sat up, throwing the covers off. *So much for the breath work.* He grabbed a tunic from the back of his chair and packed his bags.

The walk across campus to the armory was depressing. Angels were noticeably paler, the vita rationing finally starting to show. Bellies stayed full on wheat and barley, but he knew too well the early symptoms of starvation. Stubborn indoctrination maintained their cheerful dispositions, but there was no telling how long that would last. Thankfully, the trees Philistina had planted in the meadow were already beginning to mature.

The doors of the armory were propped open, and Joseph was inside polishing black chest plates hanging from pegs. "Yours is right there," he said and pointed to a uniform.

"What kind of material is this?" Michael ran his finger along the cool black surface. "Some kind of stone?"

"Almost," Joseph said. "The armor itself is steel, but it's plated with an obsidian alloy. Scholars say it can be infused with enhancements, but they're not quite there yet. They're working on plating our swords with it too."

Michael wasn't about to do anything to his sword, but the armor looked sharp. "There are scholars in our Order?"

"Quite a few," Joseph said as he rubbed some kind of oil on the black plate.

"What about Azrael?"

"High Master Azrael?" Joseph paused. "No. He can't know about any of this. How do you know Azrael?"

Michael cleared his throat. Now was as good a time as any to come clean, especially knowing how much Joseph despised Baalael. "I arrived here before you sent the invitation because I received a Calling to come. They want me to be an artist, and Azrael is giving me lessons."

"Art lessons? Why didn't you tell me?"

"Same reason you didn't tell me you were at the wedding to recruit me for a rebellion," Michael said. "Less is more. And Baalael had just tried to have me mauled, remember?"

Joseph's face soured at the mention of Baalael's name, and he went back to polishing. "Fair."

"Besides," Michael said, picking up a helm by its long, crimson horn, "I have no interest in being an artist, and they have no problem letting me pursue the Games."

"All the more the reason to qualify then," Joseph said. "Stay away from Azrael. He's dangerous."

"Dangerous?" Michael put down the helm. "I thought the scholars were just creepy precepts with better skillsets."

"Spoken like a true commonborn." Joseph shook his head. "Listen to me—scholars are ancient as the lords and their wisdom reaches back before history. Azrael is their High Master. Lucifer doesn't even know the extent of him. Under no circumstance should he be trusted or informed of anything. Avoid him best you can. When you don't understand something, consider it a threat."

Those last words gave Michael pause. "Is that also one of your philosophies? To destroy what you can't understand?"

"I didn't say destroy him, I said avoid him. It's not my philosophy, but there's wisdom in it still."

"Words from the Black Manifesto, then?"

"You'd know if you read it."

"I did read it." Or at least, he skimmed it. "I find the Military Manual much more interesting."

Joseph paused his polishing, his lips curling just slightly. "It's not often a dancing bear gets the chance to leave a legacy of words." He set down his rag and reached into the armoire. "Before I forget..." He pulled out a folded, crimson cape and handed it to Michael.

"What's this?"

"You'll wear it when you enter and exit the pit."

Michael unfurled it. The red cape was similar to Joseph's, except the bottom hem was embroidered with black snakes that were almost reminiscent of flames, and Lucifer's sigil was sewn on its back.

"It's a Legion Commander's cape," Joseph said. "You're not there yet, but optics are important. We want everyone to associate this cape and its sigil with competence and power. You'll wear it during the tournaments, and my hope is that you'll eventually earn the right to wear it outside of the arena, in the fields and in our camps."

"A legion is over two thousand soldiers," Michael said, holding up the cape. "The most I've led is five, including myself."

"You'll be training with the larger groups while we travel. War is new to everyone, but there's an edge to you I've not seen in anyone else. More than ambition."

Ambition was a virtue in the Black Manifesto, but it had been Joseph's words that turned Michael's obsession into purpose. *I fight for justice,* he wanted to say, but he couldn't tell his secrets to Joseph. It was bad enough his own mind was accessible to the lords—there was no reason to have his secrets floating around two minds.

"For what it's worth," Joseph said, "I'm glad you're the candidate who turned out to be our Champion. I think you can earn much more than this red cape and an athletics trophy."

Michael had every intention of earning more than that, but he asked anyway. "Such as?"

"I think you can take the pearl helm from that graceless pig and become Master of the Games," Joseph said, plainly. "The rules of the Games will supersede our Military Law while you're in that pit. It'll be the only opportunity we have to face down a superior."

"We?" Michael furrowed his brow. "You want justice then? For what he did to you?"

"What I want isn't relevant," Joseph said. "What is relevant though, is that when Baalael loses that vote—and he *will* lose—he'll make a move to usurp power. And as the Principality of the military, he'll be able to do it too. Senior leadership have all trained under him at one point or another. Then the whole world will be in danger. Lucifer's too blinded by family loyalty to see what's right in front of him—he's an idealist. But nobody will follow Baalael if they see he's weak. If you can claim Legacy and defeat him in front of the world, he'll be powerless." Joseph smirked. "If he happens to lose his hands during the fight, even better."

"Is that why you wanted to scout a Champion outside of the military?" Michael asked. "So they wouldn't be loyal to him?"

"Partly," Joseph admitted, wiping his hands on a clean rag. "But we also felt strongly that the best talent might still be out there, so we compromised and sourced fighters from within our ranks, and then sourced you. Asher and Zillah were chosen carefully: Asher would do anything for glory, and Zillah bleeds honor. She'll protect this world at any cost. The Games are the only place to stop him without breaking Military Law. Lucifer knows none of this, so please... this conversation stays between us."

"Impressive strategy." Michael raised his eyebrows. "But what's to stop Baalael from cheating again? Like he did with you?" It was a problem Michael needed to solve anyway. Might as well try and get some help with it.

"Things are different now than they were then," Joseph said. "If I have my way, he won't be able to cheat. I'm working on it."

Michael laid the cape over his armor. "I'll do my best to lead us to victory, then. And if I do, the pearl helm will be mine."

"Good," Joseph said, then blew on the oil as if to dry it. "I just wanted you to know how much was at stake before you got in there later. This is more than a public relations effort. Now suit up, soldier. Let's see how you look in uniform. And shave that rodent from your face. We need to look presentable."

"Yes, sir." Michael bowed the salute, and Joseph bowed in response, but as he did, a golden locket tumbled from under his chestplate and clinked to the floor. There was a picture on the inside panel.

Joseph snatched it up and shoved it back into his armor.

"I didn't take you for the jewelry type," Michael said.

"I'm not. This brings luck in that arena. She was the greatest fighter I've ever trained. In fact... you remind me of her sometimes."

21

X

"This one can dance, and this one, he sings! This one makes jewelry: bracelets and rings. No matter our Calling, or if we have wings; we can have fun, and learn some new things!"
-Heaven's Handbook, Mindsets, Part 4, "On Learning"

"**B**UBBY?" ANTOINETTE CALLED OUT. "Bubby, where are you? Everyone will be awake soon—they'll be looking for you."

She refused to call him X when nobody was around, even though he insisted on it. *Bubby* was cute and childish. At thirteen, he hadn't been either of those for quite some time.

He sat in his underground fort sharpening his sword with the whetstone he stole from the equipment closet. It was so sharp it could split a hair, but he still didn't know how to wield it, so he just kept on sharpening. Baalael had begun teaching the other children to fight, and it wouldn't end well for him if he couldn't protect himself. Or Gabriel, for that matter.

"Bubby?" Her voice got closer, and footsteps crunched twigs near the secret entrance. "Please say you haven't run away again. Oh dear..."

X rolled his eyes and stuck his head through the thick, leafy canopy. "I'm here, Antoinette."

She ran over and crouched, pushing some brush aside. "Bubby! If they find this place they'll put you in the cellar again."

"You'll be punished too if they hear you call me bubby." He went back to sharpening the sword.

She crawled inside and raised her eyebrows. He'd constructed quite the underground lair out here, safe from the prying eyes of the manor. He dug the hole with the shovel he stole from the landscaper, then nabbed a saw from the shed to cut the branches that framed it out. The hammer and nails were easy to nick from the maintenance closet, as were the brackets and washers. The oil lamps were a little trickier, so he stole two for good measure.

"I'd never have spotted this if you hadn't called back."

"That's the point."

The entrance to the fort blended perfectly with the landscape. You could walk over it without ever knowing you were stepping on a door. He continued scraping the whetstone along the sides of his blade, the fire from the lantern dancing in its reflection.

"If they ever find this place, Bubby..." She glanced around. "I shudder to think—"

"They won't," he cut her off. "They're full of themselves, and being full of yourself makes you dull."

"Sometimes I wonder where you find all your courage."

So did he. The punishment for his painting stunt should've broken him, along with every punishment after that. But once you've spent a full movement locked in pitch darkness, alone, there's not really much you're afraid of anymore. They should've kept simply being mean. It was when they became cruel that the fear left him.

"I know you like to take things," she said, her gaze moving over the clutter of stolen things he'd stashed down there, "and I won't tell anyone, but someone *will* come looking for *that*." She gestured to his sword.

"I found it."

"Where?"

"In the woods."

Doubt colored her face, and he couldn't blame her.

"If anyone comes looking for it, they won't need much of a reason to blame you. Are you sure nobody was around when you found it?"

He thought of the figure that watched him pull the sword from the tree. He shrugged, and then lied. "Nobody was around."

"Oh." She picked up the lantern and stepped to the corner. "Is that a new drawing?"

X dropped the whetstone and snatched his sketchpad away.

"Drawing is better than playing with swords, Bubby. What do you plan on doing with that thing? It's too sharp."

He wouldn't answer stupid questions. Part of him wanted to take the butt of the sword and knock some sense into her. She was an adult, yet she did nothing to change his situation. Or her own. The other part of him loved her because she was kind, even if she did let everyone walk on her.

"Bubby, look at me." She knelt down and pushed the tuft of black hair from his eyes. She'd never stop calling him that stupid name. "Not even gladiator swords are that sharp. Just because we heal quickly, doesn't mean we can't feel pain at the end of a blade."

"How would you know?"

She smirked before taking the sword off his lap. She examined it, feeling its heaviness and moving it around in her hands. "It's got good balance and weight. The steel's strong, but there's flex to it." She cocked her head. "This is too well made to have been discarded in the woods. I know you lie, bubby, but please don't lie to me."

"I found it. Swear on my honor..."

"*Honor?*" Her face paled. "Where did you hear that word?"

"In a book. *Essays by the Ancient Gladiators.*"

"Deidre's acquired quite the library for herself—that book was banned well before I was born. And you've become quite the skilled thief, getting into her personal study."

He shrugged. "Why'd they stop printing it?"

She stared at him, as if deciding whether or not to answer. "Joseph the Champion had a philosophical streak—he wrote most of those essays. But after a while, the Council decided that his ideas were dangerous. Ideas like 'honor' combined virtues like humility and honesty with forbidden things, like power and pride. The lords feared such concepts could confuse the masses; maybe unleash more ideas they couldn't control. So, they stopped printing it, and collected the copies from our libraries and destroyed them. The one asset you have going for you is that you're *not* educated."

"That makes me ignorant."

"That makes you *free*," she said. "You've not been taught what to think—not by the Handbook, and not by anyone here."

"How do you know so much about honor?" X cocked his head. "And swords?"

"You think you know me, little bubby?" Her lips curled. "I was a fine athlete before we met. Archery, running..." she widened her eyes, "*fighting*."

She twirled the sword under her arm and whipped it up into position. X made a little "o" with his lips.

"Before I was sent to perform these... *domesticated arts*, I was trained by Joseph the Champion."

"*You*?" His eyes went wide.

"Don't look so shocked," she chuckled. "Joseph had come to our village one song looking for young angels interested in learning the physical arts. Angels that weren't likely to be called to the arena. He assigned trainers to those of us who were, but took a liking to me and trained me himself. Eventually I became more interested in Joseph than I was in the sword." She smirked. "I ruined many a kerchief that way. "

"You're a *gladiator*?" His eyes went wide.

"No, but something like that. I didn't learn to entertain, but I still learned from the best."

"Teach me." He grabbed her sleeve.

"That's too risky." She freed herself. "For both of us. I'm not here to swing a sword, and if I do there will be consequences. I dare not even think of what they'd do to you."

"*Please.*" He grabbed her again. "If Baalael plans on making the others fight, what do you think he has planned for *me*?"

"Just keep out of sight, bubby. Don't make unnecessary trouble for yourself."

"Trouble finds *me*. I can't hide from it."

She sighed. "It wasn't supposed to be like this. Nobody planned on you showing up. There's so much going on that you can't understand. You need to lay low. Just be like a shadow and don't vex them."

His nostrils flared. "Who do you think they're going to practice on when they learn to swing those swords? You're only worried about getting in trouble yourself."

"That's not true!" She lay the sword back on his lap. "I'm an adult and I've chosen this; whatever it may bring me. It's *you* that I fear for. Baalael has the absurd idea that you're a threat, and he keeps your existence concealed from everyone."

"If they really thought I was a threat, wouldn't they treat me better?" X had heard those whispers, and they utterly baffled him. "I don't even know who I am! How can I be a threat to anyone?"

"I don't know. But that's why they keep you a secret, and treat you as they do."

"And *you* help them," X spat.

"I have no choice, bubby." She put her hand on his again and her eyes welled. "There are things you can't understand."

"When I run, he finds me. When I hide, he finds me. I have to fight."

"He's a god, bubby. *You cannot fight a god.*"

"I can try...."

"You *can't*," she rasped, gripping his chin. "He's done things... unspeakable things. If he knew how much you stole he would cut off your hands—and wounds like that never really heal, even if the limbs eventually grow back. You need to show him you're harmless. Stay quiet like a mouse and stop stealing."

X had spent countless silences, awake, playing that very threat over and over in his mind. He'd been caught stealing once, and the threat of losing his hands was enough to never get him caught again. No more drawing. Or painting. No hope of learning to swing his sword. But to obey would be to submit, and he could *never* do that.

He clenched his jaw. "You say you can fight, but what good is that when you're a *coward*? Or maybe you're just as cruel as they are."

Her eyes welled further, which gave him an odd sense of satisfaction.

"You have no idea the strength it takes to restrain myself and hold hope. There's more at stake than you understan—"

"It's simple to understand!" he growled. "You're a coward, and my life is *worthless*."

"Don't say that!"

"I only wish there was a way to end it."

His words hung in the air, and her blinking eyes overflowed. More than a measure passed without words.

"I suppose you're not wrong about my being a coward," she whispered, "but your life is not worthless, sweet angel. You were never worthless."

"Then *teach* me. Let me at least have a chance when the brothers come for me. They'll come for Gabriel too, because he's soft and slow."

She rubbed her arms as if warming a chill, blinking the tears away. She picked up the sword and traced a finger along its edge, the cold steel glinting.

When she looked up again, there was something in her eyes. A fierceness Michael had never seen before. "If we do this, you must follow all of my directions... I'll train you during the silence when everyone's asleep, and when you're out here hiding, you must run and do all the exercises I show you. Without speed and strength, training means nothing. I'm no gladiator, little *X*. I'm far worse than that. My training exceeds anything Baalael can teach the little snogs on this estate. Lords are weak without their birthright. They're overconfident and dull and can't train up a real fighter. Never repeat that—but know that they are. And you can't breathe a word of this to anyone. Not a word. Do you understand?"

He nodded, afraid to say anything, lest she change her mind. He'd talk her into training Gabriel later.

"We'll store our equipment in this burrow. Anything you don't have, you'll steal. You'll follow my orders without question, and push yourself until you can't anymore. Those are the conditions of my training." She bore into his eyes. "Do you have any questions?"

He paused and swallowed hard. He did have *one* question.

"I read something else in Joseph's essay...."

She narrowed her eyes.

"He said anyone called to the arena might become a Champion, and that if a Champion can win the Final Battle, they might claim *Champion's Legacy*."

"Is that why you want to learn?" She narrowed her eyes. "You dream of being called to the arena and taking Baalael's title?"

Master of the Games. When she put it that way, he felt ashamed. Not ashamed to want to get into a pit with that miserable god, but ashamed because he was a nobody, and would probably never even get a Calling, much less to the arena.

"I won't train you to entertain delusions." She crossed her arms. "Is that the real reason you want to learn?"

He shook his head. "I swear—I was only curious. I just want to learn to protect myself."

She examined his face like she could detect a lie, but she couldn't. Nobody could ever detect his lies, which was what made him an excellent thief.

"Good," she said, "because I won't be teaching you to fight as a gladiator. Gladiators are skilled fighters, but the arena is for entertainment."

He knitted his brow. "If I won't learn to fight as a gladiator, what will I learn?"

She stabbed the sword straight through the ground, and it wobbled. "You're going to learn how to *crush* any angel who ever tries to hurt you. And let them have fun healing *that*."

22

Michael

"First impressions become a bias, whether one likes to admit so or not. Impressions stick, so make sure others see exactly what you want them to. Optics are everything."
-Black Manifesto, Chapter Two, "On Power"

MICHAEL WASN'T HAPPY ABOUT having to shave his beard, but if Baalael was going to figure out who he was, realistically, a few whiskers on his chin probably wouldn't prevent that.

He pushed the thin curtain of the armory window aside and watched as angels from the Second Hexant poured in from the ferry making their way through the arena, waving little flags that represented their home crossings. The smell of rootroast pastes and snog fritters made his mouth water as more cooks from the outdoor eatery popped up in makeshift kitchens and prepared food for the fans. It smelled delicious, and probably was, but none of it had any vita. That was only distributed to residents now, and in rations.

Servants from the Order of Light peppered the bleachers in their long black robes, handing out crimson flags with Lucifer's black sigil. As the official sponsor of this new squad, nobody blinked at his sigil branding.

And if the Two/thirteen performed the way Joseph was so confident they would, Lucifer would win the entire realm's trust through sports.

But not everyone believed they'd qualify. In exchange for the extra competition, the Second Hexant officials would get to send *two squads* into the championship battle, which they gladly agreed to. The consensus among the other athletes, however, was that this new, amateur squad from "Technology Island" would be the first to fall. Nobody was afraid to fight a bunch of "desk chairs".

But soldiers weren't trained in the same way gladiators were. And soldiers—or at least these soldiers—had more than a little glory to fight for.

"Chestplate's a little snug 'round me belly," Bernard said, grabbing the excess slab that peeked out from under his faux-obsidian abs.

"Lay off all that wheat and you'll be fine," Joseph said. "Soldiers don't need to ration manna. The Order's made arrangements for us."

"Michael," Hoot leaned into his ear. "I meant to tell you—the angels who attacked us in the darkness wore similar armor."

"They wore these uniforms?"

"No. Black and silver, but the style was similar."

"Obsidian must be the new trend," Michael said. "Might've been locals protecting what little resources they had left. You should've stated your business."

"How could we state our business when we were running?"

"Thieves run."

"... I don't know." Hoot looked down at his wrist guards. "These uniforms just feel dark."

"They are dark," Michael said, "and if you don't get comfortable with the darkness, it's going to eat you up. You'd better swing that sword out there."

An awkward beat passed before Michael changed the subject. "What about Philistina?"

"She's waiting at the sidelines with the rest of the triage techs."

Michael patted Hoot's shoulder and then clapped twice to get everyone's attention. "This is a brawl, not a ball! Let's get moving!"

Michael clipped his cape to the tips of his chestplate and Zillah finished slipping daggers in the sheaths at her calves. Everyone fastened their helms and picked up their shields.

This otherwise sweet bunch looked fairly terrifying in their obsidian armor and scarlet horns. Their shin and wrist guards sported sharp spikes at the top, and they marched to the front of the armory and stood in a straight line, just like they'd learned in training.

Michael slipped on his black helm by its red, twisted horns and stood in front of them. "Remember—we're not here because anyone saw fit to recognize our potential as athletes. Nobody saw what we were capable of except ourselves. We've worked hard and earned this opportunity, so have pride in that. Pride is alright when you've earned it."

"And these uniforms..." Joseph appeared next to him. "These uniforms are more important than any one of us individually. The world needs to trust us so we can protect them. Be fearless and stay focused. Dispatch your enemies quickly, and with efficiency."

Hoots' gaze dropped to the floor, but Michael stomped and it snapped up again. The squad marched into a vertical line behind him, and Joseph opened the door. Their steps locked in a synchronized rhythm like an ominous drumbeat against the stone path, and Michael could feel the wind as it billowed his cape behind him.

Fans stopped in their tracks and stared as the Two/thirteen advanced from the armory. Other gladiators in plain, brown leathers stood frozen, gazes fixed.

"First rule of engagement," Joseph said as he marched beside Michael, "is *fear*. If you can get your enemy to fear you, the fight's already half won. And anyone who fears you will want to join you, so our recruiters will be at the ready after every tournament."

Everyone gawked as they marched, one unit, stomping in sync around the perimeter of the pit. The crowd stayed silent, and those broad-chest-ed fighters who had been strutting around like peacocks just a few measures ago now stood motionless, apprehension glazing their eyes.

"Nobody's calling us 'desk chairs' now," Michael mumbled.

Gladiators might have looked strong, but under all that strength and armor they were just ordinary, weak-minded angels that had never tasted a drop of real pain. All it took was something a little different... a little darker to rattle them up. Flirting with the idea of pain was the whole allure of the Games, but when the wings hit the wind, even the gladiators were weak.

The squad got to the lip of the pit, and Joseph made a show of ceremoniously removing Michael's cape and folding it carefully. Photo-machines flashed on tripods as sports journalists were the first to shake from their stupors. The world had never seen anything like a soldier before.

Michael threw a hand signal, and the Two/thirteen bowed before their opponents, then descended to the dirt. The other twelve squads parted to make way for them, exchanging nervous glances.

Michael moved his gaze upward. The haze was thick, and healing would be slow. He wasn't worried about himself, Zillah, or Asher, but Bernard preferred attacking with brute force rather than his sword, and Hoot... well, Hoot preferred not attacking at all.

Philistina waited in the first row with the rest of the triage techs, all in plain white robes with a purple triangle sewn in the shoulder. Normally they'd just minister to the angels in the healing circle as they soaked in the light. But now that the light was dimming, they'd actually have work to do.

A snare drum popped and rattled, and the entire crowd stood and harkened to attention. Two of the three judges appeared, wearing yellow robes with the gray judge's sash. Michael recognized them as former long-time Champions, gladiators who held the title for several symphonies. They walked the perimeter of the pit, stopping in front of Joseph and bowing the salute. Joseph bowed back, and they continued to their seats at the head of the pit. Between their seats was something like a throne, which was reserved for the Master of the Games.

A luminous blue light flew toward them from behind the campus gates, tremendous wings outstretched from either side of him. A lord in full glory. The Lord of Victory, also known as Baalael, Master of the Games. He was the third and tie-breaking judge.

His wingspan was nearly the width of the whole pit, and dust kicked up from the ground with each powerful thrust, whipping everyone's hair around. Shadows stretched out from every angle as his bright glory basked everything in blue light. He was a marvel of beauty for anyone who didn't truly know him.

He landed at the edge of the pit, nearly blinding the crowd, and held up his hand. All his glory condensed into a bright orb centered around his ring, then shot in the direction of the well. A wingless Baalael emerged from the light wearing the signature pearl armor of the Games.

Show off.

He stopped in front of Joseph, chest out, with his hands clasped behind his back. Joseph bowed the gladiator salute, but Baalael didn't bow back. Instead, a sweat broke out on Joseph's forehead as his muscles went taut and he shook. Slowly, he lowered to one knee and bowed before the cruel lord.

Michael gritted his teeth. Joseph would never do that on his own—he was being forced. Baalael grinned as he turned his back to Joseph and sat in his glorified armchair.

The first judge stood up and held a whistle to his mouth and Michael readied himself, but another bright orb approached from the sky, and everyone looked up.

This was a golden light, much brighter than Baalael, and it sailed on a stream of song. Graceful white robes floated ethereally around him, and his wingspan was nearly the size of the whole arena. A drumbeat pulsed from him that rattled the ground, and sounds of cello and violin built up to a crescendo. The crowd began clapping along.

Underneath him marched an entourage in black robes, all holding baskets. "Manna cakes and vita frittes! Hot and fresh!" the servants hollered, swarming the stands and giving away the provision along with crimson and black flags. The crowd cheered wildly, grasping for the food.

Baalael watched with his eyes narrowed, and Michael chuckled.

Lucifer landed and beamed his glory to the well. He approached Joseph and kissed him once on either cheek, garnering even more applause, and then sat in the stands with everyone else, humbling himself next to the commonborn. Everyone waved his little flags and cheered.

Now *that* was pure genius.

The judge raised the whistle to his lips again and the squads got into position. It blew, and Michael signaled. The Two/thirteen formed a circle, backs to one another, and lunged into offense as the chaos of thirteen battling squads broke out.

It didn't take long, however, to realize that the other gladiators were avoiding them. Zillah was able to pick some off at a distance with her daggers, but the rest of them had to practically chase down opponents. Maybe their uniforms were a little *too* intimidating.

The numbers in the pit were dwindling, but optics were a key part of this mission. The Two/thirteen needed some kind of show.

Michael left the formation and went to the center of the pit, flinging his helm and his shield to the ground. Then he tossed his sword, rendering himself defenseless.

"What are you doing?" Hoot hissed.

The crowd took notice and began fixing their eyes on where he stood, center pit.

"This is too dangerous!" Hoot ran over. "You'll get hurt."

"Don't let me get hurt, then." Michael opened his arms wide and slowly spun.

Several of the opposing gladiators inched closer, and began to circle.

"A whole loaf of manna for anyone who can land a shot," Michael called out.

They swung at him, but Michael danced between their striking swords. He pivoted behind one and dropped him with a sweep from behind, stomping his wrist and taking his sword. The crowd stood up, eyes on Michael, clapping and hollering.

The other gladiators began to back away, so Michael tossed that sword and beckoned them forward again. Lucifer was now on his feet, cheering with everyone else. Two more gladiators lunged from either side, but Michael ducked and spun, flinging the one at his right into the one at his left. They tumbled and he pounced like a cat and swiped one of their shields, swiftly using it to bludgeon their faces. Light exploded from their wounds and they pulled their flags.

The crowd got louder, every section now cheering for Michael regardless of what flag they held.

A little more than half a dozen gladiators remained fighting at the far end of the pit—two other squads trying to pick one another off. Wouldn't it be something if they all tapped out, and only the desk chairs ended up representing the Second Hexant? Everybody loved an underdog.

"Formation!" Michael threw up a hand signal and the squad formed a V behind him. "When I call the next move, don't hesitate. We need them all to tap out at the same time."

"What are you trying to do?" Asher asked.

"Be the only ones left."

They advanced, and the gladiators stopped fighting each other and turned their attention to the Two/thirteen. Michael clapped his wrist guards twice, and the squad broke V, fanning at his flanks before charging. Bernard was the first to employ the signature shin stomp that Michael had taught them—not the kind of thing you learned in gladiator school. A series of painful crunches, followed by screams echoed from the opponents—all but one.

Hoot volleyed his opponent while the rest were moaning in the dirt, on the brink of tapping out.

"Zillah!" Michael barked. "Finish that!"

She flung a dagger through his challenger's sword arm, and he pulled his yellow flag.

The crowd erupted. Hollers and whistles filled the air, and anyone who'd waved another flag now waved Lucifer's. Even Lucifer waved a flag wildly, cheering between bites of a root sausage roll. Lord or common-born—angels loved their sports.

Michael glanced at Philistina, who rolled her eyes and went back to healing. Joseph bolted into the pit and grabbed Michael into a bear hug, lifting him from the ground, and the rest of the squad joined them. The first judge announced the winning squad—the only winning squad. The Two/thirteen would represent the Second Hexant in the Games... *alone.*

23

Michael

THERE WAS STILL ABOUT half a song's worth of travel left before they arrived at the military camp that would lodge the squad for the better part of the Games. Biting wind blew in from underneath the tent fabric as Michael wrapped himself tight in the wool blanket Mary had knitted for him. He was glad she'd made him pack it.

The waning light on the mainland seemed to take the heat right along with it, and the squad made camp in the woods at the outskirts of a village near the Two/ten crossing. Even the mountainous regions of Fourth Hexant, famous for their ice-capped peaks and snowy terrain, had a more pleasant cold than this. At least you could snow-skip and bob there.

This cold was nothing like those glistening slopes where light bounced into shimmering rainbows and angels made merry. This was a gray cold. A looming, bitter cold. And kindling a fire was now on the long list of things a soldier would need to be proficient at.

So they pitched tents and traveled by horseback while the rest of their entourage and triage techs rode in a carriage, opting to lodge at the estates and inns offering hospitality to the traveling athletes. And that was all fine with Michael— at least when things weren't going so well, you didn't wonder when it would all fall apart.

The crackling fire and whipping wind outside were the only sounds that broke the silence in their tent. That and Bernard's snoring.

Michael lay awake by the soft glow of his lantern as he studied the Military Manual. He was fascinated by this concept of *law*—legitimizing actions and words—that Joseph fleshed out. It was a series of verbal and physical conduct codes, enforceable by punishment. Between the ages of around four and fourteen, Michael never knew when his punishments would come, or what they would be for. And after that, Mary never chided him for anything. The law though—it felt balanced. Everyone agreed to a set of expectations and were held accountable to them.

"You're awake?" Philistina's face peeked through the opening of the tent and Michael shot up. She retreated outside, and after scrambling out of the covers, he followed her.

Birds chirped, which meant the first bells would be ringing soon, and a dusting of tiny flakes covered the cold, rocky soil. The snow muted the silence even more, and he regretted not bothering to put on his sandals.

"You're talking to me now?" he whispered, toes freezing.

She ignored him and wiped her hand across a rock, collecting some snow and inspecting it. "It shouldn't be falling here."

"I asked you a question," he said, rubbing the warmth back into his arms. They could lament about the world falling apart later. She hadn't so much as looked at him since the opening tournament.

"You should see yourself when you fight now." She dusted the snow from her hands. "You wouldn't like you either. You're arrogant and proud. The opposite of who you were back home."

"You never saw me compete in a real tournament back home. I'm not arrogant when I fight... I'm competent."

"You strut around like my sisters. Like you're better than everyone else."

"Strut?" He guffawed and blinked the snowflakes off his lashes. "You think I'm arrogant because of my posture?"

Her eyes narrowed. "Precisely because of your posture. It's like someone jammed a stick right up your—"

"You're both up early." Joseph emerged from the tent stretching, and Michael straightened. "First bells haven't even rung yet."

Michael cleared his throat. "Wanted to get a head start on our travels."

"It's too early for lies." Joseph yawned. "You didn't get any sleep either." He put his hands on his hips and surveyed the layer of white covering the ground, snowflakes settling in his dark curls. "Can't fault you for not sleeping, though. We never know what we'll wake up to anymore. Suit up and prepare the horses. I'll distribute the rations before we head out."

"Yes, sir." Joseph went back into the tent and Michael turned to Philistina, but all that remained were her footprints heading in the direction of the inn. Despite the myriad of snowflakes that cluttered the air, the forest felt suddenly empty.

They packed up the campsite and Michael clipped his gear to his saddle before distributing the rations: four small sacks of dried vita that tasted like uncooked broccoli. He didn't take one for himself, relying rather on the provision from Mary's care package. The musty vita from his village was a delicacy compared to this one. Philistina had been smart and packed provisions of her own from the meadow. That vita wasn't too bad.

The squad mounted their horses, looking sharp in their uniforms even if their teeth did chatter. But Asher sat aloft his horse wrapped in a quilt.

"Take it off," Michael sighed. "It's not part of the uniform."

An emotion crossed Asher's face too quickly to evaluate. "Why would I take it off? I'm cold."

"We can't risk being seen parading through the villages like we're afraid of a little cold," Michael said. "And we definitely can't ride into camp clutching knitted quilts."

Asher deadpanned him.

"Chain of command," Joseph said, appearing beside them and mounting his horse. "He's your Champion and he's right; that quilt isn't uniform. They'll distribute warm cloaks and footwear once we arrive. The time to stretch your limitations is now."

Slowly, Asher removed it and shoved it into one of his bags, but he didn't look happy.

"Let's move," Michael said, nudging the horse with his heel. "If we don't stop, we can make camp before the second verse."

They traveled slightly deeper into the center and headed for the southernmost point of the Two/eight crossing. Every village they passed had the gloom, some more than others, but they didn't encounter any active *storms*—as Philistina and Hoot had called them. Instead, they saw the evidence of past storms: broken trees, debris fields, and even some manors and shops reduced to complete rubble. When all was said and done, they would have to revisit the infrastructure and establish new building standards that could withstand the new weather—especially those towering wind funnels that leveled everything in their paths.

On a brighter note, the village inhabitants were even more enthusiastic about the Games than usual. Even in these conditions, they held feasts and tournaments celebrating that one movement of the symphony when everyone was a dedicated sports fan.

Granted, the spreads were thin. Manna rations had become a practice everywhere, and even the wheat loaves looked flat. The fruit and vegetables were undoubtedly smaller, but angels still made due, erecting stands all around their stadiums as they gathered to cheer for their home squads in the local tourneys.

Word had spread through the Second Hexant about the Two/thirteen, largely due to Michael's antics in the qualifier. They rode through the villages to virtual parades, angels laying palm and cypress branches in their path as they cheered them on. Posters hung in the town squares with Michael's image, arms spread and helm off, surrounded by opponents. Photojournalists feasted on the unorthodox spectacle.

Stands and shops traded placards with his image and amateur stats, along with flags that had Lucifer's sigil in exchange for rations of manna and obsidian. Some villages had even started fashioning the obsidian into small, flat pieces they called *coins*. Wares were no longer given away—if you wanted something, you had to give something in exchange, just like he did at that inn. Givers now called themselves merchants, and he didn't mind the strange custom gaining traction. After all, he'd never been comfortable receiving from someone without doing something in return, as if he'd needed their charity.

Philistina refused to so much as look through the carriage window. She kept her face buried in a book, only occasionally lifting it to glare at Michael through slits.

When they finally dropped Philistina and those servants off at the inn, she slammed the carriage door so hard he thought the window might shatter. He was starting to understand why her sisters considered her so disagreeable.

The squad continued past the village to a narrow, unpaved road that led through a forest, and eventually came to a clearing. The military camp was surrounded by an ugly stone wall with cast iron gates that opened to dozens upon dozens of wide black tents, with the occasional red one.

The smell of mud in the camp was thick as they rode through, voices bellowing commands over the ambient sounds of clanging metal and grunts somewhere out of sight. Other soldiers trudged about in the same obsidian armor that the squad wore, except they were covered in thick, black cloaks and had more appropriate footwear for the cold. Blazing fires peppered the camp where soldiers kept warm, sharpening steel or brewing up stews.

About halfway through, they passed a roped-off black tent significantly larger than the rest. Guards lined the perimeter, and a smell so rancid hung around it that Michael buried his nose in his elbow. He had never smelled anything so foul. Before he could ask, a fierce roar came from inside, followed by another. Then screeches and thrashing. Michael's hair stood on end.

"What on the Throne was *that*?" He eyed the structure, grimacing.

"That information is for red capes only," Joseph said. "Real red capes."

The whole squad had buried their noses too. That smell was just *awful.*

"This camp is equipped for a full swarm of soldiers." Joseph changed subjects as they rode past. "The big tents sleep a throng, which is where you'll be staying. We're still building, though. Eventually this will hold a whole legion."

"Can't imagine the kind of havoc that many gladiators can reap," Hoot said.

"Soldiers," Zillah corrected.

"What happened to peacekeepers?" Bernard asked.

"Peace is guaranteed through strength," Michael said, and Joseph smirked at him.

He didn't need any black book to teach him the art of manipulation.

They dropped their horses by makeshift stables and Joseph escorted them to their tent.

Straw-filled beds lay on the ground in rows. They'd be staying here with the other four squads in their throng. The Might that was to lead them slept in a red tent across the way. Michael hoped to meet him sooner rather than later.

They set their things down and settled in while another soldier distributed warm cloaks and boots, which they were grateful for.

Joseph raised his hand before Michael could receive his cloak and shook his head. "He gets the red hem. He's their Champion."

"Black's good enough for the rest of us..." Asher mumbled.

"Everyone's tired," Joseph said, glancing at Asher. "Go to the chow tent and have some dinner, then get rest. You begin training with the whole swarm at the first bells."

Asher shoved his cloak in a bag, and Michael opened his mouth to say something, but Hoot put an arm around his shoulder and whispered, "Everyone's tired, Michael. Let's get something to eat."

Michael was up before the first bells—well before, in fact. He'd managed to get some sleep from the sheer exhaustion of being awake through two consecutive silences, but it was that deep kind that made him wake up more exhausted. He fed the embers under the water pot and heated it, pressing a fresh pitcher of coffee for his squad, and then snuck one of Mary's vita biscuits for breakfast.

When the birds began chirping, he woke the squad and distributed their rations with fresh cups of coffee. When you lived with Mary for that long, some things were just bred into you. They took their breakfast outside, enjoying what was left of the silence.

"Why do you look so disturbed?" Hoot asked after they ate, lacing up his boot.

"Silence will break soon and the throng's still asleep," Michael said. "We're supposed to start training at the first bells."

"I'm sure they have a system in place. We've only just arrived."

"You know how Joseph makes us all run laps when one of us is lazy?" Michael said.

"Yeah..."

"If they're late, we're late." Michael fixed his gaze on the red tent. "I don't want to run extra laps. I'm waking up the Might."

Hoot took a breath to protest, but Michael went back into the tent before he could. He filled a cup with black coffee and set out for the red tent. Joseph stood nearby, talking with another high-ranking officer in a red cloak. They locked eyes from a distance and Michael nodded, acknowledging them. He pushed the fabric of the Might's tent aside and entered.

The Might lay on a proper bed, asleep under the covers. Michael cleared his throat. "First bells are about to ring and everyone's still asleep in there, sir. I brought you coffee."

"Who are you?" the Might grunted from under the pillow, and Michael set the mug down next to him. "And why are you in my tent?"

"My squad arrived at camp before the end of the last chorus. I'm Michael."

"Not the fake fighters from that island," he moaned and rolled over.

Michael frowned. "I thought you could use some coffee—to help you wake up. The swarm's about to run late for training."

"So?"

"There are consequences for being late. It says so in the manual. My squad's traveled a long way and I don't want them exhausted before they can even start training."

"Read your manual again, soldier. I'm not punished for my crew. It's not my job to wake everyone up."

"Leaders set examples," Michael said. "They'll do what you do."

"Your problem, not mine," he said. "Wake them up yourself and get out of my tent... before I put you out of it."

Michael stepped closer to his bed. "I won't let my squad get punished because you're lazy."

His ginger head popped off the pillow. "What did you just call me, *soldier*? I'm your superior and you'll respect that."

"Respect is earned." Michael stalked closer. "And you're not doing a good job earning mine."

The Might grabbed the mug and swung it at Michael's face, but Michael grabbed his wrist mid-swing. He swung his other arm, but Michael caught that one too before head butting him. He cried out and clutched his face as tiny beams of light condensed into blood that escaped from between his fingers. He threw the blankets off and left the tent in his nightgown.

Michael would pay for that one. He followed the Might outside and watched him enter the tent, calling out to wake the soldiers up.

"Well done." Joseph patted Michael's back and he jumped.

"Snuck up on me..." Michael exhaled.

"Enemies don't announce their arrival," Joseph said. "Pay better attention. Cornelius has been complaining about that one." He gestured to the wounded Might who was now leaving the tent.

"Cornelius?"

"The Furie of this swarm. That throng your squad just joined never shows up on time, so I suggested enforcement of our code. He argued with me because that Might is Baalael's little pet." Joseph smirked. "Then you came out with a cup of coffee. I bet that woke him up."

"He swung at me and I lost my temper," Michael said. "I'm sorry. I didn't mean to break rank."

"If he assaulted you first then you'll just have to clean a few chamber pots. Besides, Cornelius barely knows the law himself. It's been no easy task turning these angels into soldiers."

"I'm sure the Might will report me."

Joseph rolled his eyes. "Cornelius needs to get rid of that little rat and he knows it. Baalael only installed him in this camp to spy on them, and he gets away with everything because of it. Now, do me a favor and go show them what real discipline looks like."

The swarm did make it to training on time, which pleased Furie Cornelius. Each squad was identified by their crossing of origin, followed by their number of registry. Being that no other squads were registered from the island, the Two/thirteen retained the same name.

Squads lined up in rows of five throughout the field, and the first exercises they ran were marching exercises. Cornelius clapped in a rhythm, and the soldiers would follow, even if it was completely out of sync with the Music of the Spheres.

Battle training followed, and Michael's squad excelled considering they'd never trained in large groups before. Hoot still wouldn't go on offense, but his defensive acumen impressed everyone, and his little trick with that healing stone kept him in the fight. Zillah was given wooden bars to throw instead of blades, and a dozen angels soon walked around with slow-healing lumps on their heads.

Michael knew how to capitalize their strengths and mitigate their weaknesses. Bernard was like a bowling ball, so you sent him out first, and Hoot would move like the wind to protect him. He kept Zillah on the inside so she had clear shots, and Asher picked up dirty fighting quicker than Michael could teach it.

It wasn't long before Furie Cornelius was using the Two/thirteen as the example of what the others should be doing. The Two/thirteen fought dirty. The Two/thirteen watched each other's backs. The Two/thirteen and their Champion had a near psychic connection where no sooner was an order given, than was it meticulously executed.

Three songs went by, training through the verses and into the choruses. The Might whose nose Michael had broken kept at a distance, but he was awake well before those first bells and making sure everyone else was too.

Until now, Michael hadn't realized how superior their training under Joseph had been. To say nothing of the training he'd received from Antoinette. Still—there was some kind of magic when the Two/thirteen worked together. The squad absorbed everything Michael taught with such ease. And he didn't question it either—he'd take any bit of luck that came his way. The Two/thirteen stood out from the other squads, and he was alright with that.

It meant that it shouldn't be long until their squad elevated rank—that is, so long as other angels' ambitions didn't stand in their way. For every few dozen soldiers that were impressed by them, there was a superior officer cracking their proverbial knuckles. Leadership here was lazy and proud—bad mixture. And the Furie wasn't too sharp. Nobody in their direct line would be looking to acknowledge their shining accomplishments any time soon.

Better to get ahead of these things. If Joseph was game to go along with Michael's plan, they might be moving up the ranks sooner than anyone thought.

Let everyone else rely on the Black Manifesto to learn how to thrive in this dark new world. Michael would rely on experience.

24

X

"Let every word you say be true, a lie will steal a piece of you."
-Heaven's Handbook, Virtues, Part 1, "On Honesty"

X LAID STOMACH DOWN on the bed, turning a page in one of Joseph's essays. A desk chair was propped under the doorknob so no nannies could come barging in. He couldn't afford being caught with stolen things, much less a *book*. As far as they knew, he couldn't even read.

Gabriel tapped the secret knock and X swung his leg, knocking the chair out of place. He came in, out of breath from the trip up the stairs and closed the bedroom door.

"Here..." Gabe held out a mug and a roll. "You must be starving."

X swung his legs over the side of the bed and took the food. "Bold move. Now put the chair back so you don't get caught lifting."

He scarfed down the contents of the mug. It was cold, but the manna was soft and sweet. He plucked up juicy morsels of rootroast with his fingers and shoved them in his mouth, the gravy spilling down his hands and the side of his lips. "I can't believe they let you leave the table with all this."

"They didn't." Gabriel paced. "One of the kitchen maids set it aside for the gardener.... I think she wants him to pick up her kerchief."

"And you took it?" X raised his eyebrows. Gabriel would usually scavenge dish scraps after dinner to feed X, but he'd never take food that wasn't already headed for the compost bin. He didn't like to break the rules.

"Don't look at me like that!" Gabe plopped into the desk chair and pulled another manna roll from his pocket. "I brought this for you too, but I need to calm down." He shoved it into his mouth and got flour on his chin— both of them.

"Have you thought about my question?" X asked.

"All I do is think." Gabe chewed harder.

X dipped the bread in the mug. "It wasn't easy talking Antoinette into training you alongside me. They're all learning to fight. What do you think that means for you?"

"I go with them to the pits."

"Yeah, to clean the equipment and run them water."

Gabriel frowned. "Baalael won't let me train with them. I'm too soft."

It was true, but X wouldn't say it. He wiped a finger on the inside of the mug and licked it clean. "Before you know it, he'll have the archers using you for target practice and you won't even complain for fear of hurting their feelings. You need to learn to protect yourself. Just let Antoinette train you—"

"I don't like breaking the rules."

"You broke the rules by bringing me dinner."

"Doesn't mean I liked it." Gabe jammed the rest of the roll in his mouth and X winced. If he got any bigger, he was going to bust out of his robes.

"The rules are dull," X said. "The adults are dull. And you're dull for listening."

"That doesn't help," Gabriel said with his mouth stuffed. "It's all just so confusing. Not letting you eat with us is wrong, but stealing is also wrong. Learning a sport is good, but breaking rules is bad. Saying 'yes' would make you happy, but that would mean I'm lying."

"The only thing confusing you is that stupid white book you're always reading. You know you're already lying by reading it, right? What do you call that? A lie of commission?"

"Omission." Gabriel pushed up his glasses.

"Yeah, that. There's probably a reason they don't allow that thing in here. Look how confused it makes you."

"Lord Baalael extended his training program to the whole village...." Gabe perked up. "Maybe they'll just fight each other?"

"Or maybe even *more* angels will use us for target practice. If nothing else..." X glanced at the crumbs on Gabriel's robe, "the exercise will do you good."

Gabe slumped. "I still don't like lying."

"Sneaking isn't lying. Technically."

"It's dishonesty."

"It's *creative honesty.*"

"What if I hurt someone?"

"They'll heal right up. *They* don't get locked in the cellar."

"What if you laugh at me."

"Laugh at you?" X sat up straight. "Why would you think that?"

"The others make fun of me whenever I run, because I'm fat."

X's nostrils flared. "So run even harder to prove them wrong."

Gabriel wiped a tear that escaped. It was so easy to make his brother cry, and he did it frequently, though never intentionally. "Don't pretend you don't see what I see, Gabe. He's teaching everyone to fight—except you—and obviously me, but they leave me out of everything. Do the math. You're not safe anymore."

Gabriel put down his roll and squeezed his eyes closed. Little drops rolled down his pink cheeks, under his glasses. "I don't think life is supposed to be like this."

"I don't know how life's supposed to be," X said. "I only know how it is. You need to be stronger, Gabe. Just try."

"We're not supposed to step a foot through those doors after the silence falls."

"So we'll climb through the window." X smiled. "Problem solved."

"It hurts to lie, even though sometimes I have to. It's like I lose little bits of myself."

"You're going to lose *big bits* of yourself if you don't learn to fight back," X said. "They push you around now—imagine when they get good with that steel."

Gabriel's gaze roamed the wooden floor planks, and X set aside the cup and knelt before him. "Just start with exercising. You can't feel bad about exercise."

"I don't like exercising."

"I don't like running, but I feel better after I do. If you try it and don't like it, you can stop. And I'll stop bothering you."

"And I don't have to use a sword? You swear?"

"She made me build strength first. And speed. I had to walk around blindfolded to learn to use my other senses better. She doesn't just put a sword in your hand. C'mon, Gabe..." X stood up and cocked his head. "Manna biscuits and milk?"

Gabe sat there a long beat before looking up, but then a smile tugged his lip. "Vita butter and jam."

"Black tea and honey?"

"Rootroast and mash."

X stretched out his arm and looked at Gabe, expectantly. "A sword and a shield?"

"No sword!"

"I'm the sword," X said, "you can be the shield."

Gabriel smiled as he gripped X's arm and shook. "Fine. You be my sword, and I'll be your shield."

25

Michael

"The animals are all our friends, should they live in trees, or in dens. Just above those pointy claws, are furry, fluffy, friendly paws!"
-Heaven's Handbook, Truths, Part 2, "On Species"

"A WAGER?" CORNELIUS ASKED Michael, turning in his seat.

"If my squad wins," Michael said, "you get a competent Might and your force will be stronger. Then you can demote the Might causing you so much trouble. If we lose, you get my entire collection of obsidian chips."

Not that Michael had any obsidian chips.

Joseph had scheduled the Two/thirteen in some local tournaments to muster up support for the Order. Cornelius sat in the mezzanine of the small arena, enjoying the bloodshed, and contemplating Michael's proposal.

"And how did you come by all of this obsidian?" Cornelius' eyes glossed over as he drained the last sip of empyreanol from his cup. He eyed the bottle on the table, and Michael poured more into his glass.

"Before I was Called to the Eastern Island, I worked as a miner, sir," Michael lied. "By the sweat of my brow I'd dig through mountains, mining precious stones to export to the Holy City. I took a liking to obsidian, and being that it wasn't in any high demand back then, I began collecting it. We'd use it in our gardens... it's excellent for drainage, and very decorative. The black really makes the flowering bushes stand out."

"I suppose that kind of work would account for your strength." Cornelius sipped the empyreanol and scrunched his face. "But I'm not inclined toward gambling."

Of course he wasn't. He was too afraid of word getting back to Baalael that one of his pets had lost his spying vantage. "You can't lose, sir. I'd be a dedicated Might and the whole Swarm would run smoothly as my squad. Or, you get a load of obsidian—more than you can carry."

"You think I don't know how to gamble, child?" Cornelius spit, his words now slurring a bit. "No need to repeat yourself. One might say the fanfare's gotten to your head."

"It's possible."

"Is my Champion tempting you to gamble?" Joseph appeared next to them and handed Cornelius a mug of ale to supplement his empyreanol. "Drink up, old friend."

Cornelius took a sip. "He's got some set of wings, your Champion here."

"So I heard," Joseph said. "Voices carry in these halls. Seems like a bet you can't lose, Furie."

"I won't anger Lord Baalael by interfering with anyone he's installed into our ranks."

"Ah..." Joseph smiled, "our esteemed Principality. I'd think he wants what's best for the legion. Wouldn't you?"

"He wants what's best for himself," Cornelius scoffed. "That bumbling snog he's installed has been nothing but a thorn in my sandal."

"You have authority over your soldiers, Cornelius," Joseph said. "You can promote and demote whomever you please."

"That's bearscat and you know it." He sipped the empyreanol. "You know how the game works.... Lords always call the shots, old world or new. Baalael's ruthless. I won't incite his wrath."

"Fear is weakness, Cornelius." Joseph sat in the seat next to him. "You know that."

"Fear is wisdom," Cornelius said. "I learned that from you. A little fear of Baalael might've done you some good."

"I'm not weak, old friend."

"No... you were never weak. A little stupid, maybe."

Michael noticed the muscles in Joseph's jaw clench, but before Joseph could respond, he said, "All due respect, Furie... you're speaking to our Greater Dominion. You should mind your words."

"Mind your own words, soldier." Cornelius looked drunk and affronted. "You're speaking to a Furie."

So much for goading him with a bet.

"Michael may yet be a Champion," Joseph said, "but he's becoming the face of this movement—and that's by design. Word of his victories spread like fire, so I'd be less worried about Baalael's pets if I were you, and more worried about Lucifer's."

"The election hasn't happened yet," Cornelius said. "Baalael's just as likely to become Sahtan as Lucifer is. I won't chance getting on his bad side."

"All Baalael has is a bad side," Joseph said.

"I won't argue that." Cornelius sipped his drink and settled back in his chair.

"Ignoring incompetence in the leaders beneath you puts the whole legion at risk," Joseph said. "And that puts my dominion at risk. I won't tolerate such incompetence."

"What?" Cornelius laughed. "You'd replace me now?"

"When the walls of that Throne Tower open up and its Cherubim and Seraphim pour out," Joseph said, "you'll be *begging* me to replace you, so you don't have to stand before that disaster of an undisciplined swarm."

"Sir..." Michael interrupted, addressing Cornelius, knowing he'd have to leave them soon to fight. "I'm willing to go out there right now, unarmed and defenseless, and fight two squads by myself for the chance to make sure the group around my squad is secure. Consider my offer... please."

"Fight two armed squads alone? With no weapon?" Cornelius burst out laughing. "I'd give you *my own* position if you could do that, soldier."

Michael cocked his head. "I'm sorry, sir... Could you repeat that?"

"I said *I'd give you my own position if you could do that.*"

Joseph and Michael exchanged a glance.

"And I would..." Cornelius laughed, downing the last of the empyreanol. "Delusion is delusion. Your little stunt in the papers most definitely went to your head. Maybe you laid down your sword, but you still had a squad behind you."

"*Greater Dominion is witness...* sir," Michael said.

"Excuse me?" Cornelius erected in his seat.

Joseph smiled.

"*Greater Dominion is witness,*" Michael repeated. "Your words were just witnessed by a superior ranking officer, which makes them binding by Military Law."

The Furie's face fell. "I was joking...." He looked to Joseph. "Tell him I was joking."

"We have laws, Furie." Joseph stood up. "As a ranking officer, you should know better than to speak arbitrarily in front of a Dominion—and the Greater Dominion at that. Like Michael said, *I am witness.*"

"You jest," Cornelius said. "Surely you don't mean to hold me accountable for a joke while I'm half inebriated—while we're out here enjoying some sport."

"It's bad enough you've proven yourself a coward and a drunk." Joseph leaned over the concrete shelf, his eyes following the brawl in the pit and his dark curls blowing in the breeze. "But please don't demonstrate ignorance of our laws as well. Rank or not—we are soldiers, one and all. We are held to a higher standard."

Cornelius bit down on his knuckle. "I can't believe you're doing this to me."

"Perhaps your time will be better spent praying that Michael cannot win your wager," Joseph mused. "If he does, I'm sure he'll be more than willing to replace that inept Might with you. At the very least, you're more competent than he is. And unlike yourself... Michael doesn't cower before gods."

Lights flashed in Michael's face as the journalists snapped photos and clamored for his attention. They screamed out questions and held quills as they waited for him to say something.

He climbed out of the pit, panting, his side throbbing from that one speedy bub who managed to land a boot square in his rib. Blood oozed out from the wound on his shoulder, and the roar of the crowd was deafening.

No matter how beat up he was, he still did better than the first time he was defenseless in a pit. But back then, it wasn't by choice.

The crowd chanted his name, and the other soldiers from their swarm went wild in the stands. Merchants sold Lucifer's flags like they were hot manna cakes, and all Michael wanted to do was get back to his squad.

Hoot and Bernard rushed over, blocking him from the mob, and Bernard handed him a pitcher of water.

"Thanks," Michael said, downing it as they trudged forward, trying to get away from the pestering journalists. His eye throbbed and he could feel it swelling. "How bad do I look?"

"Not nearly bad as them..." Bernard poked his chin toward a line of angels lying on the ground, moaning. Triage technicians tended them.

"That was incredibly stupid," Hoot said as they ducked under the stands and into the gladiator hole. "What were you thinking going out there like that? You didn't even give us an explanation."

"I couldn't." They headed toward the exit and into the hallway. "By the time I convinced the judges to let me pull this stunt, they were already in the pit waiting to fight each other. I had no choice."

"But why?" Hoot said, and Michael stopped walking.

"I made a bet."

"A bet?" Hoot's jaw fell. "You went out there alone in no armor, no sword... nothing—to win what? Manna? Obsidian?"

"Rank," Michael said, and continued walking. Asher and Zillah tailed them as they cut through the stone halls under the arena.

"Rank?" Hoot asked. "I don't understand..."

They emerged into the gray outdoor light and Joseph stood there waiting, Cornelius behind him. Joseph saluted them, and Cornelius stepped forward, his posture humble. He bowed the salute and un-latched the crimson cape from his plate and clipped it on Michael.

The ride back to camp was thankfully uneventful. Joseph issued an immediate decree ordering all soldiers to report to the training field, where he announced Michael as the new Furie to cheers and applause, the majority of those fighters having just attended the tournament. Michael's first order of business was to publicly shame the Might who'd been lax on the job and appoint Cornelius to his position. Let the sniveling bub go back and cry to Baalael, where he'd receive even less mercy and probably be punished for his inability to keep his rank.

The music had settled into the outro, and most of the swarm were back in their tents. Hoot, Bernard, and Zillah sat around a fire outside, talking about their lives before the darkness. Asher had been quiet, opting instead to segregate himself inside with his face buried in the Manifesto.

"Sure ya don't want some roast snog before ya go?" Bernard asked, holding a stick full of charred lumps over the fire.

Michael grimaced and waved it away. "I'm not hungry. Thank you."

"We don't even have coriām," Zillah said, rolling the "r" in coriām as if offended by the way Bernard had been pronouncing it. "How can we stomach snog without coriām?"

"Where I'm from we use salt." Bernard bit a hunk from the stick and smiled.

"We don't have that either," Zillah said.

"Once I'm settled," Michael said, "we'll figure out a new Champion for the squad. Recruits are still coming in. Maybe you'll each get a squad of your own. Your training's superior to anything I've seen here."

"Before you leave..." Hoot stood up. "Are there any extra rations? It's fairly dim here. Angels out there might need our help."

"I'll find out and let you know."

They began getting up to salute him as he left, but he motioned them back down. The formalities, now that he climbed rank, would take some getting used to.

He made his way through camp to the crimson tent reserved for the Furie and watched soldiers carry out the last of Cornelius' things. He pushed aside the heavy fabric and entered.

The tent's interior was lined with plush, thick tapestries that not only kept out the cold, but gave the tent a feeling of unnecessary decadence. The floor was made of polished wood, rather than cold, hard soil, and there were enough oil lamps to not only warm the space, but keep it bright. Sweet incense burned, pushing out the smells of mud and iron while gold tassels adorned the edges of decorative fabrics that would've been put to better use as blankets for the horses.

At least there was a writing desk and a chair—it wasn't completely useless in there.

He stepped inside and sat on the bed, bouncing a little. The quilt was thick and soft, and the pillow was fluffy, covered in satin.

He stood abruptly and dragged the mattress outside.

"You...." He summoned a soldier passing by. "Take this into the field and burn it. Bring me one of the straw beds from the empty tents."

The soldier looked at him like he was crazy. "Are you sure, sir?"

"Do I look unsure?" He loomed over the shorter angel. The soldier picked up the bed and scurried off, the edge of the mattress dragging in the dirt.

He sensed someone behind him. "That you, sir?"

"It's late and nobody's here," Joseph said. "You can stop calling me sir."

"You held Cornelius to code at a casual event," Michael said. "How do I know you won't do the same to me?"

"Cornelius is an ambitious dungshoot who could give a rotting snog about his soldiers." Joseph entered Michael's tent and paused in the center, staring at the empty spot where the bed had been. "Already burned it, huh?" He put his hands on his hips.

"How'd you know?"

"I did the same in my first crimson tent. As a visiting Dominion, I should be sleeping here, you should be in the Might's tent, and the Might should be sleeping with the squads."

"So why aren't you?"

"Because that part of the code is Baalael's nonsense. After I wrote the manual, he skimmed through and peppered it with pomp. But you shouldn't ask anyone to do anything you're not willing to do yourself. I pitched my own black tent... which is nice because I can keep an eye and ear on everyone without them knowing I'm there."

"At least there's a table and desk in here," Michael said.

"I demanded them for official tents," Joseph said. "Baalael thinks dangling luxury in front of these soldiers creates ambition."

"Doesn't it?"

"The wrong kind of ambition. Soldiers need to observe a different kind of code if the realm's to be free to live by whatever principles we want. Fortunately, Baalael's too self-obsessed and lazy to put any real thinking into this. Pomp won't win our freedom when we're facing what's in that Throne Tower."

"Speaking of freedom," Michael said, "these villages will begin running out of vita soon, if they haven't already. The precept was asking about rations for them."

"Trees of Life still produce around here, though much less than they did. The scholars have come up with some technologies to keep a limited supply flowing, but those facilities haven't been built yet. For now, we're paying farmers in obsidian coin to supply the rations stored for this area."

"Stored in that big tent?" Michael asked. "The one with the guards?"

Joseph shook his head before regarding him. "No. But you should know what's in that tent now that you're authorized."

"What about the rations?" Michael asked.

"I'll show you where those are too. But for now... follow me."

They made their way through camp, which was now silent for the most part as the soldiers retired for the silence. The only sounds were the crackling fire pits and occasional neighing of horses.

The wide, black tent from earlier was still roped off and guarded by soldiers, but the stench had somewhat dissipated. Still, Michael resisted the urge to cover his nose. The guards crossed their arms and saluted before handing them an oil lantern with a tint to the glass.

They pulled the fabric aside and Joseph paused at the entrance, asking, "Have you wondered why the Military Manual said there would be mounted fighters, but none have been at training?"

"I assumed they weren't here," Michael said.

"That's only half true." Joseph stepped inside and Michael followed.

It was so dark in there that Michael couldn't see his hand in front of his face. They stepped forward, slowly, and his boots made a clicking sound on the sticky floor. A low growl crept across the darkness and Michael froze.

"What was that?" Michael asked, then something shuffled above him. His pulse quickened as he whipped his head around.

"Peace," Joseph said. "They're trained to only attack on command. They won't hurt us."

"Who won't hurt us?" Michael's voice pitched up, every instinct in him blaring like bells.

"I know you've heard of light runners," Joseph said, and Michael nodded, his eyes darting from sound to sound.

"How can there be light runners with no light?" Michael blinked and focused into the nothingness. Then, as his vision adjusted, little pairs of yellow eyes with peaked black slits for irises stared back at him, blinking. They were all over the tent—above him, in front of him, to the side of him. Joseph twisted the lever on the oil lamp, and it slowly grew brighter.

Cats—dozens of huge cats, black as pitch and big as oxen stalked the air, their gazes fixed like they were ready to pounce.

"Our silent scholars have figured a way to adapt the light runners to the darkness. We call them *shadow chasers.*"

Michael stepped on something soft and wet and nearly slipped. He grabbed Joseph's arm and steadied himself, then yanked the lantern from his hand and brought it down to the floor. Piles of reddish, purple mush lay there, mangled with fur. The stench now assaulted him as he stood in its source. "What is that!?" he gagged, slamming his hand over his mouth to prevent his dinner from escaping.

"A deer. Or at least, it was a deer," Joseph explained. "Things that thrive in the darkness can't eat from the Tree of Life, and they won't touch the flesh of any fruit. Their feeding is difficult to witness, but it's a necessary sacrifice."

Michael was speechless.

"You're not to speak of this to anyone unless they're authorized. Do you understand?"

After a few rancid breaths, Michael nodded, barely able to speak. "You... said they'd be mounted... by who?" It was hard to get words out without losing his food.

"Not who," Joseph said, "But what. I won't tell you that now… Some learning curves are best taken slowly."

He put a hand on Michael's back and led him from the tent. When they hit the fresh air Michael gasped, allowing that putrid, rancid stench to empty from his lungs.

"You'll meet their riders when we crown the Sahtan," Joseph said, "after the vote. For now, go get some rest. It's been a long song."

Michael squeezed his eyes shut, trying to push the image away. But that pile of blood and ooze carried on behind his eyelids, morphing into old memories of his own spilled blood and deep lacerations. Soft, bruised flesh that ached and stunk, and seemed little more than meat.

But then those eyes would come and bring comfort. Those glowing green eyes.

"Michael…" Joseph snapped his fingers, "are you alright?"

He blinked, then held his breath for a long beat. "I'm fine," he said, shaking it off. But those memories would be back in his dreams later. And bad dreams, unfortunately, were the only dreams he ever remembered.

26

X

*"The hand that feeds you, owns you. And if you're foolish
enough to eat, then you deserve whatever you get."*
-Black Manifesto, Chapter Four, "On Reliance"

"**A**RE YOU SURE YOU don't want to practice those new forms I
showed you in a proper spar?" Antoinette twirled one of the
wooden swords X had "borrowed" from the equipment shed. "These
can't cut you."

"That's okay," Gabriel said, hopping through the obstacle course. "I'd
rather not hit anyone."

"Your brother's very cute." She turned back to X. "Are you ready to
practice?"

X nodded and lifted his sword—barely. He was so tired. Antoinette
advanced on him, dirt and twigs crunching under her feet as she shuffled.
She swung and he tried to block her strikes, but his arms kept getting
heavier.

"Keep your sword high...." Her delicate shoe pivoted under the petticoats. "Where's that defense I taught you?"

X dropped his sword and leaned on his knees, already winded. "I don't
feel right. Maybe I'm not getting enough sleep."

"But you've been sleeping more than usual," Gabriel chimed in. "You should have more energy now that Matriarch Deidre's finally letting you eat proper meals."

"Maybe my body isn't used to so much food," X said. "I usually eat whatever scraps Gabriel can bring me, and scavenge what's left from the Mother Tree."

"Too much food slows me down too." Gabriel pulled a half-eaten tart from his pocket.

"Proper meals should only make you stronger," Antoinette said. "I knew Deidre's sense of charity would eventually kick in."

He sat on a rock and slumped, feeling the sudden need to lie down. "I don't think I can finish the session."

"That's alright." Antoinette set down her sword and stepped over to him, rubbing his back. Her warm hand made him aware of just how cold he was. "You're burning up. I can't imagine what could..." she trailed off and went silent for a beat. "May I check the back of your arm?"

"Why?"

She didn't answer, but rather slid the collar of his robe down slightly. She let out a little gasp and Gabriel ran over.

"What *is* that?" he asked.

"I'm not entirely sure," Antoinette said. She licked her finger and rubbed the spot. A sharp pain radiated from it.

"It's not coming off." She bit her lip and pulled up his sleeve to reveal small purple splotches all over his arm.

His face twisted. "What are they?"

She gently ran her thumb over one. "They look like bruises."

"Bruises?" Gabriel pushed up his glasses and examined X's arm. "I thought those only came from falling off a roof?"

"Or something equally serious that requires long healing time." Her face darkened. "Have you had any accidents you didn't tell us about? Did somebody do this to you?"

"No," he said. "And I didn't fall off any roof."

She scratched her head. "And you haven't noticed them?"

X shook his head.

"They must be from the sparring," Antoinette said. "But that doesn't make sense—bruises don't come about that easily. And you're eating everything they give you? Not skipping meals out of protest or pride?"

"He's eaten more than he ever has," Gabriel said. "His plates are loaded. They used to only let me bring him leftover snog, but now they prepare full meals just for him."

"And there's vita or manna in every meal?"

"Manna... tons of it..." Gabriel trailed off and knitted his brow. "But his manna looks different from ours. It has small brown specks in it, and they coat it with honey."

"Specks? That's grain bread, not manna."

X didn't have the energy to contribute to the conversation anymore. He eyed a soft patch of grass and wished he had the energy to get up and lay in it.

"Gabriel... go climb the Mother Tree and get some fresh vita right now. I don't like this one bit."

"There is no more," Gabriel pointed. "The cooks have been plucking it clean before any ripen. And they're draining the sap for extra cream."

She turned back to X. "When was the last time you ate from this tree?"

"I don't know...." He wanted to close his eyes and nap. "Half a movement ago. Maybe more."

Her nostrils flared. "Blasted, deviant angels! How could I be so stupid to think they'd change! They must be putting honey on wheat or barley loaves so you'll taste the sweetness and won't know the difference. They're starving you!"

"How can you eat so much and still starve?" Gabriel asked.

"You will starve if your body can't absorb nutrients. We need vit—"

"His skin doesn't look right..." Gabriel cut her off, his voice suddenly trembling. "He's turning gray!"

X could hear them talking, but lost all interest in what they were saying. It would be so nice to lay down and dream. To just sleep for a little while. He closed his eyes and a pair of bright green orbs stared back at him, seeped in darkness. *Hello again.*

"What if we take his robe off and lay him in the light?" Gabriel asked. "Will that help?"

"Light is for wounds," she said. "I'll go to the agorium and fetch—"

"Antoinette!" A hard-edged voice pierced the air from the direction of the manor. It roused X alert.

"Deidre," Antoinette said. "Quick—hide the swords and cover the obstacle course."

Gabriel dropped their swords into the underground fort and dragged a tarp of loose vines over the course. They peeked through a clearing in the leaves.

"She's looking for me," Antoinette said. "Hurry...."

They hoisted X's arms over their shoulders and dragged him away from the hidden refuge. X's back and legs ached something fierce, but no matter which direction he looked, those bright green eyes stared back, watching, making him feel safe.

"Over here, Matriarch," Antoinette called out.

"There you are." Deidre puckered her lips and stomped toward them. She picked up her black dress and stepped over the roots and vines, annoyed. "What are you doing all the way out here? And so late?"

"Late?" Antoinette laughed. "You mean early. We're gathering firewood before the first bells."

"We have plenty of firewood," Deidre said. "You waste your time. Get the child ready. He's going to practice with Baalael and the brothers."

Deidre had never adopted the name X either. Whenever she referenced him, which was never directly, she simply called him "the child."

"What kind of practice?" Antoinette asked.

"Fighting. Or whatever it is the little savages do."

"He's not a part of that," Antoinette said. "Besides, he's not feeling well."

"Not feeling well?" Deidre's sour face morphed into a grin. "Excellent. Get him ready."

"Matriarch Deidre," Gabriel pleaded, "X has to rest."

She looked at him like he was something that crawled across her food. "Be quiet or we'll send you to the pits next. I don't think a round, squishy thing like you would last very long."

"I must object." Antoinette crossed her arms. "I'm not sending this child to do anything physical. He needs a proper meal and a bed."

Deidre's nostrils flared and she grabbed X by his hair, yanking him to his feet. A jolt of pain surged as she dragged him out of the brush and back through the field. He let out a low moan. Everything ached. He didn't even have the energy to be angry. He just wanted to sleep. Gabriel and Antoinette protested behind them, but Deidre ignored them.

They entered the manor and walked straight through the main hall and through the front door where a wagon waited. Lord Baalael sat, fully armored, in the driver's seat, and the rest of the children sat in the wagon. She opened the door and shoved X on board, slamming it with a resounding thud.

They took off, Antoinette and Gabriel running behind them. Deidre grabbed Antoinette by the collar and yanked her back. Antoinette cocked a fist and landed it square in Deidre's jaw, knocking her to the ground. She laid there motionless as Antoinette picked up her petticoats and continued the pursuit, Gabriel struggling to keep up.

"Run, fatty, run!" the brother they called Hariel shouted, then burst out laughing. The rest of them joined in. X stared, somewhat dazed, at the widening distance between him and the only two friends he had in the world. Those glowing green eyes lingered in his periphery, but he knew they weren't real. They were just something his mind would conjure to console him.

By the time they pulled up to the pits, X was half in a dream of darkness. Sweet, peaceful darkness. Lord Baalael opened the wagon door and the brothers all but stepped on X as they climbed out.

"Come on, X," Lord Baalael said, "time to fight."

He stared at Baalael, whose cold gray eyes had come to define his whole face. If he wasn't so cruel, he could have been beautiful. Were all of the lords like that? Cruel and beautiful?

"Why must you be so *difficult*?" He reached in and hoisted X's limp body over his shoulder and closed the wagon door. "Don't take it personally. You're helping the world. We need to understand what happens when angels are starved of vita. And better still, when my children learn to forfeit mercy, their confidence will receive a much-needed boost. You're doing a great service for all."

Lord Baalael's words were a jumble of syllables, with no rhyme or reason. Exhaustion began morphing into euphoria, and the only thing X could really understand was that the green eyes still watched. They were right there, floating in his little private cavern of darkness. He smiled.

"Rather than plead, you smile at me?" Baalael laughed. "Too bad I don't trust you... your pride is a bit like my own."

They climbed into the pit and Lord Baalael set him on his feet, propping him against the dirt wall. X held on to the side and tried to focus his gaze on what waited in there for him. In the center of the pit was a thick wooden pole that had a strawman tied to it. Lord Baalael yanked the dummy down, dried grass falling from its sleeves and pants. He tossed it to the side with a thump; its lifeless face stared into the sky.

He grabbed X under the arm, a sharp pain radiating where his hand gripped. X tried to protest, but couldn't. His eyes moved to the edge of the pit where at least a dozen brothers stood, fully armored in leathers and holding real swords. Metal swords. Baalael dragged him to the pole and propped him there, then tied both wrists above his head.

"Formation!" Baalael commanded, and the brothers formed a line and harkened—backs straight, chests out.

"One at a time!" Baalael yelled. "I want to see each new offensive strike executed meticulously, and without mercy." The brothers stared straight ahead, no sign of reaction from any of them. "If you show mercy—harken now—*if you show mercy, I will show you none.* Is that understood?"

"Sir, yes, sir!" they bellowed in unison.

"NO!" Antoinette screamed as she approached. "What are you doing!?"

She jumped in the pit, Gabriel huffing behind her as he tried to keep up. Lord Baalael's ring glowed, and he held up his hand. She crashed, full speed, into a wall of nothing, and went flying back out of the pit, landing on Gabriel. They were rendered motionless, their faces contorting like they were in pain. Not a limb on their bodies budged.

"You'll be chastised for that later, angel." Baalael turned back to the fighters. "Commence!"

X closed his eyes as footsteps drew closer. A whoosh filled the air, followed by an incredible pain in his side. Then another to his thigh. His chest. Then the side of his head. Pains, both dull and sharp, bloomed all over his body in a nonstop assault. More feet crunched the dirt, followed by more blows, and more pain.

His head hung from his torso like an apple about to drop from a tree. He forced his eyes open, and purple light filled the air around him. His life force. He closed them again as his body jerked on its own, gasping for breath. Warmth ran down his skin in different spots. First, a little, then he was covered in it.

Blood.

He let his eyes close, and saw the glowing emeralds behind his eyelids, watching him. The pain dulled to a distant ache, an echo of terror that he moved further and further from. The glowing green eyes gave him a nod; it must've been alright to sleep now. They could stay awake and keep watch. X took a breath and drifted into the darkness.

"He's at the brink," someone said. A needle poked his arm. "That should do it...." The voices were fading in and out, but he couldn't open his eyes.

"There we are.... Now write that down so we know for the future." Words were being said, but their sounds had no meaning to him.

"He lives?" Lord Baalael's voice joined in like an untuned cello that ruins a song.

"Yes."

X barely opened his eyes. There were shadowy figures around him—angels in dark hoods and pure white masks. He couldn't see their faces, or their eyes.

"Put him in the cellar away from the light," Baalael said. "Record every change and keep him breathing—but just barely. Test subjects without records aren't easy to come by."

27

Michael

*A **Proper Meat Pottage**- 2 full rootroasts, freshly picked. 2 deep spoons of oil from the olive—or butter from the sap of a Mother Tree. 1 large onion, chopped fine. 2 fists of carrot, celery, mushroom and 'taters, cut into chunks. 2 deep spoons of vita flour. 2 cups of ale. 3 cups of water. Half a cup of dried tomaters, soaked n' mashed. 4 sprigs of rosemary and a punch of salt. *Coat rootroast in flour then brown in oil. Add onions 'till they sweat. Add veg, then tomater paste. Now, pour yer ale to loosen all the snog bits from off the bottom— good n' tasty, that snog. Add water, then cover 'n cook on low for half a verse.*

-Excerpted from Matriarch Mary's personal recipe book.

"GOOD OVERTURE, SIR." HOOT stepped through the slit in Michael's tent and bowed the salute as Michael drew out marching formations on a sheet of paper. "Swords have all been sharpened and bed checks are complete."

"Was everyone up to code?" Michael asked, too engrossed in his training strategies to bother to look up.

"Not at first, but they are now," Hoot said. "A few squads will be running extra laps later, but overall, they seem eager to improve."

"And accountability is the only way they will," Michael said. "How'd our squad like their new accommodations?"

"No complaints, sir. Better to deal with Bernard's snoring than an entire throng's snoring."

"Good." Michael put down his quill. "You and Zillah go prepare the camp to depart—the swarm will march to the training field together."

Hoot started to bow the salute but paused. "One more thing, sir..." he said. "Philistina came to camp earlier, and it wasn't easy to convince her to go back to the inn. I didn't think it was wise to escort her to your tent because of her... disposition."

"She was angry?"

Hoot nodded. "But I convinced her to go back to the inn and wait to hear from you."

"Send word that we'll complete her mission right after the next official tournament. Then I'll make arrangements to have her transported back to the island with her samples."

Hoot nodded and bowed the salute before leaving, and Joseph entered as he left. Michael stood and saluted.

"At ease." Joseph watched Hoot disappear into the busy, buzzing swarm of soldiers. "I've got to hand it to you, your idea of having a personal guard to handle tasks was a good one. I wasn't sure if it was pure pragmatism, or just a way to keep them at your side."

"A bit of both," Michael admitted, focusing back on his work. "Mainly because I trust them... well, most of them. But also because managing the operation of two hundred and fifty soldiers is a lot."

"As Greater Dominion I've been dealing with recruiting and war strategies... not field operations. You're the first leader that's come up with meaningful changes instead of letting me theorize everything. It's nice to have help."

"It's mostly just common sense." Michael popped a few coffee beans and crunched down, the strong flavor pepping him up. "I guess I learned most of it from Mary."

"Tastes better when you drink it, you know"

"Already did," Michael said, dipping his quill and tracing over the formation strategy he drew. "Hits faster this way. I'm usually more tired when I wake up than when I lay down."

"To each their own." Joseph glanced at the page before stepping over to the coffee press and fixing himself a cup. "Nice sketch... We have an important meeting later, you and I. A Duke from the First Legion named Asmodeus will arrive during training.... He's a very old friend. He's going to handle the matter of Lord Baalael's ring."

Michael looked up from his work. He'd been waiting for word about this. "I look forward to meeting him."

"He'll be impressed with what you've done here. This Swarm's performance is measurably better than when Cornelius was leading, and he was one of the better Furies."

"I appreciate the vote of confidence, sir."

"Soldiers are following your example, working late and waking up early. I've heard them from inside my tent saying that you don't sleep because you're some kind of lord sent in disguise to test them."

Michael chuckled. "They wouldn't sleep either if they saw what was behind my eyelids."

"That bad since the shadow chasers?" Joseph put the cup down.

"I'll adapt." Truth was the shadow chasers didn't make a lick of difference in Michael's poor sleep. "I'd rather spend the silence reading your Military Manual anyway. I don't know what I'd do without it."

"That warms me." Joseph smiled and took a sip. "I poured all of myself into that book. I'd always dreamed of a great, organized force—a fellowship in arms."

"May I speak freely, sir?" Michael laid down his quill.

"Of course."

"It's not that I don't like the Manifesto… But this thing you've created, I can't put it down. It's like nothing I've ever heard. Where did you come up with it all?"

"I wrote the bulk in a single sitting, many symphonies ago. Maybe what happened to me at the hands of Baalael conflicted so greatly with my indoctrination that something entirely new emerged." He raised his eyebrows. "Or maybe the Almighty inspired me because he wanted a worthy foe. I don't know."

"I wanted to say thank you. That manual takes the chaos from my head and puts it into neat little piles that can be managed."

"Me too," Joseph admitted. "But you must be careful, Michael. The military serves the Order of Light—not the other way around. Never confuse politics with honor, and never show your sentiment again, not to me or anyone else. It can be used against you. That's where the Manifesto's advice shines. It's better to demonstrate these sentiments by enforcing our laws swiftly, with strength and fairness. I tell you this now because Asmodeus is a solid ally, and a good friend—but he has the kind of ambition that could never fully adhere to our code. He's a good soldier… but he's motivated by politics and power. We'll be hard-pressed to find soldiers who love the honor code more than themselves. Asmodeus is not one of those angels."

"Understood," Michael said.

"Good. Friend or not, we can trust Asmodeus so far as we understand his motives, and how his actions on our behalf will ultimately benefit himself."

Joseph and Asmodeus stood at the top of the hill observing as Michael led the swarm in training, their red cloaks billowing in the frigid western wind. The sky didn't churn dark, but rather remained in the damp, cold gloom that it'd been since they'd arrived at camp.

Training went even better than usual. Every soldier was clean-shaven, their armor polished and pristine. Michael had begun implementing systems of checks, making sure the codes of dress were being adhered to. They moved in a choreographed oscillation between marching and fighting, and their helms made them appear as carefully arranged bulls, locking horns as they engaged in mock battle.

Michael even led the endurance training by running extra laps himself and promising double rations to any squad who could match him. Running was entirely unpleasant, but it was also a reliable means of mentally conditioning oneself to endure discomfort, and the swarm proved better motivated by reward rather than punishment.

Accomplishments and progress were recognized now, creating a sense of competition that focused on improvement. Complacency was punished with exercises designed to make better warriors, rendering progress inevitable.

Soldiers bumped chests, smiling, and a new kind of brotherhood was emerging, similar to Michael's own squad, but manifested a hundredfold. More than ever, the spirit of being a part of something brought its own kind of light to this impending darkness.

The chorus transitioned to the outro, and Michael signaled the swarm to pack it up and get ready for dinner. The Two/thirteen took up formation behind him and Michael led them to the hilltop where Joseph stood with Asmodeus.

"You are a beast, Furie Michael," Asmodeus said in a thick, inner First Hexant accent as he crossed his arms and saluted. His skin was covered haphazardly in black markings, symbols, and pictures, and he was shorter and leaner than Michael expected. Michael returned the salute, and must've been staring a little too hard at the Duke's markings.

"You like my ink?" Asmodeus laughed, his teeth sharpened into fine points, some even covered in gold or silver. "The First Legion brands accomplishment, instead of sticking puny little pins on our cloaks. Do you like?"

In all honesty, it looked distasteful. "I'd think we would want the whole of our force to be uniform."

"Great idea," Asmodeus drawled, winking. "Maybe the rest of you should get branded too."

Michael took a breath to respond, but Joseph raised his hand. "Asmodeus is as strong willed as you are, Michael. Hash it out over dinner, which we'll be taking in the village. You may want to release your guard. We have some... sensitive business to tend."

"Asher, Zillah..." Michael turned to the squad. "Return to camp and make sure the Mights are all doing their jobs. Hoot and Bernard, take the ride with us for good measure. Make sure no wandering ears find their way into our conversation."

Zillah turned on her heel and marched away, but Asher's gaze lingered on Michael.

"Something you want to say, Ash?"

He shook his head, slowly turning to follow Zillah down the hill.

They headed north toward a village that stretched over the border into the First Hexant. The sky grew notably darker as they got nearer the populated parts, the horses almost instinctively walking closer together.

"Can't see a snogs wart 'round here," Bernard said. "Throne only knows what's past that tree line."

"We must learn to love the darkness," Asmodeus said, his immense black horse the only one of the herd looking entirely calm. "If there is anything in that brush, it has more to fear of me than I have of it."

"The First Hexant's seen the worst of the darkness," Joseph remarked. "Not accounting for Asmodeus' ink."

"You can't fear what you are." Asmodeus looked back at them, the black symbols stretching up his neck and into his face like a scarf. "If you want to rule the darkness, you must first become it. The Almighty must find a new weapon, yes? How can darkness destroy itself?"

"The Almighty?" Hoot asked, and Michael panicked.

"There are different theories about what's causing all this," Michael cut in, trying to mitigate the damage. "Some say weather and some say luck. Some say other things. Nobody really knows."

Asmodeus chuckled. "Listen to your Furie. Whatever he says is what I meant."

A noise came from the brush, and they harkened.

Hoot pulled his reins. "Did you hear that?"

"Could be an animal," Bernard said.

"Or someone who needs help out here...." Hoot said.

Michael rode into the tree line and signaled Bernard and Hoot to follow. Fog slithered across the forest floor, and the sounds of blowing leaves mingled with those of crickets and frogs—at least there was still life in these parts. They looked around, but saw nothing, so they retreated back to the road.

"Was probably just an animal," Michael said, nudging his horse with his heel, and the rest did the same.

A series of dull orange lights defined the village just ahead. As they got closer, it became apparent that gaslamps were affixed to the tops of poles that were dug into the ground. The light was significantly more degraded here. Fire pits speckled the nearly desolate center of the village agorium, filling the air with the smell of burning wood and ash as angels stayed huddled around them, rubbing their hands together for warmth. Their heads turned from the fires and watched the group as they rode by.

"Why ain't they home by the hearth?" Bernard asked.

"They are not from here," Asmodeus said. "They come from neighboring villages seeking respite. This dense gloom is a beacon to them. It is worse in other places."

"We need to minister to them," Hoot said with a sense of urgency. "I have a double dinner ration, and so does Bernard from our training rewards earlier."

"We will," Michael said. "After, though."

"They're hungry now... sir," Hoot said.

"We'll see what else we can get our hands on before we approach them," Michael said.

Asmodeus laughed. "Will you all save the whole world from the darkness, then? Furie Michael?"

"That's enough, Asmodeus," Joseph warned, and Michael was grateful. Asmodeus wasn't lending to Michael's whole "peacekeeper" narrative one bit.

"I am only playing with the Furie," Asmodeus said, turning and stretching a wicked smile with those jagged gold teeth. "He is strong. I like him."

They stopped in front of an inn between two boarded-up shops, and disembarked their horses.

"Keep an eye for anything out of sorts," Michael told Hoot and Bernard. "We won't be long. You have your rations, right?"

"I'll skip my dinner," Hoot said, not looking Michael in the eyes. "The angels here need it more than I do."

"I as well," Bernard said, but without the resentment.

"I'll make sure they have food," Michael said. "Food security means peace, and I intend to keep my word—"

Hoot turned sharply toward the alley. "Did you hear that?"

"Hear what?" Michael looked around.

Hoot crept along the edge of the inn and peeked between the buildings. "Who's there?" He called out, but no one answered. "I could've sworn I heard footsteps. You didn't hear anything?"

"No," Michael said. "Which doesn't mean it didn't happen, so stay vigilant. Where there's hunger, there's danger." Hunger could drive an angel so mad that he started seeing things. Mangled deer flesh flashed in his memory and he grimaced. "I don't even want to think about what they'll start eating if they get desperate enough."

"Which is why we need to feed them," Hoot insisted.

"We will," Michael said, "I'm from the Jolly Bub. We don't let anyone go hungry."

Michael followed Asmodeus and Joseph up the creaking wooden steps of the inn while Bernard and Hoot kept watch, waiting with the horses. To his surprise, the atmosphere inside was lively despite the dim light. Soldiers of various skin tones were covered in ink and filled tables lit at the center with candles, laughing and drinking, mouths filled with silver and gold spikes. They were all First Hexant soldiers, and their presence was unsettling.

Asmodeus and Joseph had been waiting by the door, and when Asmodeus stepped into the dining area, the entire room got quiet as everyone's gaze followed him. Michael and Joseph tailed him, the three of them being the only red-capes in the room.

"This is my domain, is it not?" Asmodeus spread his arms as he strutted across the dining area. "I am important here... like a lord. I have no birthright to power, so I just take it. Isn't that right, Joseph, my friend?"

"It certainly is, Az."

"When we finish recruiting," Asmodeus slapped his chest, "I will be the Power over a Legion. I will command many."

"I have no doubt, my friend," Joseph said before exchanging a glance with Michael.

A servant of the Order met them in her dark robe and sat them in a room at the rear of the establishment. Michael made sure to sit facing the door with his back to the wall, and Joseph sat right next to him. A breeze blew in from an open window just to the side of them that was big enough for an angel to crawl out if he needed to.

Asmodeus wasn't exactly the kind of angel Michael would label as predictable, and sitting in an establishment where he commanded at least seventy soldiers meant that having a nearby escape route wasn't the worst idea.

Asmodeus banged on the table twice, and the servant rushed away, returning shortly with a tray of mugs. He rambled off a list of dishes to prepare, some that Michael was familiar with, and some that he wasn't. She scurried out of the room and Asmodeus held up his mug.

"A toast," he said, "to old friends, and new ones… and to the enemies of my enemy, which make the best friends of all." They clinked their mugs and drank.

"The First Hexant has split in two," Asmodeus said, putting his mug down and wiping his mouth with his arm. "The outer circles are dark now, worse over the villages. The inner circles, not as bad. But they grow worse."

"Are all the Hexants like that now? Split in two?" Michael had been so wrapped up in recent events that he hadn't stopped to consider what conditions might have been like around the Jolly Bub.

"The First Hexant is the worst," Joseph said, "But the darkness has begun blooming over every Hexant."

"Do you worry for your family?" Asmodeus asked, a grin teasing his lips.

Michael wasn't about to give any information relating to anyone he cared about, so he shook his head. "They can fight for their Hexant if they want to survive. My loyalty is to my squad. And to the other soldiers that will fight with us."

"He really is brutal," Asmodeus turned to Joseph, laughing. "He lacks mercy even for his own Matriarch."

Michael didn't comment—let Asmodeus think whatever he wanted. How this all would turn out was anyone's guess, and attachments could eventually become targets.

The servant returned with several trays of food—more than they could eat. She placed bowls and woodenware before them, but Asmodeus reached right into the trays and ate with his hands, scooping both rice and stew before shoving them in his mouth and sucking the juice from his fingers. Mary would've fallen out cold on the floor.

"What is wrong?" Asmodeus paused, eying them both. "Are you not hungry?"

"Of course we are." Joseph smiled and served himself a roll with butter, and Michael spooned a scoop of pottage into his bowl.

He gave a nod of thanks and stuck his fork into a dense piece of saucy rootroast. It was darker than usual, and smelled a little different, but didn't appear burned. He stuck it in his mouth, his face somewhat tensing from the unexpected flavor. And texture. He chewed and swallowed, but an off taste lingered. A strong taste. He didn't like it. He downed some ale and took another bite, but it was just as bad.

Joseph slipped him a look and subtly shook his head.

Michael downed more ale and shoved a heaping piece of bread into his mouth. "I'm sorry—what did you say was in this pottage?"

Joseph rubbed his face and sighed, and Asmodeus stretched a wide, unsettling grin. "Do you like it? It is good, no?"

"I can't say my palette is... used to this taste." Michael dragged the napkin across his lips. "Exactly what spices were used to prepare this rootroast?"

"And who said this was rootroast?" Asmodeus broke out in a laugh and wiped his hands. "You are in the First Hexant now, Furie. I can hear your stew *oinking*, I think. How do you like the taste of fresh pig?"

Michael jumped from the table and wretched the contents of his stomach straight into the napkin. Joseph buried his face in his hands as Asmodeus howled in laughter.

"Asmodeus, enough!" Joseph slammed the table. "I'm your superior, so cut it out. We know life's hard out here and we respect you for it. You don't need to make my new Furie lose his whole stomach."

"He should have eaten the beans then." Asmodeus roared, practically crying.

"Never mind the food." Joseph pushed his plate aside and leaned on the table, folding his hands. "We need to tend business. Michael, sit down."

Michael took a deep breath and shoved his chair back, sitting in it as he glared at Asmodeus.

"Listen," Joseph said, "Asmodeus was on my squad. He fought by my side for many symphonies, and he has as much reason to despise Lord Baalael as I do."

"I am sorry, Furie Michael." Asmodeus was still laughing. "I only wanted a little fun. But know, I am loyal to my friends, and that never changes. Do you know who climbed into that pit and collected Joseph's bloody hands from the mud?"

The question was rhetorical, so Michael focused on his breath—in at the tip of his nose, and out through his mouth. He retained composure, allowing the putrid flavor to dissipate.

"Me," Asmodeus pointed to himself. "I picked up my Champion's hands—the hands that teach me everything I know. I picked them up and washed them. And I cried for my friend."

"I'm sorry," Michael said, letting Azrael's exercise calm him from the impulse to feed Asmodeus to the pigs he so ravenously ate. That poor pig.

"None of this 'I am sorry,'" Asmodeus waved. "The Black Manifesto preaches vengeance, and vengeance we shall have... but that is not the only vengeance I seek."

"Lord Baalael also summoned Asmodeus' match, Jezebel, to serve him," Joseph explained. "Against her will."

"He burns his triangle into her palm over and over like she belongs to him," Asmodeus growled, baring his sharp teeth.

"Lucifer believes in free will," Michael said. "How would he allow that?"

"Lucifer doesn't know," Asmodeus said.

"Jezebel believes she's submitting to Baalael to protect Asmodeus," Joseph said. "Baalael told her that Asmodeus betrayed Lucifer, and Baalael threatens to expose him if she doesn't comply."

"Is that true?" Michael asked.

"Of course it's not true," Asmodeus said. "I would never betray Lucifer.... He will be our Sahtan."

"So just tell her the truth, then," Michael said.

"He can't." Joseph sighed. "If he does, Baalael *does* have something to reveal... that Asmodeus betrayed Jezebel."

"I deserve beautiful servants too, do I not?" Asmodeus defended himself. "Baalael has many proofs of my infidelities. But I love Jezebel. She is *mine*." He spit out that last word and Michael cocked a brow. "I go along with this charade manufactured to torment me, and I tell what *is mine* to subjugate herself to him."

Asmodeus' concept of pairing was... interesting. "What's the point of Baalael tormenting you?" Michael asked. "Because you picked up Joseph's hands, eons ago?

"Lords aren't like us," Joseph said. "When they love, they love immeasurably. But where they have no love, it's vicious. Baalael torments anyone who means anything to me. Asmodeus was my best friend and most loyal compatriot. But... this situation with Jezebel... it can be used to our advantage."

"That pig cannot burn a triangle with his ring on," Asmodeus said. "So my Jezebel will take it when his hand is naked, and replace it with this..." He pulled out a perfect replica of Baalael's ring, complete with his sigil in the center of the blue stone.

"This way," Joseph said, "he won't be able to cheat when you claim Champion's Legacy. Not without his ring."

"How can she do this if Baalael can read her mind?" Michael asked. "If she even thinks of betraying him, he'll know."

Asmodeus laughed a long, low cackle. "You do not know my Jezebel. She is like a goddess—the goddess of lies. Her lies are so good, so realistic, that she sometimes believes them herself. She will not slip up and think wrong thoughts."

"I still have to make it to the Final Round so I can fight him," Michael said. "The Hexant Champions might be a tougher fight."

"Your reputation already washes the world like honey-sweet blood," Asmodeus said. "If someone else could beat you, I would not be here, would I? Joseph has been looking for the right Champion for a long, long time."

Michael looked at Joseph. "I thought you didn't care about justice—that you wanted to protect the world?"

"I don't want justice," Joseph said. "I want *revenge*. And if my revenge protects the world, even better. A Champion can't claim Legacy twice, so I've been looking for someone with your potential since my hands first healed. You just happened to come along when the stakes were highest."

"Lucky me." Michael wiped his mouth again, in case any of that pig grease clung to his lips. "If you can swap that ring and I make it to the Final Battle, I'll do better than remove Baalael's hands. I'll remove his head."

"Now you're talking!" Asmodeus nearly leapt across the table and grabbed Michael's cheeks, planting a kiss on his forehead.

Before Michael could revile him, something banged outside and they all jumped from their seats. Michael bolted to the window and leaned out. Footsteps echoed in the alley, but he didn't see anyone.

"What is it?" Asmodeus appeared next to him, looking outside.

"I don't know," Michael said. "Probably one of those angels from the square looking for food. Maybe you could have your servant put those beans and the manna in a jar for me?"

"Of course," Asmodeus said. "Beans and bread to save the world. Would you like to bring the rest of the pottage?"

Michael looked at him with disgust.

"Don't be naive, Furie Michael," Asmodeus said. "When an angel is starving, they will be willing to eat more than that pig you just spit out. If you are not careful, they will eat you too."

28

Michael

*"Within every angel is a divine spark; a direct connection
to the Almighty himself. Most, if not all, will live their
lives giving lip service to this fact, never truly knowing its
meaning. Should conditions ever change, however, the few
who ignite this spark will prove truly exceptional."*
-The Guide to Utopian Principles and Ethics, Section II,
On Internal States

MICHAEL STOPPED HIS HORSE and scanned the square as Hoot unclipped a sack of rations from his saddle. The gloom had lessened slightly, making this grim new reality even more visible. Angels huddled around dying fire pits dressed in tattered, ashy robes. Pallid skin clung to their faces, lines creasing the edges of their eyes and mouth. "How bad do their homes have to be to come here and live like this?" Michael asked, rhetorically.

"'Tis painful to look upon," Bernard said.

Nearby, the roar of a cheering crowd could be heard from the arena where amateurs fought to get the crowd warmed up for the second tournament of the Games, where the Two/thirteen would be fighting the other winners of the eastern Hexants later. Manna cakes and other nutritious foods were sold to those with something worthwhile to trade, while right here in this once bustling market, angels with nothing went hungry.

Michael should've kept focused on his plan and not listened to Hoot. This was depressing.

"Where's your Almighty now, precept?" Michael mumbled as he jumped from his horse, swiping the sack of rations from Hoot's hand. Seeing these pitiful things hunched over fires in a little more light made him realize they probably didn't look much worse than he did when he was starved. He had a sudden, overwhelming urge to punch the pious precept in the face. "Suffering and starvation too inconvenient for your Great Overseer?"

Michael handed rations to Bernard and sent him to the north end of the square, then turned his gaze back to Hoot and waited for an answer.

Hoot didn't respond—the perfect picture of self-control, as always. Which was even more irritating.

"I'm your superior, and I asked you a question."

Hoot's gaze remained fixed on the huddled, miserable angels. "Perhaps you should focus more on the fact that the suffering and starving angels have been too much an inconvenience for *you*." He dismounted calmly, and approached a group with the rations.

Michael thought his face would explode. "What's that supposed to mean?" He stormed after him.

Hoot handed out rations, ignoring his question. The wretched creatures snatched up the rations and scurried into an abandoned building.

"Answer me!" Michael spun him around and narrowed his eyes.

"You're only here helping because of me," Hoot said. "And that's a fact, whether you enjoy hearing it or not. So before you go judging the *Great Overseer*... judge yourself."

A thousand emotions clamored for Michael's mouth at once and he stuttered. "Y-you think anyone with the power to stop this and doesn't cares a *single lick* for us? You think he'll do something to save them?" He motioned the whole square full of vagrants and howled a laugh. "You lug that big leather book everywhere like it means something! He's not coming... he doesn't care about saving us! Nobody cares!"

"I care," Hoot said, again calm as he distributed the food. The backs of Michael's eyes stung as if he could cry, but not for sadness. He genuinely didn't feel anything for the starving angels. In fact, they were lucky! If they weren't such sorry sacks, this would make them stronger. It was his rage at Hoot that wanted to condense into tears, but he shoved them back down because emotions were useless and irrational.

"You're about the only one who cares," Michael muttered.

"Big surprise..." one of the vagrants warming their hands by the fire said. "The arrogant wingbag's being an arrogant wingbag again." She pushed the tattered hood away from her face, revealing two blonde, spiky buns, and Michael's eyes bulged.

"Don't look so shocked," Philistina said. "Hoot's not the only one who cares about anyone other than themselves."

"What are you doing out here?" Hoot asked.

"Helping... feeding... healing," she said. "Not everyone's like Michael with their heads up their—

"Whoa..." Hoot held out his hand. "Why are you dressed like that?"

"Easier to help if I look like one of them. When I look clean, they steal everything."

"Steal everything?" Hoot furrowed his brow. "I guess it makes sense, they're starving."

She guffawed. "The ones who are starving aren't stealing, which is why they're starving. The angels you just fed have been taking everyone else's food and hoarding it in that building to trade for obsidian. They don't even need it... they live a few villages over in the Second Hexant where it's brighter than this."

"Resources are running out," Michael said, suddenly defensive of their resourcefulness. "They've got to do what they've got to do."

"You would say that." Philistina rolled her eyes, and someone snatched the sack of rations from Michael's hand.

"Hey!" Michael started after him, and Philistina laughed.

"Don't bother," she said. "Donalus is a master at hiding. You'll never find him."

"You know them by name?" Michael was stunned.

"Of course," Philistina said, like it was the most normal thing in the world. "How can you help angels you don't even know?"

"Generosity flows easily from abundance," Hoot said. "We'll all find out who we truly are now."

She got up and pulled the hood back over her head. "Well, I've got to get back to work. I need to go steal from the thieves and redistribute those rations before they take them out the back door again."

"You can't go in there alone," Michael said.

"I'm not." She put two fingers in her mouth and whistled. A soldier in full armor, no helm, stepped from one of the abandoned shops. His chest and arms were covered in ink just like Asmodeus, and his sharp teeth glistened with gold and silver.

Michael pinched the bridge of his nose. "Tell me... please... tell me you're not hanging around the soldiers here. Tell me you're not *that* mad."

"What's the problem?" Philistina asked. "They look exactly like you with those ridiculous outfits. They just like to... draw on themselves. He helped me get my samples. At least he's not wearing a silly cape."

Michael held a hand out to the approaching soldier who stopped a few yards away, saluting him. "That's enough for this song, soldier. You can go back to your camp; we'll take it from here."

"Are you sure, Furie?" He said in that same inner First Hexant accent as Asmodeus.

"I'm sure," Michael said.

"Hey!" Philistina made a face. "You can't tell him what to do!"

"Actually," Hoot said, "He can."

"Maybe the femme will enjoy meeting with me later, then? After the Games?" The soldier eyed Philistina like a ripe piece of vita. "Maybe she would like to *hold my hand* when my squad wins our battle later?"

Hoot looked like he was going to fall over.

"This femme is my charge," Michael said, straightening to full height and stepping in front of her, "and under my care while we travel. She'll be with me after the Games."

"I'm not your charg—"

Hoot shoved a ration into her mouth before she could finish.

"I see, Furie Michael," the soldier bowed, winking. "You will be the one to hold hands with her, then. Good for you." He saluted them, then turned on his heel and left. Philistina spit the manna out and took a breath to berate him.

"No, you don't..." Michael held a hand in front of her face. "You have no idea who you're dealing with. *I* barely have any idea who we're dealing with. They eat pigs, Philistina. Like—*eat* them. With sauce and bread. And the Throne only knows what else they're eating out here."

She went silent, her face a mix of confusion and horror.

"Sorry we didn't get to your samples yet," Michael said, "but now that you have them, you're going back to the island. Finish out this tournament here as our triage tech, and then I'll have Bernard and Hoot escort you back. They have plenty of time before the final round of tournaments. You all need to understand what angels are capable of—*truly* capable of...." His gaze roamed over the three of them: Philistina, Bernard, and Hoot. "Maybe then you'll all stop being so naive."

A light drizzle made the pit slippery, covering everyone in mud from their shins down. The air was mixed with the scent of sweet blood and sweat as Michael's hilt bashed into a gladiator's inked face, the light from his wound condensing into spatter. The Two/thirteen battled the

winning squads from the First and Third Hexants for the Eastern Dominion Championship, and even though the others didn't wear military
uniforms, the few inked faces revealed there were First Hexant soldiers
among them.

Michael theorized that Joseph and Asmodeus weren't fully hedging
their bets on him as the only Champion who could take Legacy, because
the First Hexant squad was particularly fierce. But if there were any
doubts that Lucifer hadn't rigged the Games in their favor to promote
his own flag—it was snuffed out with the ambitious glints in the eyes of
their inked opponents. Anyone capable of taking down Michael would
take his growing reputation too.

Well... good luck with that.

Michael called a formation and Asher broke to the wrong side. Two
fighters lunged and Michael couldn't cover Zillah's left, as planned. She
caught a blade to her throwing shoulder and the judge tapped her out
before Hoot could get to her with the stone. Michael shot Asher a glare
before leaping over an ax and kicking someone in the face.

He glanced at Philistina who received Zillah in the healing circle.
She put her to the back of the line, tending soldiers from the opening
tournaments whose bleeding was worse, and hadn't been controlled yet.
She returned Michael's glance with a glare and shook her head. The
light—or lack of it—made healing all the slower.

Both squads were attacking the Two/thirteen as if they weren't also
competing against one another for the same title. *The enemy of my enemy
is my friend,* he remembered Asmodeus say. Michael's reputation had
definitely made them a target.

He kept a keen eye on that soldier from the square he met earlier with
Philistina. He kept trying to position himself behind Michael, and Zillah
wasn't there to pick him off.

"Asher, get back in position!" Michael yelled after he disappeared
behind him too. Asher at his rear made him nervous. It was bad enough
half the pit was piling on him.

"I'm covering your back," Asher huffed, metal clanging.

"I don't need you back there," Michael said. "Get back in position!" An elbow flew at Michael's head and he ducked, but Asher still wasn't in his periphery. Hoot blocked defensively and Michael continued volleying swords with multiple fighters, using his shield as a bludgeoning tool whenever possible. The soldier from the square jumped into the action against Michael, totaling four military-trained angels coming at him at once. Hoot kept glancing his way, finally breaking his defense and going on the attack to help Michael.

It's about time.

Bernard swung around from behind and bear-hugged one of their opponents, body slamming him to the floor, but the bub flipped him over and they wrestled in the mud like swine competing for the last bit of snog.

More fighters piled on, and the soldier from the square launched an aggressive attack. His sharp, silver teeth almost glowed against his inked black lips.

Someone swept Michael from behind and he went down. Four angels closed in, and suddenly a sword was slicing straight for his neck. Hoot blocked it and drove them back, and Michael stabbed his sword straight through the groin of that soldier from the square. The fighter's eyes bulged as light blazed from his skirts. He went to his knees and blood pooled beneath him. That was the worst injury yet. The others didn't waste a breath, doubling the attack.

Philistina came running toward the pit, and Michael glanced her way but couldn't take his eyes from the fight. "What's she doing!?" he yelled to Hoot. "She has to wait in the healing circle!"

"Oh no..." Hoot's sword clanged as he went on total offense now. "She's coming in."

She ran and slid under the sword volley, yelling incoherent insults at Michael with her healing stone glowing in her hand. She pulled out bandages to stop the bleed.

"Get out!" Michael commanded her, but she utterly ignored him.

"What are we going to do?" Hoot yelled as a sword whizzed by her head, narrowly missing her.

"Stop the fight!" Michael jumped back and held up his sword, but the angels kept coming at him. He backed to lure the fighters away from her, but Asher now decided to jump in front of him and start fighting. He whipped his head toward the judges—two former champions and Lord Baalael—who sat watching, unperturbed. "STOP THE FIGHT!" Michael screamed, but they ignored him, and the gladiators came at him even harder.

The tip of a sword glinted, and cut the air like silk toward Asher. He flipped backward, curling around it like a ribbon. Its long, dark shadow passed over the dirt, then over the feet of the angel from the square. It was heading directly for Philistina's neck.

The blue stone in Michael's hilt must've caught the light from Philistina's stone, because it flashed bright. Then, what felt like a thousand daggers pierced every inch of his back as his body went taut. Without thought or intention, he lifted his sword high and plunged it into the dirt. In that very instant, a blast of energy quaked the land and air in every direction, sending everyone and everything in the entire arena flying backward. The bizarre coincidence stunned him. Then...

Utter silence.

He snapped out of it and ran to Philistina, stepping over the angels scattered on the floor and knelt beside her. He picked her up and propped her against his arm.

"Wake up, please wake up...." He gently shook her.

She blinked, then slowly opened her eyes.

He let out a deep breath.

"The ground and the air..." her eyes darted from side to side. "They convulsed..."

"Are you alright?" Michael asked, examining her face.

She pushed herself up slowly, shaking off whatever just knocked her over. "It must be another kind of storm," she said, bewildered. "A quake—another symptom of the darkness."

Michael nodded. He had no idea what it was. All that mattered was that she was alright.

"Michael!" Hoot ran over to him. "Are you two okay?"

"We're fine," Michael said, and Bernard appeared next to them.

In the stands, everyone began to rouse, climbing back to their feet.

"Are you both alright?" Michael looked to Hoot and Bernard.

"We're absolutely fine," Hoot said. "Whatever that was, it hit everyone in the arena."

"Everyone..." Bernard looked around, "except the three of us. And Zillah." She stared at them from the healing circle.

The other gladiators stayed on the ground, staring at the Two/thirteen with horrified looks in their eyes. One by one, they pulled their flags.

"We must've gotten lucky," Michael said, his eyes moving over Philistina. "I don't know what new kind of storm that was, but its timing was fortunate."

"A new kind of storm..." Hoot looked around. "One that erupts from the ground with no warning of its wrath."

"It's been raining," Michael said. "The other storms come with rain too."

The first judge stepped to the center of the pit and declared the Two/thirteen winners of the Eastern Dominion Championship—by default. They were the only fighters left standing.

29

Trudy

"If you encounter a nuisance, there's no need to be vexed;
often such troubles, prove themselves blessed!"
-Heaven's Handbook, Virtues, part 7, "On Temperance"

T RUDY CHECKED OVER BOTH shoulders as she crept through
the creaking, massive front doors of the Crimson Tower. The
solid obsidian slabs were so heavy that she nearly burst an eyeball
trying to open them.

"Flappy," she rasped, her gaze darting around the translu-
cent-gold-paved roads of the Holy City. "Where are you?"

A little chirp came from one of the ruby planting pots at the side
of the black veranda, and Trudy scurried over and knelt, examining
the bird. Rumors were spreading of some new kind of storm, so she
wanted to make sure Flappy hadn't gone off exploring.

The bird was fine, but her little eyes roamed Trudy's drab black
robe disapprovingly.

"It's only temporary until we find what we came for," she whispered
to the bird. Well— she really whispered it to herself. Being among Lucifer's servants was a miserable task, and Zuriah had been incensed that

she agreed to travel with him. But she couldn't pass up the opportunity to be so close to the inside of this thing.

She pulled a manna biscuit from her pocket and broke it up, sprinkling the crumbs into the dirt. "That'll keep you for a bit," she told Flappy. "Don't wander too far."

She stood up with a grunt, her vision taking in the immense ruby monolith that Lucifer called home—the Crimson Tower. A small red light blinked from behind a black lens above the door, and she smiled up at it and waved.

Winging cameras all over this monstrosity...

Unlike photo-machines, cameras were a sophisticated means of capturing moving pictures and sound. She'd worked on plenty of camera software back at the logistics hubs. They were necessary to coordinate operations, which made her all the more suspicious of Lucifer's home. What kind of operations was *he* trying to coordinate? Or did he simply not trust anyone?

And cameras were just the tip of the Tower's complexity. The amount of technology Lucifer employed for even mundane tasks was obnoxious, not unlike the Tech Center. And it required more cleaning than a cathedral, with the added decadence of its solid-ruby walls and ancient art.

She turned away from the Tower and leaned against its decorative black fence. It was nicer to peruse the gem-laden landscape of the Holy City, and doubtful that the other building's interiors were as augmented as this one.

The shimmering skyline was a kaleidoscope of color, its towering spires like majestic icicles carved from jewels like jasper, emerald, and topaz. Floating high above the center was the Throne Tower, a castle that sparkled with every color from the city itself. Nobody knew the type of stone it was carved from, but it refracted all the colors from the city in a rainbow-like dome that erupted from its crystalline facade. Because of that, the sky here was still bright, almost true to its original nature. It was nice to feel light warming her face again.

And that wasn't the only thing erupting from the Throne Tower. The Music of the Spheres blared from its windows, sailing across the light to the furthest reaches of the world. Her nannies used to teach that the seraphim and cherubim played it eternally, but nobody had ever actually *seen* a seraphim or cherubim— so it was anyone's guess how the music was really made, or travelling at the same volume throughout the Circles.

She'd only been to the Holy City once, and that was for a University field trip. Commonborn seldom roamed these golden, residential streets unless they were here for work or to tend political business. It had been bustling then, but with the lords all having been Called away and the Council dissolved, the city was nearly empty, save those who would be gathering for this event in the Crimson Tower.

It was a shame she had to visit the majestic city under such unfortunate circumstances. She would have loved a bit of sightseeing. But there wasn't time for any of that now.

"I dare not imagine you just fed a manna ration to birds." Almog, Lucifer's stiff-necked *Master Servant* emerged in a black robe from the doors behind her.

"Apologies, sir." Trudy turned away from the beautiful vista and back toward the tower. He must've been watching the cameras. "It was my own ration."

"The rations assigned to you must be eaten by you," Almog said, his pale white hair even lighter than his skin. "Disobedience won't be tolerated by the Order. Be not deceived by the light around us. The city imports its food—shortages are just as real here as they are anywhere else."

"The original Mother Tree looks healthy from here," Trudy said, glancing at the distant foliage that peeked from between the city's shimmering spires, beneath the Throne Tower. "Can't we take those fruit?"

"The very infant pod of Lord Lucifer himself hangs there," Almog tisked. "We do not eat from sacred ground."

She wanted to laugh in his face, but thought better of it. "I'll not waste my rations again, sir."

"Good." Almog's face remained stoic as he motioned her back inside.

The foyer of the Crimson Tower stretched at least three stories high, its walls carved from solid ruby. Chandeliers cut from onyx dangled over their heads, and the cold black floors were covered with intricate and ancient rugs woven by the most skilled crafters. But that was where the artistry ended. The furnishings and accents were laden with sleek, technical-looking designs.

"These are your duties in preparation for His Masterships event." Almog pulled a list from the inside of his robe and handed it to Trudy. His hooked cavern of a nose pitched an annoying nasal tone to his voice. "Only authorized servants will be permitted on the first floor during the event, of which you are *not*. You and the other trainees need to be out of sight before the silence falls. Is that understood?"

Trudy eyed the list, nodding. Based on the little bit of context she gleaned in the previous songs, Lucifer's little book club was about to choose their leader. Fortunately, *the event* had the whole place in such an uproar, that they'd never notice her snooping around the rest of the tower.

Thwop.

Something crashed into her ankle and she yelped. A low-hovering, beige disk zoomed away. She cursed the rogue machine under her breath and rubbed the ache. "That's the third time the floor cleaner's crashed into me," she said. "I think the sensors are faulty."

"There's no time to repair vacuum disks," Almog said. "You will sweep the rugs by hand."

"Won't they crash into the walls and damage them?"

"These walls are solid ruby," Almog huffed. "I'm not worried about *vacuum disks*."

Trudy folded the list and shoved it in her pocket. "Has there been any more word of the quakes?"

"Only the one at the Games," Almog said, "But best assume the worst. The Almighty's turned vengeful. All the more reason to make sure Our Lord's event goes smoothly."

And all the more reason to snoop more efficiently. "Understood, sir."

"Good." Almog turned on his heel and started down the hall. "Get to work."Of all the things she envisioned doing to save the world, polishing Lucifer's ruby walls was not one of them. This was worse than keeping his dry-cleaning schedule. She dipped the rag in vinegar and wiped, the acidic smell nearly choking her.

The garish luxury of a lord. Zuriah's words played over in her head. He was right. What was the matter with wallpaper? Or wood? And this blasted ruby streaked so easily. Another flat, beige disk whizzed directly at her and she nearly fell into her bucket avoiding it. "Stupid, broken machines..." she grumbled. The only thing worse than overusing technology was not maintaining the technology you overused. Throne only knew how many sensors were broken on those vacuum disks.

She checked the hall both ways and eyed the camera looming at the other side. She opened a panel of her robe, and turning away from the camera, slid a qube from her inside pocket. She initiated it safely from within the dark confines of the fabric and connected to the world network.

Fortunately, she'd been on the team that designed the only camera software that existed, and was able to access Lucifer's account with her old administrative credentials. The whole system only existed so that one logistics hub could virtually be in the same room with the others, so his extensive use of it was more than suspicious. It was clear though, as she viewed the sheer amount of surveillance on her hologram, that he didn't trust the very angels pleading loyalty to him. What a terrible way to live. His little Black Manifesto might have touted freedom, but such a lack of faith in friends was anything but.

First, she set the camera feed in the hall to loop its previous footage of her cleaning. Once she did that, she relaxed and placed the qube flat on the floor. Then she set the entire list of cameras on a playback loop, all save the ones on the first floor where the event would be held. She slid the qube back into her pocket, and took her bucket and rag with her—just in case.

If Lucifer possessed the kind of technology needed to access nature itself, there would need to be some kind of high-density data center to host it. A space filled with machines and servers. Somewhere that had a proper cooling system and moisture control to maintain ideal mechanical conditions.

She began her search in the rooms at the end of the hall, checking wardrobes, closets, and wall panels for any kind of secret access panel. She moved down the hall and searched room by room, in the backs of beds and under carpets, behind wall tapestries and paintings.

By the time she was finishing up on the eighth floor, the outro of the song was well underway. The guests of "the event" would start arriving soon.

She resumed her snoop-cleaning. Every floor was like its own home, replete with bedrooms, living areas, and a kitchen. A single one of those silken bed coverings would've taken half a symphony to weave... but he found machines to make those too. Even the art on his walls lacked the texture to have been made by real, angelic hands.

Imagine using machines to create your art? Where is the joy or love in that? What a terrible world he would lord over, given the chance. She shivered at the thought of a world where creativity was outsourced to lifeless metal and circuitry. *Technology is meant to enhance life, not replace it.*

But the abundance of technology, she learned, had brought his servants comfort. After all, what better than artificial light to help you forget the darkness? Under those black robes, most of them were terrified. And they all trusted Lucifer to keep them safe.

She had to commend his cleverness, though. His little tale about the Creator gone rogue was ingenious. Scare them, starve them, then show up to save them.

Manifesto or not—angels were painfully naive.

The thick aroma of savory dishes and hot bread rose from the first floor and her stomach rumbled, but she just laughed to herself. Most of that food didn't have vita in it anyway. It wasn't a real feast—just a counterfeit.

Exhausted, she moved on to the third floor, nearly falling over one of the confused vacuum disks as it zipped up the stairs. The event was starting now, and she had no idea how long it would last. She searched, lifting more carpets and checking floorboards. She inspected more storage rooms and went through every last inch of closet space. She checked for hidden panels in the bathrooms... but there was nothing.

She considered that he could have been storing the hardware offsite somewhere, but technology that powerful would need a formidable base of operations. It would be difficult to hide among the villages, or stretches of forest between them where angels frequented. And with access to the whole world, it only made sense that it would be located somewhere in the center, in or around the Holy City. And it only made sense to keep it somewhere he had total control over, at all times.

There had to be *something* here, somewhere.

She searched the second floor, her eyelids now heavy and her thoughts sluggish. The fear that she might not find anything hit hard. Even worse—if his system didn't exist, and she was wrong about him... then nature itself was failing, and there was no hope for the world.

She went into the bathroom and splashed cold water on her face, steeling herself. She couldn't think like that. She had to hold hope. And there was still one last place to search—the basement.

She retrieved a lantern from the utility closet and found the old servants' stairwell. Lucifer made a show of sharing his space with the commonborn, so these dusty, dark corridors went completely unused.

Her feet ached as they hit the creaking boards of the ancient stairs, and her muscles screamed for vita and a hot bath. She passed the first floor, gingerly, and continued down until she came to the basement door.

A whizzing noise came up behind her and she whipped around, nearly dropping the lantern. A vacuum disk careened head on, inches above the stairs; she must've forgotten to close the door behind her. She shoved the basement door open just in time for the disk to whish through without crashing.

She exhaled. Last thing she needed was a loud bang underneath Lucifer's precious event.

She lifted the lantern in the windowless basement and her heart absolutely sank. There was equipment in the corner, but nothing beyond what she expected to supply a Tower that size. Otherwise, the cellar was just an empty footprint. No doors or rooms or tunnels... nothing beside the four stone walls.

A sob rose up her throat and she clenched her eyes shut.

She wanted to scream—down the Throne with Lucifer and his stupid event. Down the Throne with the lords and the scholars, and down the Throne with Almog and all the mindless pets that licked Lucifer's sandals. They would all taste death—every last one—and there wasn't a blasted thing Trudy could do about it. Sandoval and her Matriarch and all her sisters too. The whole world was doomed.

And right as the sob was about to escape her lips, that winging piece of junk came whizzing straight at her again. She cocked her leg back and kicked, meeting the vacuum flat on its edge. Pain ripped through her foot as the disk went flying backward, clear across the basement. It headed straight for the wall and she winced in anticipation of the sound.

But no sound came.

She straightened, lifting her lantern higher and stepping toward the wall. The vacuum disk had disappeared. Her gaze roamed the gray, concrete floor searching for it.

Nothing.

Suddenly, the disk emerged *from the wall* and came whizzing back. Her mouth fell open.

She hurried to the spot it emerged from and stopped short, putting her palm just in front of the cold stone bricks. Slowly, she touched it, and her hand disappeared into the wall. She yanked it back, then, slowly, waved it through again.

Hologram.

Her pulse quickened and she lifted the lantern, carefully stepping through the wall.

The space was no larger than a dressing room, with a single light source glowing in the middle of a huge steel door. No, not a door—*a vault*.

A blue holographic sphere floated in front of the latch, and inside of it hovered alphabetical glyphs. She put her index finger near the sphere, and the glyphs rushed to the border of the orb. Three yellow circles then appeared above it.

She furrowed her brow. It was some kind of passcode lock. She moved her finger closer to the letters, and the first of three yellow circles blinked.

A lock that required a password, and three chances to get it right.

Her pulse quickened and her lips curled. This was it— it had to be. But with only three tries, she couldn't risk a half-hearted, rushed attempt. She'd hacked passwords before—never for dishonest purposes, of course, but angels were infamous for forgetting their qpistle credentials. She already had a script written to crack codes, but never had to deal with a limited amount of tries before.

If she entered the password wrong three times, it was likely that the system would send some kind of alert to Lucifer. But, if she could figure out what passwords he used for other things, there was a strong chance she could crack this one. When you had to log into multiple systems, different passwords were a pain in the wings. Angels usually kept their passwords consistent. This was her only shot.

She had administrative access to his camera system already, and though his actual login credentials weren't visible, it would be easy to run her cracking script there first. Then, she could run the script on his qpistle account, where there would also be an unlimited amount of tries.

She stepped back through the wall and headed up the servants' stairwell. The vacuum zipped past her and she smiled at it. Who would've guessed that a few broken sensors in a bucket of bolts might turn the whole world around. *Talk about luck.*

30

Michael

"When we analyze the overt and covert complexity within the systemetry of an angel's ability to think and reason, the functioning thereof remains a mystery to be marveled at. It is that very thing which gives rise to our consciousness and will. And without a will, what would an angel become?"
-Treatise on the Relevance of Piety to Nature by The Esteemed Professor Zuriah

T HE MINSTRELS PLAYED A string sonata from the corner of Lucifer's sitting room, making Michael almost forget that the silence had fallen. Lords, both known and unknown to him, swarmed the place as they chatted with silent scholars and decorated military officers alike. Black-robed servants kept to themselves, doling out refreshments and cleaning empties with near the same precision as a military march.

Michael stretched his head to relieve the itch from his new, over-starched version of a uniform that was to be worn at all formal events. Lucifer's home, while a marvel, was hard to appreciate when your neck felt like something that got stuck to Shemliel's not-so-fresh-shaven chest.

"Ready to hit yourself in the head with a hammer yet?" Joseph sipped casually from a flute glass as he smiled, nodding to other officers as they passed. He looked sharp in his crimson uniform, with its sleek obsidian buttons and embroidered insignias.

"I don't know what's less comfortable..." Michael squirmed, "these uniforms or this room." He slid a finger under his collar to let some air through.

"Don't show discomfort," Joseph said casually, "it makes us look weak. These lords need reminding that not all commonborn are easily cowed." His gaze moved to Baalael, who was draped in sheer fabrics like his siblings, lounging and chatting on a sofa while servants catered to them. Michael dropped his hand to his side and fixed a serious countenance, ignoring the itch.

"Look at the bright side," Joseph said, taking another long sip, "you'll finally get to see who mounts the shadow chasers."

"That's the bright side?"

"Bright side, dark side..." Joseph downed the rest of his drink and snatched another from a passing tray. "It's all the same now."

Michael eyed his drink. "Wine and thought trolls might not mix well...."

"Ruby blocks telepathy." Joseph sipped again. "That's why Lucifer's constructed his home from it. But keep your voice low—there are devices that record images and sound everywhere. The vote's happening here for an extra layer of protection. It's harder to conspire when you can't silently communicate. Though I'm fairly certain he gets a kick out of doing this right under the Almighty's nose."

Michael sniffed the air. "Is that empyreanol?"

"Nectar of the gods." Joseph sucked another long gulp and grinned. "You might want to get yourself a glass for this."

Michael cocked a brow. This room was the very last place to lose control. "No thanks."

"Don't say I didn't warn you."

A bell tinkled from the center of the room and the minstrels stopped playing. Michael and Joseph exchanged a final glance before fixing their attention on the center of the room. Lucifer's Master Servant, Almog, placed a glass funnel into a translucent jar, and poured a small bag of sand into it. "You have until the last grain falls to cast your vote," he practically intoned through that giant nose. "Choose well."

Joseph and Michael got into the queue and dropped their votes for Lucifer into the bowl, then headed back to the spot where they were standing. A highly decorated officer stood there looking eager, apparently waiting for them.

"Greater Dominion…" The officer bowed his salute. "My fondest greetings."

"At ease, Ramiel," Joseph chuckled and pulled him into a hug. "How are you, old friend?"

"I'm well, brother. I was looking forward to seeing you here."

"As was I, brother. Michael, meet Ramiel. He's the Lesser Dominion over the western Hexants. *Almost* my equal, but more importantly, one of my oldest and dearest friends. We've fought on many a squad over the symphonies."

Michael saluted. "An honor to meet you, Dominion."

"Michael's a Furie in the Second Legion," Joseph said. "But once we're done recruiting there, I suspect he'll climb rather quickly to Commander."

"An honor, Michael," Ramiel saluted him. "Your reputation precedes you. They're already putting on plays of your unarmed victory in my home crossing."

"Even Asmodeus likes him," Joseph said with mirth.

"Speak of Asmodeus, and he shall appear!" A lean, dark arm crept around Ramiel's shoulder and Asmodeus' head popped up between them. "Are you getting our squad back together without me, my Champion?" His gold and silver teeth gleamed in a wide smile. "Michael, has Ramiel told you how our Champion would make us run like wild animals when he trained us? We can outrun a herd of gazelle, still, the three of us."

"Good times," Ramiel said.

"This was before you needed five fighters," Asmodeus said. "Angels were tough then. We were brutal."

Ramiel laughed. "Don't let him fool you. Az would clear the pit for bugs so none were injured before we fought."

Asmodeus wagged his finger. "Because I get no credit for defeating a bug. They can dig their own pits if they want to fight."

"We need to get together and fight for fun," Ramiel said. "Blow off some steam. Like the old songs."

"Nothing's much fun anymore," Joseph sighed. "Life's gotten too serious."

"And where is your squad, Furie Michael?" Asmodeus asked. "Or should I say, your *guard*? Smart angels find ways to keep those they trust close. Furie Michael... he is smart."

"They're escorting one of our triage technicians back to the island," Michael said. "They'll be back in time for the final tournament."

A high-pitched bell tinkled again, and they all harkened.

"I hate to leave you all," Ramiel said, "but I need to get back to my cohorts for the crowning."

Almog appeared in the center of the room again in front of a glass bowl, now filled with folded pieces of parchment. The last grain of sand fell through the glass and he said, "Time is up." Three more servants joined him and began counting the ballots.

"Not so fast..." Baalael's eyes flashed a bright gray as he dangled a flute of empyreanol from the couch. "I want my administrator to count the votes as well."

"I assure you, Lord Baalael," Almog said, "Lucifer has arranged a triple check of the count. Your administrator is not necessary."

Baalael stood up, his casual toga and lax demeanor a complete disgrace as the Principality of their military. Nobody holding power over six legions should be walking around with their nipples exposed. It was either nipples or war. It couldn't be both.

"Defy a lord, Almog?" Baalael said, and a breeze stirred from inside the room—a predictable flex from that wingbag. "Would your master really encourage that?"

Almog grew even more pale than he already was. "No, m'lord. But Lucifer's given me explicit direct—"

"So far as I'm aware," Baalael cut him off, "no Sahtan has been crowned yet. I am a lord, and I require that my administrator, Deidre, confirm your count."

Deidre?

Michael could feel the life force drain from his face as one of the servants standing behind Baalael's couch stepped forward and pushed her hood back. She was even more gaunt than he remembered, as if somehow her cruelty had etched itself right into her face.

"Are you alright?" Joseph whispered. "You look worse than when you saw that deer." Michael nodded reflexively and took a deep breath—just as Azrael had shown him. He couldn't lose his calm. Not here. Not now.

She stepped to the bowl and reached in, but Almog pushed her hand away.

"It's alright." A melody blossomed in the air, soft and mellow. Lord Lucifer descended the wide ruby staircase and adjusted his cufflinks. Everyone straightened. His clothing matched the military uniforms down to the very last stitch of his trousers. Crimson and black. *Optics are important.*

Lucifer was so much smarter than the grape-eating, overfed cows he called siblings.

"We have nothing to hide," Lucifer said, a charming smile in the center of his jaw. "Deidre may count the votes if that pleases you, brother. I trust that all lords, scholars, and officers have cast their vote?"

Almog nodded. "They have, m'lord."

"And the sacrifices?" he asked.

"They've cast as well, m'lord," Almog said.

Michael turned to Joseph. "Sacrifices?"

"You should've just drunk the empyreanol when you had the chance." He shrugged and took another sip.

Servants appeared at every window and drew the dark shades closed, turning the room black as pitch. Lucifer's eyes blazed a bright yellow, and then the hearth and candles spontaneously lit, their flames licking upward and turning everyone into a dancing and ominous shade of orange.

"Some of you know how partial I am to dramatic lighting," Lucifer said, "but more importantly, sensitive events will take place here, and for that we need privacy. Foremost, I'd like to thank you all for traveling to my home. I know for some it's been a long journey.

"We begin a new epoch as we take this final step to etch ourselves into history, birthing new rituals that will ensure we are still thriving when darkness takes the world—and long after that. Our scribes have prepared the scrolls on which this first historic entry will be written. The election of our first Sahtan." He paused and everyone applauded, clinking their glasses.

"While votes are being counted," Lucifer continued, "I'd like to update you with some very encouraging news. Our campaign to win the trust of the masses has enjoyed more success than we could've hoped for." His yellow gaze roamed the room until it landed on Michael. "This soldier's courage and creativity in the Games have garnered more affection than any gladiator in history, and nothing could make me prouder. If you've been following the papers, then he needs no introduction."

Lucifer waved Michael forward, and he froze. He wasn't expecting this.

"I'd like to formally introduce you all to the face of our movement …."

Joseph nudged Michael forward, and hesitantly, he stepped to the front of the room, keeping his face turned away from Deidre. He bowed the salute, unsure of what else to do, and Lucifer waved it off and kissed him once on either cheek.

"When the masses see Michael," Lucifer put a hand on his back, "they see themselves. Already he's advanced to the rank of Furie in the Second Hexant, and he represents what every commonborn may accomplish if they have the courage and intelligence to do so. He is the very face of freedom, and the Order of Light has big plans for him. As a token of my appreciation, I'd like to present him with a gift."

Lucifer reached into his frock and pulled out the looking glass—the one Michael had looked into when they first met.

"This is from my own personal collection," Lucifer said. "Should you ever forget what you're capable of, or what your future may hold... glance into this and remember: *the world is yours.*"

He handed the mirror to Michael. Last time, the reflection barely resembled reality. Now, it wasn't so far off.

"Thank you," Michael said.

"Michael will calm any vestige of apprehension in the populace during the final tournament as he leads the Second Hexant to victory. Let's show him our appreciation."

Applause filled the room, and all of the military officers who had been seated stood up. After a few beats, the bell tinkled again and they quieted as Michael made his way back to Joseph, slipping the looking glass into his inside pocket.

"We have reached a consensus, m'lord," Almog announced. "The votes have been counted and confirmed."

"The powers that be have spoken," Lucifer said, clasping his hands behind his back. "Let the recording of our new history begin."

Almog announced the results. "Twenty-five votes in favor of Lord Lucifer. Twenty-two in favor of Lord Baalael. Thirteen votes in favor of Lord Astorath. Nine votes in favor of Lord Azazel. Eight votes in favor of Lord Mammon...." Almog hesitated, suddenly looking uncomfortable and mumbled, "And one vote in favor of Asmodeus."

"You cannot know if you do not try, eh?" Asmodeus' whispered, cackling in Michael's ear.

Almog pulled a black case from under the table and removed a glossy, obsidian crown. The glow from the candles danced on its dark surface, and two twisted horns protruded from either side, perfectly matching the horns on their military helms.

Almog pulled his hood low, covering his face. "Powers that be!" His nasal voice bounced from the walls. "Bow before your new Sahtan."

Each of the glowing-eyed gods moved to the center of the room and huddled around them. They lifted the crown in unison and placed it on Lucifer's head. One by one, they fell to their knees and kissed his sigil ring. Baalael went last, and while he knelt, Lucifer lifted his face by the chin.

"My sweet brother," Lucifer said, "life force of my branch, and treasure of my soul. Those in whom we trust the deepest, we keep the closest. I confirm your appointment as Principality of War, and I name you lead advisor of my Council and second in command. Should anything happen to me, you will reign in my place."

Baalael looked up at him, his eyes filled with hunger.

"Are you ready to present your gift?" Lucifer asked him.

Baalael nodded, and Deidre escorted a servant to the center of the room.

"Try and hold your dinner down for this one, eh, Furie?" Asmodeus whispered in Michael's ear.

The servant was covered in a black hooded robe, and Almog retrieved a golden chalice and a plain, steel dagger. He dragged the dagger across the servant's hand and light flashed before blood pooled in the chalice. Deidre wrapped a cloth around his hand and the servant stepped back.

"That wasn't nearly as bad as you feeding me pig meat," Michael hissed back at Asmodeus.

"Don't worry, Furie," Asmodeus said, "the show is not over yet."

Lucifer dipped his thumb into the chalice and traced an upside-down triangle on Baalael's forehead. "Principality of War; I seal you in blood."

Baalael stood up and stepped to the side as Lucifer and the lords repeated the ritual with six other servants—Azazel, Astorath, Mammon,

Leviathan, Belphegor, and Abaddon. Michael was familiar with Azazel and Mammon from campus, but the others he didn't know. He anointed each of them as the Principality of a respective Hexant to serve as the governing arm of the Order.

Each lord presented a servant as a gift, and each gift cut their wrist and bled into the chalice that Lucifer had used to anoint them. It was crazy, of course. Blood rituals and all. But the world was crazy now. It wasn't so big a deal that Joseph and Asmodeus should be doling out warnings. It wasn't like he'd never seen blood before.

"You have received our gifts," the lords of the new Council chanted in unison, their voices like a chorus. "Now receive our sacrifice."

Lucifer lifted the chalice to his lips and gulped it, blood spilling from the sides of his lips and running in straight lines down his chin. Michael winced a little. Then the first servant disrobed, exposing his naked body. He closed his eyes and stretched out his neck, and Almog slipped behind him and slit it wide open.

Michael gasped as light exploded from the servant's wound, but instead of condensing to blood, the light beamed straight into Lucifer's open mouth. The next servant disrobed and did the same. Then the next, and the next, until all six had lavender beams of life force spewing from their opened throats straight into Lucifer.

Asmodeus could barely contain his cackling as Michael stood there, jaw gaping, in complete shock.

First, their eyes went black. Not black like obsidian, or onyx. It was a black so dark that it seemed to inhale even the light from the candles. Then the blackness spread like vines from their eyes around their faces, down their necks and to their torsos until the blackness swallowed them whole.

"It's a necessary sacrifice," Joseph put a hand on Michael's shoulder. "They volunteered for this. It was their will. To sacrifice themselves for the greater good, and they'll be honored as heroes for it."

Lucifer's yellow eyes grew brighter as their life force drained into him. What was left where they stood were six impossibly black figures. Six shadow forms that were so dark, they appeared like a void in the very fabric of existence.

"Are they gone?" Michael rasped. "*Dead*?"

"Not in the way you use that word," Joseph said. "They live still, but they're part of Lucifer now."

"What have they become?" Michael asked, barely able to string together the sentence. "Are they still angels?"

"They're the *absence* of angels," Joseph said. "They've become demonstrations."

"Demonstrations?" Michael asked. "Of what?"

"True faith in the Order. In our ideals. We call them *demons* for short. Those six will mount the shadow chasers in the Great War against the Almighty. Lucifer was the one to consume them, so their shadows serve him now."

Asmodeus slapped Michael in the back, finding all of this hysterical. "Look at the face on you! You never disappoint me, my friend." He handed Michael a glass of empyreanol. "Drink this, it helps."

Michael downed the empyreanol as applause filled the room, and the demons disappeared into the shadows. Servants opened the shades, and slowly, chatting voices began to fill the room.

"Not that the show is over…" Asmodeus cracked open the front door and discreetly motioned them to follow, "let us convene our own council."

Once outside, Michael gulped down the fresh air and blinked his eyes in the bright light. He tried to keep his stomach contents inside as Asmodeus led them down the black veranda steps to the glassy golden road in front of the Crimson Tower.

"Can't be too careful," Joseph said once they were about ten meters up the road. "Lucifer has eyes and ears everywhere."

"Did you see her there?" Asmodeus hissed, any vestige of his giddy countenance now gone. "Rubbing his shoulders while he pawed her like an animal. I want to see him in pieces, Furie." His nostrils flared wide. "Scattered around the pit like that pig I fed you."

"Have you spoken to Jezebel?" Joseph asked. "Did you give her the new ring?"

"Of course I have spoken to her," Asmodeus spat. "That pig is stupid and easy to sneak around. She will switch the rings during the silence before the Final Battle."

"So, we're set," Joseph said. "Michael, are you ready to do this?"

Michael's throat bobbed.

"You are afraid of him?" Asmodeus crinkled his brow.

"No...." Michael took a deep breath, held it, then let it go. "But we just watched six angels get their lives sucked out until they became *nothing*. I need a measure...."

"You are still thinking of that?" Asmodeus cackled, the flippancy with which he changed moods growing entirely more disturbing. "You never cease to cheer me, Furie. This is the way things are now."

"Light once defined everything," Joseph said. "Now, Heaven embodies lost light."

"HELL!" Asmodeus declared, cackling at his clever acronym. "Welcome to *Hell*, Furie Michael! Don't worry... you'll get used to it."

31

Michael

"Silent scholars were inspired to forge the rings when the first commonborn Mother Tree sprang up. They are simultaneously a catalyst, and a valve that controls the flow and intensity of power. It could not be risked that the newer species might be tempted to worship the gods."
-The Guide to Utopian Principles and Ethics, Section of Addendums and Later Knowledge

MICHAEL PUSHED OPEN HIS tent curtain and stepped into the gloomy gray air of the One/three crossing. A First Legion campsite had been hosting them as a courtesy, due to their proximity to the Colosseo, the immense arena where all final tournaments of the Games would be held.

On the horizon, the Holy City's glimmering Rainbow Dome was the centerpiece of Michael's vantage point, and a sharp contrast to the gray and dismal gloom that encroached on the edge of its glow. From this far, the Throne Tower was little more than a tiny spike pointing up from a brightly colored helm. The Almighty stayed locked safe within those walls, basking in the light, while he condemned all his creation to suffer a fate worse than even Michael had ever suffered. It was another level of cruelty.

Michael shook his head and turned away. It was better to embrace a darkness that wanted you, than chase a light that had forsaken you.

"Horses are ready, sir." Hoot appeared before him in full armor. "The squad is gearing up for the Final Battle."

"How was the ride with Philistina?"

"Quiet," Hoot said. "She's not exactly enthusiastic about all this."

"Better for you then. She's not exactly gentle with her words either. Have the rations been distributed yet?"

"Yes, sir. All except yours."

"Keep it, I have my stash. Take what's left in our reserve and finish it with the others—we can't chance anyone getting weak or winded in the pit later."

Hoot opened his mouth, but closed it again.

"What?"

"I already packed the reserve in case we come across any hungry angels."

"You can't just *give away* our reserves, Hoot. Besides, there are still some Trees of Life here. There shouldn't be hungry angels."

"But there are," Hoot said. "First Legion is controlling the trees so they can distribute rations in neighboring crossings."

"Fine," Michael sighed, "but the squad needs at least a triple ration."

Hoot started to protest, but Michael shook his head and began walking. "I don't want to hear it. I'm not taking chances with this battle and I don't care if the whole realm starves, so save your breath."

Hoot didn't respond as they crossed the dirt path to the stables.

The camp smelled like iron, horses, and mud, and Michael's red cape commanded acknowledging nods and salutes from the soldiers engaged in various duties. Michael glanced back at Hoot, ready to further justify his position, but the precept kept his head down, which was oddly frustrating.

This was like when Gabriel would get quiet after Michael delivered a proper chiding for letting others pick on him, then would drown his sorrows in a tin full of sweet cakes. Gabriel would get quiet too, and that silence grated him.

Michael stopped short and turned. "You're like a pious splinter in my behind, you know that? Just take the reserves to whoever you want."

"What about the squad?"

"I'll give them the last of my stash. Just know that you're encouraging the angels out there to be weak. Better to teach them how to source what they need rather than giving everything we need away."

"Everything we have was given to us."

"We're working for it. They can become soldiers and work for it too. At least use the rations to try and recruit. A lifetime of easy living's made everyone soft and lazy."

Michael resumed walking, shaking his head. The precept would've made a much better son for Mary; always trying to feed everyone and fix their problems. It was hard to dredge up that kind of sympathy for angels who'd never so much as suffered a hangnail. In some ways, the darkness was a great equalizer.

The squad was already mounted on their horses and waiting, and Hoot gave Michael one final nod, mouthing, *"Thank you."*

Long caravans of angels filed across the plains, riding toward the stadium like streams of water desperately seeking their source. Angels loved their sports—that was a given—but it was almost like they were clinging to the Games now as a last vestige of normalcy.

The squad was especially enthusiastic about the match, chatting and planning their moves the whole way there. Michael kept them far from the caravans, not wanting to waste time on autographs or pictures. It wasn't that he didn't enjoy the attention. It was a great vindication of the steaming pile of dung his life had amounted to before meeting Joseph. But his focus was elsewhere now. It was time for justice.

The Colosseo was just beyond the border of the One/two crossing, a mere Circle away from the Holy City. His breath caught as the massive, circular structure came into view. Its fortified stone walls were topped by a series of seventy-two swirling concrete spires, each flying a flag that represented one of the realms Crossings.

The irony was that the Two/thirteen had no flag on a spire, because the island had never been considered a Crossing. But that didn't matter, because Lucifer's flag was sprawled wide across the immense entrance archway.

He drank in that single, long beat, free of ambition and justice and vengeance. He had made it—he was about to fight in the Final Battle of the Games.

The Colosseo was situated among some of the most ancient, common villages in the Second Circle. The light around the stadium itself was fairly bright, which was odd given its proximity to high populations. It was common knowledge by now that where more angels resided, the darkness grew deeper.

The grass at its base was brown and withered—no flowers or animals—but the light remained decent, and Michael wondered how.

Long lines stretched from the entrance and curved around its walls, the familiar scent of fried foods filling the air as merchants sold flags and posters of the competing athletes. There was no shortage of voices calling out Michael's name to advertise their wares. The squad rode around to the rear entrance, which was cordoned off by ropes and military guard.

Joseph waited outside for them, having opted to stay at the Crimson Tower with Lucifer rather than in the camp.

"Earlier than I expected," Joseph said, then motioned them to follow. They went through the elaborate marble entrance and into a winding, concrete corridor that led to the gladiator hole under the stands, where athletes stretched and practiced their forms.

"I'm near parched as a sand squirrel!" Bernard smacked his lips, and everyone looked at him. "Thirsty..." his gaze darted among their confused faces. "It means I'm thirsty. Air's too dry down here."

"Me too," Hoot said.

"There's a fount in the corner," Joseph pointed, "along with some nice fruit and crackers. I hope you've all eaten your rations—there are none here for the athletes."

Bernard rubbed his belly and saluted. "Full as a fork fiddler."

"I don't want to know..." Hoot patted Bernard's shoulder and they headed toward the refreshments.

"Michael and I have some business to tend during the opening fights," Joseph said to Zillah and Asher. "We'll be back in time for warm-ups."

"Where are you going?" Asher asked. First thing to come out of his mouth since they'd met by the stables.

"Tending business," Joseph repeated. "Officer business."

Asher didn't make eye contact as he tightened his sandals. "I only wonder when our *Greater Dominion* might remember the promises he made to the rest of us."

"Asher..." Michael warned, but Joseph held out a hand.

"You promised us glory before we ever agreed to go to that forsaken island," Asher said. "Before *he* was even a thought."

"Don't bring me into this," Zillah groaned while she leaned into a stretch. "We're fighting in the Games. And winning. It doesn't get more glorified than that."

"If I wanted to live under a shadow I would've stayed in the orchard." Asher finished tying his sandal and stood upright. "You never mentioned being anyone's lackey."

Michael stepped in his face, so close he could feel the heat rising from Asher's skin. "Why don't you go re-read the military code about insubordination."

Asher glared back for a few beats, nose to nose with Michael, and Joseph put a hand on Michael's chest. Asher grabbed his satchel and stormed off.

"Let him cool down," Joseph said. "I did make promises when I thought he could be Champion. Had I not enticed him to come here, he'd have advanced past soldier by now."

Michael regarded Joseph for a beat, then relaxed his shoulders. "I just hope I can trust him out there."

"He'll be fine," Joseph said, motioning Michael to follow him into the corridor. "I'll talk with him. Maybe transfer him somewhere he can move up the ranks a little quicker."

"I think transfer's a good idea," Michael said. The whole point of a guard was to be surrounded by those you trusted. And he didn't trust Asher. Not for some time now.

Michael scanned the corridor for cameras as they padded lightly through the stone halls. There were none, but the beams of light that shone through the open-air windows to the stone floor were a rare sight these songs. "What's with the light around here? Can it heal Baalael if I succeed?"

"Nobody heals from a missing limb," Joseph said. "At least not for a good while."

"It's pretty bright out here."

"This isn't the kind of light you think it is," Joseph said. "That ritual you saw in the Crimson Tower does more than create demons to ride the shadow chasers. The lord who consumes the life force also controls it, and that energy can be used for things—like a battery. Brightening up the atmosphere is one such use. Lucifer's also using it to help grow food. But it's not strong enough to heal anything significant."

"Seems a high price for spectators to see a fight better."

"Now more than ever we need the Games," Joseph said. "Angels are practically making pilgrimage here. They're desperate for more than food. They're desperate for hope. Light gives them that. You'll give them that. When you lead the squad to victory, they'll love you, and when you leave Baalael in pieces, they'll fear you too."

"That's a good thing?"

"Of course. Everything they associate with you, they'll associate with this uniform. The military is the connection between the Order and the masses. To do our job properly, we need more than their love. We need their fear." Joseph shouldered open a heavy wooden door.

"Fear?" Asmodeus stood behind a wooden table in the center of a small, stone room. "What do you think you know about fear?"

"We know nothing of fear," Joseph answered, pulling a chair out and sitting. "We know only valor and courage."

"Good answer, my friend."

"Do you have the ring?" Joseph asked as Michael sat down. Asmodeus tossed a metal band on the table, and it twirled on its side until tipping over with a clink. It had a blue oval stone set in the center, with six encircled black stars etched underneath. *Baalael's sigil.*

"The pig cannot tell the difference between the real and the fake," Asmodeus said. "I will hold this one for safe keeping."

"You ready for this, Michael?" Joseph asked.

Michael nodded. If they only knew how ready he was.

"There's no room for error," Joseph said. "Don't waste your energy in the match—let the squad show off a little. Treat it like a warm-up. Keep it entertaining; don't get winded. After you win, the judge will bring the trophy into the pit and ask the squad to name their Champion; it's tradition. When they do, cross your arms to your chest in a half salute. That's the refusal. Then claim Champion's Legacy."

"Did you get all that, Furie Michael?"

"Don't accept the trophy, cross my arms to my chest, claim Champion's Legacy. Simple enough."

"That's a soldier." Joseph patted him on the back, and Asmodeus put the ring back in his pouch and shoved it deep into the groin of his armor.

"It'll be safe down with my pisser." He grabbed his crotch and yanked it before spitting on the floor. "That's what I think of a god and his power. If I could have a million eyes, I would use them all to watch you cut that pig into pieces."

32

Michael

*"When things don't flow in accord with our plans, let's
look for even bigger hands!"*
-Heaven's Handbook, Virtues, Part 2, "On Faith"

T HE SQUAD STOOD AT the precipice of the gladiator hole and
looked out into the arena. Sweat and fresh blood perfumed
the air as plumes of dust rose beneath the amateur gladiators' feet,
rallying the crowd for the main event. Lucifer's servants flooded
the stands and doled out rations as angels tripped over one another
and grasped at them. They gave away crimson-and-black flags as
journalists snapped away, leaving no doubt as to who was providing
for them.

"They look tough," Bernard said, looking straight across the arena
into the other gladiator hole. The Western Dominion Champions
stood in a horizontal line behind the fence in their leathers. They
didn't wear military armor like the Two/thirteen, but by the way
they carried themselves, you knew some were soldiers. They had
chewed through the competition on their side of the realm too,
though with less dramatic fanfare.

"I'm sure they are tough." Michael pushed back from the fence and faced the squad, "Everyone's clear on opening forms? These fans need to have some fun.... They've had a rough go lately."

They all nodded except Asher, who hadn't so much as looked at Michael since he'd gotten back. When this was all over, his transfer would be imminent. If Michael could've retired him from the squad right then, he would've, except they needed five to fight.

In the Colosseo, all three of the judges sat on silver thrones at the head of the pit, the Master of the Games sitting highest and center, looking bored. His presence there was mostly symbolic... unless of course, some angel, mad with ambition, claimed Champion's Legacy.

Michael spotted Asmodeus in the stands with a crew of other inked-up First Legion soldiers. He cheered the amateur fight, yelling what Michael could only guess were enthusiastic obscenities that made the others laugh. Asmodeus' eyes landed on Michael, and he grinned wide before grabbing his groin.

After the archery, javelin and running competitions, winning gladiators from local crossing tournaments got to warm the crowd up for the final event. Three amateur fighters remained in the pit—two against one, and the one didn't last very long. He hit the floor hard after a femme clobbered him with her shield. He pulled his flag and tapped out, then the rest of the winning squad rushed the pit and embraced their still-standing fighters. Even as amateurs, to fight and win in the Colosseo must've felt tremendous. They cheered the whole way out.

Silence descended as the outro notes faded, cueing the main event. A composer holding a stick stepped in front of the balcony orchestra and began waving his arms to a high-paced allegro. Cellos and violas chirped tense notes in rapid succession, and the Two/thirteen readied themselves at the stairwell.

A troupe of costumed jugglers and acrobats appeared in the perimeter field. This kind of show was customary before the main event. The balcony orchestra blasted as angels in shiny white leotards tumbled and hurdled, flipping from one another's shoulders in perfect sync with the pulsing music.

They descended into the pit, leaping like frogs, and the crowd cheered. They performed to the beat, each doing some feat that moved to the upbeat music. In a final stunt, one of the more elaborate acrobats cut clean across the pit in a speedy series of cartwheels, flips, and jumps until he came to the other side. He launched himself over the dirt wall and landed at the judges' feet. He bowed before the Master of the Games, then kissed his cheek with a dramatic pause. Michael rolled his eyes. He then knelt low and kissed Baalael's ring.

The show ended with an explosion of confetti in Lucifer's signature crimson and black.

The sky dimmed sharply, and the orchestra stopped playing.

A beacon of light exploded from behind the stadium and new music crept over its walls. A drumbeat, soft at first but growing louder as the crowd got to its feet. Lucifer ascended on high, his glory shining in every direction and casting dark shadows behind the spectators. He looked like that twinkling dot in the painting from the Great Hall of art. What did they call it? *The morning star.*

Violin notes broke out in a fury as Lucifer thrust his powerful wings and flew to the center of the arena, crimson-and-black robes floating like silk carried on waves. Two twisted horns flanked the temples of his crown as he turned his head, perusing the crowd. Journalists fell over one another, snapping photos as the crowd erupted into praise, flailing their arms as if worshipping him.

It really did take so much more than brute force to lead, as Lucifer said when they first met. And he had a positive genius for it.

"I trust you've all had enough to eat." His voice was a melody above his music, bouncing from the concrete walls, and everyone cheered as they waved their black-and-crimson flags. "The Games are the most vital and unifying aspect of our culture, so I've made it my mission to ensure their continuity through these difficult times."

He paused, allowing the crowd to respond with praises. Michael signaled the squad and they pulled on their helms, climbing up the stairs from the gladiator hole and on to the grassy perimeter.

"Please extend your warmest welcome to our Eastern and Western Dominion Champions as they fight for the realm," Lucifer announced. "May the best squad win." He dropped from the sky like a dart and fireworks blasted behind him, sprays of gold and red and blue. He shifted back to common form as he landed in a squat.

A *positive* genius for it.

The Two/thirteen marched around the arena to the deafening roar of the crowd. They stopped before Lucifer and saluted, and he made a show of embracing Michael and kissing both cheeks before unclipping his cape and folding it. The other squad simply filed down the steps and into the pit, but the Two/thirteen did another perimeter march as the spectators cheered on their feet. They broke formation and leaped into the pit, one by one. Michael went last, landing in a controlled tumble followed by a crouch, and the crowd went wild.

Angels loved that stuff.

Optics. Everything was optics. And the more they loved Michael, the less Lucifer could say after Michael amputated his beloved brother. It was a win-win for everyone.

The squads got into position, facing off from either end of the pit. The first judge blew a whistle, and Bernard knelt as Zillah took off from his back like a grasshopper. She chucked half a dozen blades and the opponents scrambled, abandoning whatever form they started running, and scattered toward the walls. The Two/thirteen came up from the inside in a single unit and broke off into one-on-one offense.

Michael volleyed swords with the biggest of the bunch, conserving his energy and letting the team pick up as much slack as they could. He kept a keen eye on Asher who fought a few meters away, and kept his own fight light and entertaining, employing more dancing skill than anything else.

Hoot was pivoting and evading in his usual style, but at least he swung his sword. Maybe he thought the light over the arena would heal any wounds—or maybe he finally found his will to survive. Either way... he put on a good show.

Bernard was the first to score a tap-out, barreling in and hoisting a poor bub over his shoulder before letting out a wild roar and slamming him to the ground. He belly flopped on top of him and finished him off with a crunching headbutt to the jaw.

Zillah's blades moved like the spokes of a wheel, leaving lavender light beams and ribbons of cut skin in her wake. Michael looked for Asher, but he kept disappearing. He finally popped up behind Michael's opponent and bashed the giant's head with his shield, dropping him to the dirt. A yellow flag appeared below the angel's cuff.

"Truce," Asher said to Michael. "I was out of line before, brother. I'm sorry."

Michael nodded and patted his shoulder. He still didn't trust him. Five on three now.

Michael found a new target but stepped aside when Bernard jumped in, letting his bear-like mitts pound the opponent in a cascade of blows. He hit like a piece of construction equipment.

Five on two.

Zillah, Hoot, and Asher surrounded the remaining two fighters. Michael took off in a sprint, light as a cat and came up from behind, bashing their two heads together. Dazed, they stumbled around. Michael signaled the squad to stand down before signaling Hoot to engage. The precept fought them both, and the crowd cheered as he danced around them, showing off his skill and defensive forms.

He signaled Zillah next, and she twirled and twisted her swords into a blur, tumbling and leaping better than the acrobats. When she was done, the opponents were cut in ribbons. They pulled their yellow flags and the fans roared. Five on Zero.

Match over.

Lucifer grinned as the whistle blew. Crimson and black confetti rained down as the squad embraced one another. Tears streamed down Hoot's cheeks and Bernard roared into the sky, beating his chest. Zillah let out a howl and even Asher pumped his fist as endless photo-machines flashed, nearly blinding them.

They were living every child's dream. They had done it—they'd won the Games. At least for this symphony, they would be considered the greatest athletes in the world.

The backs of Michael's eyes stung as he recalled all those times he stared into the empty postbox. He knew something special was inside him, he just needed the opportunity to prove it. In this instant, he did.

Joseph came running and leapt into the pit, practically tackling the squad as he joined their ecstatic huddle. He gripped Michael's hair. "You were a diamond among glass, Michael! You did it."

"We did it." Sweat dripped down Michael's face, confetti sticking to it. "They did it. You did it."

Joseph grabbed him in a hug, whispering, "But the true gift is yet to come. Don't forget to do as I instructed."

Michael nodded, and as he did, his gaze moved over the stands where the First Legion sat. "Where is Asmodeus?"

Joseph looked toward his empty seat. "I'm sure he's here somewhere. Might be 'taking the piss' as he likes to say."

The first judge descended into the pit holding a Golden Gladiator—the trophy that would be engraved with all their names and live in the Second Hexant's Hall of Fame forever. The squad lined up, shoulder to shoulder, keeping Michael in the center as Joseph backed away. A hush fell over the crowd as the judge lifted the trophy above his head.

"The winner of this symphony's Gladiator Championship is the Second Hexant, represented by the Two/thirteen!" he bellowed, and howls and cheers erupted again. "Who is the Champion that will accept this honor on behalf of your squad?"

In unison, the squad responded, "Michael!" Then the crowd repeated it, over and over, until the stadium rattled with their chanting. "Michael...! Michael...! Michael...!"

Michael stepped forward and the judge held the trophy out to him. Rather than receive it, he crossed his arms to his chest.

The judge hesitated, confused. "What are you doing?" he whispered. "Take the trophy."

Lord Baalael leaned forward on his throne.

Michael made no eye contact as he took a deep breath. "I claim Champion's Legacy."

The color drained from the judge's face. "You don't know what you're doing," he hissed. "Just take the trophy."

Michael held fast.

"Are you mad?" the judge rasped.

"Champion's Legacy!" Michael cried it at the top of his lungs, and the roaring cheers faded. The squad whipped their heads toward him, confusion clouding their faces, and the Colosseo went so silent you could hear a feather fall.

Lucifer's yellow eyes flashed, but his expression was unreadable.

"You stupid angel," the judge huffed. "You stupid, foolish angel!" He took the trophy and stormed back up the steps.

"What are you doing?" Hoot yanked Michael's wrist. "Nobody claims Champion's Legacy."

"You don't need that much glory!" Zillah hissed. "Forget the Manifesto. You're the greatest athlete in the world right now—"

"Clear the pit!" the third judge stood from his throne and announced. "Clear the pit and make way for the Master of the Games!"

"Michael, please," Hoot was on the verge of tears. "Don't do this...."

You would think they were all around to witness what happened to Joseph. Maybe everyone really did cower before the gods.

"Clear the pit!" the judge yelled louder. "The Champion claims Legacy and challenges the Master of the Games to battle!"

Baalael stood up, muscles rippling under his gleaming, white plate. He fixed the pearl helm to his head.

Pig...

The word echoed in Michael's mind and he scanned the stands for Asmodeus, but he was still missing. *If I could have a million eyes, I would use them all to watch you cut that pig into pieces.* There was no way Asmodeus would miss Champion's Legacy.

Michael looked to Joseph, who stood in front of the Gladiator hole with his arms crossed. Joseph gave him a nod, and Michael tried to gesture toward Asmodeus' seat, but Joseph didn't understand.

"All rules remain the same," the judge announced, "with the addition that the Master of the Games must refrain from using glory to his advantage."

Michael's gaze combed the stands again, but Asmodeus was nowhere to be seen. More of his crew was missing now, and a knot tightened in Michael's stomach. The crowd murmured as Lord Baalael descended into the pit and stepped to the center.

"If it's a show you want," Baalael said in the confident voice of a god, "it's a show you shall get!" He bowed with his arms wide.

"Let him remove his ring, then." The words were out of Michael's mouth before he could think. "So he won't be tempted to use it."

"Lords cannot lie!" the judge chided him. "To imply you don't trust him is blasphemy, and that will not be tolerated in this aren—"

"I will oblige," Baalael called out, and slid the ring from his finger. Had they known it would be that easy to get him to part with his ring, they could've saved Jezebel the trouble.

"Let it be known..." Baalael announced and raised the ring over his head, "that your gods need neither birthright nor glory to dominate even the strongest of your kind. We are ancient and skilled and wise. And if I can do what I'm about to do without my power.... imagine what I can do *with it*."

He flipped his ring at the judge who fumbled to catch it.

Michael glanced at Asmodeus' seat again, and it was still empty. *...I would use them all to watch you cut that pig into pieces.* Asmodeus wouldn't miss this.

Something was wrong. Terribly wrong.

And just like that, Michael was a powerless child again.

Baalael got into position, and flashed the same kind of grin he would before tossing X into the cellar. Memories flashed like an old picture book, and Michael tried to focus on his breath. Slowly in, slowly out.

Baalael met his gaze, and numbing tendrils pulsed in and around Michael's head as he felt the lord prodding into his mind. Baalael froze, something like shock and recognition crossing his face. He narrowed his eyes and stepped closer.

Michael stepped back and tried to regroup. He breathed, just as Azrael had shown him. He needed to focus; to remember who he was *now.*

Justice. I'm here for justice.

Michael's throat bobbed as he pulled the sword from his scabbard, the scraping noise like nails on a board. Sweat slicked the insides of his hands, and he got into position.

The judge blew the whistle and Baalael attacked. Instinctively, Michael blocked, but his head wasn't right. He was bumbling. Panicking. The clanging of their swords echoed from the arena walls and Baalael drove into him like an armed herd of oxen, much more grit than grace. Michael's bones rattled from the sheer weight of the blows.

It wasn't long before he could taste the salty sweat pouring down his face. He could barely keep up with Baalael's volley, and began to stumble backward. Joseph loomed over the edge of the pit; distress clear on his face.

Memories flashed so vividly that he nearly forgot which reality was the present one. Was he tied up again? Starving? He felt weak. Pathetic. Ashamed. He wanted to curl up in a fetal position and wait for those bright green eyes to comfort him. Life had never been fair. Never. He'd made it all this way, and was at the precipice of the promised land... but he couldn't walk in.

When your heart feels dry and cold, and faith is nowhere near. Stand firm and don't look down. Stand firm, it's only fear.

Gabriel's voice whispered up from the center of Michael's gut. Over and over, he sang that little song.

Michael blinked. His sword was locked with Baalael's and he was down on his knees, losing. Gabriel's voice became louder than the scraping steel. Louder than the roar of the crowd.

Gabriel. Who Michael was forced to *abandon*. Gabriel, who this pig-god probably tortured and disposed of and erased his existence.

Michael grabbed his sword by both edges and let out a guttural roar. Baalael's eyes flashed as Michael stood up, forcing him backward.

Michael's foot landed square in the center of the pig's pearl chestplate and sent him flying backward. He pounced, training and rage and justice and revenge surging through him like lifeblood. He danced around the lord, untouchable, moving like a phantom. His elbow crunched Baalael's jaw and the lord cried out. It was like music to Michael's ears.

The whole crowd was on their feet now. Michael didn't let up, striking faster. Harder. Baalael stumbled back to the wall.

You're going to pay, Michael thought with direct clarity. *You're going to pay for everything you've done.*

Michael would cut off his head. No—he could cut out his heart, then his head. Then take his hands and his feet, and feed them to Deidre. Maybe let Asmodeus throw him in some pottage.

Something lifted Michael slightly from the ground and sent him stumbling back. He glanced at the floor expecting to see a rock or a root, but there was nothing.

He refocused on Baalael, unleashing a new fury of blows. This pathetic sack had no right to hold the title of Master of the Games. He was weak. Unfocused. He was nothing without his birthright.

Michael spun, sending a solid elbow cracking straight into his neck. Baalael let out a groan as Michael pivoted behind him, kicking hard and sending him stumbling forward.

Joseph was at the edge of the pit, roaring and cheering him on.

But Baalael didn't go down. Instead, he turned on a heel and launched an aggressive counter, his eyes now glowing fiercely. Michael pushed him back again and side-stomped his shin. Baalael's face darkened.

Then, again, something lifted Michael from his feet and sent him stumbling backward. His limbs turned to lead, and an invisible weight pushed back at him.

"Tired already?" Baalael landed a kick to Michael's chest, knocking the wind from him. Michael tried to counter, but his limbs were so heavy he could barely swing his sword. The lord blocked him easily, striking back swiftly and slicing shallow wounds into Michael's ribs.

Michael looked for Asmodeus again, but he still wasn't there.

It was now like he had two dozen sandbags dragging him down, the invisible force pushing him to his knees. Baalael sliced both of his cheeks with the edge of his sword, and warm blood ran down to Michael's neck.

He tried to fight back, but it was like moving through deep waters—everything was so heavy. He tried to turn and run, but a golden shield crunched his head, and down he went.

The weight became unbearable on the ground, threatening the very breath in his lungs. The crowd stood on their toes, silent, as Baalael ripped off Michael's helm and threw it. Michael saw double as he struggled to push himself up—but the weight. He glanced at the judge, but he wouldn't be tapped out for shallow cuts.

He could hear Hoot and Bernard and Zillah screaming to pull his flag, but he couldn't move his arms. And when he tried to call back to them, the invisible force strangled him.

"How...?" he rasped, looking up at the lord looming over him. "How are you doing this?"

Baalael's sandaled foot smashed his jaw, and the pain rippled down Michael's neck as teeth came loose. Everything was a blurry haze.

Slowly, Baalael knelt, his golden shield and nacreous armor coming sharply into focus. His gaze moved to a sigil ring that was clipped to his groinskirt. Michael squinted.

"You ambitious little fool..." Baalael pulled his head up by the hair and whispered in his ear. "You thought you could take my ring? I have loyalties *everywhere*. Asmodeus is being gutted as we speak, and the acrobat produced a timely delivery." He leaned in closer. "I never trusted you, Michael, from the instant I laid eyes on you in that pit. But it wasn't until *just now* that I realized who you were...."

He sheathed his sword and rubbed a thumb along the swelling lump on Michael's cheek. "That mind... it's so quiet. Not a single thought. Not even the murmur of a hum. I couldn't hear you then, *little X*, and I can't hear you now." His eyes narrowed. "So, the question remains.... *What are you?*"

Michael choked up blood as something crushed him from the inside.

"Tell Asher I said *thank you*. He'll be rewarded greatly for this."

Baalael let go of his hair and yanked Michael's arms flush to the ground in front of him.

Michael struggled to pull his arms back, but couldn't. Terror rose up his gullet and he whimpered, unable to even form the words to beg. *Please. Not my hands... don't take my hands.*

Like a clay pot in the hands of an angry god, he was about to be broken.

"I could drain you into nothing. I could *consume* you," Baalael spit as he drew his sword from its scabbard. "Keep your shadow as my pet for eternity and use your life force as a reading lamp. But you'd have no mind left... nothing to suffer with." He placed his foot on Michael's wrists, crushing them under his weight. Tears trickled from the corners of Michael's eyes, betraying him. All this time. All this work and planning. Just to end up in a pit helpless again.

"If memory serves me correctly," Baalael said, "weren't you a painter too?" He raised his sword like someone about to split a plank of wood over a tree stump. "I suppose you'll have to find new hobbies now...."

A whooshing sound cut the air followed by a sharp, crushing pain in Michael's wrists. His head jolted up; the invisible force completely gone now. Light exploded from the ends of his forearms and condensed into thick, purple rivers that gushed from the ends of his arms. Gasps filled the arena, along with a single, lone scream.

His scream.

Two bloody hands lay here, and his eyes rolled to the back of his head. Everything went dark.

33

Trudy

*"Not all setbacks set us back. If our goal is worthy, then
the lessons we learn will all be drawn together at once in a
majestic symphony of inspiration."*
-The Guide to Utopian Principles and Ethics, Section IV,
On Belief and Faith

T RUDY HUNCHED ON THE bed, her index finger tapping furiously as millions of potential passwords flashed through her qubes
hologram. Her script should've cracked both passwords by now, and
been well on its way to figuring out the vault. But it hadn't even cracked
his camera account yet.

With a grunt she got up and checked the hallway. Still clear. There
were only two or three servants left in the Crimson Tower, including
herself, but she didn't need anyone poking around or asking what she
was up to.

Flappy played lookout in the front, perched at an open window over-
looking the veranda in case Lucifer and his sycophants got back from
the Games early—but at this point, they wouldn't even be early. She was
cutting it close.

The hologram blinked green and she darted to the bed.

She cocked a brow at the incredibly complex string of letters, numbers and glyphs displayed. This was no mundane password featuring your best friend or pet's name—this was an attempt at security in a system he didn't control.

Even more reason to believe he had something to hide.

She gave her neck a good stretch and copied the jumbled string into her data crystal. If she could crack at least two of his passwords, there was a good chance she could crack the vault.

She slipped the qube into her pocket, along with a small candle and a match. She pulled up her hood and scurried through the hall to the servant staircase, where she descended to the first floor.

She checked around, and the only movement came from a light breeze that blew in from an open window. Flappy swooped in and let out a little chirp before perching on Trudy's hand.

"Shhhh." Trudy raised a finger to her lips. "You remember where the study is? At the end of the hall, like I showed you..."

Flappy side-eyed her.

"Just checking... stop being so sensitive. The instant you see that carriage coming up the road, come get me."

Flappy launched into the air and back through the window, and Trudy gently padded the carpeted hall that led to Lucifer's personal study.

A camera eyed her from the edge of the ceiling and she smirked as she passed it. The whole system was looping footage from earlier, so it could stare all it wanted. She set her gaze on the cherry-stained door at the end of the hall and scurried over to it, checking over her shoulder. She grasped its golden handle.

It wouldn't budge.

Locked.

Ugh. She gritted her teeth, chiding herself for being so preoccupied with breaking into accounts that she didn't consider breaking into doors. She leaned over and glimpsed between the door and the frame. There was a little stretch of metal securing the lock, so she jangled the handle, softly at first, and then harder.

Why can nothing be easy?

A noise startled her and she whipped around. The edge of a tree branch tapped the hallway window, and she exhaled. She leaned against the door and pinched the bridge of her nose. They'd be back any beat now, and she couldn't even get into his study, much less crack his qpistle password. It was like everything was working against her. If only some-one was here to help her think. Zuriah or Philistina....

Or Hoot.

She pulled a long, sturdy pin from her bun and slid it behind the locking mechanism, the way he'd done in the darkness. Carefully, she moved it around, applying pressure while being careful not to bend it. She kept at it, pushing the handle and shimmying her pin. After a few measures, the lock made a clicking sound.

Her eyes went wide as she pushed the handle down. She slipped into the study and left the door open just enough for Flappy to fit through.

She backed into several black robes hanging on hooks beside the door, nearly knocking them down. *Servant robes?* He probably wore them around to spy on whatever whispers he couldn't hear from the cameras. She stepped farther in, more careful this time.

The walls were lined floor to ceiling with leather-bound books, some of which were so ancient that the binding was peeling and frayed at the edges. She was tempted to pull one out and marvel, but there was no time for that. Marble busts were elegantly placed about, giving the place a museum-like feel, and in the center of the room sat an obsidian desk, its legs covered in decorative patterns that were probably carved by Raphael himself. At least this room wasn't sleek and sterile like the inside of a qube.

Something chirped behind her and she jumped. It wasn't Flappy, though. In the corner of the study was a glass case with small round holes in it. Little brown and white birds flitted around, perching on sticks that had been strategically placed for them. What a terrible thing—to keep birds in a cage like that. She liked Lucifer even less now. She tapped on the glass and cooed, pulling some leftover manna crumbs from her pocket and sprinkling them through the little air holes. The birds hopped from their perches and pecked at the crumbs.

Who fed them while Lucifer was away? Maybe one of the servants stayed behind to take care of the sweet little—

A black snake pounced from under the wood chips and latched a little brown bird in its mouth. She gasped, panicking, and clawed the glass, searching for a seam or some way to open it. The snake closed its mouth and swallowed, pushing the bird through in a lump. It struggled under the snake's skin and she could barely stifle her scream. A mouthful of lunch came hurtling up her throat, and she slammed a hand over her face.

Chirping. Furious chirping as the rest of the birds scattered back to their high perches. She stumbled backward, nearly knocking over a carved bust of Lucifer.

She had to get it together. If she smashed open that case and set all the birds free, she'd blow her cover and the entire world might soon look like the inside of that glass.

She steeled herself and ran to his desk, whipping open his drawers and shoving papers and items aside. If there was a single shred of a doubt that Lucifer was behind the darkness, it had vanished. What kind of twisted, abomination of an angel *enjoyed* death? Kept it in their study for entertainment, even?

She spotted a square black case at the bottom of his drawer and opened it. The qube had a Universal Technologies symbol on it—a work device. Not as good as a personal one, but it would have to do. With a squeeze, the device initiated and projected the login hologram. She pulled the data crystal from her pocket and loaded her script. Potential passwords flitted through the login field as she glanced at the door, her knee bouncing with a fury.

"We left the carriage in the rear courtyard...." A voice carried through the hall and she nearly fell off the ostentatious chair. "See to it that it's washed." Almog's voice became clear. "Our Lord will be delayed in his return."

She bolted to the window to see a carriage parked behind the tower—*behind* the tower. They must've taken the back roads and come through the rear. Her life force thundered as failed password attempts flashed in the hologram. Footsteps now echoed through the hall, and Trudy's gaze darted around in search of somewhere to hide.

Come on... She stared at the flitting hologram.

"Did you hear something?" another servant spoke now.

"I only hear birds," Almog said. "Be sure to collect more before we depart for the island. We don't want our Lord's pet to starve."

Pet? They called that flesh-eating death-worm a *pet?* She couldn't decide if it would be better to hide or to clobber them both with a bust if they walked in. Better them than the birds.

Or Flappy. She swallowed hard.

"Is the door to our Lord's study open?" Almog asked as footsteps grew quicker and louder.

The hologram blinked green with the correct password, and Trudy loaded her data crystal and copied it. She yanked it free and shoved the qube back into the drawer before gently closing it.

The footsteps were right by the door now. Her eyes darted desperately for somewhere to hide as a hand appeared on the door's latch.

Wild chirping and banging came from the hallway and the hand pulled back, footsteps now scattering.

"It's in my hair!" Almog yelled. "Get it out!"

Flappy.

Trudy darted to the hanging robes and pulled her hood up high, latching it on a hook and pressing her body flush against the wall. It wasn't exactly cover, but it was her only option. A breeze hit her as the door swung open, and multiple footsteps rushed inside, heaving.

"The case is still sealed," the servant said. "That bird must've gotten in from outside."

"This door is supposed to be locked," Almog said. "Someone will be drained for this." His incensed voice was right next to Trudy's head.

Drained? She bit her lip.

"Check the schedule for who was last in here cleaning—" Almog paused. "Why are you looking at me like that?"

"Your shoulder, sir," the other servant said. "The bird must've... relieved himself."

Almog let out a disgusted sound. "Feral little beast! It's on my neck too!" His footsteps stomped from the room, and the other followed. Trudy waited for the sound to fade down the hall before letting her breath out. She unhooked herself and counted to ten before cracking open the door to peek out.

She stepped into the hallway and ran toward the servants' stairwell. Flappy landed on her shoulder, her warm little feathers nuzzling into Trudy's neck. She opened the door to the stairwell and stepped inside, making sure to close it behind her this time.

She lit her candle and eased down the old staircase, wincing every time a step creaked. When she got to the bottom, she shouldered open the basement door. Flappy leapt from her shoulder and whooshed across the room directly through the holographic wall.

"Slow down," she rasped. "You could've crashed and broken your beak!"

Trudy stepped through the wall, and Flappy was hovering over the glowing blue orb that was the vault's security system.

"It's now or never, Flaps." Trudy knelt and set her qube and candle down on the floor, pulling the data crystal from her robe and slipping it inside. A hologram appeared, and she logged herself in. Flappy swooped in front of her face and hovered there, chirping like mad.

"Stop making a ruckus," she hissed. "They'll hear you!" She opened her cracking script and typed a few lines before feeding Lucifer's two nonsensical passwords into the script. A cursor blinked as it analyzed them for any sign of a pattern. Flappy chirped loud in her ear, but she shushed her.

A smaller hologram emerged in the air spelling out three potential passwords for the vault. She stood up and raised her finger to the glowing blue orb.

Flappy landed on her hand, almost pushing it through. "Not now!"

The bird chirped indignantly, but she ignored her and put her finger to the orb again. The letters, numbers, and glyphs that floated inside came rushing to its transparent shell, and carefully, she selected the first string of characters that her program predicted.

The orb brightened as it processed the password, and she held her breath.

It turned red, and one of the three yellow dots disappeared.

Two more tries... She took a deep breath.

Flappy swooped dangerously close to the orb and she winced. "I'm going to put you in that stairwell if you don't stop," she rasped, and then pulled the last vestiges of manna crumbs from her pocket and sprinkled them on the floor. *That should keep you busy for a while.*

Trudy raised her finger to the orb again, carefully copying the second string from her hologram. Her whole body tensed as the orb brightened, processing the new password.

Please, please, please...

It blinked red right before the second yellow dot disappeared. She pressed her palms against her eyes. If she got it wrong again, there was a very strong likelihood that this system would alert Lucifer, or even set off an alarm.

Her breath grew ragged as she analyzed the two original passwords with her own two eyes. She couldn't make heads or tails of them.

She glanced at the next password her script predicted, and her hand shook like a leaf in a storm as she raised it to the orb. Whatever it meant to be "drained"... she hoped it wasn't too bad, because she'd definitely be drained if this didn't work. She took a deep breath and—

Flappy shot into the air and darted at her face. She flinched backward and reached for the wall to steady herself, but almost fell through the holographic stone. She regained her footing just in time to see the little bird's tiny talon grazing the edge of the orb. Flappy plunged into it and her tiny claw struck one single letter and brought it to the surface.

Trudy grabbed two fistfuls of hair and dropped to her knees as the blue orb grew bright, processing Flappy's password.

"We have to go!" Trudy swiped for her bird but missed. She had to get them both out of there, but as she lunged again, the blue orb turned green, and the heavy latch clicked.

She froze.

The password blinked green, signaling the door was open. A single letter hovered above the green orb—the one that Flappy had selected.

X.

With a long, slow creak, the vault opened, and a cold, artificial light buzzed inside. It was about the size of a dressing room, and appeared to be some kind of... what? Storage closet?

Where were the quantum servers? The hardware? Where were the rack mounts and the fans?

White, featureless masks hung on the wall, and a stack of old art supplies were discarded in a rubbish bin. A small, tattered robe hung on a hook—nothing that would ever fit Lucifer. She touched its hem, feeling along the edge of the gritty fabric. A tiny device was sewn into it, and to anyone else it would have appeared like an oddly placed button, but she knew a tracking device when she saw it. They would use them at the logistics hubs when they sent important parcels, to make sure they didn't get lost in transit.

She turned her attention to the plain desk, cluttered underneath with file cabinets. She opened one. There were files labeled *endurance trials,* and other hand-drawn charts that she didn't have the context to understand. She shuffled to the back of the cabinet where some folded up parchment was jammed into the corner. Letters—between Lords Baalael and Lucifer.

They were short letters, and didn't say much. She let her gaze roam over the words, and it was clear they spoke in some kind of secret code. Lucifer did this often, having secret meanings for ordinary words. She would watch him have entire conversations where someone present in the room wouldn't understand half of what he really said. It was like taking inside jokes to the next level—with none of the humor. The fact they kept these records on paper was also telling. Digital communications were all stored somewhere.

She couldn't quite grasp what the letters meant, but whatever this "X" thing was, they feared it—both of them. Which meant that Trudy needed to *find* this "X" thing.

She searched more files to try and gain context until she exhausted every page in those cabinets, but it was useless. Everything was labeled by numbers and dates and variables. Whatever they were documenting, they covered their tracks well. X could've been anything. Baalael said it was "silent" and of "unknown origin" and "belonged nowhere."

What did that even mean?

She slammed the file cabinet shut as disappointment flooded her. She was no closer now to finding how they were corrupting nature than when she was back on the island. She only knew Lucifer feared something he called "X," which could have been anything in the world.

She glanced at the creepy white masks on the wall and grimaced. This was all for nothing. She'd come all this way... taken all this risk...

She closed the vault with a click, Flappy nuzzling into her neck. The blue orb appeared again, securing the lock, and she stepped back through the holographic wall.

Pulling her hood above her head, she ascended the steps back to the first floor and casually walked down the hall, not bothering to respond to Almog or the other servants questioning where she came from.

She couldn't stand this place—couldn't stand them. They were all a bunch of unthinking, sandal-licking lackeys. Especially Almog, the "Master Servant." How mindless do you have to be to accept the title of "Master Servant"? What an oxymoron.

Moron. It wasn't a real word, but it had a nice ring to it. She stepped into the main foyer and unbuttoned her robe, pulling out her arms and letting it drop to the glossy, gemstone floor. She glanced down at her green trousers and yellow tunic. It was nice to see color on herself again.

"What do you think you're doing?" Almog chased after her. "Pick that up! Where do you think you're going?"

She shouldered open the heavy, obsidian door and stepped into the light. In the distance, the Throne Tower floated high above the Holy City, oranges and pinks and yellows radiating from its crystal walls. The Music of the Spheres spilled from its windows, sailing over the air and into the whole world.

"Where in our Lord's grace do you think you're going, angel!?" Almog burst through the door and demanded, his normally pale face now twisted and red.

"What do you think is up there?" She pointed to the Throne Tower and asked casually.

"Did you hear a word I said?" he spat. "How dare you ignore me and discard our sacred garment to the floor? Our Lord will be back soon. Get inside and pick it up! There'll be a price to pay for your disobedience."

The Throne Tower? She rubbed her chin. If there was any such equipment that could power—or unpower—the entire world, it would need access to the entire world...

"Hello?" Almog said, waving in her face.

Pulsing violin notes launched through its high windows like gulls taking off from their nests. Those notes would travel to the very last drop of the Endless Sea—there wasn't a cubit of their world that the Throne Tower's music wouldn't reach...

The Throne Tower!

How could she not have thought of it before? The Throne Tower already had access to the world. How else could the music have played at the same volume, no matter where you were? A giddy feeling rose up from her feet.

Maybe this wasn't a big, fat waste of time after all....

"Are you listening to me?" Almog dug sharp nails into her shoulder and spun her around. She grabbed both of his cheeks and pinched them. Hard. Shock lit in his eyes.

"Go suck a tomato, Almog. I'm going back to campus."

She skipped down the stairs and Almog stuttered. "You... you can't just... How will you get back?"

She rolled her eyes as she stepped onto the golden road. There were more abandoned carriages and light runners in this city than she could count. She could alternate between land and air, now that she knew what to look for.

"You should try using your head for more than a hood-rack, Almog. Lucifer favors you because you follow him blindly, but don't get it twisted..." She turned and walked backward, meeting his gaze. "Figuring out that the Handbook is childish doesn't make you smart. Not if you just go and follow someone else's ideas blindly. *Master Servant*..." she chuckled to herself. "You're a *moron*, Almog. A real, live *moron*."

34

Michael

"Be careful how your words are strung, no weapon cuts quite like the tongue."
    -Heaven's Handbook, Virtues part 2, "On Kindness"

MICHAEL COULD'VE SWORN HE was slowly bobbing over waves of some kind, but there was no water to be seen. He swooped into valleys of invisible currents, a sweet darkness engulfing and flooding his senses. It was like the velvety chocolate from one of Mary's piping-hot, cocoa cakes—except this sweet darkness pressed into the brink of his awareness, and plunged him to the depths of those ineffable swells. If fear so much as flirted from the edge of his periphery, those bright green eyes would show up and lock on him, two emerald orbs in a sea of nothingness, covering him in safety so he could finally rest.

These waters might cleanse you, if you let them, the eyes had said once, without words.

But I am already clean, Michael thought back.

Then the wave's crest would come, with all of its attendant chaos and flashes of life. Hoot's face, twisted with grief, jostling and bouncing as if riding through a storm. Bernard's voice in a panic, stumbling on words. Philistina's cold expressions, her movements curt and resolute. Strangers said things he didn't want to hear—didn't want to remember. Muffled sentences about bleeding and life force. And hands.

He willed himself out of those peaks and back into the valleys, time and time again. This time, the descent was different.

He found himself breathing deeply the scent of freshly trimmed grass. Both the peaceful darkness and the chaotic light were gone. How long had he been standing in this field, next to the garden? It felt like longer than it should have.

The sky was overwhelmingly brilliant and bursting with color—more brilliant than any sky he'd ever seen. It was a golden backdrop, streaks of sea-foam green and pink and tangerine dancing as if they were alive. Light sliced through pillowy mounds of cloud creating beams that glazed the grass in delicate washes of orange and gold. And as the sky danced, so did everything around him: the wind and the plants and the water near the horizon, all alive and moving with the sound of the music.

Such was the light. If only he could *be* that light. But he did have the next best thing...

A thrill pulsed through him as he recalled his art supplies that waited in the garden. He ran toward the thick, flowered canopy and high foliage walls. His body was awkward as he ran, his strides neither graceful nor swift. Light bounced in his eyes and the insides of his chubby thighs chafed. The arched entrance of the garden was covered in tiny purple flowers, and he was met with the sweet, green smell of honeysuckle and rose. He pushed through the vines and stepped into a bright cacophony of fruit and petals and leaves and twigs.

In the center was the Mother Tree, its thick, braided bark exploding at the top into a leafy, flowered canopy. Plump yellow fruit hung ripe on the branches, and birds flitted and chirped while bright dots of light danced through the leaves and scattered on the ground below.

In the center of the thick bark was an arched slit of brilliant yellow light, outlining a wooden door that was slightly ajar. Michael craned his neck to peek inside, and could just make out the image of a tall angel with wings. It was a statue, made from concrete or stone.

Wings. He should like to have those one song.

He ducked under a branch and scurried to the easel set up by the hedges. On a small table was laid out all of his art supplies: paintbrushes, lined up in order of size, tubes of pigmented oil and a palette with dollops of smooth, thick paint. And they were laid out in the correct order—the order of a rainbow.

There were guidelines to painting, and if you wanted to make something beautiful, you followed them. Of course, following guidelines was up to you... but if you opted not to and ended up with a dark mess all over your canvas, you had nobody to blame but yourself.

He pushed the heavy hood from his head and picked up one of the thicker brushes. His fingers were small and fat, like little sausages. He dipped it into the thinner, and then dabbed it in a bit of ochre and cadmium yellow before patting the excess on his robe. Gently, he slid the paintbrush across the canvas, leaving a wash of gold in its wake. It was always a good idea to coat your canvas first with color—thin layers were the best way to capture living light.

The white canvas transformed into a sky, and then he dipped the brush again into the thinner, but when he lowered it to the palette, he could no longer find the ochre or yellow. Nor the green or the blue. They were all gone.

His gaze moved across the dollops. Dirt browns and moss greens; deep purples that were the color of bruises now crowded his palette.

The light around him dimmed, and he strained to distinguish the hues. The music grew dissonant and the notes pulsed quicker—like an untuned violin playing to the beat of a broken phonograph. X's breathing got shallow, and his gaze darted up. The statue's wings turned black and crumbled off as the leaves and fruits on the tree withered and fell.

Death.

"Where are you, X?" Deidre kicked through a bush and invaded the garden, and X whipped around, darting back through the viney curtain. He was in the field behind Deidre's manor now, and made a run for the woods. His breath quickened as he crossed the tree line and ran toward his fort. Deidre pursued and the sky flashed and crackled as he ran toward his refuge.

"Leaving so soon, Michael?" Baalael was in front of him and he stopped short, slipping in the mud and leaves. The wet ground opened up, revealing sharp, silver-gold teeth. It began to swallow him as he clawed the edges of the soil, grasping at the dead roots and grass.

"Don't forget these..." Baalael tossed something his way and they hit the ground, slightly bouncing in his direction with a thump.

In front of him lay two bloody hands, and he glanced at his bloody stumps, realizing he had nothing to grasp on with. He tumbled down the gullet of the world like a boulder from a cliff.

Michael jolted awake as a gut-wrenching scream exploded in his ears.

"He's up!" someone cried out and footsteps scurried around him. "Keep him tied down or he'll rip off the dressing again."

Burning pain seared up his arms, and light was everywhere—blinding light. Blurry figures leaned over and around him as he struggled to sit up, but something held him down, just like when he was held down in the pit. He roared like a beast as he tried to free himself.

"Peace, brother..." The blurry image of Hoot sharpened into focus above his face. "It's alright. You're alright. You've been out a while."

Michael heaved and spat, "Let me see my arms!"

"You need to keep still so you can heal," Hoot said. "We had to restrict your movement. Whenever you come to, you're not in your right mind."

He was briefly startled by the dark circles under Hoot's eyes. The precepts face was sharp and thin, almost gray.

The memories raged in like a river—Asmodeus disappearing. Baalael's pearlescent armor. Being crushed under some invisible force. *The ring.*

"What happened to me?" The question fell out of his mouth. He knew exactly what happened, but he needed to confirm it. Dreams and reality were still too woven together to think straight.

"Don't worry about that just yet." Hoot patted his sweaty forehead with a rag, and then bowed his head and started mumbling words.

"What are you doing?" Michael yanked his arms, almost flipping over whatever they had him tied to. Hoot mumbled louder until his voice became clear, and his words obvious.

He was *praying*?

An ancient, guttural rage blasted up from Michael's belly and exploded from his mouth, spit and sweat spraying as he struggled to break free. "Empty words to an absent God mean nothing to me! Unbind me! That's an order!"

Someone shoved Hoot out of the way and slammed Michael flush on his back.

"Don't you *dare* speak to him like that!" Philistina growled, inches from his nose. "He well near *drained* himself keeping you alive! They all did!"

"Drained himself?" Michael screwed up his face. "What are you talking about?"

"When there's not enough light to fuel my healing stones, our own life force will do."

The other angels behind her came into focus. Bernard and Zillah. They almost looked as bad as Hoot. And some white-haired angel with a bushy mustache stood there too.

"Zuriah and I barely managed to save *them*," Philistina growled, "because they nearly died saving *you*."

"Just get him out of here with those prayers," Michael growled back, right in her face. "If the Almighty listens to any prayers, he only does so for his own amusement."

"Fine." Hoot raised his hands. "I'll stop... and I'll go if that's what you want. But just know we weren't the only ones who saved you. Joseph left us by the ferry and went back to the First Circle. He's the one who found the light runner and carriage to transport us. I left him with a healing stone, but he was already half dead. We don't know how he fared after that."

"And where was your Almighty then?" Michael turned his head and spit on the floor.

"You'd be dead if it weren't for them," Philistina snapped. "You have no right to treat him like that."

"Don't be so sullen...." the angel with the bushy mustache sat on the cot next to him. "Your friends love you very much. Be grateful we were able to capitalize on the healing properties here in the meadow.... It's not an ideal circumstance, but it's better than nothing."

"Who are you?" Michael's wrists were throbbing.

"Zuriah. Professor Zuriah—Master of the Natural Sciences, and apparently, pioneer of the healing arts now. Philistina designed this glass structure around us so the healing properties of the meadow could be amplified."

Michael's gaze moved around to the metal frame that held the small, glass hut together. Next to him, a long tube stretched from a clear bag of fluid that hung on a pole. It went into his arm.

"Don't be concerned about that," Zuriah gestured the tube with his bushy mustache. "I managed to isolate some healing properties of the vita fruit through chemical extraction and dilute them in a basic solution. We're feeding it directly into your life force through a small incision. It was the best we could do before you were awake to eat. But I suggest utilizing it as a therapy in addition to eating for the next few symphonies, or until you're fully healed."

The next few symphonies. Dread closed in on him. Everything was over. All he'd accomplished—gone, just like that. He dared not look down at his wrists. He was a charity case again, except now, he couldn't even earn his keep.

"You want me to eat?" Michael moaned as another sharp pain moved up his arm. "I can't even hold a fork!"

Bernard brought him a bottle with a straw. "Empyreanol," he said. "It'll help with the pain 'til they come up with something better."

Michael put his lips around the straw and sucked, letting the strong liquid sear the inside of his mouth and throat. When he looked up again, everyone was silent, looking at him the same way he looked at those pathetic creatures that were huddled around the village fires, starving.

"You should've let me die."

"Michael—" Hoot started.

"Get out."

Nobody moved.

"I said GET OUT!"

Philistina threw a roll of wound dressing at him. "If you want so badly for us to be gone, *fine*. Save yourself."

"He can't even brush his hair," Zillah said.

"If losing his hands didn't teach him to stop being an arrogant wing-bag, he'll never learn." She stormed out and Zillah wiped a tear from her gaunt cheek before following. Professor Zuriah quickly checked the tube and bag one last time before stepping through the low entrance, and despite Michael's demands, Hoot was the last to leave.

The precept paused at the door, the shadows under his bony cheeks a shameful reminder that not only was Michael unfit to lead, but there was truly no overseeing force of good that cared about any of them. If anyone didn't deserve this, it was Hoot.

Yet the stupid fool clung to his piety the way a child clings to a pacifier.

Michael fixed his eyes on the precept and narrowed them. "Just. Get. Out."

35

Michael

*"What is enough? And should we not consider such matters
as subjective? The fundamental flaw in our logic begins
when we fail to embrace our individual selves, and what
we desire. There is no objective cap on "enough." No true
morality in denying oneself "more." Let each for themselves
decide in light of their own constitution, what enough shall
be in any given circumstance."*

-The Black Manifesto, Chapter Five, "On Vice"

M ICHAEL SHOT UP IN his cot, heaving, as the first bells of the
overture rang out. The remnants of his sleep phantoms faded
as he bit his shoulder, making sure he was really awake. The dreams had
become so bad that one too many sips of empyreanol meant that the
terrors might just show up whether he was asleep or not.

He missed the songs where he would sleep deep, yet wake up exhausted as if he'd been training the whole time. Exhaustion was so much better
than this—at least caffeine could fix that.

Now, nothing could fix him.

The burning above his groin indicated it was time to empty that last
bottle of empyreanol he finished before passing out, or, to "take the piss"

as Asmodeus would say. There was no reason to shuffle all the way to the pond and not capitalize on the trip, so he leaned over and sucked down the last few gulps from the bottle next to him.

"Dreams any better, sir?" Bernard appeared at the opening of his glass hut, and Michael dropped back to the pillow and closed his eyes.

"I already saw ya wake up, sir," Bernard said. "No use in pretendin'."

"Leave the bottle there," Michael grunted and pointed his bushy chin to the end table. He paused. "Why's that bottle so small?"

"Professor Zuriah thinks too much empyreanol slows yer healin'."

"Tell Zuriah not to do me any favors," Michael said. "I need it for the pain."

Bernard set the bottle down and picked up the old one. "Maybe I could stay and help ya shave? Or comb yer hair... Can barely see ya under all that brush."

"I'm fine."

Bernard sighed and regarded Michael for a long beat. "Won't ya just talk to Hoot? That's what precepts are for, ya know. We all need a little help upstairs from time to time. Besides... he's real broken up about how ya left off."

"I don't want to see any precept."

"He's not just any precept," Bernard said, "he's one of us. Ya didn't have to yell at him like ya did when he tried to visit last time."

"I don't need vapid platitudes or birdscattery proverbs from that Handbook, least of all now. And stop calling me sir—I'm not your Furie anymore."

"I'm just disappointed, is all," Bernard said. "And Hoot'll be too."

"It's about time I'm not the only one used to disappointment around here."

That fact that Michael's rage at the Almighty was landing on Hoot wasn't lost on him. He just didn't have the energy to separate the two. Especially when that last bottle of empyreanol had already begun morphing into a raging headache, making the urge to piss even worse.

Bernard slumped his shoulders and left. They should've all been back at the camps anyway, making themselves useful to the world. Not resigning to a miserable, useless existence just because Michael had to. Maybe if he rejected Hoot long enough, the precept would go back to Joseph and fight in the war that would free the lot of them from the darkness. That would be a lot more useful than empty platitudes. He was probably doing Hoot a favor.

Michael sat up and stretched his neck, then ripped that stupid tube from his arm. His sleeping gown was covered in sweat and yellow stains because it was too much of a hassle to change it without hands.

Michael the Champion, hero of the realm... Unable to pull up his own gown to take a proper piss. But every overture, he had a ritual, and pissing was only one part of it.

He swung his legs over the side of the bed and hopped down, steadying himself. It was hard to understand just how important every appendage was for balance until you lost a couple. Or, maybe he was still drunk.

He passed the basket of fresh, peeled vita that Zillah faithfully left every silence before he woke up. At least she had the decency to not stick around. The trees Philistina had planted in the meadow were thriving, but the food would be put to better use feeding angels who actually wanted to live.

Just knowing Zillah lingered on campus because of him gnawed at his insides. She'd been the most disciplined and reliable soldier of all—never complaining once and invaluable in battle. She was a born soldier, but she also insisted on letting him ruin her life, which only brought more guilt.

The sky above the island had become nearly as dim as those depressing villages now. And if it was this dim here, then those villages must've been dark as pitch. The realm was good as done and there wasn't a snogging thing he could do about it.

"You out here?" he called out, lifting a bandaged stump to his mouth out of habit, as if he could whistle with it. "Bentley, you stubborn old rock... where are you?"

Looking for Bentley was the next part of his ritual.

Drink, donkey, piss, drown... in exactly that order.

The beast had to be close, munching on grass or fallen fruit. He hadn't seen him since they'd arrived on Eastern Island. Unless the poor beast was laid out starving somewhere, unaware that the meadow even existed. That would break Mary's heart.

Hard to believe how worried he'd been about his four-legged friend when they first arrived—right up until the point he had better things to think about. He'd memorized an entire Military Manual and its codes of loyalty, but left a defenseless animal in a dying world alone without a second thought.

Maybe when the island ran out of vita, desperate angels would drag Michael off and use him for food like they did to animals in the First Hexant. He deserved as much.

And what of the Jolly Bub? Mary and Shem? Were they huddled around a refuse bin too? Starving and terrified of the darkness? Michael was supposed to be a soldier— supposed to be loyal. But he was none of it.

Philistina had been spot on with her assessment of him the whole time. And he wasn't even a good liar anymore—couldn't even convince himself of his own snogwash.

He pressed his eyes closed and let them spill over, like they did on every trip to the pond. There was nothing left to hide behind.

No competence. No justice. No vengeance.

No hands.

He dropped to one knee and clenched a watermelon-sized stone between his forearms and lifted it to his chest. He struggled back to his feet and trudged toward the shimmering pond. Critters scampered from his path as his feet splashed in at the edge. He descended deeper and deeper.

First, he relieved himself, the piss warming his legs in the cool pond. Then, hugging the stone tight, he took the final step and plunged.

He opened his eyes under the bright blue water, just in time to see fish and bubbles scattering through sharp rays of the bright meadows light. He inhaled a huge gulp, reflexively choking and forcing the water in deeper. Maybe this time, he'd stay down there.

But there was no such luck. His first time doing this, he'd learned that breathing must be little more than an olfactory function necessary for comfort, but not life.

Still, his little ritual brought some twisted sense of comfort.

Something yanked him up by the hair and dragged him from the pond. He dropped the stone as he hit the dirt, choking up water through his nose and mouth.

"Are you dull?" Joseph got on his knees and pounded Michael's chest, forcing more water out of him. "Do you know what I went through to get you back here so they could help you?"

Michael rolled over and coughed.

"Baalael's out there raising up an army and you're here drowning yourself in pond scum. Death won't come that way, you know."

"I know." Michael rasped. "How do you know?"

"Tried it already," Joseph said. "I dreamed up death way before it was a thing."

Michael rubbed his throat with a wet, bandaged wrist and sat up. "Why are you here?"

"I've got a mind to make you run fifty laps around this meadow and do a hundred pull-ups, stumps and all," Joseph said, grimacing down at him. "You made a commitment, and that commitment doesn't end because you decide to end it."

"I didn't decide to end anything." Michael pushed himself to his feet, pain radiating from his bloody bandages. "It took two symphonies in real light for you to hold a sword when you lost your hands. All I have is some glowing grass and a glass hut. My commitment was ended for me."

"You smell like a distillery. How much have you been drinking?"

Michael shrugged and started walking back.

"You're a disgrace." Joseph pursued and pulled a brown package from his satchel. "This is for you. Take it."

"I don't want it."

"You don't even know what it is. Hoot's team worked an entire movement on this. Your friend Philistina designed it."

"She's not my friend anymore." The dirt mushed under his feet and he wished he'd worn sandals.

"Apparently, she is," Joseph said. "She would've brought this herself, but since I was coming anyway, she asked me to bring it."

Michael ducked into the glass hut and sat on the bed. "You mean she can't stand to be in my presence."

"Maybe that too," Joseph said, holding the package out. "But who could blame her? Open it."

"And how do you expect me to do that?" Michael waved his bandaged wrists in the air.

Joseph leaned into his face, his dark olive skin and eyes almost a mirror of Michael's. "The self-pity act is getting old. Figure it out, soldier."

Michael held his gaze for a beat, then gripped the stupid package with his stumps and dropped it on the mattress. He leaned over and bit into it, ripping the paper away and spitting it out.

Two semi-transparent, handlike apparatuses lay on the ripped brown paper. Copper, or maybe brass parts were visible on the inside, and leather straps were wrapped around them with buckles on the ends. The surface didn't look hard, but it didn't look soft either. Michael soured his face. "What am I supposed to do with these?"

"Put them on?" Joseph suggested. "They said you can use them until your hands grow back. It's more than anyone did for me."

"What?" Michael said. "Jab my stumps in like spears? She's mocking me—sending gloves when I have no hands."

A femme's silhouette appeared in the doorway; spiky buns slightly uneven at the sides of her head. She waltzed inside. "Lightning from the storms rarely strikes the same place twice," she said, casually. "Did you know that?" She picked up one of the handlike apparatuses and turned it, slowly. "Unlike stupid, which repeatedly strikes in the exact same spot. You must have a target on your back."

"How do you expect me to wear gloves when I have no hands?"

She narrowed her eyes. "They're not gloves. The fingers and palms are mechanical, and if you can control that reckless will of yours, the quantum nodes should read the pulses from your wrists and allow you to control their movement." She paused and sniffed at the air. "You stink."

"Thank you." Michael attempted to cross his arms, but failed. "I don't need these. Sorry you wasted your time."

"You should be ashamed of the way you treat the angels trying to help you," she said. "Do you know how hard Trudy, Zuriah, and I worked on these? Or how much you've hurt Hoot by singling him out and refusing to see him? Do you understand what he went through to save you?"

"All the more reason not to inconvenience any of you anymore." Michael averted his gaze. "Take the gloves and go. I don't need your pity. Or charity."

"What you need is a decent shave and a change of clothes," she spat. "Maybe try a bath with soap instead of pond scum." One of the mechanical gloves came flying straight for his head and he ducked. It smashed into the glass behind him, rattling the whole structure, and she stormed out.

Joseph raised his eyebrows. "Why haven't I recruited her yet? She's got great aim."

"Because neither you, nor anyone else would be able to domesticate her."

"That's a catch right there...." Joseph retrieved the glove and laid it back on the mattress. "Once your hands heal, you better seal that one with a star."

There was no reason to legitimize his comment with a response.

"Despite what your friends may think..." Joseph sat on the bed next to him, "I didn't come all the way here merely to transport fancy gloves across the island. I wanted to update you."

Michael couldn't even muster a facial expression that made it appear like he cared.

"The rules of the Games protected you from any military consequences, as we knew it would. Lucifer's a stickler for organization, so he agreed with me about which jurisdiction the Final Battle fell under."

"I'm sure he wasn't happy I challenged his brother."

"No. But he respected your ambition.... Of course, he thought it was glory you were after. The bad news is that you won't be able to maintain the title of Furie while you're off-grid healing. You'll have to start from scratch when you return, but you'll work your way up swiftly, just like before."

Michael laughed in his face. "I was crushed in front of the world."

"The fight with Baalael didn't damage your reputation," Joseph said. "If anything, your courage to battle a god strengthened it. Nobody expects any commonborn to be a match for a lord, even without his powers."

"But I was a match for him." Michael's eyes narrowed. "His sigil ring was hidden in his armor, and he crushed me under some invisible force. Asher betrayed us. I don't know how he knew, but he did."

"He was lurking outside the inn when we met with Asmodeus," Joseph said. "Baalael promoted him to Commander over the Second Legion."

"Where I would've gone once we finished recruiting..." Michael grumbled. Mathematically impossible. His bad luck had to be mathematically impossible. "What about Asmodeus? Baalael said he had him gutted."

"He tried, but Az tore those poor soldiers apart—drained them clean into shadows with his bare teeth. Now he's got a handful of demons he doesn't know what to do with. He's awaiting tribunal, but he's maintained loyalty to us. Said he acted on his own."

"Why didn't Baalael tell Lucifer we were involved?" A tribunal sounded kind of nice to Michael. Befitting, actually.

"Tribunals aren't Baalael's style. He'll torment us slowly so long as we draw breath."

"Ah." Michael lifted his wrists. "He's doing a great job so far."

"This isn't over yet," Joseph said. "I'm gathering evidence that Baalael is building a force to overthrow the Order. At the right time I'll present it to Lucifer. I have it on good word that Asher's a part of that too."

"He'll never believe that about his own brother."

"Once Lucifer sees evidence," Joseph said, "he won't be able to unsee it. The love he has for his brother will turn into something far more vile than we can imagine. The gods are like that."

"Why tell me all this? The whole war will be over by the time I heal. My fate's already sealed."

"After the war," Joseph said, "the military will be more important than ever. Who do you think will enforce the laws of the world? "

Michael furrowed his brow. "But laws are for soldiers…"

"Laws are for everyone in the new world, Michael. That's why each Hexant has a governing Principality. Otherwise, they'd be out there trampling each other for a piece of bread."

Still, none of it mattered. Odds were that his hands would never heal without the light. Michael hauled up his legs and leaned over, sucking down a straw full of empyreanol. He laid back down, feeling the warmth rise to his head. "I'm tired. If you could scoot back to campus and grab me another bottle of empyreanol, I'd appreciate it."

"You can't check out forever, Michael…" Joseph shook his head. "I'm disappointed in you."

"Then you're in good company. Oh… and get the big bottle, please. Ignore anything Zuriah says."

36

Michael

*"If we're not shy and move our feet, we never know just who
we'll meet!"*
-Heaven's Handbook, Mindsets, Part 4, "On Courage"

"**T**HAT'S NOT HELPING, YOU know." Zillah's accent filled the
glass hut as she stood like a soldier in the doorway, her glossy
black hair tied in battle braids. Michael leaned over his bottle, sucking
down the last sip of empyreanol. "We can hear your screams all the
way from the pits now. Excessive consumption will only make your bad
dreams worse."

"Says you..." Michael buried his face in the pillow and groaned.
He was half mad nearly every song now, depending on when Bernard
brought his bottle. And he hadn't shown up this overture. "Leave the
new bottle on the table."

"I didn't bring any empyreanol," Zillah said, "and Bernard's done
watching you rot away."

Michael blinked tightly, trying to somehow push back the headache.
Zillah wore the traditional leathers of a gladiator, no doubt wasting her
time in the pits with the amateurs on the island. "You should be back at
the camps with Joseph. Not playing hero to a bunch of desk chairs."

"I was invited to this island just like you." She stepped inside and set down a basket of vita. "I have my free will, and I choose to stay."

Michael reluctantly sat up, his head now swimming as it begged for more drink.

"You need to eat something." She held up the basket. "The Almighty himself couldn't consume that much empyreanol."

"I've been eating just fine."

"You eat barely enough to survive," she said, "much less heal. But that is not the only reason I have come. We need to talk about Hoot."

"There's nothing to talk about."

"You have hurt him deeply with your words," she said, "and he too is now growing withdrawn—"

"Shhh..." Michael raised his arm, "did you hear that?"

She looked around. "Hear what?"

A slight neighing sound came from outside and Michael pushed himself up. It wasn't quite a bray, but close enough. "I think I hear Bentley...."

He fumbled from the bed and, gingerly as he could, stepped from the hut. He ventured into the tree line toward the pond with Zillah following. They stopped behind a wide tree bark and Michael craned his neck. Something moved in the clearing, but it was obscured by more trees.

"Who's Bentley?" she whispered.

"My donkey," Michael said. "Haven't seen him since I got here."

"How do you know it's not a deer?"

"Deers don't bray. Or neigh."

They snuck closer to get a better look, carefully avoiding anything that could go crunch. He angled himself for a better view of the clearing.

"That's no deer," Michael said, disappointed. "But it's no Bentley either."

The white winged steed with the silver horn leaned over and grazed with machinelike precision.

"It's beautiful," she whispered, "and it cuts the grass better than Bernard."

"Never mind." Michael kicked leaves, annoyed, and the steed perked its head before running off. "Not who I was looking for."

He started back for the hut, his head pounding. He was going to have to go get a bottle himself if he wanted the ache to go away. Or worse, if he didn't want his dreams to come to life.

Zillah followed close, and her words definitely sounded louder than they actually were. "We need to talk about Hoot," she said. "Please. He has not been himself."

"There's nothing to talk about." Michael ripped a flower from a bush and threw it to the ground. "Nothing personal against the precept. I just want to be left alone."

"He didn't deserve your scolding."

"Never said he did. It wasn't personal."

"Then why demand he stay away?"

"I wish you'd all stay away." Michael pushed a branch from his path and it bounced back, almost hitting her.

"You threw a tantrum when he approached to check on you. It's cruel, and Hoot doesn't deserve it. He's probably the only one who can help you get through this. Let him minister to you."

"What can minister to me is another bottle." Michael ducked under the low frame of the hut and sat on the bed, his back to the door as Zillah loomed from behind. "Zillah... I can barely stomach the pious when things are going well, much less a precept praying over my mangled body. Can't you see the irony in that? Asking the Almighty to heal something he could've prevented in the first place? Hoot's the epitome of everything wrong in this world. He should've chosen a different Calling."

"We don't choose our Callings. You know that."

"Give him a copy of the Black Manifesto. Maybe then I'll be able to tolerate him."

"You haven't even read the Manifesto."

"Of course I have. I was a Furie."

"There was never even a crease in that binding," Zillah said. "You placed the book in your tent like a prop."

"I skimmed it," he admitted. "*Thoroughly* skimmed it. There's nothing in there I didn't already know. I could've written the book myself."

"What about our code, then?" Zillah asked. "The soldier's code? What about honor and loyalty to your brothers in arms?"

"A praying soldier is good as dead," Michael said. "Soldiers shouldn't put faith in anyone but themselves."

"Soldiers should put faith in soldiers," Zillah said.

"I can't stomach weakness, Z. The precept is weak. He's always been weak."

"Well, I can't stomach losing faith in another brother," Zillah said. "I've already lost it in Asher; don't make me lose it in you too."

"If Hoot needs comfort, let him read his little white book. Far away from me."

"I don't read a *little white book*," another voice interjected. Hoot stood in the doorway and dropped a large sack to the ground with a thud. "I read a big, leather-bound book, which is too long and complex for your simple mind to understand." His voice was flat. Harsh. "No offense."

Michael closed his eyes and pinched the bridge of his nose, his whole body throbbing now. This was way too much before his first piss. "How long have you been standing there?"

"Long enough."

"Don't take it personal, Hoot. I'm not fond of talking to Zillah, either."

She acknowledged Hoot with a nod and glared at Michael. "I'll leave you two to talk. Please, Michael, don't disappoint me."

At least he gave them all something to agree on: he was one big disappointment.

Zillah left them in the most awkward silence that could possibly exist, and a long measure of it passed before the precept spoke.

"I brought some things from your quarter," Hoot said. "I took the liberty of packing a bag for you."

"My door was locked. How'd you get in?"

"A sliver of wire and a pin."

"You picked my lock?" Michael's eyebrows lifted. "That's not very precept-like."

"An angel with nothing to hide has nothing to fear from a lock being picked."

"What's that supposed to mean?"

"Locks either protect the dishonest, or protect from the dishonest. I'd like to think neither of us fit those categories."

"Where'd you learn to pick a lock? They teach you that in the *big leather book*?"

"No." Hoot cleared his throat. "Azrael asked me personally to bring your art supplies, and I obliged because he was my mentor. The other items I grabbed as a courtesy."

"Your mentor?"

"While I was in University."

"How did he know I'd have supplies in my room?"

"You'll have to ask him that," Hoot said. "Now that you have the gloves, Azrael said there was an assignment for you."

An assignment? "You've got to be kidding me." A stabbing pain ripped through Michael's head and he winced. He needed more empyreanol before his dreams came to life, which happened whenever the spirits left his system.

"I assure you," Hoot said, "I'm not. You might want to clean yourself up before he gets here."

Michael's hand began shaking—a symptom of the empyreanol drought.

"If you need help cleaning yourself up, I can—"

"I'm fine, Hoot," Michael cut him off. "If you want to help, you can get me another bottle."

"I'll get you nothing to pour down your throat," Hoot said, firmly. "We've all agreed that your pain reliever is doing more harm than good.

But before I leave, I need to ask you a question. An important question… Is that alright with you?"

"No…" Michael's vision started to double, and he blinked. "But I feel like you're going to ask anyway."

Hoot leaned over and pulled a book from the sack, plopping it on Michael's bed. It was the drawing book Gabriel had gifted him as a child, Angelic Anatomy.

Michael's face darkened. He didn't have many sentimental items, and didn't appreciate anyone touching the little bit he had, precept or not.

"Where did you get it?" Hoot asked.

"An old book shop," Michael lied. "You shouldn't go snooping around, touching things that aren't yours."

"This book is very rare," Hoot said. "There are only a dozen in existence."

"And?" Michael tried to hold his gaze, but his vision started fragmenting.

"And I collect them," Hoot said. "Do you know where the book shop sourced it?"

"I have no idea," Michael said, wishing he would leave. He needed that bottle before he started seeing things. He might have to drag himself half-dead across the island to get it.

"Then tell me where the book shop is, and I'll ask them where they sourced it. Is it in your home crossing? Your village?"

Michael screwed up his face. "I can't remember details." His mind was too clouded to come up with any lies. He leaned over and sipped from the empty bottle, draining any drops he could.

"You're not exactly a librarian, Michael," Hoot said, curtly. "You own exactly two pieces of literature from what I've seen, and this book happens to be one of the rarest in the world."

"I should trade it for obsidian, then," Michael taunted. Maybe that would make him go away.

"You'd have to take it from me first." Hoot swiped the book from the bed. "And good luck doing that without hands."

Michael was taken back, even through his pain. "You act like a soldier *now* for an old book? What's that book to you anyway?"

"I don't cast my gems into vomit," Hoot said. "It's none of your business."

"Tell me..." Michael's vision fragmented again and he nearly fell over, but his curiosity was genuinely piqued. He knew little about the book, or where it came from. He only knew what it meant to him. He steadied himself. "I'm sorry for acting like a wingbag, Hoot. Please... You're not an artist, so why do you care about an old anatomy book? Is it for the scientists?"

"No."

"You're an antiques collector?"

"No."

"Then what?" Dark spots were appearing in Michael's periphery, and he tried to ignore them. "Sit. Please... Forgive the way I acted. I meant no harm. Tell me why you want my book."

Hoot stared at him for nearly a measure. He must've looked a pitiful thing, because the precept's face softened. He sat at the edge of the bed. "I don't want your book," Hoot said. "I only want to know where you found it."

"Why?"

Hoot leaned on his knees and stared off, his expression distant. A measure passed before he spoke. "Learning's always been more than a Calling for me—it's a passion. I've never missed an opportunity to visit the ancient libraries and museums. While at University, I'd travel to the Holy City two, maybe three times a movement just to see the antiquated works with my own eyes, and to learn more about our history.

"I was fortunate to have seen the original version of this book. The *Anatamous Angelakos*. They keep it encased in diamond. It's said that no angel could have created it—not even the silent scholars. The images inside are more than simply our anatomy—which nobody could have possibly known back then. They're the blueprint for every angelic species in the world. Our original designs. The first book is older than both the lords and the silent scholars."

"Who made it, then?"

"The Almighty himself," Hoot said, "with his own divine hand. Only a dozen copies were created—hand drawn by Lord Raphael."

Michael raised his eyebrows, but even that hurt. Had he known how rare and special the book was, he probably would've taken better care of it. "Raphael is here on campus," Michael said, temporarily losing his train of thought, but then snapped back. "If you collect the copies, why don't you just ask him where they are?"

"I don't merely collect the copies to collect them," Hoot said.

"So, what then?" More dark spots emerged in Michael's blurring vision, and he shook his head. He eyed the empty bottle, wishing something was in there.

"When I was a child," Hoot started, "almost too young to remember... I was playing alone in the field behind our manor. I was different back then, and young children don't take well to different if their indoctrination is... less than ideal. When my isolation became too much for me, I dropped to my knees and prayed, begging that the Almighty take away my loneliness. To protect me from the bigger brothers in my manor."

A breeze rustled some leaves up against the top of the glass, and the sky above them appeared to lighten. Michael blinked hard, refocusing his eyes and his mind. When the empyreanol emptied from his system, he couldn't tell reality from dreams.

"After I said the prayer," Hoot continued, "I noticed something in the woods partly covered in dirt, so I ran over to it. Two books lay side by side. I thought maybe the books were the answer to my prayer. Maybe there were games inside that would give me something to do, so I wouldn't feel so lonely. I brought them back to my room and hid them deep in my chest so that my brothers wouldn't find them."

Michael harkened, and the sky above them now swirled, slight ribbons of light and color amid the gray. Something caught in Michael's throat, and he cleared it, blinking. Had Zillah even woken him up? Or was he still asleep? He couldn't focus. He needed more empyreanol.

"During the silence while everyone slept," Hoot said, "I took the books out. Neither contained any games. The first was a copy of the Handbook, which I was unable to read because I barely knew my letters back then, and the other was a copy of the *Anatamous Angelakos—Angelic Anatomy*—like the one you have here. Being that I had no talent to draw, I feared my prayer had fallen on deaf ears. But I refused to believe it—I refused to give up hope."

The blotches in Michael's vision started taking form, and dread filled him. He felt like he was floating on those waves again, between the crests and the valleys, where anything was possible. His head swam with confusion as Hoot's story grew more and more familiar.

He *had* to be dreaming again. At any beat, the sky would crack and fall dark. Deidre would smash the glass with a hammer, or Baalael would set the meadow on fire. He clutched the sheets, feeling the sweat forming at his brow.

"Shortly after," Hoot continued, gazing off as Michael's limbs shook, "my prayer was answered. One song, I sat alone eating my lunch in the field like I always did, and a raven-haired child appeared from behind the tree, out of nowhere, literally manifesting from nothing. My prayer had been answered—the Almighty sent me a brother."

The air left Michael's chest as he braced for the storm, squeezing his eyes shut and closing his forearms around his face. The tendrils of his memory wrapped around what he so desperately tried to forget.

"Are you alright?" Hoot finally turned to him, harkening with concern.

"You have to go..." Michael panted and scurried from the bed, crouching on the floor. "Get out before Deidre comes... the light above us won't stay. It's a lie—it always comes before they do. Baalael and Deidre—they're coming."

Hoot's eyes went wide as the wind picked up. Michael clawed at the fallen pole from Zuriah's contraption, but he had no hands to grasp it with. He couldn't protect them. Couldn't save them... "Find Antoinette! *Find her and get out!*"

The precept ran to him, dropped to his knees and gripped Michael's shoulders, searching his face.

"Get out of my dream!" Michael screamed, shaking. He could hear the crashing and the storm before it even arrived, like a rush of pure chaos. "Get out before they come! I can't protect us without my hands!"

Hoot dug his fingers into Michael's shoulders and forced him still. "This isn't a dream, Michael! It's the empyreanol leaving your system."

Michael looked up, his eyes searching frantically.

Finally, they landed in Hoot's gaze. Something familiar beckoned to him... something in the precept's gentle brown eyes.

"Michael, listen to me," Hoot said, "the raven-haired child had no name... *but we called him X.*"

Michael froze, and the chaos in his mind came to a screeching halt. The only sound now was the rustling of leaves and the chirping of birds. Hoot dug deep into his pocket and pulled out a pair of crooked spectacles, slipping them on his face.

Michael blinked, unable to find his voice as he searched the precept's face.

"*Gabriel?*" he rasped.

"It's me." Hoot's voice cracked as he nodded, his eyes now glistening. "I'm here. There was barely a chance, but I had to try. I saw the book in your room... and it's so rare. I was afraid to hope. I prayed so hard to find you again...."

Michael looked around for Deidre, or Baalael. Or the storm... But there was none of it. "The sky..." Michael pointed, his bandaged wrist shaking.

Gabriel looked up. "I can't explain why it's lighter, but I promise you... this is no dream. I'm here."

The world around them shrank. Deep in Hoot's eyes, hidden inside the adult, was *Gabriel.* Where he had once been round and soft, he was now chiseled and hard. The face Michael remembered cowering with fear now stared back at him, steadfast and strong.

Michael buried his head into his brother's chest and wept. "I abandoned you," he whispered. "I *am* X. Mary calls me Michael, but that's not who I am."

Gabriel rested his cheek against Michael's head and held him, his warm body lending life to Michael's cold, clammy skin. "I think it *is* who you are, though. *Mi kah e El.* There's an ancient tongue few know about, spoken only by the silent scholars. It's the source of our naming conventions. *Mi kah e El* means 'I am your gift from the Almighty.' And that's what you are, Michael. It's what you've always been. When you're better, I'd love to hear about Mary. And the story about how you got your name..."

37

X

"Vita heals from the inside, and light heals from above; but the most powerful cure for anything, is truly a Matriarch's love."

-Heaven's Handbook, Truths, Part 1, "On Family"

IT HAD BEEN THREE, maybe four songs since anyone shoved anything resembling food under the door of the cellar. If X's pain had been severe when he was consuming everything except manna, it was now unbearable with his stomach completely empty, and his throat parched as sand. He rubbed the hem of his robe in the wetness that had once been a puddle, and sucked whatever moisture he could from it.

He wanted to sob, but he was too weak and dehydrated to spare even a single tear. He checked the far end of the cellar again. Those glowing green eyes cut through the darkness and remained fixed on him, watching, as he teetered at the edge of a fading sanity. Starvation, isolation and darkness would do that to you, apparently.

He had told Antoinette and Gabriel to stop coming, but that wasn't why they stopped. Baalael had posted brothers outside the cellar door, and given explicit instructions to spare no body part should anyone approach with food or drink again.

The last of the mercy that X had received was whatever had spilled under the door from the jug of water Antoinette had thrown in Hariel's face when he refused her entry. The last sound X heard from that exchange was Lord Baalael's voice interrupting them, followed by a dull thump and the sound of someone being dragged away. Antoinette should've had her guard up. Underestimating what this estate was capable of had always been her weakness.

He could barely tell the music from the silence anymore. His mind filled the darkness with voices that weren't really there, which probably should've worried him, except that the vaporous echoes were a welcome distraction from the throbbing pain that pulsed through his body.

The bolt on the door unlatched and he partly roused from his stupor. The light from outside assaulted him and he crawled into the shadow, his joints and limbs sending bolts of pain from the sudden movement. He shielded himself, squinting.

One of those hooded angels in their blank, white masks approached holding a long needle. He grabbed X by the arm and jabbed the thing in, sucking his life force into a sterile, glass-like tube. Why couldn't they just remove his head and be done with it? Could someone remain aware without their head? Maybe then he could finally go to sleep without worrying about having to wake up again.

"Stand up," the angel said from behind the white mask. X furrowed his brow. He could barely bend his knee, much less get on his feet.

Without another word, the angel grabbed him by the arm and dragged him across the concrete floor, the cold, hard surface scraping the skin off his knees. Once outside, the light was unbearable, even with his eyes closed, and the blaring music assaulted his ears as if two songs were playing different melodies, out of tune, both at once.

Someone pried his lids open, and he screamed as the blinding light virtually seared his eyes.

"Dilation is over eighty percent now," another robed angel said from behind a white mask. His voice was dull, emotionless. "Load him into transport for the next round of endurance trails." He was slung over someone's shoulder and dumped into the back of what he could only imagine was a carriage, from the strong smell of the horses.

They began moving, the floor beneath him jostling with every bump and sending more pain searing through his body. Slowly, the light creeping through his eyelids became tolerable again, and little by little, it healed at least his superficial wounds. He opened his eyes.

The carriage and horses kicked up dust on the road behind them, and he recognized the route to be the one that led to the village fighting pit. He didn't have the strength to jump, and with the way he felt, the fall might break him. What could they possibly benefit from fighting someone who was already so weak? They couldn't be learning anything, so what was the point? Besides cruelty for the sake of it. It didn't make sense.

The carriage came to a stop and two of the brothers unlatched the gate and pulled him out. He managed to stand up, although barely.

"Mercy is for the weak," Lord Baalael's voice preceded his presence as two brothers gripped X by the arms. He towered over the young, fighting horde who were fully dressed in leathers and standing straight, most of their hands clasped behind their backs. "If someone is unwilling to obey or comply, what does that make them?"

Several of the brothers raised their hands to answer the question.

"Hariel?" Baalael called on the largest and oldest of them.

"An angel unwilling to obey or comply is a threat, sir."

"That is correct. And what are they a threat to?"

"Our way of life, our security, and our food, sir."

"That's right. And what would happen if we made a habit of showing mercy to threats?"

"We would cease to exist."

"That's very good, Hariel. And has X here been obedient or compliant?" Lord Baalael moved his gaze to another brother. "What about you, Andres? What is your answer?"

"He has not been obedient, sir," Andres said.

"That's right. He's been a very, very disobedient angel. So what does that make him? What does disobedience to my orders make X?"

"A threat," Andres said.

"And what are threats?" Baalael cupped his ear so that Andres spoke his answer louder.

"Threats are objects to be destroyed, sir."

A chill ran over X's skin and he eyed the grip the brothers had on his arms. He tried to pull himself free, but he was just too weak without any food in his system.

"That's right," Baalael smiled. "He is an object. So take him to the pit, and anyone caught showing mercy will be considered disobedient and noncompliant. Anyone caught tolerating another showing mercy will also be considered a threat... so on and so forth. Do you all understand?"

The brothers nodded.

"Go."

Panic produced a surge of energy through X and he yanked one arm free, but something smashed the back of his head and he stumbled. Hariel gripped his arm again, and they dragged him to the pit, shoving him over the edge of it. He landed hard on his face, the pain now fading into numbness and panic.

The brothers filed down the steps and X crawled to the opposite side of the wall, stumbling once and face-planting on the ground. The brothers fanned out from either side behind Hariel, and X scurried into the corner, glancing in every direction.

"NO! I'll not tolerate it anymore!" Antoinette came running from the woods in a long, blue robe, screaming. "Don't lift a single hand to him, you little abominations!"

"Ah," Lord Baalael stepped to the opposite edge of the pit and crossed his arms. "Looks like we have two threats with us for this session. Very good. The more mental training, the better." Gabriel came running behind her, winded, his round cheeks flushed purple. "Make that three," Baalael said.

"It's over," Antoinette called out. "I've renounced my oath and I've already sent letters to the Council and the Ministry of Education to let them know about what's taking place here."

"That was very kind of you," Baalael said. "I'm sure they'll appreciate the time you took to write those before throwing them in the garbage." The ring on his hand blazed a bright blue and suddenly he was standing behind her. He grabbed her hair and lifted her from the ground. She let out a yelp, and bright blue wings of light beamed from his back and they began hovering.

"No!" She screamed as she dangled there, clawing to get him off.

"Antoinette and I are going to take a little trip. In the meantime...." He kicked Gabriel hard in the back and he went flying over the edge, slamming into the center of the pit. "Practice on both of them." He twisted Antoinette by the hair until she was face to face with him and said, "I preferred to keep it simple and use the angel with *no* records for the testing and training... but being that you're making simplicity impossible, it looks like someone else's records will have to disappear." He turned back to the brothers. "Remember... no mercy!"

They began ascending and Antoinette reached into her blue robe and slid out a long, steel sword. X's sword. "Bubby—take it!" She tossed it into the pit and it landed with a thump. He practically fell over to grab it, but it was too heavy to lift.

Gabriel moaned from the ground and rolled over, his excess weight jiggling with the motion. The brothers eyed one another, holding back smirks, and started for Gabriel.

"No!" X rasped, trying to get their attention. "I'm the threat! Not him!"

"You can't even stand up," Andres called back. "At least he's got a little fight in him... he'll be more fun."

The stone on X's sword caught the light in an odd way, and a surge of energy pulsed through him. His hand gripped the hilt and he straightened to his knees, lifting the sword with one hand. "I'm the one you need to destroy..." his voice was stronger this time, "because I'm the one who'll come back and have *no mercy on you.*"

They surrounded Gabriel, whose gaze was wide and terrified. He held his hands in front of him and mouthed the word *please.*

The sword's stone caught the light from another angle this time, almost appearing to glow, revealing some kind of mark at the center. Strength suddenly rippled through X and he rose to his feet, breath heavy and eyes fixed.

Hariel kicked Gabe across his face and he slammed to the floor, whimpering. The others pounced, unleashing a flurry of kicks as Gabriel curled up in a ball.

X took off and leapt into the melee, cocking his sword and descending with a barrage of strikes just like he'd practiced. Bright lavender light burst from the wounds in the wake of his blade, and shock rippled through the faces of Gabriel's assailants as they stumbled back.

He got between his brother and the threats, lunging at anyone still standing.

"Stop!" Hariel scrambled to his feet, the wounds to his arms knitting themselves back together. "Give us a few beats to regroup..."

X stalked him, sword lifted. "Threats are objects to be destroyed." He got in his face, and before Hariel could retreat, X bashed his forehead into the angel's jaw with a loud crack before kicking him square in the chest, knocking him to the ground. The others hollered, but none dared interfere. X climbed on top of Hariel and cocked his fist back, smashing it into Hariel's face over and over until he was unrecognizable.

"Stop!" Gabriel yanked X's robe from behind. "You'll be no better than them!"

X shoved him to the ground and picked up his sword, angling its hilt for Hariel's eye socket. But before he could bring it down, the weight of it became unbearable again, and he lost his breath. The burst of energy vanished as quickly as it came.

He stumbled and coughed, catching himself with the sword like a walking stick. Gabriel was under his arm in an instant, dragging him out of the pit. "We have to get out of here."

"Baalael's back," Andres spit out. "You're done now, X."

The blue orb that was Lord Baalael sped toward them as X's strength drained from his body.

"We have to go," Gabe panted.

Baalael drew closer, and Gabriel ran the best he could with the weight of X slung over his shoulder.

"We won't make it," X said, retracting his arm and falling to his knees. "Run!" he commanded Gabriel. "You go alone!"

"I won't leave you." Gabe pulled at his arm.

"No..." His energy was so drained now he could barely speak. "Please... just go."

Baalael landed behind them, his light impossibly bright as he yanked X by the neck and flung him like a limp rag. He landed in some patchy grass with a hard thump and rolled several cubits, the pain now completely unbearable.

"Let's see how much angels can endure..." Baalael's foot smashed into his jaw with a loud crack, "... before they finally stop breathing."

Baalael lifted X from the ground and launched his body through the air so that he crashed into the side of the carriage. He was drifting in and out of consciousness. He was lifted again and thrown into the back of the carriage, coughing up light which quickly condensed into honey-sweet blood in his mouth.

X could hear the others boarding behind him, but he didn't have the energy to open his eyes or worry. The carriage jolted forward, and his breath shallowed to a near halt. Once again, those two green orbs blinked to life behind his closed eyelids. He wanted to reach out to them, but he knew that was impossible... so he sat quietly, in the darkness of his mind, locked in their gaze.

Shortly after the carriage stopped moving, he was being dragged. A loud, scraping sound indicated they were back at the cellar, and he was tossed on the hard, concrete floor.

He was still in and out of consciousness when he heard the distinct sound of liquid spilling, followed by the striking of a match and a *whoosh*. Warmth engulfed him, and he welcomed it, all the while gazing into those beautiful green eyes.

The door slammed shut, and he became aware of the distinct odor of smoke, like the wood chips they would burn to add flavor to rootroast. Someone pounded on the door, crying. Antionette? What a waste of energy. Better to just go to sleep and get it all over with.

Heat began to sear his skin and he choked, which was inconvenient. He just wanted to sleep. Then something crashed and a fierce wind blew, so he forced one eye open to see what so fervently insisted on disturbing his rest.

A figure emerged from the doorway in a blur of speed and X was suddenly being carried. His robe was stripped from him, somehow, and he was naked. His skin was charred and gray, but it didn't matter. He wrapped his arms around the stranger's neck and tried to stay asleep.

He was placed inside a carriage, plush and soft on the inside, and a pair of cool hands laid on his stomach, pushing some kind of energy inside him. The stranger pulled a blanket from under the seat and covered him. They jolted forward and X forced open his eyes only to see Gabriel running after their carriage, red-faced and panting. His robe was all burned up, and X wanted to call out, but he didn't have the energy. He rasped his brother's name in a haggard, weak voice. "*Gabriel...*"

He put a hand to the glass for a beat, but it slid down as Gabriel grew smaller with the distance. The stranger put their hands on either side of X's head and everything went dark again. Except for the emerald eyes. They stared back from the nothingness, as if they had been waiting.

X found himself standing on the doorsteps of a strange manor wrapped only in a blanket, holding his sword. The air was silent and smelled of lavender, and a satchel was next to him, but its contents were unknown. He squeezed his eyes shut and blinked, unsure if he was dreaming. When had he left the pits? And where was Gabriel?

The door opened, and a roundish femme with pink rollers in her hair stood there in a nightgown and slippers. She furrowed her brow and leaned over, eye level with him. "Could you be the gift I've been waitin' for all this time?"

"I..." X shook his head. "I don't know about any gift."

"Never you mind..." She fingered the small amulet around her neck. "Have ya got a name I can call ya?"

He shrugged, unsure what to say. If this *was* a dream and he had to pick a name, he certainly wasn't picking "X".

"Might I call ya Michael, then? Would ya like that?"

He straightened, and then nodded. *Michael*. It was a good name.

Then he wondered when he would wake up in that cold, dark cellar again.

"Don't drift off, Michael." She booped his nose and picked up his satchel before leading him inside the house. "Yer all skin n' bones. I'd reckon a hot meal might put some color in those cheeks. There's a batch of hot manna cakes coolin' in the kitchen, and I just milked our Mother Tree's sap to churn some fresh butter. How does that sound?"

He suddenly became aware of the glorious aroma all around him, and his starving stomach rumbled.

"Let's get ya dressed, then, so we can put some food in that belly proper."

"Thank you," he whispered, still unsure if any of this was real.

She pulled a wool robe from the hallway closet and placed it around his shoulders. "This'll take away the chill. If you were lost before... well... yer found now."

"What do I call you?"

"Mary," she said. "Matriarch Mary." She pulled him in a tight hug and held him there. Tears stung the backs of his eyes and something broke. He stood there, weeping in her strong, warm arms. For the first time in his life, he felt *safe*.

"There'll always be a place for ya with me, Michael." She kissed the top of his head. "Welcome home, son."

38

Michael

"Selfishness might be generalized as the inversion of all load-bearing virtues in the utopian framework. Where an overwhelming sense of self is present; no enduring beams may be found."
-The Guide to Utopian Principles and Ethics, Section III, On Existence

THE PAINTBRUSH LEANED AGAINST the inside of an empty jar where the bottle of empyreanol once sat. Michael's glove contraption hovered just above it, and he knitted his brow, focusing. The glasslike appendages were heavy and foreign on his wrists, the leather straps wrapped tight around his forearm almost to the elbow.

It had been fourteen songs since his last sip of spirits, and during that time Gabriel kept close, pitching a mat on the floor and not leaving his side. Michael had relented to being shaven and cleaned up, but left his hair long to remind himself that he could no longer be a soldier—not without hands. Or rather, not without real hands.

He willed the fingers to grasp the brush, breathing slowly in, and slowly out, as Azrael had shown him. But his mind kept drifting back to images of Gabriel being locked in a cellar, or starved, or beaten. Or all three.

"These things don't work." Michael let the fake hands fall to his side. "I've been at this for three songs and I can't even get a finger to twitch."

"You've *only* been at this for three songs," Gabriel corrected. "Have some faith in Philistina and the team. You've got the best minds in the world pulling for you."

Gabriel pulled up a stool and sat. "Focus on your breath. When your mind is still, picture the fingers closing around the paintbrush."

"I *am* focusing on my breath. You sound like Azrael."

"I should—he was my mentor."

There it was again: that gap between the angel who sat before him and the pudgy, defenseless brother whom Michael had abandoned.

"This is frustrating," Michael said. "And you not telling me how you escaped, or where you found refuge, or *if* you found refuge is frustrating. This is all frustrating"

"I'm not trying to frustrate you," Gabriel said. "Your body and mind are still recovering from the empyreanol and near starvation. To say nothing of your wounds. Zuriah said stress will set you back."

"It's more stressful not knowing," Michael said, growing agitated.

"I'll tell you everything when you're strong enough to handle it."

"Don't treat me like I'm fragile!" Michael stood up, his volume escalating. "I got into a pit with a god—*with* his ring on—and I survived! All I've done is survive. I'm not fragile, Gabriel—"

Gabriel smashed a palm over Michael's mouth and pushed him back on the bed. "The only time that name's been murmured since I left home was when you barely whispered it twelve songs ago," he hissed. "Names carry on the wind heavier than words. They're decipherable and unique. I've been hiding all this time—just like you."

He kept his hand there several beats before finally removing it, and Michael sat, shocked. He was right. Maybe Baalael knew who Michael was now, but there was no reason to expose Hoot's identity.

"I'm sorry," Michael said, forcing himself to be calm. "But you want me to focus and move these limbs, yet all my mind shows me is how they punished you because *I left*. The same way I left my donkey... and Mary and Shem. All of them. Your silence only makes me imagine the worst."

"There are parts of my story I just don't think you're ready to hear," Gabriel said.

Michael harkened. "So, they *did* hurt you?"

"They didn't hurt me," Gabriel said. "They never got the chance."

His words hung in the air for a beat before they settled in, and Michael closed his eyes, relief washing over him. "You figured out a way to escape?"

"Something like that...." Gabriel shuffled in his seat and cleared his throat. "We should get back to—"

"No—" Michael cut him off. "Please. Tell me the parts you want to tell me. But I need to know. I can't focus on anything until I do."

Gabriel sighed. "Alright. But no questions. I tell the story my way, or not at all."

"Fine," Michael said, eagerly. "Did you make it to the next crossing and find another estate? Ask them for help?"

Gabriel glared at him, and Michael looked away. "Sorry. No questions."

He answered anyway. "I didn't think going to another estate would be wise. We know how strangers like to believe 'children with vivid imaginations.' So the first thing I did was steal a map and a compass from the Agorium."

"*You* stole?" Michael raised his eyebrows. "Why not just take them honestly? It's not like there were shortages back then."

"I was too paranoid to be seen or speak to anyone," Gabriel said. "And I needed to know how to get to my destination, which was in the Second Circle. My heart had always been set on University, but I was only fourteen, and I needed somewhere to live until then. I knew that the silent scholars ran the Universities using few words, but in their home, they took a vow to utter no words at all… which meant they couldn't ask questions. So I had to get to the monastery."

"The monastery? You planned this all on your own?"

Gabriel crossed his arms.

"Sorry," Michael grumbled.

He resumed the story. "It took the better part of a symphony to get there on foot. Rather than steal anything else, I stayed off the main roads and ate from wild groves, living in the same robe I wore when I left. By the time I showed up at the monastery, my sandals had more holes than a crumpet.

"Azrael was standing in front of the iron doors when I arrived. I wasn't even sure he was real, he was so stiff and tall. But when I climbed the marble steps, he simply opened the door and led me inside, otherwise ignoring me. The scholars inside tarried to and fro, like they were engaged in some deep task, but no one breathed a single word. Nor could I see their faces to see if they even noticed my presence. Eventually, I just made myself comfortable… I slept in their studies, ate from their kitchen."

"Exploiting their vows of silence," Michael murmured. "Nice."

Gabe winked. "I learned from the best…. After about a movement, things I needed started popping up. A new robe in my size, or new sandals. Books that I could read… and during the silence, I'd sit in the study and read them out loud to myself, just so it felt like I was talking to someone."

"Must've been lonely."

"Not really," Gabriel said. "Every overture I began going into the courtyard, where you could see the Throne Tower and the rainbow dome above the Holy City. I'd meditate on them and pray…. I could feel the Almighty communing with me. After that, I'd join some of the other scholars while they practiced the gladiatorial arts. But they didn't fight each other. They practiced the forms slowly, and it became part of my meditation, and my routine. That's why my forms are so solid. It would be three symphonies before I conversed with another living soul, and that soul turned out to be Azrael."

Michael found himself oddly relieved that Hoot found solace in his meditation and prayer, in spite of who he prayed to. He felt a little stupid now that he was so hard on him. Michael had Mary and the Jolly Bub, but all Gabriel had was prayer.

"I have one burning question," Michael asked. "Please... don't get angry."

Gabriel cocked a brow.

"The name... Why Hoot? Why not choose something that sounds strong—like Rocquiel or Bensonite?"

Gabriel smirked. "Those sound like construction materials. I never chose a name. During the silence when I'd read aloud to myself, Azrael would pass the study and make the sound of an owl."

"I thought they couldn't speak inside the monastery?"

"They can't utter *words* inside the monastery," Gabriel corrected. "The vow says nothing about uttering sounds. It comforted me—like he was offering his approval for my being there. Later, I'd find out from him that he made those sounds—hoot hoot—because owls are silent during the songs, and only noisy during the silence. Just like I was when I would read aloud instead of sleeping. You'd never tell by how serious he is, but Azrael has a strong affinity for children.

"He keeps a gallery's worth of framed artwork in his study that were clearly made by children, or a child at least. Mother Trees and garden flowers drawn in colored wax or painted."

"There used to be art competitions for children to learn from the masters—remember?"

Gabriel took a deep breath and shuddered. "How could I forget? But no, he wouldn't apprentice from any competition. That's not what the Master Scholar does. Anyway, I suspected my mystery robes and books came from him too, which I later found out they did.

"After three symphonies of my own silence in the monastery, Azrael handed me an invitation—a Calling to study at the University of Utopian Ethics and Psychology. It was addressed simply to 'Hoot.' He never asked about my name, or where I came from, so I never told him. I stayed in the monastery during my tenure studying, and when I graduated with honors, I was sent all over the realm to work in different capacities, until I was finally called here."

"Well..." Michael swallowed, blinking back the emotions crowding him. "I'm sorry I abandoned you. I'm sorry I was too much of a coward to make my way back there. I found... *other ways* to deal with my guilt."

"You have nothing to be guilty for," Gabriel said. "You were a child, and experienced things the world would never understand. The Almighty never lost sight of me, Michael. Never. I've always had someone taking care of me. It just wasn't you."

Michael really wanted to believe that. But he just couldn't. "And what exactly is it you do here? On campus? Besides playing sports."

"I help bring out the best in individuals... which brings us current. Now that you know I wasn't skinned alive or burned, or starved, you should be able to focus and connect with those hands."

Michael sighed before nodding, and he lifted the appendage to the paintbrush.

"Picture yourself holding it," Gabriel said. "Picking it up with confidence. Don't let any other thoughts into your mind."

Michael visualized the fingers pinching the handle, then pulling it flush into his palm. He closed his eyes, looping the action in his mind.

After several beats he opened one eye, but the fingers hadn't moved.

He tried again, this time with his eyes open. He focused so hard that beads of sweat formed on his forehead, but the stubborn thing wouldn't budge.

There might have been more of Philistina in this invention than she'd care to admit.

"You're trying too hard," Gabriel said. "Let it..." A cloaked figure moving through the meadow caught their attention. "Azrael," Gabe said.

"How can you tell?" Michael asked. "They all look the same."

"The cincture."

"The who?"

"The rope around his waist," Gabriel said. "A master's cincture is the color of wheat, but the High Master's cincture is black. Azrael is the only High Master. Remember… no names."

"I thought you trusted Azrael."

"With every bit of trust I'm capable of," Hoot said. "So… no names."

Azrael seemed to glide through the meadow. The scholars all had a disconcerting presence, as if some nonentity loomed within those mysterious hoods, but Azrael was the worst of them. His size alone could raise the hackles of a tree, and his speech was even worse.

Hoot scrambled to meet him outside, bowing low when he arrived. The scholar wasted no time in getting to the point of his visit.

"A portrait is required," Azrael droned in his slow, monotone voice. "She is one of two crown jewels in our creation. Michael will execute her portrait, and she will be called Eve."

"A portrait?" Michael glared at him. There were so many reasons why he couldn't do this—his hands being only one of them. Once this project launched, it was over for them all.

"High Master…" Hoot said, "with all respect, Michael's made progress, but he's still learning the new apparatuses. I'd recommend giving him a little more time."

"There is no time," Azrael droned. "He must accept the task, or leave the island."

"You said you would find me for my next lesson," Michael said, exasperated. "Not to actually *paint* something."

Azrael didn't respond.

"There's a whole horde of professional painters on this island," Michael gestured to the campus. "Lord Raphael himself is in there."

"You've received the inspiration," Azrael said, "so you must paint it."

"I didn't receive any inspiration…" Michael lifted his heavy appendages. "I can't even get these things to work!"

Azrael waited until Michael calmed down to respond. "You cannot get the hands to work, because your will centers on yourself. You are selfish, self-centered, and self-absorbed."

Michael's jaw slacked. This was the *second time* that scholar berated him without even knowing him! Before he could respond, Hoot placed a hand on his shoulder and squeezed, his expression warning Michael to stay silent.

"Art is the act of preserving and protecting what is good," Azrael said with inflection. "Learn to do that, and you will connect with the gifts." He unraveled a scroll and held it in front of Michael's face.

It was the request, in writing, signed by Lord Raphael. Without a goodbye, the scholar turned on a heel and departed, disappearing into the dense trees.

"Did you hear what he said to me?" Michael hissed. "He called me selfish and self-absorbed! Why didn't you back me up?"

"You don't rebut the High Master," Gabriel said. "You were called here as an artist. So far as they're concerned, that's your job."

"Even if I *could* paint that portrait," Michael lowered his voice, "I wouldn't. Do you know what happens when this project is complete?"

Gabriel cocked his head.

"It's over," Michael said. "The Almighty's replacing us with whatever they're building in that machine. It's all a punishment—the darkness, the storms... everything."

"A punishment?" Gabriel grimaced. "For what?"

"Lucifer wrote a book that ran contrary to the world's indoctrination, and his ideas spread beyond the pages. Now we'll all be destroyed for it."

"There's no shortage of theories about what's causing the darkness," Hoot said, "but that's the most ridiculous yet. Even if it were true, that should make you take this assignment all the more. If the other artists could paint this in a fraction of the time, how much more would you delay the project if they were waiting on you? You're at a considerable disadvantage."

Michael wanted to argue, but the precept had a point. "You might be smarter than I give you credit for...."

"I'll leave that point unchallenged," Gabriel said. "But I'll warn you that Azrael's not an angel to be trifled with. They'll discharge you if you don't complete something they assign, and you won't be able to heal without Philistina's glass. If you agree to paint this, you really have to try."

"Paint it with what?" He lifted the heavy appendages. "My toes?"

"Azrael said that your will wasn't right," Hoot said, scratching his chin. "He called you selfish and self-absorbed..."

"Thanks for the reminder."

"I'm serious," Hoot tilted his head slightly, his eyes thoughtful. "What was your motive to pick up the brush earlier?"

"Well..." Michael searched his mind. "If I was going to rot here while the world took a piss, at least I'd have something to do."

Gabriel quirked a brow. "I can see what Azrael meant."

"You want me to muster up some noble cause to slop paint on canvas while everything falls apart?"

"No, I want you to think about what usually motivates you to do good things."

"I don't know...." Michael shrugged. "Because they need doing?"

"Give me an example."

"Alright..." He closed one eye and thought back. "Okay—I'd always wake up before the first bells and do any extras that Mary needed done. Fix things, clean stables, mop floors... things like that."

"Why?"

"So that I wouldn't be a burden," Michael said. "She gave me a place to live... fed me, treated me as her own. I felt like I owed her a debt."

"So doing those things made you feel like less of a burden?"

Michael nodded.

"So you did them to make *yourself* feel better?"

Michael made a face.

"What else?"

"Well... I went above and beyond training you. And the rest of the squad. I wasn't required to do any of that."

"Why did you do it?"

"So we could get to the Games... and win."

Hoot narrowed his eyes. "*Why?*"

"So that I could challenge Baalael. And chop him up."

"Wow." Hoot raised his brows. "Okay then... You need to find a motive that's bigger than you. Azrael said that art should *protect and preserve* what's good. Maybe rather than focusing on what you want the hands to do, focus on *why* you want them to do it. What is it you want to paint?"

"I don't know."

"Azrael said you've already received the inspiration. Is there anything you've sketched, or wanted to sketch, that's worthy of preservation and protection?"

Michael grimaced. He had no idea what inspiration Azrael was talking about.

"There must be something, Michael..." Hoot stepped inside the hut. He grabbed Michael's sketch pad from the art supply bag and started flipping through the pages.

"What about this one?" Gabriel held up a still life; an egg leaning on a vase.

"Nah."

He flipped through more. "This one?"

That was Michael's sketch of the Mother Tree at the Jolly Bub. The tree with a pod for everyone but him. "I'll pass."

Hoot huffed, nearly at the end of the book. He paused and looked up. "What about this one?"

Philistina smiled at Michael from the page, and memories of her laughter immediately echoed across his mind. A warm feeling washed over him, and he took the sketch pad. "This might be workable...." He cleared his throat.

"Good!" Hoot sat again by the paintbrush and motioned Michael to do the same. "Now, hold her in your mind as you picture the hand closing around the brush."

Michael put his hand next to the jar. He pictured Philistina's face. Her buns. Her snorts when she laughed.

His wrist began to tingle, and then the tingling turned to an icy burn. Not painful—*alive.* The thumb and middle finger twitched and their eyes went wide.

"Keep going, Michael!" Hoot leaned in. "You're doing it!"

The hand closed around the brush, pulling it flush into its palm and gently cradling it.

"I can't believe it..." Michael whispered, shocked. The hand moved without effort, holding the paintbrush exactly as he would have with his own natural hands. He twisted his brow and looked up to Hoot. "How'd you do that? Get me to hold the brush?"

"Sometimes we just need a change of perspective." Gabriel grinned. "I'm a precept, remember? Getting you in the right state of mind is my job."

39

Michael

*"No feeling is more exhilarating, no experience so sublime
as the crash of true inspiration. For a sparkling, fabulous,
glorious instant, the directions are clear. All things are now
possible."*

-From the Ancient Essays of the Lord of Aesthetic,
Raphael

H E MUST'VE SKETCHED PHILISTINA'S image a hundred times
before he painted it, five hundred if you counted the little
thumbnails he did to study the shapes and colors. Azrael periodical-
ly checked on his progress, never mentioning the profound delay he
must've been causing. Likely because Michael was genuinely trying.

Gabriel stepped into the hut dressed for the pits, and dropped a sack
on the floor. "Looks great. Azrael asked me to tell you to let the paint dry.
He'll be here with Raphael in the overture to collect the finished work."

"I can't get the nose quite right...." Michael bit the inside of his cheek
and stepped back from the painting. "And the color is off."

"Stop being a perfectionist." Gabriel gestured to the sack. "A package
came for you."

"The post is still operating?"

Gabriel shook his head. "Only if you can find a herald brave enough to travel by foot. But this didn't come via post. Soldiers dropped it off by the ferry. Joseph sent your things from camp." He slipped a looking glass from the top of the bag and handed it to Michael. "You shouldn't leave this in the bag, though. I'm surprised it hasn't broken already."

"I don't think it's real glass." Michael took the mirror. "Some kind of technology. It was a gift from Lucifer."

Gabriel rested his hand on the hilt of his steel. "There's one more thing Joseph sent." The blue beryl stone of Michael's sword glinted as Gabriel slid it from his scabbard. "I'm sure you'll be happy to have this back in your possession."

Flashes of the last time Michael held that sword played like a bloody picture book. Gabriel gave him a reassuring nod and held the sword out by its blade, the hilt facing Michael. "Go ahead," he said. "The sooner you face this, the better."

Michael nodded, the sudden thought of empyreanol invading his mind. He reached out with his synthetic fingers and willed them around the handle. They curled, forcing it into his palm. He couldn't feel the cool metal against his skin, or the shape of its handle. The sword that used to feel like an extension of his arm now just felt awkward, and reminded him of everything he wanted to forget.

Gabriel's tone grew somber. "The violence on the mainland is getting worse, and the darkness pushes closer to these shores too. Trudy confirmed it."

"Trudy?"

"My friend, and the leader of the team I work with," Gabriel said. "They're monitoring the storms."

Mary. Bentley. Shem. There was nothing Michael could do to help any of them.

"The sword's too heavy for me." Michael offered it back. "You hold on to it."

"I'll leave it on the dresser," Gabriel said. "You need to face the fear."

"I'm not afraid of the sword," Michael said. *I'm afraid of who I am without it.*

"You *will* wield it again, Michael. Give time to time. Joseph lost his hands too, and he eventually healed."

"Joseph had the right light and an abundance of vita."

"You have Philistina, Zuriah, and Trudy," Gabriel said. "Don't underestimate them. They've created an entire new discipline of healing arts. Many will be helped because of your misfortune."

"Comforting," Michael mumbled.

"On a lighter note..." Gabriel's expression lifted. "Philistina is no longer jabbing a finger to the back of her throat at the mention of your name."

"That's a lighter note?"

"Her portrait in oil might be just the thing to make amends."

"You said they're coming in the overture to collect my painting," Michael said. "I can't give it away."

"You can though..." Gabriel pulled a tube from his pocket and handed it to Michael. "It's digitizer, from Azrael."

Michael vaguely remembered the substance from his tour in the Great Hall of Art.

"You spread it over your painting," Gabriel said. "It turns the image into a three-dimensional rendering that can be input into the computer system. You keep the original. That's technology for you."

"Closest we'll ever get to divinity...." Michael grumbled before pocketing the tube. The painting wasn't very good, and Philistina might just as easily be insulted by its inaccurate proportions and crooked nose.

Gabriel craned his neck and looked over Michael's shoulder.

"What is it?" Michael followed his gaze.

"I thought I saw something move in the shadows," Gabriel said. "But it's gone now. Anyway... consider giving Philistina the painting after they come to collect the image. She might be a little salty, but she's been working hard to heal you."

"You can be honest," Michael said, still not believing he was letting anyone see his artwork. But they'd already seen him half-crazy and drunk and covered in piss. Did it really matter that he couldn't paint? "It won't hurt my feelings."

"It is stunning." Zillah clutched her leather breastplate as she stepped up to the canvas, examining it. "I never could have ever guessed you had such a delicate touch for paint after dodging your sword."

Bernard and Hoot leaned in over her shoulder. "The likeness is unreal," Hoot added. "It's her right down to the last freckle."

Bernard stroked his battle beard like a learned scholar as he hovered over the work. "'Tis infinitely better than some of the scat I've seen those lords hang up."

They meant well, the lot of them. But Michael knew it wasn't the art they were affirming, but rather, their empyreanol-addicted, handless, muck-up of a friend.

There were only two opinions you could never trust: that of anyone with motives of their own, and that of friends.

"Her nose is crooked and the butt's too big." Michael tossed a rag on the table and trudged outside, giving his back a good stretch in the process.

"I don't know what you see..." Zillah followed him, "but what I see is beautiful. You've captured more than that angel's image. You've captured her spirit."

"Yer too hard on yerself," Bernard chimed in behind them.

"Artists are always too hard on themselves." Purple curls bounced on Lord Raphael's head as he sauntered through the tree line and into the clearing. Lavender light blazed from his eyes as he gracefully pushed stray branches from his path.

"Lord Raphael..." Hoot bowed low. Michael was about to do the same, but something like a shadow flickered next to Raphael like it was fleeing him. Michael blinked, and it was gone.

"Oh, stand up, Hoot." Raphael flicked a dismissive hand. "Any friend of Trudy's is a friend of mine." He hugged the precept warmly and greeted everyone else with a kiss on either side of their cheek. "It's an honor to be among some of the finest athletes in the realm. Congratulations on taking home the Golden Gladiator."

Bernard grinned like a fool and Zillah raised her chin. Michael just gave a subtle nod—last thing he wanted to remember was the Games.

Raphael looked at Michael and said, "I'll have you know that I haven't traveled from this island so that my glory could remain in that well to aid in your healing. I was grieved terribly when I learned of your hands. My brother can take those Games too far sometimes. I'm sorry."

Michael mustered the most graceful smile that he could. "Thank you."

Raphael gave him a once over. "I hear you've completed our puzzle."

Michael tilted his head. "I don't know of any puzzle."

"Of course you don't." Raphael squeezed his shoulder. "The puzzle connects us as artists. It's the process of discovering something greater than the sum of our parts, and then coming together to build it."

Michael frowned; Raphael's words didn't make a lick of sense. "I don't have much training. The painting isn't even really done."

"Art is *never* done," Raphael said, a note of zeal in his eyes. "We only stop working on something when we can no longer grow from it. Azrael's been checking your progress. If he says it's ready, it's ready."

"It's not as good as the work they do in the Great Hall," Michael said. "I'm just warning you."

"It'll be exactly what it's supposed to be." Raphael stepped past him and ducked under the low frame into the hut. Zillah gave an encouraging nod before grabbing Bernard by the hand and heading back toward the pits. They probably didn't want to see his work decimated by someone who actually knew what they were doing.

"This must be the healing house that Trudy's team built..." Raphael looked around, the tips of his purple curls grazing the glass ceiling. "Inspiration is certainly not reserved for art, that's for sure."

Raphael turned toward the easel, and Michael was suddenly filled with the urge to run. The lord leaned in close before stepping back for a better view. "This *is* our missing piece..." He clasped his hands together. "I can feel her essence bursting from the canvas."

"What about the perspective?" Michael grimaced. "The nose is crooked."

Raphael dismissed him with a wave and opened the tube of digitizer, then pulled a qube from his smock.

Michael turned to Hoot, whose expression said *just shut up and take the compliment.* So he did, still bothered by the painting's obvious flaws.

Raphael smeared a clear layer of digitizer over the canvas. First, the image quaked, then, a semitransparent version of the painting peeled off itself and floated into the air. As it grew more opaque, the background popped and turned into a three-dimensional version of the meadow. Philistina's lying form stood up and dusted herself off. She looked at her hands, turning them over, and did a little spin and curtsy to her onlookers. Then, she turned directly to Michael and stuck out her tongue. Michael gasped, then the whole image beamed into the qube.

"She'll be a live one," Raphael smirked. "You've truly captured the spirit of your subject."

"And he keeps the original, right?" Hoot asked.

"Otherwise, it will be hung in a museum," Raphael said. "Whichever he prefers."

"A museum?" It was bad enough so many eyes already saw the original. "No, thank you."

"Up to you," Raphael said. "And as a tribute to the painters who contribute key pieces to our puzzle, the great artists of Mankind will be named after us. They will be those who chisel great statues, or paint chapels for the Almighty."

"I could see it now," Hoot smirked, "the Angel Michael painting the ceiling of a famous chapel. I think I like that idea."

Michael frowned. "Mankind? Is that who you're making in there?"

"The crown jewel of all artificial intelligence," Raphael said. "I painted Adam, and you have painted his more dignified counterpart, Eve."

"Does that mean the project launches now?"

"Soon," Raphael said, tucking the qube into his smock. He thanked Michael graciously before bidding them goodbye, and left.

"You should wrap up that painting," Gabriel said. "I left a roll of paper in the corner."

"Why?"

"Because I told Philistina you had a gift for her. She'll be here to pick it up soon."

40

Michael

"You can stay put, or you can run far, but wherever you go, that's right where you are!"
-Heaven's Handbook, Mindsets Part 3, "On Learning"

T HE ROLL OF TAPE crackled as Michael stretched a long piece from its holder. It kept sticking to the material of his hands, and was nearly impossible to peel off. He set the painting down on the square of brown paper laid out on his bed, making sure it was centered. Philistina looked up at him from the canvas with her crooked nose and big butt.

"You won't seriously embarrass yourself by giving this to her, will you?" a voice hissed.

Michael harkened. Was that voice in his head?

"Who's there?" he called out.

Birds chirped in the meadow, accompanied by the muffled violin notes of the chorus outside.

Great, now he was seeing *and* hearing things. He shook his head and folded the wrapping paper.

"You're deluding yourself, fool."

That voice was most definitely *not* in his head. He darted to the dresser, shoving his stiff fingers around the hilt of his sword and willing them closed.

"You couldn't shave a bum with that blade if you tried."

He stumbled from the hut, his eyes frantically searching. A shadow twitched from the ground and he blinked.

A dark shape took form from his shadow, stretching and reaching, pushing up against the glow of the meadow. It converged into the shadowy silhouette of a femme, thin angles at the shoulders and hips blossoming into the shape of a petticoat. It turned its head, stretching and cracking, to reveal the profile of a harsh jawline and a bun. He *knew* that silhouette.

"Deidre?" His voice nearly failed him.

"In part." The whisper hissed before its head cocked at an unnatural angle, and he took a step back. He swung his sword across the shadow, but that did nothing. He swung again, but she remained there, unchanged. A low, rumbling laugh echoed from all around him, and he dropped the sword and covered his ears. The laughing grew louder.

"Don't fight my voice, child. It comes from the shadows... and you hear it because you are of the shadows."

"What do you want?" Michael yelled, pressing his hands harder to his ears.

"I want peace with you," she hissed. *"We have had our differences, you and I, but we are on the same side."*

"You left me to die!"

"I made you strong. Independent. I helped prepare you for the reckoning that is to come. And I can help you still. I've been watching you...."

"Watching me? For how long?" he dropped his arms to his side, the artificial hands now balling into fists.

"Long enough. And I'll tell you a truth that no one else will, if you care to hear it."

"What truth could you possibly have?"

"The shadows see many things. As we speak, Raphael is planning to paint right over that abomination you just presented. Of course, he'll smile and claim it's your work, that he only 'cleaned it up.' But you're not crazy, Michael. It's every bit as shameful as you think it is. They feel sorry for you—fighting was the only thing you had. That's why they gave you something to do. But you are no artist, little X. You never were. They're all just humoring you."

He lunged into the shadow and screamed, swinging his fists, but the meadow echoed with her laughter, bouncing from shadow to shadow. Michael screamed louder until his voice drowned out the horrible noise.

"Michael!?" Philistina's voice broke Deidre's laughter into shards as footsteps came rushing through the woods. Michael bolted into the hut and threw the painting behind the dresser. He balled up the brown wrapping paper and shoved it deep into the waste bin. His eyes darted around the hut, searching for something to give her.

They landed on Lucifer's looking glass.

"Sorry," he called back, grabbing the mirror from his dresser. "Just a pain in my wrist. Maybe a stitch opened."

She got to the clearing and leaned on her knees, out of breath. "I nearly... crashed into a tree... running here," she huffed. "Are you alright?"

Michael nodded, emerging from the hut. "It was just a shooting pain; I get them sometimes. This one caught me by surprise, is all. I didn't mean to scare you."

"Everything okay over here?" A red-haired femme jogged into the clearing behind her, stopping to catch her breath too. There was a little bird flitting circles around her head. "We heard someone screaming."

"He's alright," Philistina called back. "He just felt a pain in his wrist."

"Let's get that looked at," the other one said as she approached. "That was a brutal trauma you had at the Games. I'm sorry." She extended her arm. "I'm Trudy."

"Michael." He extended his and shrugged. "It'll be easier if you do the gripping and shaking."

"I know." She grabbed his forearm and shook it harder than he expected.

"I promise to make it up to you," Michael said. "All of you." *You're a burden, Michael. You're nothing.* The old voices played in his head like they were permanently stuck there. "Eventually."

"We should confirm he's not bleeding," Trudy said. "Are there clean bandages here?"

"It's alright," Michael said. "Really. I can tell when it bleeds, and it's not. The pains are common, this one just caught me off guard."

"Are you sure?" Trudy asked.

Michael nodded, and the little bird popped out from under her hair and hopped to his shoulder, chirping like mad. It made his ear itch.

"I think he likes me."

"*She*," Trudy corrected, "... seems to be yelling at you."

"You understand the bird?"

"No actual words," Trudy said, "but I get Flappy's gist. You probably gave her a scare with your screaming."

"Hoot said you wanted to see me," Philistina said. "He said you had a gift for me."

Michael caught Trudy shooting a glance to Philistina's pocket, where a tiny edge of fabric peeked out. It looked like a kerchief.

Flappy dropped from Michael's shoulder and began pecking at the looking glass in his hand, nearly breaking it. Michael shooed her off.

"She always this aggressive?"

"Not usually," Trudy said. "Maybe she doesn't like mirrors."

"Mirrors?" Philistina craned her neck.

"Not just any mirror," Michael said, raising the elaborately carved silver handle so they could see it. "It's a looking glass. An original creation by one of the lords."

Trudy's head leaned sidelong. "Which lord?"

Flappy dove in again and furiously pecked at the glass, but Michael yanked the mirror away. "The Lord of Music," he said, blocking the bird. "He crafted it himself."

Trudy's face fell as Flappy darted from every direction, trying to get at the glass. Michael swatted, and handed the glass to Philistina. She hesitated, avoiding Flappy's assaults, but then took it.

"Look inside," Michael said. If anything could impress her, it would be the technology used to make that mirror. Certainly better than a crooked image of herself with an elongated butt.

She lifted the mirror to her face, and Trudy stepped behind her, peeking just over her shoulder. Michael's mouth curled into a smile and he crossed his arms, confident in Lucifer's work. He shifted his gaze briefly to the dresser where the painting safely hid.

They stared into it for a long beat, and Trudy's eyes went wide before darting between Michael and the image in the mirror. Then, Philistina's eyes welled, and the edges of her mouth quivered.

"I know," Michael said, sensing her deep gratitude. "It can be overwhelming to see yourself like that."

"Is this what you find beautiful?" Philistina rasped, covering her mouth. Her face flushed and two big droplets fell from her eyes.

Michael stammered, unsure how to answer. He stepped behind her and looked at the image in the mirror.

It was an image of Philistina looking nothing short of a goddess. Her hair was silken, down to her waist, and adorned with flowers and braids. Her many layers of colorful, feminine robes blew in the breeze, and her lips were painted a bright shade of red. She moved with aloof grace, and around her sat her plain-looking sisters, staring with envious expressions.

"You look beautiful here," Michael said. "What's wrong?" He dared to put his arm around her shoulder and she flinched.

"I'm not beautiful to you now..." Her lip quivered. "You think I need to *change*. To be anyone other than who I am. That I need to look and be and act like *them*...."

The sky above them began to churn, the colors that emerged during his reunion with Gabriel now morphing into dark, charcoal swirls. Something rumbled deep in the clouds, and the wind picked up.

"What's the matter?" he yelled over the wind. "Don't you like it?"

Philistina dropped the mirror on the ground and it shattered on a rock. Whisps of her buns came loose in the wind, and Trudy searched the sky wildly as Flappy fought the wind with all her might. Something flashed in the distance.

Michael stepped back, and Philistina's chest heaved as she raised her gaze—two narrow, rage-filled slits. She took a deep breath, and bellowed three crushing words. "I HATE YOU."

Lightning crashed between them and everyone flew backward, hitting the ground. A terrible ringing assaulted Michael's ears as he oriented himself. Philistina and Trudy lay on the ground, dazed.

Animals ran frantically into the clearing, confused. He pushed himself up, still reeling from the blast and stumbled over to them. He reached for Philistina, but she slapped him away. She stood up and took off.

Something thumped on the ground, followed by another thump. Then another, and another.

Birds. Dozens of birds fell from the trees and spotted the grass.

"No!" Trudy rasped. "No, no, no...." She crawled through the grass, lifting the birds until she came to one and froze. She let out a wail.

"Michael!" Hoot ran into the clearing, calling to him. Bernard and some stranger were right at his heel.

Louder thumps now joined the chaos as bigger animals hit the ground. Squirrels and chipmunks, a fox and a deer.

Bentley.

Michael took off, fast as he could. He screamed Bentley's name as he leapt over rocks and roots, his eyes scouring as branches whipped him in the face.

"Michael wait!" Hoot, Bernard, and the stranger took off after him.

"I have to find Bentley!" Michael tried to whistle, but he couldn't with those hands. If only Mary was there—her whistle could travel a whole Hexant.

He darted past the pond, leaping over the poor dead animals in his path. His only hope was that he'd seen several deer still standing, still able to run. Maybe the larger animals didn't all die.

"Michael, stop!" Hoot called out, still in pursuit of him.

His foot caught a root and he flew, smashing into the ground. One of his hands went flying, and his friends caught up with him.

"We have to find him...." Michael heaved, trying to push himself up, but his ankle was twisted something awful. He tried to whistle again, but couldn't.

"Ya trying to wreck yourself?" Bernard huffed, out of breath. "Or wreck us? We ain't runnin' laps like we used to."

"I have to find Bentley," Michael said. "But I can't whistle with these pissing hands!"

"Say no more," Bernard said and put two fingers into his mouth. He took a deep breath, and a sharp sound rang through the air, broken into short staccato bursts—the exact way Mary taught Michael.

"Where'd you learn to do that?"

"'Tis a whistle for everything back home. 'Specially for callin' yer donkey."

"Help me up." Michael reached out and Hoot gripped him, pulling him to his feet.

"There's news," Hoot said, his face rife with concern. "A herald's arrived. Your brother Shemliel sent him. It's about the Jolly Bub."

The hackles rose on Michael's skin. "What about the Jolly Bub?"

Hoot hesitated, and a shadow moved over them. Michael whipped his head toward it, but it came from above. The white-winged steed circled the sky just over their heads.

"It's your Matriarch," Hoot said, and Michael's stomach dropped. "The Jolly Bub's been attacked. They're the only estate in the village still able to grow food, and it's made them a target."

"Mary?" Michael could barely get the words out. "Is Mary alright?"

Hoot nodded. "But she's hurt."

"I have to go." Michael stumbled away. "I have to get home."

"What about yer donkey?" Bernard asked, and Michael froze. Bernard whistled again, and the shadow circling overhead got bigger. Wind from the thrust of the horse's wings whipped around them as he passed and came to a landing not three meters away.

"Someone answered the whistle," Bernard said. "But it wasn't yer donkey."

The horse rested its wings on his flanks and trotted to them, its silver horn producing a glow of its own.

"Never seen an animal give off light like that," Bernard said. "But I never seen a flying horse with a silver horn either. He must've eaten half the meadow."

The horse approached, and Bernard walked up to it, inspecting his face. "Didn't that donkey of yours have two different eyes? One green and one brown?"

"What of it?"

"Odd thing to have in common."

Michael stepped closer and had a look for himself. He also had the same little gold specs in his irises.

"When you said there was 'more than a bit of the Almighty's magic' around here for the animals to graze on... what did you mean?"

"Ain't it obvious?" Bernard said. "Meadow's rife with glory from the lords. The critters grow bigger and stronger. Get a sheen to their coats and run faster."

"And... if an animal was in the habit of gorging himself? If it ate nonstop?"

"Wild animals ain't in such a habit."

"Bentley's no wild animal."

"I suppose if an animal *gorged* himself on glory from the gods, there's no telling what might be."

Michael cocked his head. "Someone get me something to eat—anything."

Bernard dug through a tiny satchel clipped to his belt and pulled out a handful of almonds. "I chew 'em when I'm peckish."

Michael took the nuts and let the horse smell them, before snatching them away. The horse tossed back his muzzle, and then locked Michael's in his mismatched gaze.

Three, two…

Two stomps and a *majestic whinny*. Michael ducked the mucus spraying from the horse's muzzle and almost wept with relief.

"Bentley! You snogging beast! You've eaten yourself into a god!" Michael wrapped his arms around the horse's warm, thick neck and kissed him. Bentley nipped his arm, and Michael fed him the nuts. "Forgive me, old friend," Michael whispered in his ear. "Forgive me for leaving you."

"Ever ridden bareback before?" Hoot asked.

"Yes," Michael said. "But not without hands."

"Hoist us up," Hoot said, and Bernard held his palms together. The precept climbed up and held a hand out to Michael. "You still have two arms, so hold on to me."

"Send the herald to Joseph," Michael said to Bernard as he shuffled on the horse, the wings making it even more awkward to get on. "Get Zillah and meet us at the Jolly Bub. It's the fifth village in the Three/five crossing. Take the fastest horses you can find, and come quickly."

Hoot nudged Bentley's rear and turned him around, heading back toward the hut.

"Where are you going?" Michael asked. "The mainland is west."

"We're not going anywhere before we get your sword."

41

Michael

"It's always better to have one, than two if someone else has none."

-Heaven's Handbook, Virtues Part 4, "On Charity"

"Look there." Gabriel took one hand off Bentley and pointed in the distance, making Michael feel unsteady.

"Can you please steer with two hands?" He clung tighter with his thighs.

"There's a bright spot before the horizon," Gabriel called over the wind. "The darkness hasn't taken the whole crossing yet."

Michael was never a fan of great heights, even less so while riding a flying horse, bareback without hands.

Rays of golden light and swirling color broke through a space just big enough to see from where they were. "It's either very far away," Michael said, "or it's not very big. It almost looks like a beacon."

"It is a beacon," Gabriel said, tugging Bentley into a turn and making Michael's head swim. "Because it shines in the direction we're headed."

Michael knitted his brow and examined the terrain below: the treetops—or what was left of them—the roads, manors, roofs, and ponds.

The Jolly Bub sat on its hill, lit like a candle in a cave. "That light's not distant," Michael said. "It's shining right on the Bub."

They began their descent in long, dipping swoops that made Michael's stomach drop. They passed through a few low-hanging clouds, but Bentley's powerful wings easily dispersed them.

Silver hooves crunched down on the gravel road as they came to a bumpy landing. Michael's stomach threatened to evict its contents.

"Are you trying to make me sick?" Michael swallowed down.

"I assure you," Gabriel said, "I'm not. Bentley did that on his own—I have no idea how to land a horse."

Michael wiped his mouth. "Good thing we didn't think of that before we left. Jolly Bub is just up the road."

Bentley came to a steady trot as they made their way to the estate. He looked like some kind of equestrian god against this backdrop. The village wasn't the darkest he'd seen, but it was dark enough. The sky was filled with shades of gray and the grass was limp and colorless. Only the most zealous of leaves clung to their branches, and not a one was green. It was one thing to see life disappear around you, and another thing entirely to see it disappear in the only place you ever called home.

But at the edge of Mary's property, the world sprang to life again. The lavender still flourished, awakening Michael's senses with the smell of home. The groves and grass were healthy enough, save some yellowing in the trees, but it wasn't that much different than when Michael left. Everything was terribly overgrown, though, and the white picket fence lining the property had been torn down and rebuilt with bare wood in several spots. A knot formed in Michael's stomach.

The lack of normal activity around the manor put Michael on edge. "Do you see anyone?" he asked.

They slowed to a stop. "No," Gabriel said, "but maybe we should walk him the rest of the way. Might not be wise to announce our arrival."

"Because walking next to a shimmering, winged horse is less noticeable than riding one?"

Gabe shot him a look and they dismounted. Michael rubbed the soreness from his thighs as best he could with his one attached hand, and Bentley gave himself a good shake. His other hand was lying in the meadow somewhere. "Hopefully, word gets to Joseph, and he sends reinforcements."

"It's odd how the light's surviving here," Gabriel said. "What are the chances someone has a qube for me to send word back to Trudy and the team?"

"One of those square, brass things?" Michael laughed. "You'll be more likely to find a chamber pot at Mary's."

"Light means healing," Hoot said. "So I'm hopeful about your Matriarch."

"Me too."

Thwop. Michael ducked as something whizzed by his head. Gabriel drew his sword and Bentley took off in a run. An arrow lodged into a tree at the side of the road, and they fell into a fighting stance, their training kicking in.

Michael's gaze traced the invisible line between the arrow's end and the direction it came from. Someone was perched in one of the trees.

Michael shielded his eyes. "Ahab?"

The angel lowered his bow. "Michael?"

"Stand down," he said to Hoot. "He's one of Mary's sons."

Ahab climbed down and ran toward them, greeting Michael with an awkward hug. His tunic was dirty and tattered. "Sorry, brother. I thought you were foe. What was that you were riding?"

"Long story we don't have time to tell," Michael said. "This is Hoot."

"I know who Hoot is...." Ahab smiled like a fool and stretched an arm in greeting. "Hoot's your second shield—best defensive wielder in the world."

Michael had already forgotten about their fame. Hoot blushed and shook Ahab's arm.

"We heard about Champion's Legacy," Ahab said, his gaze moving to Michael's wrists. "We practically had to tie Mary down so she didn't run straight to the center of Heaven in her slippers to find you. Had things not gotten so bad so quickly here, she might have done it."

"I'm glad she didn't...." Michael motioned Ahab's bow. "Since when do you nock arrows?"

"Since the village turned dark," Ahab said. "I've been practicing."

"Thankfully you're not any good yet."

"Let's hope I am soon," Ahab said. "The light's made us a target. Shemliel didn't want to worry you, but we're running low on brothers."

"Low on brothers?" Michael's stomach dropped. "Has anyone been lost?"

"Not sure what lost means," Ahab said, "but Mary's throwing us out left and right. Won't let most of us step foot on the property. And I just can't bear to leave them undefended, so I stay perched in that tree with my bow."

"Mary's alright, then?"

"Alright enough to chase us away with that broomstick of hers. Because of this...." He slipped a small, black book from his waistband. "New ideas, Michael.... We'll need them to get through this. But Mary's old-fashioned. You can have my copy. It'll open your mind in ways you've never dreamed."

"So she can put me out too?" Michael pushed the book back. "No, thank you."

"Aren't you even curious?"

"Maybe we should go check on Mary?" Hoot cut in.

"We should." Michael patted Ahab on the shoulder. "Good work out here. And I was only joking that you're not any good—you nearly took my ear off."

Poor Ahab. His indoctrination ran so deep that he didn't even think to just lie about having the book. It would be a steep learning curve for him.

The white, wooden gates that once greeted everyone had been ripped from their hinges and tossed on the ground like scrap wood. The signage that read *The Jolly Bub, all are welcome,* clung by only one nail, creaking as it swayed in the breeze.

They approached the manor, its windows mostly broken and boarded up. The front door was gone, and replaced by a sheet of wood that had been poorly installed. Had Michael been here, he could've repaired these things. The brothers of the Bub had never been very handy. The one time Mary truly needed him, he wasn't there.

"Let's check the perimeter of the property," Michael said. "Stay together."

They moved like they did back in the camps, back in training. They crept alongside the manor, visually sweeping the area and rounded the corner, making sure the yard was clear.

Michael did his best to stay at the ready, but he felt completely useless. He was out of shape, out of practice, and weak. To say nothing of having only one fake hand.

Gabriel was strong, though—not only trained but well-practiced. Michael would put him up against half a dozen average fighters easily, maybe more.

"You still have your forehead and legs, you know," Gabriel said. "You've done enough damage with those in the past."

"I wasn't complaining."

"Not out loud, you weren't."

"You some kind of god now? Reading my thoughts?"

"I don't need to read your thoughts to know what you're thinking," Gabriel said. "You forget, these aren't the first wounds I watched you recover from. And if you don't get a more positive attitude, there will be more. Believe that."

Michael pursed his lips, but there was a nagging truth to what he said. There always was with him. He had to go off and become a precept, now fully mastering the skill of wedging under Michael's skin like a splinter.

"Don't look so depressed, stranger!" Shemliel emerged from the back door with a pair of pruning shears. "It's about time you got here."

"Did you trade your belly for a smaller model?" Michael jogged to him, and they met with a warm embrace.

"Ugh..." Shem gripped him in a hug. "I've missed you so much. I can't believe you went and did that to your hands. I can't leave you alone for a measure."

"No, you can't." Hoot smiled and stretched out his arm. "I'm Hoot."

"I know," Shemliel said. "I read the papers—well, I did when they still printed them. Shem wrapped his hairy arms around Hoot and nearly squeezed the breath out of him. "Thank you for taking care of my brother."

"He's a precept too," Michael said. "Bet you didn't know that."

"That's good," Shemliel said. "It means Mary will let him in the house. Vouch for Michael and she may let him in too."

"Mary's alright?" Michael asked.

"She is. Got knocked around a bit, but I was able to force-feed her enough vita to heal up. The light's strong here too."

"And Lilith?"

Shemliel bit his lip. "No harm's come to the Violet Rose, but we don't speak much anymore. It appears we have a difference of... principles."

"I'm sorry to hear that.... What's happened here, Shem? Where is everyone?"

"It's not as bad as it looks. Mary sent a good thirty of us out to distribute food to the migrants in the agorium. She was letting them camp outside the Bub, even giving our rooms to the ones who would swear on a Handbook. But they all fled after the attack. Now they just huddle around fires in the markets, begging and freezing."

"Ahab said she sent the brothers out."

"Almost three quarters of us are gone." Shemliel took a deep breath. "It's that blasted book. She'll have no part of it... and Mary's never been one for compromise."

"The Black Mani—"

"SHHH!" Shemliel shoved a hand over Michael's mouth. "She's got ears like a donkey," he hissed. "You're her favorite, and she's worried about you. But make no mistake... you'll be out that door quicker than you came in. And she'll do it so kindly that you'll thank her. She's stronger than all of us, Michael."

He removed his hand and Michael nodded.

"Mother Tree is bare...." Michael glanced over. "What about the groves?"

"They took everything in the attack, but the trees are already budding again. Should have fruit soon. And there's still plenty stashed in the stable cellar. They didn't even think to look there."

"Was anyone else hurt?"

"All of us, but we have good light here." He pulled his tunic down to reveal a big bruise on his shoulder. "I took a pretty good beating, but I'm proud of it. Felt like I could've been on your squad for a beat." He huffed a laugh. "But there's something else I need to talk to you about."

He bid them walk to the edge of the property, and spoke in a hushed tone. "I don't know how much you know about what's going on, but a revolution is happening. There are lords who blame the Almighty for the darkness, and there will be a revolt against the Throne Tower. They have forces—fighting forces—and they wear your uniform."

Michael went still as his gaze crept to Hoot. He never did fully explain the whole nature of the military. Hoot's eyes had slightly widened, but he kept quiet in front of Shemliel.

"So far they've been keeping the peace and helping with food," Shem said, "but I thought you should know."

"No worries, Shem." Michael waved his wrist. "I won't be wearing that armor any time soon."

"And there's one more thing," Shemliel said. "The real reason I called you back home. It wasn't only food they were after in the attack. They left a message... For you."

"A message?" Michael knitted his brow. "What did they say?"

"That your torment's only begun. That no one, or no thing you love will ever be safe."

Chills covered Michael's skin. He should've known it. Should've known Baalael was behind this.

"I don't know what you're mixed up in, Michael, but Mary doesn't know what they said. Nobody does."

"Did they wear uniforms?"

"Different than yours, but yes. That's why I sent the herald."

"We have to fortify this place," Michael said. "And get steel into the hands of every brother left here."

"She won't have the violence. She's not going to compromise."

"Hoot can convince her."

"Me?" Hoot's eyebrows went up.

"Yes, you," Michael said. "You wear a sword and carry a Handbook. You're a precept and a gladiator. If you convinced me to strap fake hands on myself and paint a pretty picture, you can convince anyone of anything."

"He might not be wrong." Shemliel shrugged. "Mary holds angels of the cloth in high regard."

"Hoots a Master Precept too," Michael said. "Lived in the monastery nearly his whole life and apprenticed under the High Master."

"Azrael?" Shemliel lifted his eyebrows. "You're the best chance we have, then. We were helpless as babes when they invaded."

"The Jolly Bub is good," Michael said. "It needs to be preserved and protected."

"Go inside and see her, Michael," Shem said. "She doesn't know I sent for you.... She'll be so happy you're here. She needs to smile again."

Michael's heart sank. There was one light he couldn't bear seeing go out, and that was Mary's.

"But go through the front because they attacked through the back door, and she still jumps when it opens."

Michael gritted his teeth, but he needed to stay peaceful right now—for her. They left Shemliel and headed toward the front.

When they were out of earshot, Gabriel said, "Did you know we were going to revolt against the Almighty?" His voice was calm. "Don't lie to me, Michael."

Michael cleared his throat. "I had... an inkling."

Gabriel stopped walking. "Unacceptable."

"We're not in uniform anymore." Michael threw up his hands. "What does it matter?"

"It matters."

"I'm sorry. Okay? I shouldn't have lied to you."

"You shouldn't lie, period," Gabriel said. "That's always been a problem for you."

"I wasn't lying about keeping order," Michael said. "Keeping the peace. The world's a mess right now. We both want what's best for everyone, we just have different ways of getting it."

"When you convince someone to do something under false pretenses, you steal their free will. Is that what you wanted? To steal my will?"

"No," Michael said. "I wasn't thinking that deeply into it. I just wanted to recruit, and you showed so much promise. It was wrong. I acknowledge that now and I'm sorry. You preach forgiveness... so do it. Forgive me."

Hoot stared into Michael's eyes for a solid measure. "Fine. I forgive you. But don't give me a reason not to trust you again. Forgiving doesn't mean forgetting. Don't ever lie to me again, Michael."

"I promise. On Mary and on this house I promise."

"No need to swear on things that aren't yours to swear on." Hoot started walking. "It's done. I forgive you. We move on."

He took the lead as they rounded the manor and headed to the front door, if that piece of flimsy wood could even be called a door. Michael was afraid to knock, lest it fall in, so he called to her.

There was no answer, so gently, he slid the wood aside and they went in.

Colored light streamed in through the stained foyer window, along with brighter spots where the window had been broken. Shards still littered the corners by the stairs, and the mirror above the curio had been shattered.

In the dining hall, next to them, a thick layer of dust sat untouched on the tables, and dried blood stains littered the dull wooden walls. For an instant, he saw the past. Smiling faces around the many tables, clinking cups and making merry. Mary whipping around with her endless energy, serving food and picking up plates. Demanding everyone's honest opinion about her recipes. He should've appreciated those times while he could.

They carefully stepped around the shards and headed toward the kitchen. The pantry door was ripped from its hinges, and everything inside was gone. Mary hummed a melody to the jangled sound of pots and pans.

"Mary?" Michael called out.

"Is that you, Shemmie?" She called back from the kitchen. She stepped into the hall wiping her hands on her apron and looked up.

Her eyes met Michael's and she froze. Dark circles hung on her face, and she was thinner and more hunched than he remembered. Tiny streaks of white lined her temples and ran under her bonnet. She needed more vita, but she was probably half starving herself so others could eat.

"My son!" She dropped the wooden spoon and ran to him, wrapping her warm arms around his waist. "My son, my son!" She nearly squeezed the breath from him.

He put his arms around her too, and choked back tears. He kissed her head, and she still smelled like warm buttered biscuits.

She grabbed his bandaged hand and her face contorted with grief. "I shouldn't have let ya go," she sobbed. "My poor son..."

He was lost for words.

"Mary..." Hoot gave Michael a reassuring look before introducing himself by his full title, "I'm Master Precept Hoot, and I'm here to minister. I've heard so very much about you, and I'm humbled to be in your home."

She stepped back, wiping her eyes, and grabbed Hoot's hand with both of hers. "My Michael is good," she said. "The others blaspheme with that book. But not my Michael, *my gift*... He brings you here in the name of the Almighty. I'm so proud of my son."

Matriarch Mary had called him son from the instant he arrived at the Bub, but it always felt awkward to him. The word hit differently this time.

"Hoot is a brother to me," Michael said, his voice shaky.

"If he's a brother to you," she straightened, resolve shaping her tired face, "then he's a son to me. We've plenty of room after the migrants fled, and after yer other brothers were put out. That's if yer both stayin'... which I hope ye are."

There was a hint of the old Mary in her voice now. Shemliel was right, he needed to be here. "Of course we're staying," Michael said. "I saw Shemliel outside."

She grabbed the banister and started waddling up the steps. "He told ya 'bout the attack, then? You should know it might not be safe here before ya settle in."

"He told me everything," Michael said. "Hoot and I are going to help get this place cleaned up and back in order. We're going to teach the Jolly Bub how to defend itself."

She stopped and looked back. "Ya don't mean with swords? Or those blasted arrows? They're not just for sport anymore, Michael. I know you're an athlete, you and your friend. I read it all in the papers—I was so proud. But there's angels out there hurtin' one another with blade 'n bow now. I can't take the sight of it, Michael. The violence. The Almighty must weep himself sick. I could never sanction such use of swords; it'd be an affront to our principles."

"I give you my word with the Holiest of Holies as witness," Hoot said. "We wouldn't do a thing on this property that would put you at odds with the Almighty or our principles. But if you value all that is good and right, and if you hold these things dear, you will allow us to teach you how to defend them."

"I've seen bubs cut clean open and bled out in the market," Mary said, "for naught but a bit of manna and a coin, when they could've shared and both been alright. How could I let me own sons act such a way?"

"To stand idle while what's good is cut open and bled out, is to allow it to go extinct, and that would be the greatest sin of all," Hoot said. "We must preserve and protect it. For those who are strong and able, it's our duty. That doesn't oppose the principles in our Handbook, it preserves them."

She paused at the landing and stared at Hoot for a long beat. Then she led them to a room with two beds. "If ya want more privacy, you can take your own rooms. But if they come again seekin' shelter, you might need to double up."

"This will be fine, Mary," Michael said. "Thank you."

"The sheets and blankets are fresh, and if ya need clothes, there's plenty in the closets."

She started for the hall, but then paused in the doorway. "Master Precept Hoot?" She looked back.

"Yes, Mary?"

"If I let ya teach me sons to fight... how do ya know they'll never use their swords against what's good? Become like those liars and thieves in the market?"

Hoot took a deep breath. "I don't. But I do know that if we don't teach them how to fight, they'll have *no choice* but to become like those liars and thieves in the market. Because there will be nothing good left to fight for."

42

Michael

"If someone is unwilling to cooperate, find the stakes and raise them. Most will relent at the first sign of pressure. If they still don't cooperate, they cannot say they weren't warned."

-Black Manifesto, Chapter Two, "On Power"

"YOU HAVEN'T CHANGED MUCH, Michael, I'll tell you that." Shemliel hoisted the sack of dried, whole vita higher on his shoulder as the three of them walked the road toward town. Hoot picked up the fruit that bounced out occasionally, blowing them off and putting them back in the bag. "You still get more done before the first bells than I can in a half a movement. I don't know how you fashioned a new door so quickly."

"Symphonies of practice." He glanced at Hoot. "And a little help. They learn a lot more at those monasteries than you'd think."

"Speaking of learning," Shemliel said, "after we get these swords, how long before we'll be able to use them without losing a finger?"

"Not long," Hoot said. "What's more important is that you're all in shape; not easily winded or tired. Even Ahab's running laps while we're gone, albeit outside the property."

Michael cringed. He hadn't run a lap since before his incident.

"I can't believe Mary's letting you both train us," Shem said. "After she heard about the violence, she forbade swords near the house."

"Hoot's doing the training," Michael said. "He's a master at defensive forms, driving opponents back and tiring them out. I can barely hold a sword, much less wield it."

"That's if we can even get the swords," Shemliel grumbled, hoisting the sack higher. "Obsidian's worth more than food these songs."

"They only want obsidian because it buys food," Michael said.

"I don't know about that," Shemliel said. "It's like some of them worship obsidian now. They go mad for more."

"The blacksmith's no fool," Michael said. "I've dealt with Marcus before. He's pragmatic."

They crossed the agorium, and it was every bit as depressing as Michael expected. Hoot distributed the vita from Mary's cellar, along with the cloaks she sent with them. Her fingers were calloused from all the sewing.

Stands where hand-fashioned fabrics and jewelry were once given away now stood in ruins, their broken beams and countertops leveled by the storms. Shops were boarded up, and the rodents that scampered through the open cracks were the only sign that critters still lived. Nothing was being produced anymore, as if every angel picked up one song and decided to stop creating altogether.

"Blacksmith's just up the road," Shemliel said. "But we're being trailed by some unsavories, so we'd better hurry."

Michael checked behind them. A group of angels walked not ten meters behind, their eyes shifting as they picked up speed. He counted six in total.

He hadn't brought his sword, not that he could wield it anyway. But it might've been a good deterrent to have two of them armed. They didn't have time for this.

Michael took the empty bag that Hoot still carried and brought it up to Shemliel's sack, pushing a load of dried fruit in with his forearm. He walked straight over to them.

"Here." He held out the bag.

The bubs exchanged glances, and one of them flashed a dagger in his waistband. "We don't want this bag. We want *that* one." He pointed to the sack on Shemliel's shoulder.

"You can't have that one. But I'm giving you enough to eat for a dozen songs." Michael reached the bag out a little farther. "Take it."

"Don't I know you?" The one who did the talking narrowed his eyes.

"You definitely do not," Michael said. "Take the food so we can be on our way."

Slowly, he reached for his blade, and Michael sighed. "Next time we'll take the back roads..."

He pulled out the blade, and Michael walloped his face with the sack, dropping him like a rock. *Good thing we brought the whole fruits.* Two more tried to grab him and Michael's elbows flew up, crunching their jaws in. Hoot was by his side now, sword drawn.

They ran off and Michael tossed the sack at them. "It's there if you're hungry! Pissing snogs!"

"Michael!" Hoot said. "Language."

"They get their hands on a blade and think that makes them tough..."

"A blade doesn't make the fighter," Hoot said. "The fighter makes the fighter. And it looks like you've still got some fight in you."

The blacksmith's workshop was at the end of a lonely dirt road, just on the outskirts of the agorium. It was at least double the size that Michael remembered, with a full extension now jutting from the back of the building.

"Let me do the talking," Michael said. "Marcus favors me. I polished his steel and extracted oil for his fuel when I would get supplies here."

"Ahead of your time," Shem said. "Trading labor for goods."

Michael stepped through the broad open doors first, the familiar scent of smelting metals filling the air. But there was something else in the air, a smell he couldn't identify.

Fires blazed everywhere, and hammers clanked anvils that were set up in clean lines across the building. Michael looked around at the faces—the ones not covered by shields, anyway. He recognized many of them: potato farmers and weavers, stone masons and even the baker.

"It's like the whole agorium moved here," he mumbled to Shemliel. "At least they look well enough."

"Michael?" A metalworker in a leather apron approached. "It's you? Truly?" He lifted his shield.

"Nunziel?" Michael smiled, and Nunziel hugged him.

"What's everyone doing at the blacksmith's?" Michael asked. "I see half the agorium here."

"It's the only job that can earn any coin."

"You look well." Michael stepped back. "I take it Marcus feeds you?"

"He's got a connection for vita, so we buy it with the coin we earn. The labor is long and hard, but it's better than starvation."

He removed his leather gloves to reveal calloused, hardworking hands. Michael also noticed that his pairing triangle had disappeared completely, so he dared not ask about Darlene.

"What's that smell?" Michael sniffed. "Not steel or iron... it's something else."

"Obsidian, like the armor you wore in the Games...." Nunziel hesitated. "I was sorry to hear about your han—"

"I'm fine," Michael interrupted. "Go on about the obsidian."

"We mostly make sword, shield, and coin here. We can't work fast enough to meet the demand."

"Swords?" Michael cocked his head. "From obsidian?"

"Plated in an obsidian alloy," Nunziel said. "Some kind of proprietary mixture that comes in slabs before we melt it down. Once you chisel the edge, it's sharper than a razor."

Michael remembered Joseph mentioning the silent scholars working on obsidian enhancements.

"Can I give you some advice?" Michael leaned in. "Nick the scraps of obsidian on the floor and melt your own coin. I can see them from here."

Nunziel looked offended. "We sweep those scraps for Marcus—they belong to him! '*Even when desire roars, never take what is not yours.*'"

"That Handbook's not going to feed you, Nunz."

"I'll make an honest living, or none at all."

"What's taking so long?" Shemliel came inside and stopped short when he saw Nunziel. He wrapped him in a hug, and Nunziel's eyes widened when he saw what was in Shemliel's sack.

"You'd better get that out of here," Nunziel warned. "Marcus won't like that kind of abundance floating around."

"Where is Marcus?" Michael asked.

"Around back," Nunziel said. "Follow me."

He led them to a separate, smaller building behind the workshop.

"Be aware, my friends," Nunziel said. "Marcus has much responsibility. His manner has become impatient, even harsh."

"I'll make note of it," Michael said, and Shemliel raised his fist to knock on the door, but it opened. Nunziel scurried away.

"They never have a nice thing to say about the hand that feeds them," Marcus said, watching Nunziel retreat to the workshop. "They must think I'm half deaf with the way they speak right outside my door." He regarded Michael with a cool stare. "Nice to see you again, Michael. Come in."

He turned his back and went inside, apparently resuming the task of packing parcels into shipping crates. Shemliel and Hoot filed in behind them and closed the door.

"We need swords," Michael said. "About three dozen."

"That'll cost you," Marcus said, not bothering to look up. "Materials are scarce. What kind of swords are you looking for?"

"Steel."

"That'll cost even more," Marcus said, "assuming I have enough on hand. Do you have coin to pay for it?"

"We have vita..." Michael gestured to Shemliel's sack. "And plenty of it."

Shemliel dropped it on the floor and Marcus turned around, his eyes flicking wide before becoming aloof again. He let out a short grunt and sat behind his desk, shuffling through some papers. His clothing was fine now, made from multiple layers of smooth, glossy fabrics, and jeweled rings cluttered both of his hands.

"You're doing well for yourself in spite of conditions," Michael said, but Marcus kept reading.

Hoot nudged him from the rear and gestured to one of the parcels getting ready for shipment. The paper had splayed open, and inside sat a glossy black shield with Baalael's sigil emblazoned in silver. Michael's eyes flashed, and Hoot silently warned him to remain composed.

Michael took a deep breath and tried to sound casual. "I see you've put some of our givers to work."

"I have...." Marcus mumbled while running his jeweled finger down a page. "You're an honest, hard worker, Michael—we can train you too if you're interested. I'm always looking for honest, hard workers."

"I'd feel bad taking the work away from someone else..." Michael cocked a brow, "unless you have a well-resourced patron that could guarantee everyone work."

"We have a very well-resourced patron." Marcus licked his finger and turned the page. "With an insatiable appetite for armor and weaponry."

"And who would that be?"

"Trade secrets are trade secrets, Michael." Marcus glanced up. "I'm afraid you're out of luck. Our patron requires all of the steel that I can procure for the next symphony. I can order iron, but it's doubtful the delivery will ever arrive. I do have copper, though."

"Copper?" Michael frowned. Copper was a terrible material for swords. "No bronze?"

"No."

Didn't seem to be much of a choice. "How long before they're ready?"

"They're ready now," Marcus said. "New smiths forge them while training."

"New smiths? How bad are they?"

"Better than nothing," Marcus smirked. "You're welcome to go somewhere else, if you can find somewhere else."

"How much?"

"That sack should do."

"The whole thing?" Michael grimaced. "Steep price for copper.... You'll pay the workers in food then?"

"They'll be paid in coin like they always are, and they can buy their food from me, like they always do."

"Where are you sourcing your vita?"

"Our lord supplies."

"You mean your *patron*...." Michael cocked his head. "So let me understand this.... Your patron supplies food, and you *sell* the food to your workers?"

"They can purchase their sustenance elsewhere. It's up to them."

"There's barely any *sustenance* to go around. How much for a single ration?"

"Two ounces of coin."

"How much is a forger paid?"

"An ounce per song." Marcus' tone grew impatient. "Do you want the swords or not?"

Hoot cleared his throat, and Michael got the hint.

"What about scabbards?" Michael asked. "We'll need those too."

"Those will cost extra."

"Extra?" Michael said. "There is no *extra*. If you want that full sack of vita, then we need sheaths for our swords. It's bad enough the copper damages easily."

"Mind your manners, angel," Marcus said. "I'm not your Matriarch and this isn't a charity. Scabbards will cost you."

"Shemliel..." Michael growled. "Pick up the sack. We're going home."
They moved for the door.

"Wait..." Marcus held out his hand. "I might have an extra scabbard.
Or two."

Michael bolted to his desk and leaned into his face. "Don't think I
don't know that sack my brother holds enables you to steal from those
poor, honest fools in there for an extra two movements, at no cost to you
whatsoever."

Marcus' throat bobbed as Michael towered over him, a glimmer of fear
glinting through his proud eyes.

"It's bad enough you're melting down the obsidian scraps in there
to pay them and keeping their coin for yourself. They're probably half
starving and still indebted to you. The only reason I'm letting you get
away with it is because I don't have the time or patience to deal with those
brainwashed fools. Or you. So if you want your two movements of free
labor for garbage copper you could never sell, go get our swords—*and
scabbards*—and get them now."

Marcus clenched his jaw. "I no longer believe you're the *right fit* for
this operation, Michael. My offer for paid work is withdrawn."

"Remind me to cry about it later," Michael said. "After you get our
things."

Marcus stormed from the office, and Michael straightened his tunic
with his one stiff hand.

"We need to find a herald to get word to Joseph," Michael whispered
to Hoot. "We have all the proof we need of Baalael's uprising right here."

43

Trudy

"A soldier is at the ready in all measures. We take no com-
forts, no beats where the promise of war is shattered. Our
peace is offered to others. That is the sacrifice we choose."
-Military Manual, Introduction, "Duties and Obliga-
tions"

"How much longer?" Trudy asked. If it weren't for the bouncing motion of her horse, she would've fallen asleep already.

"Not much farther," Philistina said. "The border is just ahead."

They'd been traveling the forested back roads for the last twelve songs, and the terrain was dismal. The music, or what was left of it, rattled from the sky like a half-warped record. Scarcely an animal scampered by, and the silence of the forest was deafening. But the worst silence of all came from the treetops—not a single bird sang.

Trudy pushed the observation from her mind. She couldn't think of that now.

Bernard and Zillah rode up front in their military uniforms, chests emblazoned with Lucifer's sigil, making the trip that much more awk-ward. After Philistina's blood samples had proven a dead end—she was unable to find any angels in the same condition as Grahamuel—she had discovered an anomaly in the weather-mapping software. It happened to be in the same village that she came from, and that Hoot and Michael had run off to.

There was a spot that seemed to repel the gloom. It was like a beacon, and even the storms melted away before passing over it. If the software was accurate, then there was still a place that the darkness had not corrupted.

"Why we wouldn't hitch a carriage for this trip is beyond me," Zuriah huffed, swatting at the only life-form that seemed abundant: beezle flies. The herald rode behind him, a skinny, nervous angel whose eyes darted around like rubber balls. He'd probably seen more than a few things in his travels.

"Makes us vuln'rable, sir," Bernard said. "Can't move nearly as fast in a carriage as ya can on a horse."

"My bottom aches," Zuriah said. "And we're low on rations… who calculated the food for this journey? I'm starving."

"The rations are fine," Philistina said. "Maybe if half your portions didn't get stuck in your mustache you wouldn't be so hungry."

"Maybe if you'd learn to count, we wouldn't be on the brink of running out of food!"

"Enough!" Zillah's voice was powerful, but contained. "Voices carry. Let's keep them to a whisper."

Inwardly, Trudy thanked her. She was the only one besides Hoot who could shut these two up. She sat erect on her horse, leading the group with her glossy black armor and two curling horns. They made her look large and intimidating, but when they settled their camps before bed, Zillah was about as dignified as angels came. Trudy had known other angels from the outer Fourth Hexant. They possessed a certain serenity, and a deep connection to nature. Their estates were less brick and mortar, and more logs, sticks, and twine. Trudy was grateful she was there.

"There it is." Philistina pointed to a bright spot in the sky just beyond the tree line. The anomaly. Her face paled and she checked her map again.

"Everything alright?" Trudy asked.

"Fine," she snapped. "This map wasn't entirely accurate."

Trudy quirked a brow—she didn't sound 'fine.'

"We're almost there," Philistina said. "I just need to stop home first."

"Take the lead and we will follow you," Zillah said.

She let Philistina ride ahead. They came to a dirt road that gradually turned to cobble, and the loud clopping of hooves on stone put everyone on edge. Estates began to dot the gloomy hill country, and an uneasy chill filled the air.

Trudy looked in all directions, searching for anything resembling a threat. There were only two kinds of angels you encountered now on the mainland: those who wanted to beg for what you had, and those who wanted to take it. She'd prefer not encountering any of them, if it were possible.

They turned down a tree-lined road that was probably lush and green once, but now looked like her holograms when the saturation was set too low. Philistina put a finger to her lip and pulled up the hood of her cloak. They approached an estate with a sign that read, *The Violet Rose*, but there was no violet, and the roses must have long since withered away.

Several femmes were outside, all of whom stopped talking to eye the strangers approaching their property. One of them ran into the house.

Philistina kicked the back of her horse and took off through the gate, and Trudy nearly fell when the rest of their horses followed.

"Why didn't she identify herself?" Trudy pulled hard on the reins to slow down.

"Because she's a lunatic!" Zuriah slowed beside her. "A stark raving lunatic!"

Two riders shot out from behind the manor and ran toward Philistina, but she jumped from her horse before it'd come to a full stop. She darted for the door.

They turned their attention to the group now. Bernard put a hand on his hilt, but Zillah motioned him to stay calm.

"State your business, soldiers," one of the approaching riders said. He wore no uniform, but carried a sword.

"Escorting scientists and engineers on official business," Zillah said in that smooth accent, chin high. "I'll entertain no more questions. We shall depart shortly."

"Who's sanctioned your presence here?" he asked.

"I said I'll entertain no more questions."

More riders appeared and they circled the group. Trudy's breath quickened, and Zuriah's gaze darted between them. The herald looked like he wanted to cry.

"You wear Lucifer's colors," a rider said, putting his hand on his sword. "Who's sanctioned your presence in this crossing? I'll not ask again."

Another rider warned her, "You're speaking to a Might, soldier, so you'd better answer his question."

"There are no other colors to wear," Zillah said.

"Says you," the Might replied.

"I'm here under the authority of Furie Michael," Zillah said. "Of the Second Legion."

"Furie Michael?" He broke out in laughter. "The one with no hands? Wave hello for me, would you?"

Zillah's head turned to him sharply. In a flash her dagger cut the air and plunged through his eye socket. Trudy's jaw fell. He toppled from his horse, screaming, and everyone's blades swished as they drew them.

Philistina emerged from the manor, lugging some kind of machine. She moved slow under the weight of it, so Trudy kicked her horse and ran to her. Swords clanged as she pulled the reins, and Philistina hoisted the machine to Trudy's lap. She hauled herself next and they took off running toward the gate, the others joining at full gallop.

"Why'd you do that?" Trudy rasped behind her as they rounded the exit to the road, the machine barely staying put. "Why didn't you just tell them who you were?"

"They might've stopped me," Philistina panted, wrapping her arms around Trudy. "My sisters went dark long before the sky did. And their pairs are even worse. I had to get my machine."

"What is this that you risked us all to get it?"

"A tool that can do a lot of damage in the wrong hands, but it needs light to work. They would've figured it out eventually–especially with the anomaly so close."

"They've stopped pursuing us," Zillah pulled up behind them. "Probably tending their wounded. Let's get off the roads. Bernard and I will escort you to your anomaly, then go to Michael."

They headed through the brush toward the light in the sky, and crossed the tree line to a gravel road. The air was notably warmer than it was just a measure ago. Green trees lined an estate that was well kept, and light bathed its manor which sat aloft a hill. Its white fence still stood, looking well maintained and freshly painted.

"You won't need to drop us off by the anomaly," Philistina grumbled.

"Why is that?" Zillah asked.

"Because this is Michael's house."

Zillah and Bernard rode to the front gate and took off their helms. The sign looked fresh, maybe even still wet: *The Jolly Bub, all are welcome.*

The music was crisp and clear. It hadn't sounded like that in movements. They all gawked silently. It was like looking back in time.

"'Tis only a home," Bernard held his helm to his chest, "but I've never seen anythin' so beautiful."

"Bernie?" A high-pitched voice came from behind a bush and their heads whipped around. "Bernie is that you?"

A Matriarch's head popped up from behind a bush and she shielded her eyes with a pair of gardening gloves. She clutched her chest. "Well, I'll be a son of the Bub..."

Bernard stumbled from his horse, squinting in the light. "... Mary?"

It had been five songs since they'd first arrived at the Jolly Bub, and Trudy watched through the bedroom window as Hoot trained the brothers, and Michael ran laps around the yard. Mary stood watching Bernard volley swords the way a nanny might hover over a toddler. Their ancient, provincial accents were so thick that when they got to talking, you downright needed an interpreter to understand them.

Her gaze moved upward, where the clear, bright sky was encircled by the dark clouds that hung over the rest of the world. Now that she'd been here a while, though, she noticed that a few yellow leaves still dotted the trees, and there was the occasional small patch of brown grass. The light wasn't perfect here, but it was still good.

A feathery apparition brushed the nape of her neck and she rubbed it, pushing her grief back down. She clenched the locket where she stored Flappy's little feather and renewed her resolve. She would *not* accept the abomination they called death. The abomination that took her sweet lifelong friend away.

She stood up and yanked a comb through her hair. Zuriah was setting up the audio equipment in the front yard. Whatever mechanism delivered the music from that Throne Tower had to be the same mechanism Lucifer was using to deliver the darkness—and the Lord of *Music* would be intimately familiar with such a technology.

Imagine unleashing a book full of ideas that are plainly selfish at the same time you turn out the lights? He wasn't feeding those angels because he cared about them; he was feeding them so they would depend on him. So he could be everyone's savior.

But before she attempted breaching the Throne Tower, she had to gather as much intel as she could. And if she was lucky, in the process she'd find out what this X thing was.

The doorknob hitched, and Philistina came into the bedroom. She walked right to the window and yanked the curtains closed, which was a shame because Trudy rather enjoyed seeing Hoot train the brothers. But she likely didn't want a view of Michael passing by with any predictable frequency.

"Are you alright?" Trudy asked.

"Why wouldn't I be?" She slammed open a drawer and dumped her travel bag.

"Finally unpacking?"

She nodded. "Mary needs us. I'll stay as long as she does."

"Speaking of Mary, she left some extra toiletries on the desk for you in case you forgot anything. A toothbrush and some hair oil. And towels."

She shoved a bundle of clothing into the drawer. "Mary is kind. Unlike some of her sons."

Trudy peeked through the curtain and Michael passed below, running his laps. The poor thing looked exhausted, his arms thrusting awkwardly as he ran with his synthetic hands. At least Bernard remembered to bring his other one. She took a deep breath and sighed. "Did I ever tell you about the time I almost paired?"

Philistina perked her ear slightly. "No."

"Almost *dropped my kerchief* would probably be more accurate. There was an angel I was slated to work with at one of the logistics hubs. He was smart and well-read, an excellent engineer too. We got along well, and when our hands would come close, I could feel that tingling in my palm... like maybe we were destined." She chuckled. "I thought we could do something great together, something that would make the world better. Combine our talents and all that. So when the song came that we were to choose which hub we would work on, I brought my kerchief. I figured, if he picked it up, we could choose the same hub."

"And what happened?"

"I never took the kerchief from my bag. I was too afraid. When the time came to choose hubs, he chose northwest, so I chose southeast. A few symphonies later, they announced a new engine that could send our airships in reverse without turning them around. He'd designed that system... him and his new match. Someone had eventually dropped their kerchief, and he was glad to have found it. I've always regretted that."

"Why are you telling me this?"

"Sometimes it's better to take the risk than it is to wonder."

"Wonder?" Philistina looked affronted. "He's made his feelings about me abundantly clear. That if I completely change, maybe I'll be good enough."

"I wouldn't be so sure about that," Trudy said. "I don't know Michael very well, but I do know Lucifer, and Lucifer made that mirror. Anything he touches becomes corrupt. Michael didn't even seem to know what the image meant. It was like he thought the device itself would impress you."

"Figures Michael would follow someone like that...." she mumbled as she resumed unpacking. "Calling everyone 'sir' like some kind of trained dog."

"So did Hoot."

"Hoot's different. Hoot's got a mind of his own and he stopped wearing that stupid uniform."

Trudy peeked through the curtain again. "I see no uniform on Michael. I see an angel who's a little confused, and maybe caught up with some unsettling characters. I also see an angel who ran home at the first word of trouble, and who's just lost his hands to the darkest sort of treachery. Take it easy on him. Maybe there's more to it than you can see. Don't retire your kerchief just yet."

"Too late," Philistina closed the drawer and grinned. "I've already burned it."

"I know," Trudy said. "I saw you by the campfire. The good news is, I've packed you a new one in the front pocket of your bag. I split the kerchief I never dropped in half, and sewed a new hem. It was too big anyway."

"You kept the same kerchief all this time?"

"No use in wasting it."

"I'd sooner blow my nose into that thing than drop it in front of Michael. No offense."

"None taken," Trudy said, walking toward the door. "At the very least, we both have kerchiefs now…. It's not like we can grab things at the agorium anymore." She sniffed the air. "We should head downstairs—I smell breakfast."

Four long tables seating about twenty a piece sat in the dining hall, and two of them were completely empty. Trudy placed a napkin on her lap and looked at the haggard brothers sitting around her. They were tired, training nonstop through the songs like real gladiators preparing for the Games. Trudy got winded just looking at them.

She briefly wondered about her own family, and how they were faring, but the same lump formed in her throat that did whenever she thought about Flappy. The last letter she had received from Sandoval came about a movement before she left with Lucifer, and their village still maintained some semblance of order. They also had an antique obsidian chest in their basement that few knew about, so that would serve them well for a while.

"We finished fortifying the fences and the last window's been repaired," Shemliel said from the doorway as he came inside. Michael,

Zillah, and Zuriah filed in behind him. "And to think we did it all before breakfast."

Zillah was in full uniform, blades crossed at her back and daggers lined up her calves. She parked herself in the doorway like a statue, standing guard like she always did. Trudy didn't miss the glance that Michael shot toward Philistina, who sat next to Bernard and Mary, but when she raised her eyes, he looked away.

Zuriah and Hoot took seats on either side of Trudy, and Michael and Shemliel sat directly across from her.

"Qubes fully charged," Zuriah said, tucking a napkin above his bowtie. "And the audio equipment is set up and recording. Though it's preposterous that you won't tell me why." He adjusted himself in his seat.

"I told you," Trudy said. "I have a hypothesis. Once I get a little evidence, it'll be a theory and then I'll tell you." The truth was that whenever she mentioned the Throne Tower to Zuriah, he bowed his head in reverence and all logic left him. She'd have to be convincing if she was going to propose that his precious holy site could be the source of the darkness.

Shemliel grabbed a spoon from the serving bowl and dug out a heaping scoop of mush, but Michael slapped his hand. "Not until she gives the word. Where are your manners?"

"We haven't sat down for a proper breakfast since I can remember," Shemliel complained, "and you've already worked me half dead. I'm hungry!"

Trudy winced at his flippant use of the new word. She hoped he never learned what it truly meant.

Mary stood up, tapping her glass with a spoon and the room fell silent. She looked exhausted, her face like a thin barrier between the rest of the world and her tears. Bernard placed a hand on hers, which seemed to bring comfort. She adjusted her bonnet before addressing the room.

"'Tis been a while since we've sat here proper, like a family, and shared a meal. It's not much of a meal, but it'll fill yer belly 'n keep ya strong.

And I'm sorry for that.... I'd forgotten that ya can't help others if ya don't take care of yerself. But our new friend, Master Hoot, reminded me." She nodded at him appreciatively. "And we'll take care to do our part to protect and preserve what's good. Breakin' bread is good, even if we are low on bread....

"But there's somethin' else I wanted to address, in an official sort of way, before we eat. It's no secret there's less than two tables filled where there used to be four. And I know some of ya think I'm harsh for puttin' yer brothers out like that. But know it hurts me more than it does them. And I make sure they're fed. Ahab stays right in that tree, and I give him food to bring the others. But I can't have the selfishness or lyin' inside these walls. It's not how I raised the lot of ya, and I won't have it."

She looked down at Bernard, who smiled up kindly. "We're old," she said, patting his hand, "not older than all, but older than most, and we can attest to some things that most can't. I've had many a Callin' that's prepared me for this one. I've weaved and sewn, tallied numbers, and taught letters. Even more than that. We've seen this world in its infancy, like a babe from a tree, when there were just a few villages near the center of Heaven. Back then, we had no Matriarchs or nannies. We had lords, though we didn't know they was lords at the time. They raised us up in the ways of our Handbook, and taught us that goodness obliges duty, so we called 'em gods. They taught us how to love and live for others. How to stay simple, and always tell the truth...."

Michael shuffled in his seat.

"So long as the Almighty deems to see me lead the Jolly Bub, I'll run it how I see fit. We'll abide in the old ways because they're the right ways, and if ya choose to go yer own way, ya can. But ya can't do it here. There shall be no *black books* in my house... no lies, no schemin' or selfish ambition. We'll work to give of whatever we're blessed with, and trust we'll be alright. Because *service is the heart of Heaven...*"

"*And Heaven's heart doth serve!*" the brothers all announced, slapping the table in unison. All except Michael.

"Now that that bit's over," Mary said, "let's thank the Almighty for bringin' our Michael home, along with his friends. And for bringin' me old friend, Bernie... 'cuz I right well need a friend right now."

She led them in a prayer, and then a flurry of spoons clanked into bowls across the table, the air filling with chatter.

"She's really something else," Trudy said to Hoot as she dropped a scoop of mush into her bowl. "More angels should be like her."

He leaned into her ear, sucking some mush from a spoon. "Still think all the pious are fools?"

"I never said *all* the pious were fools," she hissed back.

He arched a brow.

"Okay, I never *meant* all the pious were fools."

He chuckled. "Can I make an observation?"

"It sounds like you've already made one." She placed her lips around the spoon of mush, which actually wasn't that bad.

"I don't think it's piousness that really bothers you," Hoot said. "I think it's *complacency*."

"How so?"

"I've seen you show a great deal of respect to many pious angels—even depend on them. You've been nothing but impressed with Matriarch Mary since you've arrived. Then there's Zuriah, who's annoyingly pious—even I'll admit that. There's Philistina who's pious too, though she's quieter about it."

"There's you..." Trudy said, but then blushed. "You don't bother me all that much."

"Me," he agreed with a slight laugh. "You have a great deal of respect for all of us. I think it's the complacent that you truly have a distaste for—those whose mouths move more than their feet. They talk about faith, but it's more of an excuse to be unthinking. If you pay attention, they're the first to abandon our principles when a threat is at their door. That's why you respect Mary. She believes differently than you, but she'd lay down her life for those convictions."

"Fair," Trudy said. "Though abandoning the principles that keep us helping each other, especially now, is nothing short of insanity. The system's falling apart."

"Ah. But when the survival of an individual is at stake, suddenly 'the whole' becomes an abstract idea. Those who claim piety, but lack conviction when tested, were never pious to begin with. Don't you think? Maybe it's your choices that determine what you truly believe. The character you become when you have to choose between yourself and others."

She furrowed her brow and took a bite. "You've officially talked around my head, Master Hoot. I'm a computer scientist, not a philosopher. Though I'm certain that if I gave it much thought, I'd disagree with you."

"You have to admit," he said, "it's strange how the light shines over an angel with such conviction."

"There are plenty of angels with conviction out there starving and freezing in the darkness," she said, taking another bite. "I appreciate her though. If everyone was doing what she's doing, the darkness wouldn't be as bad. But her kindness and conviction still won't grow food or stop the storms. There's an anomaly above this house, and if we appeal to delusions, we'll never understand it. And if we never understand it, we won't be able to repeat it. Her piety has nothing to do with the light."

He held her gaze for a beat and smiled before turning back to his bowl of mush. "Just thought it was an odd coincidence."

"Correlation doesn't equal causation," she said. "But Mary's still wonderful, and you're doing a good thing teaching them to protect themselves. Sitting back and hoping it gets better is foolish, and will leave a good place in ruins."

"Complacency," he winked, and she guffawed.

It was a shame she couldn't tell him about her theory. She couldn't tell any of them, at least not until she had a theory that could rival their loyalty to a floating castle. Even Philistina believed some Magical Master lived in that thing. And who could blame them; it's what they'd been told their whole lives.

A shadow flickered by the window and Trudy turned. She blinked, but nothing was there.

"Something wrong?" Hoot asked.

"Nothing," she shook her head and went back to her meal. "I thought I saw something."

Michael looked up from his bowl. "What did you see?"

It flickered again, and she rubbed her eyes. "Nothing. Maybe there's something stuck in my ey—"

Glass shattered and shards flew across the room, landing all over them. Whizzing noises were followed by thumps that hit the floor. Hoot's arm was already around her, pulling her toward the kitchen. Wisps of thin, black smoke rose from the floor, and dark tendrils stretched out from them.

Everyone scattered, Bernard throwing Mary over his shoulder, kicking and screaming as he ran off with her. Zillah had already drawn her swords and was slicing at the snakelike tendrils, but it did nothing.

"Arm yourselves and take position!" Michael bellowed, fumbling at his sword with those stiff hands. "We're under attack!"

44

Michael

"When the darkness comes bursting through your own front doors, will you be prepared?"
-Opening line from the standard Military Recruitment Letter

B LACK WISPS COILED AND curled, melting into any dark spot they could find. Michael's gaze followed them across the crevices and walls, swimming like fish at the surface of the shadows, leaving translucent ripples in their wake.

"Get into the light!" Michael commanded as chaos broke loose. Shadowy claws swiped at the running brothers like mad animals, and Zillah had already jumped through the broken glass to go after whoever was out there.

Everyone splayed in different directions, drawing swords and darting for the doors. Bernard had taken Mary to the designated hiding spot, Shemliel and Daniel behind him.

Hoot, Trudy, and Michael ran through the back door to the center of the yard near the Mother Tree, careful not to stand under its canopy.

"These things travel by shadow," Michael said. "Stay in the light or you'll find yourself face to face with one."

They eyed the perimeter of the yard by the groves, and there was plenty of shade stretching from tree to tree.

"We've got to make sure everyone's outside," Michael said. "You take the north side and I'll take the south—we'll meet in front. Make sure they stay in the light."

The three of them took off, and Michael passed a squad of his brothers stationed at their defensive positions. He pulled them away from any shadow and rounded to the front of the manor. Zillah waited there with Trudy and Hoot.

"Did you see anyone?" Michael said to Zillah.

"Two soldiers in obsidian with silver trim," she said. "Their helms were strange, though I only saw the backs— they ran like cowards. The angel in the tree said there were more up the road." She pointed to Ahab, who waved. "At least seventy."

"Seventy?" Michael did the math, and it wasn't good. "How long do you think before the herald gets word to Joseph?"

"Judging by Bentley's speed," Hoot answered, "he should've received it by now. But we can't depend on miracles."

"We finally agree on something," Trudy mumbled.

"Why is she out here defenseless?" Zillah eyed Trudy. "We need to get her a weapon."

"Trudy doesn't need a weapon." The front door slammed and Philistina lugged her clunky machine on the porch, bloody slashes across her face and clothing.

Michael's stomach dropped as he ran to her, pulling her away from the house.

She yanked herself free as her skin healed in the light. "I'm not afraid of any shadows. Trudy can help me operate this. It's better than a thousand swords—It'll melt anyone before they step foot on this property."

"Melt?" Michael's brow dropped as he recalled the device that liquified sand. "You mean to shoot this at them?"

"Is it any worse than impaling angels for sport?" she snapped. "Or watching them starve while you worry about yourself?"

"Stay focused," Hoot said. "Ahab said there were seventy soldiers out there. And we don't know how many of those... things are inside."

"Or outside," Michael added.

"What's he doing?" Trudy pointed to Ahab in the tree, who made a wide arc with his arms. He drew his bow and pointed in the direction of the road.

"He's telling us to get ready," Michael said, then roared, "Positions!"

Brothers lined the perimeter gates, copper swords in shaking hands. The few archers they did have, hobbyists at best, stood behind the newly erected parapet on the roof and nocked arrows. The sound of marching boots crunching gravel filled the air and grew louder. Michael feared the worst.

Philistina and Trudy dragged the machine to the front gate, and Michael ran in front of them.

"Stay by the steps!" he commanded. "Or I'll have you both hidden with Mary."

Philistina slipped on her goggles and shoved a bar into the grass. She smashed a button and the machine roared to life. "I'll shoot through you if I have to."

Michael glared at the stubborn, insufferable angel before kicking the dirt and moving aside.

Hoot and Zillah drew their swords as the marching grew louder, and soldiers appeared on the road. Their helms were fashioned into the heads of insects, like a swarm of beezle flies. Michael held out his hand, motioning *stop*.

The mounted soldier who led the brigade rode ahead.

"Turn back now and spare your losses," Michael called out to him. "This property is secure and its residents are trained by better angels than whoever trained you."

"That's not going to happen," their leader said, and they continued forward. Michael gritted his teeth.

Then, the light around them dimmed slightly and he could feel heat radiating. A red, blazing beam shot just over his shoulder and he winced.

It burned right through the bark of a giant tree, slicing it in half and sending the top part crackling down.

He looked to Philistina, shocked, and she smirked at him.

The soldiers stopped short.

"We won't say it again," Philistina called out. "Go back!"

Then a blue twinkle shot up in the distance and grew brighter, flying toward them.

"What is that?" Trudy squinted.

"It's Baalael," Michael grunted. "He's coming."

"Get ready!" Hoot called to the archers, and they aimed at the approaching orb.

Baalael stopped short above his soldiers up the road, his luminosity near blinding. His laughter echoed as he hovered there, and then he raised both arms.

Shadows rose from the trees and the manor's windows, linking together like a tightly woven fabric. Up and up they rose, stretching and climbing atop one another, until the whole of the property was cast under a canopy of twisted shade.

"I see you've met my pets." Baalael's voice echoed from the shadows, followed by his laughter. Philistina aimed the rod at Baalael and pulled a chord on her machine, but it sputtered.

"They're blocking the light," she said, smashing the buttons. "There's not enough energy!"

The soldiers advanced swiftly, their mounted riders clearing the fence and slashing at the front line of brothers. In an instant, Michael was in the thick of it. He quickly learned that the hands strapped to his arms worked better as clubs than instruments to wield. Arrows loosed and whizzed above their heads, but not a single one hit the targets. Swords clanged and even cracked—the copper swords.

Hoot and Zillah tore through the swarm of fly helms, taking two and three at a time. Soldiers lay on the ground all around them, but just to the side, brothers fell like rain and lay on the ground, bleeding.

"Get them to the stables." Michael began shoving Philistina and Trudy toward Zillah. "Daniel will know where to put them."

"I'm not going anywhere!" Philistina yelled, pulling out a glowing stone. "I can help them!"

"You have to help Mary!" Michael grabbed her by the cheeks and met her gaze, unflinching. "Keep her concealed, Philla. Please. *Keep her safe.*"

Something in his tone must've gotten through, because she nodded and ran off with Zillah.

Screams and whimpers trailed through the air and completely drowned out the music, and the entire front line of brothers lay bloodied in the grass, some curled on their sides, moaning, and some not moving at all. Hoot ran to them with his healing stone, but there was barely any light to magnify.

Michael darted from skirmish to skirmish, and soldiers were now sprinting from the groves into the side and rear yards. He glanced behind the manor to the stables where Mary was hidden; they remain untouched.

He choked a soldier from behind with his forearm and tossed him to the ground. He kicked another in the chest before bringing his elbow into someone's jaw, ducking and weaving the entire time, but the soldiers kept piling in. There were too many of them.

Something smashed his head from behind, dazing him, and his vision doubled. He stumbled, the sound of steel still ringing in his ears. A sword sliced right through his side, spilling purple light into the air, and warm blood spilled down his hip. Someone kicked him from behind and he fell, barely catching himself before face planting.

He glanced at the stables again, then tried to push himself up, but his head still swam. Blood pooled beneath him and someone laughed as light flooded his vision. Baalael landed on the grass with a crouch. The lord leaned over and drew the sword from Michael's scabbard, flinging it several yards away.

"Why lug the excess weight of something you'll never use again?" Baalael grinned, an invisible force pinning Michael to the ground.

"You've won," Michael croaked. "I'm not trying to fight you anymore. You're superior. I accept it. Why do you need to hurt these innocents?"

"Innocents?" he laughed. "We searched high and low for you, little X. Symphony after symphony. I worried myself sick for your wellness. These *innocents* kept what wasn't theirs. I'd like to have a few words with that Matriarch.... Rumor has it you're very fond of her."

"Leave her alone!" It took everything he had to yell it out with the breath being crushed from him. "She has nothing to do with this."

"We're just having a... challenge... locating her," Baalael said. "Everyone's so riddled with fear that their thoughts are too chaotic to read." He whistled, and two soldiers dragged an angel over with a sack over his head. "Fortunately, words work just as well as thoughts. He's as riddled with fear as the rest of you." One of the soldiers ripped the sack from his head.

"Nunziel?" Michael rasped.

"His puny little mind is gibbering so quickly that I can make neither heads nor tails from it," Baalael said. "Such an inferior species we were made to serve." He tsked. "Anyway..."

Nunziel cried, and one of the soldiers knocked a tooth from his mouth.

"Words will have to do," Baalael said. "Now tell me, Nunziel... where *did* you deliver all of that abundance that Mary so greedily consumed?"

Nunziel's face twisted as he sobbed, shaking his head no.

"Now remember your principles," Baalael said. "Only bad angels are disobedient, and only bad angels tell lies. "

Michael's gaze darted between them. "Nunziel don't!"

"I'm sorry, Michael! I won't tell lies and be like the rest of them."

"No!" Michael cried, but Baalael's foot slammed into his face, knocking him stupid. One of the soldiers unstrapped his hands and tossed them into the woods.

"In the stable," Nunziel wept. "Under a panel of floorboard in the southern corner. There's a cellar there."

Michael pushed against the force, the pool of blood broadening beneath him. Baalael motioned his soldiers toward the stable, and several squads ran up behind them as they took off.

"Tsk, tsk, little X," Baalael said. "Hoarding food while so many starve. One would think you would have compassion for the starving, given your history. You've been taking the Black Manifesto too close to heart."

Baalael lifted off as the soldiers raced to the stables. Michael railed against the force holding him down, but it was too strong. New sounds of fighting joined the chorus of violence, and then he heard wood cracking. He craned his neck, just barely, toward the stable.

The door was coming down. He caught flashes of Bernard and Zillah fighting, but more and more soldiers poured in from the grove.

A hair-raising scream ripped through all the noise, shrill and desperate, like nothing he'd ever heard. He went rigid. He *knew* that voice. It was the voice who insisted he eat when he was too ashamed to ask for food. The voice that had gently woken him from fevered sleep and bad dreams.

It was the voice who gave him a name.

A blue light glowed in the grass just a few meters away, first dim, then getting brighter. It was the stone in his sword, winking, then flashing in his eyes. Something like electricity moved through him....

45

Trudy

*"There are knowns, known unknowns, and unknown un-
knowns. So long as we remember this, we will stay humble."*
-The Guide to Utopian Principles and Ethics, Section II,
On Internal States

T RUDY DARTED FROM THE fighting through the field, searching
for any familiar face in the chaos. Tears streamed down her face
and blurred her vision as she tried to make sense of what she'd just
witnessed. She'd never seen wounds like that, so webbed and black and...

He was gone. *Gone.* Laid out, eyes staring flat, like her lifeless bird.

She stumbled and slumped over, throwing up. She wiped her mouth
on her sleeve and partly in her hair. She'd never be able to process this.

Philistina nearly bled herself out trying to save him with the healing
stone. Had Trudy not ripped it from her hands, she would be gone too.
But there was no way to heal that. No way to heal *death.*

And Mary. They had to save Mary.

"Hoot!" she shrieked. "Please! Where are you?!"

Baalael floated high under the dark canopy of shadow beings, a luminous snake ready to swallow its prey. He dangled Mary like a ripe fruit
about to fall from its tree. Trudy muttered pleas under her breath to no

one in particular that he wouldn't leave her permanently broken on the ground.

Soldiers rampaged in a frenzy, shouting and destroying everything. Torchlight could be seen through the windows as they set fires inside, and the Jolly Bub's brothers littered the grass like fallen leaves, broken and bleeding in the darkness.

She lifted her torn tunic over her shoulder and pushed forward. "Hoot!" Rage now filled her sore voice. Rage at what was happening to these good angels, in this good place. "Hoot! Tell me where your good for nothing Almighty is now!"

A soft blue orb glowed in the grass and she froze, panic rising inside her. *Hoot's healing stone?* Had he fallen too?

She dropped to her knees and crawled to it, but it wasn't a healing stone. It was the stone in Michael's sword. She snatched the weapon and hugged it to her chest, hoping nobody saw her.

Another soft glow caught her eye, just a few yards away. It was coming from one of the bodies strewn on the ground. Glancing over both shoulders, she cautiously approached.

"Michael!" she gasped.

His eyes were electric; glowing as he lay frozen. What terrible treachery had Baalael done to him now? She shook him, calling out his name, but he didn't seem to see nor hear her. Then, a thin wisp of light stretched from the sword and into his eyes.

She brought it closer to him, and his arm raised mechanically, as if reaching for it. A tendril of light stretched around his stump, and suddenly the sword yanked itself from her grip and floated to him. His eyes flashed with a blinding light before the ground quaked, and she stumbled backward.

The bandages around his wounds burst open, and his wrists began emitting light. They throbbed, then erupted like plants, visibly growing. Trudy didn't know if what she saw was real, or if her mind had finally snapped from all of the violence and death.

Michael lifted one hand in front of his face and balled a fist, before unfurling it. Five strong fingers stretched out, and her jaw dropped. He reached out with his other fully healed hand and grabbed the sword, his body now beginning to radiate light.

"Trudy!" Hoot stumbled across the field toward her, limping and wounded.

She scrambled to her feet and dashed to him, shoving a shoulder under his arm to help him walk. As they got closer to Michael, Hoot froze.

"Hoot?" she barked into his ear, but now *he* didn't seem to hear her. Bernard and Zillah came limping behind them, holding each other up. But when they got close to Michael, they froze too.

Baalael's soldiers began gathering around, lifting their helms for a better look. Michael's skin now swirled with a glowing silver-blue sheen, like a mix of beryl and steel, as if he was *made* of armor. Suddenly, his face contorted with pain, and his mouth dropped open. An ear-shattering scream exploded from him, blasting everyone backward—all except Hoot, Zillah, and Bernard.

Two silver monoliths exploded from his back and unfurled into metallic wings, looking hard as titanium, yet soft as a dove's tail. His torn tunic fell to the ground.

Michael's fiery blue gaze turned toward Hoot, and a beam blazed between them. Hoot's eyes caught with that same electric fire, and his taut form began to float.

"What are you doing to him?" Trudy screamed, but now more beams speared Bernard and Zillah. They lifted too, their bodies stiff, their eyes ablaze. Wings of pure light, like the wings of the lords, stretched out from their backs and began to whip, thrusting them higher and higher.

Trudy couldn't speak, her limbs trembling uncontrollably. Michael's sword burst into blue flames and he shot into the air, his squad launching up behind him. They shattered the dark netting over the estate, their radiance dissolving the shadows like flame to paper. Light broke on the grass again, and the wounded brothers started moving and groaning.

They sailed through the sky straight toward Baalael. The ground shook as they clashed, something like lightning and fireworks bursting around them.

Philistina appeared and fell at Trudy's feet. She was covered in dirt and grass and tear stains marked her face. She still held the healing stone. "What's happening?" she wailed to Trudy.

"I don't know!" Trudy said. "It's Michael... it's all of them. I don't understand it...."

One of the bright, fighting angels swooped away from Baalael and carried Mary. He descended and landed in front of Trudy and Philistina, coddling her in his arms. The soldiers nearby scattered.

Bernard laid Mary gently in the grass.

"Is she alive?" Trudy dropped beside her and pushed a tuft of hair from her face. She had so many questions, but that was the most pressing.

"She's passed out," Bernard said, his light dimming and his wings fading back to nothing.

"What just happened?" Trudy demanded. "How did you fly?"

"I don't know." He looked as shocked as she felt. "I only know that I'm under the Arch. I don't know what it means, or how I know it—but I do."

More soldiers and their horses now stampeded from the front of the estate toward the back, yelling things like "there's too many of them," and "fall back!" Trudy, Bernard, and Philistina carried Mary to the side of the manor, placing her flush against the wall where she wouldn't be trampled.

"What's happening now!?" Trudy yelled over the mayhem as soldiers whizzed by, a fresh chorus of clanging metal and battle sounds now filling the air. New soldiers appeared in crimson and black, with long horns on their helms instead of insect eyes. They chased the others into the groves.

"Herald must've got word to Joseph," Bernard smiled. "Backup's arrived."

46

Michael

"Dreams are the landscapes of other worlds, links to our deepest selves and bridges to the unknown. All should take care to heed their dreams, that is, if they can re-member them."
-The Guide to Utopian Principles and Ethics, Section II, On Internal States

THESE WERE MICHAEL'S FAVORITE dreams, when he danced on the air and moved through the clouds, just like those paintings he loved as a child. He savored every bit of them, knowing that when he awoke, exhausted, they would be gone from his memory.

How he was in the sky now, though, choking out Baalael, he had no idea. He didn't even remember going to sleep. And his squad had never been with him before. That was a first. But that was the thing about these sleep-fantasies. They happened in a world of their own, with memories and places built right into them. That's what his flying dreams were like.

"I won't let you ruin these for me," Michael growled in the lord's face as he held him by the throat, cutting off his air. "They're the only peace I have, even if I can't remember them when I wake up."

Zillah still hovered behind Baalael after having chopped off his wings, both of her swords blazing with the same fire as Michael's. They cut right through his glory.

Baalael clawed at Michael's arms, foam and spit spilling from his mouth. He was trying to say something, so Michael slightly loosened his grip.

"*What are you*?" he wheezed.

"What am I?" Michael guffawed. "I'm the poor sack who can't even have a nice dream without you showing up to ruin it. I finally have hands here, and instead of doing fancy, aerial sword tricks, I have to strangle you so you don't hurt Mary. Congratulations on officially polluting the last crevice of my mind, you wingbag. Now take off that ring so I can get back to my air training."

Perplexity passed over the lord's face, and Michael squeezed harder. His eyes bulged, and he slipped the ring off his finger and handed it to Hoot, who began his descent back to the ground.

The lord's gaze followed as he tried to yank himself free. There was some kind of chaos below—soldiers running amok like frenzied bugs.

"I'm only dreaming this because you left that stupid message with Shemliel," Michael hissed. "You crossed the line when you went after Mary."

Went after Mary.

A pain shot through Michael's head and his hands reflexively grabbed at it.

Baalael plummeted like a rock as images flashed through Michael's mind. Ugly images. Brothers of the Bub bleeding on the ground. Soldiers with insectoid helms. The wood of the shed cracking open....

Nunziel.

Michael dropped from the sky with the precision of a well-aimed dagger and landed in a crouch. Baalael lay there in a broken heap next to what was left of the stable.

Slowly, Michael stood up, and his dream began to fade. He blinked, confused, and checked behind himself. The wings were gone, as were his squad.

He looked down at Baalael, and soldiers with horned helms began surrounding them.

The lord was a pathetic, twitching wretch on the ground. Blood streamed from his nose and ears and his limbs were bent at unnatural angles. His mouth was wide in a silent scream, and Michael, unexpectedly, was hit with a pang of mercy. That was curious. He tried to shake it off, but found himself reaching down to help instead, unsure of what he could even do.

But then he froze.

Two strong hands were stretched out in front of him. He turned them over, then curled and stretched his fingers.

What's happening to me? Am I still dreaming?

Lucifer appeared wearing a formal military uniform, which made Michael realize *he* was naked from the waist up. He harkened, embarrassed, a confused flurry of questions invading his thoughts.

Lucifer knelt next to his twisted, broken brother and said, "You are hereby stripped of all titles. Do you understand?"

A whimper seeped from Baalael's wide open mouth. The urge to help struck Michael's clouded mind again, but before he could respond, the fullness of consciousness hit him. Memories—real memories— flooded him.

"Mary!" He gasped and turned away from the lords. "Where is she? Where is everyone?"

Trudy stepped forward. "Mary's alright. But..." Her face went pale.

"There's been a loss, Michael." Hoot stepped forward now, and the crowd parted to let him through. At the end of the opening, Philistina and Zuriah knelt over a mess of blood and mangled limbs in the grass. Michael's stomach plummeted as he ran to them.

An angel lay there, his face bruised and swollen beyond recognition. Worse than Baalael. Dried blood was caked in the thick mats of dark hair on his head, and even his arms. He lay there half naked, ripped open from torso to throat. Black veins stretched from his gaping wounds and covered his skin like spiderwebs.

The world tilted, slowing and speeding all at once as Michael realized who it was. He dropped to his knees.

Shemliel's lifeless eyes stared into the seafoam sky, and a scream lodged in Michael's throat as he gripped his own head with two hands.

"I tried..." Philistina knelt beside Shem, sobbing and clutching her healing stone. "The sword was dipped in darkness. He wouldn't heal..." Trudy embraced her.

"The obsidian," Hoot said, softly. "The sword was coated in it."

Michael's scream dislodged and he wailed, throwing his body on top of his brother. Shemliel's blood was sticky and warm against his bare chest. The sweet smell made him sick.

The crowd parted again, and Mary limped through under the support of Ahab and Daniel. She looked contorted. Disabled. She sobbed over and over, "My son, my son...."

"No!" Michael slammed the ground with his fist and shot up, rage exploding through him. He snapped the neck of the first insect-headed soldier he saw.

"You!" He pointed to the other mangled heap. *Baalael.*

Lucifer stepped in front of his brother and held out his hand. Michael was about to mow him down, but Joseph and Bernard yanked him back.

"Tell me why I shouldn't do to him exactly what he's done to my brother?" Michael raged at Lucifer. "Right now!? To all of them!"

"Because there are worse fates than death for someone like him," Lucifer said.

Michael's nostrils flared. "What fate could be worse than being gone? What fate is worse than Mary's right now?"

"It is your right to take revenge," Lucifer said. "Your offense is far worse than mine, and I offer my eternal support to you and your family. I am beyond afflicted to see you all go through this. But if you bring death upon Baalael now, he will feel but a pinch of the pain he's inflicted."

"Just come out with it," Michael spat, in no temper for word games. "What are you saying?"

"Give me a helm and a dagger," Lucifer said, and one of the soldiers quickly obliged. He stepped over and grabbed Baalael's limp wrist, slicing it open. The lord made a feeble attempt to crawl away, but Michael blocked him.

Baalael looked up, his dull gray eyes twisted with malice. He wheezed a deep breath, but instead of using it to plead for his life, he spit at Michael's feet.

Michael's boot met his jaw with a satisfying *crack*.

Lucifer collected Baalael's blood in the helm as it condensed from light.

"It's your choice now." Lucifer held out the helm to Michael. "Drink this and make him your servant, never truly alive, never truly dead. A demon, confined to the shadows forever under the force of his master. Or, drag him into that dark stable and carve him up the way he carved up your brother. Though, the damage he did to your family will last far longer than that."

Michael's chest heaved as he looked from Lucifer to Baalael. He didn't want any part of that filthy pig inside him, much less stuck to him forever. Just the thought made him sick. Demons were inverted, unnatural things, and Baalael would by far be the worst of them.

But he didn't want that abomination to escape the suffering he'd sentenced everyone else to, either.

"You do it," Michael spat. "Let him suffer forever. But I won't be attached to him. Take your own revenge, and with it, you'll take mine too."

"So be it." Lucifer raised his eyebrows before gulping down the blood, his lips turning a bright shade of purple against his pale skin. Baalael was murmuring something now as new terror filled his eyes.

The pathetic lord could barely raise his hand to shield himself as Joseph pulled a black tipped blade from his calf. *Obsidian.* He lifted Baalael by the hair and placed the sharp edge of the dagger to his throat, then slowly dragged the blade across his skin. The lord cried out in pain, and Michael savored every inch of spider-veined broken skin. The light wouldn't touch that wound, and Joseph stretched a satisfied smile.

Light exploded from him, but instead of condensing into blood, it stretched through the air as if searching for the rest of itself. It beamed into Lucifer's open mouth, and beat by beat, the cruel lord's life drained into his brother, leaving behind a blackness so dark it seemed to inhale the very light from around it.

A low hum buzzed in the distance, and grew louder. Something like a gray cloud emerged from the grove—not a cloud, though.

"What is this?" Michael swatted as a swarm of beezle flies invaded the yard.

"He's a god," Lucifer said, looking around. "We witness such a manifestation for the first time. This is what he draws to himself—flies. He's a beezle bub now... Beezlebub, Lord of the Flies. How do you like that for a new title? *Brother?*"

The insects condensed and began to orbit Baalael, zipping inside and around him. Lucifer leaned into his swirling darkness and spit, and two red eyes blinked to life where Baalael's head should've been.

"There, brother," Lucifer said. "I gave you back some of your life. Now you can see the fruit of your labors to harm this innocent family, and *betray me.*"

Lucifer knelt before Michael, his eyes blazing bright yellow, and a slow, somber song now rose from his body. A dirge, full of mourning. He took Michael's hand in his own, and a calm flowed out of him that was like the effect of empyreanol. It moved up Michael's arms and through his whole body, making his grief slightly more bearable.

"I'm so deeply sorry for your loss," Lucifer said. "And I beg your forgiveness. I was too blinded by loyalty to see who my brother truly was. I can never make this up to you, or your family..."

"But..." Joseph stepped forward and put a hand on Lucifer's shoulder.

"I'll need Joseph to step in as the Principality of War, to advise me on military matters," Lucifer said. "Which means we need a Greater Dominion strong enough to oversee our eastern commanders. There is something inside you, Michael, that I've not seen in any scholar or lord during my lifetime; and a greater foe lies just ahead. One who would allow the unforgivable to happen, like what just happened here."

"And we'll need strong leadership to weed out the traitors who followed Baalael," Joseph said.

Michael could still hear the weeping behind him, and a fresh wave of grief crushed him. "I can't think on this now," he said, blinking back tears. "Give me a song to make my choice."

"Take as much time as you need," Lucifer said. "In the meantime, we'll post soldiers to keep your family safe, and help with the cleanup. There are still deviants out there who will take advantage of what just happened here."

Hoot was staring, and Michael averted his gaze. He couldn't give an answer now—not with Shemliel still lying there.

But something had to be done. Someone had to keep them all safe.

47

Trudy

*"We try to show the path to take, to make it easy for others'
sake. If they don't listen, take a break. Let them learn from
their mistake."*
   -Heaven's Handbook, Mindsets Part 1, "On Learning"

T RUDY APPROACHED MICHAEL'S BEDROOM door and hesitated,
unsure if it was her place to have this kind of talk with him. She
took a deep breath and knocked, figuring there was already so much
harm done, she couldn't possibly make things worse.

Nobody had spoken about what happened to him—about his *change*.
About all of their changes. And now that he was leaving with Lucifer,
and unlikely to ever be welcomed back into Mary's house... she wasn't
sure she'd see him again any time soon.

The door opened and Michael stood there, a silhouette against the
light from the window behind him. She hadn't realized how young he
was until that very instant, his hair tousled and tunic unevenly buttoned.
Of course, it was nearly impossible to tell an angel's age by the way they
looked, but she could usually tell by their eyes. Michael's eyes held pain,
but they didn't hold wisdom.

"Hello Trudy," he said, moving away from the door. "Come in."

"Thanks." She looked around the room where a couple of travel bags were packed. Maybe some small talk would make this more comfortable. "Do you need any help packing?"

He shook his head. "I didn't bring anything with me. These were just some things I never took to the island."

"Is there anything we can send back to you? I mean, when we eventually get back to Universal Technologies?"

"I'll send soldiers to pack up my hut," Michael said. "I'm not sure what my schedule is going to look like, or where I'll be. But thank you for the offer."

She nodded, and stood there in silence for a few awkward beats. "There's something else I wanted to talk to you about."

He looked up from his bag.

"We all seem to be pretending you didn't sprout titanium wings and defeat a lord in the air. Can we not do that for a measure?"

Michael sat on the bed. "I don't know what happened to me. It still feels like a dream."

"It was no dream. I was there, right in front of you. I saw your hands grow back, and I saw you change. I saw your friends change by simply locking eyes with you." She motioned to his sword. "May I see it?"

He handed it to her, and she ran her thumb across the light blue stone. There was a strange glyph etched into the bottom of it. Something like a sigil, but much simpler. It was like an arch, but made of wings. "Do you know what kind of stone this is?"

"Beryl, I think."

Interesting. The same stone used by the silent scholars to create the sigil rings. "It wasn't until I brought you this sword that your transformation really began. Your eyes had already been glowing, but that light linked directly to this stone."

He shrugged. "I don't know," was all he said.

"You're not commonborn, Michael." She looked him straight in the eyes. "Do you have any idea what you could be?"

"Maybe it was some kind of fluke," he said. "I've heard of angels having incredible strength during emergencies. Lifting carriages that have tipped over, or breaking in doors if someone's trapped."

"We didn't have real emergencies until just over a symphony ago." Trudy cocked a brow.

"Maybe 'emergency' is the wrong word."

"You didn't lift a carriage or break a door. You grew gemstone armor and wings; you flew. And somehow empowered a select few around you to do nearly the same."

"I wish I had answers for you," he said. "Does Philistina still hate me?"

"She doesn't hate you. Give her time."

He looked out the window where there were horses and soldiers waiting. "I'm afraid I don't have time to give her. I'm leaving, and I won't be welcomed back here."

"Fortunate for you that Philistina doesn't live here, then. When we're finished getting this place back in order, we'll head to the island and regroup. Continue our research. The healing arts are going to be vital for everyone now."

"You've all been doing great work. Thank you again." He gathered his bags and slung them over his shoulder. Zillah appeared in the doorway, fully armored, waiting for him.

"I said my goodbyes to Hoot and Bernard, and made my peace with them," Michael said. "I'm sure you know by now they won't be coming with me."

"I know," Trudy said, eyeing the soldiers out the window clad in Lucifer's crimson and black. "Don't be surprised if Hoot comes and finds you, though. I've never seen him this torn."

"Maybe. I won't bet on it."

"There's one more thing I need to say to you, and I'll only say this once..." Trudy cleared her throat. "So please listen."

Michael furrowed his brow and set one of his bags back down.

"I know you think that Lucifer's a savior, but he's not. I worked beneath him for a long time, and he's not who you think he is. He blames the darkness on the Almighty, corrupting our world from some high tower in the Holy City. But there is no Almighty in that Throne Tower. There's no Almighty at all. And I have solid reason to believe Lucifer may be behind all of it. Don't trust him, Michael. Whatever you do, please, don't trust him."

Michael's lips curled just slightly and she could tell he was holding back a laugh.

"Is something funny?"

He shook his head. "I've just never heard someone say that the Almighty wasn't real. How do you explain all of this then..." he waved his arm widely, "the world? The trees? Me and you?"

"Symphonies and symphonies of small, subtle changes in nature," Trudy said. "Little strokes of luck when some of those changes worked out."

He chuckled again and picked up his bag. "I have to go, but I appreciate your concern and everything you've done for me and my family. Mary won't even look at me now, so if you could give her a kiss on the forehead from me, I'll be forever indebted to you."

"We'll take care of her."

"I know," Michael said. "She said Shemliel's death shattered her heart to pieces, and that my joining the *author of that book* broke the pieces into pieces. We're going to station soldiers a little ways off from the estate, but they'll keep it safe nonetheless."

Trudy smiled thinly. "You'd better hope she doesn't hit them with her broomstick."

Michael smiled back, the sadness of his brother's death lingering in his eyes the way her little bird's lingered in hers. He held her gaze for one more beat, and then left with Zillah.

Trudy watched them walk down the hall and sighed. She didn't think he'd listen to her, but at least she'd planted a seed. Maybe one song, he'd remember her words.

"There you are!" Zuriah walked up behind her and huffed. "I've been looking all over for you."

"Professor... I was just about to come find you."

"Well, sit your backside down, because you need to see this."

They stepped into the bedroom and Zuriah plopped a book down on the bed.

"Your Angelic Anatomy book?" Trudy asked. "Have you discovered new ways to heal?"

"Shhh!" he said, flipping through the pages. He landed on a page and laid it in front of her.

"What am I supposed to be looking at?"

"All of it!" He flipped through the next few pages. "These pages were blank just a few songs ago. They've always been blank! I thought they were for sketching or notes—not that I'd ever mark a book like this. But now they're full!"

Trudy knitted her brow and leaned over, examining the diagrams. It was Michael—or nearly Michael. The face was just a rough, featureless sketch, but the body was awash in silver and gemstone, and metallic wings spread out behind the angel in lines and angles that somehow came together and looked soft, like feathers.

"It's impossible..." she said, running her finger under the title of the page. "*Archangel.* What does it mean?"

"No idea," Zuriah said. "But look at the notes and the other sketches. Its life force can spread like a dome, affecting anyone under its cover. 'Under the arch', it says. That's how Hoot and the rest of them started flying around like kites!"

"How does an angel get under the arch?" Trudy asked. "They all went into some kind of trance, and before I knew it, they were off the ground." Trudy stepped to the window and watched Michael fling his bags into the back of a carriage and climb inside.

"I have no idea," Zuriah said. "I'm seeing this all in real time, just like you. These ancient books are updating themselves." He made the sign of the Throne.

Michael pulled away with the parade of marching soldiers and horses. Trudy leaned out of the window, noticing something in the forest off the side of the road. She squinted.

"Zuriah? Come see this."

He stepped next to her in the window, and she pointed to a figure in the dark trees.

"Who's that in the woods? It looks like a silent scholar."

He opened the window and leaned out. "It is," he grunted. "That's Azrael."

"How do you know? They all look the same."

"The cincture around his waist, dunce. The High Master wears a black cincture, and the rest of them wear a wheat color."

She squinted tighter, this time rubbing her eyes to make sure she wasn't seeing things. "Is it possible to see their eyes under those hoods?"

"I'm not sure. Why?"

"I think his are glowing green."

The End.

(For now)

"Farewells are just a blessing, that others prosper where they roam. Love can never truly part; for love is our real home."

Thank You for reading Awaken Archangel, Book 1 of the Universal Technologies Series! I hope you've enjoyed your trip through these pages. But, farewell is never the end, so I hope you'll join me in book 2, *Devil's Dominion*, where the Universal Technologies adventure continues! Be on the lookout for release dates.

To stay updated on new releases, free giveaways, or just to connect, come find me at:

Website/Mailing List: CJPiperata.com
Instagram: @CJ_Piperata_author
Threads: @CJ_Piperata_author
FB: Facebook.com/CJPiperata

About the author

C.J. Piperata currently resides in Southeast Florida. She began her journey as an illustrator, designer and musician in Brooklyn, NY, and attended the School of Visual Arts in Manhattan. As an illustrator, she discovered and fell in love with the world of epic fantasy. When she's not writing, you can find her reading, working on visual art, behind an instrument, or cuddling one of the many furry critters that have taken residence in her home. She has published shorts in two Grimhouse Publishing anthologies: Forgotten Lord and Wicked Ever After.

Acknowledgements

First and foremost, I want to thank you-Who-inspires. You know who you are.   ::winks and hugs::

Second, my bestest compadre and advisor on all matters psychological, Linda Levina. You have been my #1 encourager in this journey. I would have quit a thousand times without your salty, raging, don't-you-dare-quit attitude. The endless drafts you read through and probably wanted to stab your eyes out.... I'm so grateful for you. Your belief in me made me believe in myself. Still does.

Next, I need to thank my critique group, the Writers Guild. These are the most patient, informative, salt-of-the-earth kind of people and you guys have been my greatest writing teachers. You rallied behind me so many times and I genuinely love y'all. Shermon, Jacquie, Emily....

And my sister-from-another-mister, Killian Wolf and Grimhouse Publishing. Your time and patience helping develop me means the world. And the effort you put into not only creating anthologies for worthy causes, but taking *time* to help new writers for nothing in return... well, it shows what a precious gem beats inside that chest. Pelitos, you are the best. And one day I'm gona give you those damn earrings, and make you a nice lasagna lol

My editor, Dan Edelman, who's (← see what I did there lol) obsessive compulsive disorder has made me a more astute writer! And who's (← that one is correct) given me amazing encouragement along the way. I appreciate you!

My husband, for dealing with his lunatic wife, hunched over a computer for hours, days, weeks, months, years. I really appreciate that! :D And Della, because your little face and blossoming talent inspires me always!

Mary, because I'd probably be dead, or at the very least, in jail, somewhere without you... and no book would exist. Lol

Brother Joe, the original character <3 Because it's always better to ask forgiveness than permission. LOL

Toni, Nat, Sara, all in-laws and out-laws (Netsky), all my nieces and nephews (too many to mention and more on the way!) and my whole tribe of friends— you know who you are! Thank you for existing and making life worth living. Any likeness in characters is *pure coincidence.* I swear. ::wink::

Monty, my sweet little cat who is always in my heart, and passed during the time I was writing this. Wait for me in the grass in Heaven, and go find Trudy (she could use a friend after losing Flappy.) Save a place for us.

My mom. Always. Because everything I do that's worth anything is dedicated to her.

www.ingramcontent.com/pod-product-compliance
Lightning Source LLC
Chambersburg PA
CBHW061037310726
48969CB00004B/983